THE STONES OF \ ᴌ𝖳ARA

BOOK ONE OF THE EPIC FANTASY SERIES, FOR
THE LOVE OF THE GODS

CHRISTOPHER CLARGO

VISIT CHRISTOPHERCLARGO.COM

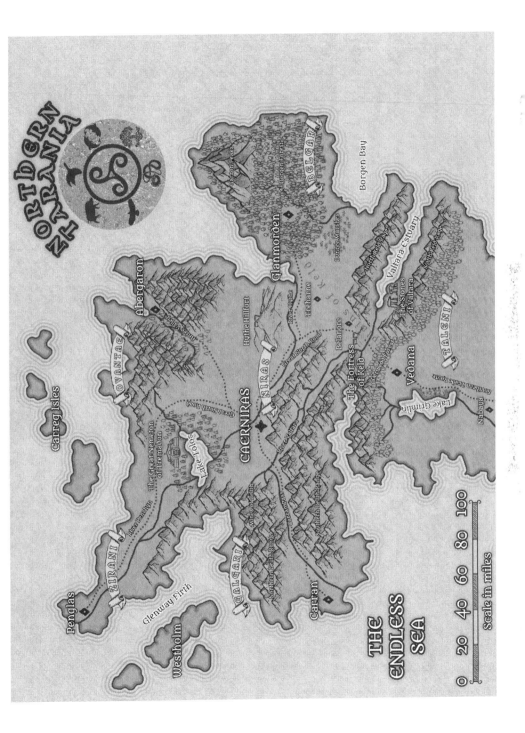

NORTHERN OVRANIA

Carreg Isles

OVANTAC
Abergaron

ZIRANI
Penglas

Westholm
Glenway Firth

GALGARI

Caeran

CAERNIRAS

NIRAS

BELGAR

Glanmorden

Borgen Bay

Veoana

TALENI

Lake Grunin

THE
ENDLESS
SEA

0   20   40   60   80   100

Scale in miles

1

TARANIAN MONGREL

Tarek slapped a coin onto the bar and nodded to a barrel of ale with a pair of crossed red swords painted on its side. "Did I ever tell you, Cara, that I know the woman who brews the mighty Red Renegade?"

Cara rolled her eyes. "Yes, Tarek—every bloody time you've had one too many Red Renegades."

"No... Have I?"

"Yes, I'm sure," she said, dipping a large wooden beaker into the barrel.

"I told you about Mari, the owner of—"

"The Renegade tavern in Belanore who brews the finest ale in all Northern Tarania?"

"No, Cara," he said, wagging his finger at the owner of the only tavern in Nabaya. "*All* Tarania."

She slammed the beaker down, spilling the dark red liquid over the solid block of polished oak that served as the bar. "If you love it so much, write a bloody ballad about it."

He tapped his nose and winked. "Maybe I will."

She stared past him and grinned. "I doubt that ballad would go down well with your usual audience."

He arched his brows and chuckled. "Oh, yes—they're a tough crowd to please." He nodded his thanks, then waded through the crowded tavern until he reached his usual bench beside the fire pit and sat down.

He swept his eyes across the circle of expectant children huddled in tight to the edge of the fire and stopped, catching sight of a boy whose face was covered in cuts and bruises. *By the goddess, Lars—Dagan made a mess of you.* He looked out into the sea of adults surrounding the children until he spotted Lars' father, Garin. Tarek nodded to him, but Garin failed to return the gesture. *Shit! I'm not looking forward to that conversation.* He gulped down his Red Renegade and placed it on the bench.

"Come on, Tarek, you said we could have one more story."

One of the youngest children was staring up at him, playing idly with a tassel at the end of her plaid shawl. She frowned, then sniggered.

"What's so funny?"

"You've got froth all over your face," she said, pointing up at his bushy beard. "You look like an old man."

The adults standing around the children laughed.

Tarek sat back and crossed his arms. "Haven't you lot got better things to do than stand around here mocking me?"

"What? And miss the best entertainment in the village?"

"He's the *only* entertainment in the village."

Tarek pulled a sour face, then grinned. "And I thought I was the only joker in Nabaya." He wiped the cuff of his tunic across his chin and returned his attention to the little girl. "Is that better?"

She nodded, then let a giggle escape from her mouth.

"Now what?"

"You still look old."

"Not as old as the Bwgan." He made a scary face and waved his arms towards her.

She screamed and dashed across the tavern floor to hide behind her mother and father. As she peered at him through the folds of her mother's skirt, Tarek waved and poked his tongue out at her.

"What's a Bwgan?"

Recognising the voice of his son's closest friend, he turned to the boy with the battered and bruised face. "That's a good question, Lars.

2

Very few people this far south would know the legend of the Bwgan; it's an old children's story from Northern Tarania."

"Da says that's where you're from."

"He's right—but I haven't been back for over fifteen years, and I doubt I ever will."

"Can you tell us the story?"

Tarek stretched his arms above his head and yawned. "Well, as my little friend said, I'm getting old." He winked at her. "It's well past my bedtime, and yours. Besides, I've already told you two stories."

The children begged him to tell them one more story and turned to their parents, promising to go to bed without a fuss.

He sighed, dramatically. "Very well. I happen to know a shorter version of the story that's in verse." He leaned forward, his face glowing in the warm light of the burning embers. "But I must warn you, children. It could frighten you.... Do you still want to hear it?"

The children nodded eagerly, then hushed.

"Then I'll begin."

A creature as old as the ancient Hen Rai,
Its home is the forest, in slumber it lies.
It waits for a movement, a scent or a sound,
Then out of the forest, the Bwgan crawls out.

As silent as a tomb, it nears its prey,
All tucked up in bed, sleeping they lay.
Then out of the shadows, it stretches its limbs,
Slithering and shimmering on the ground they skim.

It worms through windows, chimneys and doors,
Slipping past those it knows to ignore.
Until a child it finds, that brings it delight,
And steals them away, in the black of the night.

"That's not scary," said Lars, flicking his eyes at the other children whose faces seemed less sure of the fact. "Anyway, there's no such thing as a *Bwgan*."

Tarek smiled. "Maybe there is, maybe there isn't—but there's a way to make sure the Bwgan never gets you."

"W-What's that?"

"Stay away from the woods and make sure you go straight to bed when your parents tell you to. Which is right now."

"Awww."

He waved them away. "Go on, off with you. There'll be more time for stories another night."

As the children melted into the crowd of adults spread around the smoke-filled tavern, he took a deep breath and weaved his way through the throng until he stood in front of Garin and Lars.

"I-I'm so sorry about what happened the other day."

Garin placed his hand on his son's shoulder. "Look at him, Tarek. I know children get into fights over many things, but if I hadn't ripped Dagan off him, it could've been a lot worse."

"I know. Which is why Runa kept him home tonight and he won't be allowed out on his own until he's learned to control his temper."

"That was more than losing his temper. His eyes were full of rage, like a wild animal. What's that saying you Northerners have for it?"

"The Red Mist."

"Yes, the Red Mist. That's how he looked to me."

"Well, whatever it was, I'm truly sorry, Garin." He looked at Lars. "Can you tell me why you were fighting? It might help me understand why Dagan got so angry."

"Well...Umm...We were play fighting as famous warriors."

"I remember playing games like that when I was young. Which warrior were you?"

"I was Vasska the Shrewd of Kelaris, but Dagan said he wanted to make up his warrior from two people—Alun Swordstorm and Banan the Giant. When I told him you couldn't put a Northern Taranian and a Mendarian together, he got angry and said, 'Isn't that what I am?'"

"And what did you say to that?"

Lars looked down at his feet. "I-I called him a Taranian mongrel. Then he snapped and attacked me."

4

Garin flicked Lars across the head with the flat of his hand. "That's a terrible thing to say about someone. No wonder Dagan lost control."

"Please, Garin, there's no need for that. Even though those words were hurtful, it doesn't excuse Dagan's actions."

"Maybe so—but Lars needs to understand the great risk you and Runa took by marrying."

"More so for her. Which is why we moved as far away from Mendaria as possible."

Garin nodded, then creased his brows. "Speaking of the Mendari —do you think the raids on the other villages have something to do with them?"

Tarek scratched an itch in his beard and bit his lip. "Since Kaine unified the tribes, it's been quiet for years—but if he's started to push north into the Wildlands, then that would force a lot of angry, desperate people our way."

"Is that why you volunteered to help the Village Watch?"

"That's not the word I'd use," said Tarek, grimacing. "Runa gave me no choice in the matter. What about you?"

"I'd gladly help, but since his mam's death from the fever—"

"You don't have to explain yourself, Garin. It can't be easy bringing up a child on your own."

Garin laughed. "Depends if the little bugger's behaving himself— but I'd hate to think of him all alone in this world."

"You know he'll always have a place in our home."

Garin's eyes filled up. "That means a lot to me, my friend."

"You'd do the same for us. Let's just hope the raiders stay well away from Nabaya." He patted Garin on the shoulder. "Now let me buy you a cup of Red—it's the least I can do."

Half an hour later, Tarek opened the door to the tavern and looked out into the night. The pungent aroma of the sweet, smoky peat fire and Red Renegade clung to his clothes until he stepped out into the street and it dispersed into the chilly early spring air. Then, as the bright glowing disc of Golanos bathed Nabaya in her soft, pale light, he wrapped his woollen cloak tight around his body and headed home.

As he walked through the rows of wattle-and-daubed roundhouses, each wearing their peaked thatched roofs with smoke funnelling out from holes as chimneys, he considered what Lars had told him about Dagan. *So he wants to be a warrior?* Despite all his efforts, was his son destined to journey down the same dark path he had taken all those years ago? He knew that no son of his would be welcome in Northern Tarania, and Runa would fiercely oppose any mention of fighting for Mendaria. And then there was the emergence of the Red Mist. He had been around Dagan's age when he first felt the presence of his dark companion. He sighed, blowing a plume of breath into the blackness. No. If Dagan wanted to become a warrior, Tarek would have to tell him the truth about his past life in the north and train the boy to control the darkness inside of him. Then, one day in the future, he hoped his son would learn to bend the Red Mist to his will, just like he had done many years ago. The alternative was unthinkable.

"Tarek!"

He swung around to find Cerys, the leader of the Village Watch, gathered with a group of armed volunteers heading towards the south of the settlement. "What's wrong?"

"One of our scouts spotted a large group of warriors heading up the Southern Trade Route. It must be those raiders causing havoc in the South."

"Did they see who they were?"

"No. They didn't get that close."

"Shit! That would've been useful information." Tarek spat onto the ground. "How long do we have?"

"They're about two hours away."

Tarek nodded. "I'll dig out my old clansguard gambeson and get ready. I hope it still fits."

"At least you've got some protection," said Cerys, twisting her head to view the people behind her.

"Then, for their sake, I hope we stop those bastards from breaching our palisade."

As Cerys waved farewell and disappeared behind a row of roundhouses, Tarek shook his head. The villagers were woefully under-prepared and ill-equipped for hand-to-hand combat. *We'll need a barricade or a shieldwall, if there's enough shields to form the front line. But not even that'll be enough if they're Mendari.*

Although he was Northern Taranian, he rarely gave the Enorian religion of his people a second thought—but as he considered the possibility of once again facing his old enemy, he prayed to the Goddess Enora to protect his village and his family from the fanatical Mendari and their dark, merciless god, Velak.

2

ALL GOOD THINGS

Tarek had sworn to her that he would never again draw his sword, never again wear his armour and, most of all, never again take the life of another. Yet, it was Runa who opened the dust-covered chest, retrieved his gambeson and lifted it over his head. He opened his mouth to speak, but she placed her finger on his lips.

"I know what you promised, but they need you."

"The bloody thing's shrunk," he said, struggling to fasten the pair of straps nearest his stomach. "Velak's balls! Could you—"

"Shrunk, you say?" She yanked hard on the leather strips.

"Hey! Not so tight."

"That'll teach you not to drink so many Red Renegades."

Tarek snorted. "Well, it's not like there's much else to do in Nabaya."

She tugged on the last fastening, then slipped her hand inside the folds of padded linen and gripped his groin. "And what other forms of excitement do you desire, dear husband?"

He grinned. "Keep your hand there and I'm sure you'll think of something."

She tightened her grip. "Then you'd better come back in one piece."

"Dad, look at this!"

"We'll continue this conversation later," he said, easing his crotch out of her hand. Looking over Runa's shoulder, he eyed Dagan standing beside his chest, staring wide-eyed at a sheathed sword resting across his hands. "I wondered when you'd find that. Bring it over here."

Dagan hurried to the centre of their roundhouse and offered it to his father. "You own a sword?"

Tarek gripped the weapon's handle and slid it out of its sheath. The long, double-edged blade gleamed in the flickering light of the fire pit. "It's from my days serving in the Nirasian clansguard."

"You're Nirasian—did you serve with King Rodric?"

Tarek flinched inside. "Yes, I did."

Dagan's eyes sparkled. "It's beautiful—like the ones you and the visiting bards tell stories about." He frowned. "But why is the hilt wrapped in plain leather? Is there something underneath?"

"Nothing of interest to you." He snapped the sword back into the scabbard. He scruffed Dagan's dark, corded locks. "No more looking in that chest. Besides, you've got a bag to pack—just in case."

"Yes, Dad." As his son shuffled to the ladder leading to his bed, Runa placed her hand on Tarek's shoulder. "One day, he'll put the pieces together and realise who his father is."

"I fear that day is coming sooner than later." He stared at the sword. "I should've buried it."

Leaving Runa to finish preparing the provisions for the journey, he walked over to the fire pit, knelt and carefully unwrapped the leather strapping. *Hello old friend.* He inspected the sword's hilt in the glow of the flames. All along the underside of the steel guard, which was formed into the shape of a bird's wings in flight, crisscrossed a war's worth of sword cuts. *I should get those smoothed out.* He chuckled. *I could just imagine Bethan of Vedana's face when I enter her workshop and ask.* He peered closer, trailing his fingers along the smooth bone carving of the bird's body and across its tail fanning out to create the pommel. *The wren. How can such a beautiful tiny creature remind me of so much pain?*

He closed his eyes. For a moment, he stood before the red and black banners of his clan on the night of Queen Isabelle Niras's assassination. *I can never go back…nor do I want to.* He rewound the leather onto the hilt, stood and secured his scabbard to his side. Taking a few steps, he stopped and frowned. *It doesn't feel right without the rest of it.* Reluctantly, he walked over to his open chest, leant inside and opened two bundles wrapped in deerskin.

"Scale armour…and a helmet!"

Tarek glared up at his son. The boy sat with his feet dangling over the edge of his bed platform. "I told you not to look." He slammed the lid down hard, swirling clouds of dust into the smoke-filled, musty air of their home.

Dagan blinked, then looked at his mother.

"I think what Dad's trying to say is—"

"They don't fit me anymore, son. Like Mam said, I've been spending too much time down at the tavern. I'm sorry. I didn't mean to—"

The door of the roundhouse flew open.

"They're here!"

Tarek locked his eyes on the figure in the doorway. It was Cerys. "How many?"

"Over one hundred warriors approach from the south."

"One hundred? I thought you said it was a raiding party?"

"That's not the worst of it."

He swallowed hard and asked a question he was sure he already knew the answer to. "They're Mendari?"

Cerys flicked her eyes towards Runa then back at Tarek. "Yes."

"Velak's balls!" He reached for Runa's hand and held it tight.

"Not that you needed any more incentive to fight those bastards. I had no idea we had a veteran of the Mendari War in Nabaya."

"It was a long time ago. I haven't fought them since before Dagan was born."

"I'm just relieved you agreed to lead us."

"Lead you?"

Cerys frowned at Runa. "I thought you said he'd take command?"

"Runa? What've you done?"

Flustered, Cerys backed towards the entrance. "I-I'll leave you to sort this out." She wavered inside the doorway. "Make no mistake, Tarek, we need you."

As Cerys disappeared into the night, Runa squeezed Tarek's hand and lowered her eyes. "Please, don't be angry with me. You can see it in her eyes—she's terrified. The Village Watch won't stand a chance against the Mendari—unless..."

"I know. Unless I lead them."

"Thank you."

He slid his fingers through the raven-black curls that trailed down to her waist. "How could I ever say no to you?"

Looking up into his amber eyes, she mouthed, "Because you know you'd never win."

He laughed, wrapping his arms around her, and drew her tight to his body. He kissed her, then pulled away, grinning.

"What?"

"You taste of carrot and turnip stew."

"Charming. How you wooed all those women to your bed is a mystery to me."

"Well, there's only one woman for me now."

She tutted. "No-one else would have you. You've gone to look old. I'd be surprised if anyone in the North would recognise you."

He shifted his gaze away from her.

"I'm sorry. I know it's still painful for you."

"It is when I'm wearing this," he said, patting the pommel of his sword. Kissing her once more, he stepped over to the ladder and climbed up to the platform. Dagan lay on his bed, flipping a wooden knife into the air. He caught it deftly between his finger and thumb.

"Good catch."

Dagan said nothing.

Taking a deep breath, Tarek sighed and sat beside him. "I'm sorry I snapped at you earlier. You didn't do anything wrong."

"Dad?"

"Yes?"

"Why don't you talk about your life before you met Mam?"

"Hmm.... How does it make you feel when you remember the fight you had with Lars?"

Dagan looked away.

"That's how I feel when I think of Northern Tarania.... But I promise, once we're all safe from this threat, I'll tell you everything. I think you're old enough to understand."

"Well, I'm nearly twelve."

"Yes, you are." He smiled at his son and stared into his bright amber eyes. *It's like looking into a mirror of my younger self.* He wrapped his arm around Dagan and kissed him. "Come on."

"Where're we going?"

"I just remembered—there is something I can show you in my chest."

"What is it?" asked Dagan, vaulting off the bed.

"It's a surprise." He followed his son down the ladder and made his way to the chest. "No peeking." Reaching inside, he retrieved a small, plain knife and handed it to Dagan. "This is for you, if Mam is happy for you to have it."

"Perhaps I could see it before I decide whether I'm *happy* with it?" asked Runa, stepping behind the pair.

Tarek chuckled. "I'm sure there's no Mendari alive that could be a match for your mother, but, just in case, I'd feel better if you used the blade to protect her. Can you do that?"

Dagan's eyes lit up. He flipped the knife in the air and twirled to face his mother. "Can I, Mam?"

"Very well," said Runa, with a sigh. "But find something to wrap around the blade before you slice your finger off."

"I've got some leather under my bed," he said, skipping off to find it.

"It's time." Tarek led Runa towards the door and turned to face her, his expression grim. "If you hear the sounds of battle nearing, you run as fast as you can to the North Gate. Get over the border into Taleni and don't stop until you reach Vedana."

"Don't think we're leaving without you."

"But if they realise you're Mendari, they'll—"

"Shush. They won't hurt me. I have you."

He wrapped his arms around her waist and kissed her. "I love you."

"I love you too."

He drew in the warm scent of her skin. He fantasised about taking her to bed and forgetting the troubles of their world. Reluctantly, he released her. "I have to leave." With one final longing gaze, he turned, walked out of the door and headed towards the imminent battle.

3

THE DEFENCE OF NABAYA

Tarek scanned the rag-tag line of beleaguered defenders, shattered from holding back the waves of Mendari assailing the timber palisade. For over an hour, the villagers had kept them at bay, until the Mendari changed the focus of their attack. The cross bar creaked and groaned as the battering ram once again smashed against the gate. He spun around, glaring at the group of defenders pushing their shoulders against the tall beams of oak. "Hold that bloody gate!"

By the goddess, I hope Cerys has the evacuation under way. That gate won't last much longer. He turned back to the sea of terrified faces standing between them and the Mendari. "Prepare yourselves. Once those gates burst open, you alone stand between your families and the Mendari."

"How can we stop 'em with our pitchforks, scythes, and the like?" asked a woman from within the throng. "They've got proper weapons and real armour. They'll butcher us like cattle!" Many of those assembled murmured their agreement.

"Then lay down your weapons and pray the Mendari show mercy to you and your loved ones."

The gates shuddered on its hinges.

"But before you decide, understand this—I know the Mendari. They will rape, kill and destroy everything you hold dear. If they capture you, expect to be given a stark choice: turn to Velak or die as a blood sacrifice to their dark god."

The villagers spoke among themselves until they quietened, allowing a man at the front to speak for them. "What should we do?"

After several hectic minutes, Tarek gathered enough defenders with shields to form the front line of a shieldwall. He cursed: the line barely covered each side of the enclosed entrance to the village. *That'll have to do.* "Remember—every minute we hold them here is a minute more for the others to escape north."

Then, with a deafening crack, the cross bar splintered apart, and the gates flew open. The Mendari roared in triumph, rushing headlong through the gate and into the waiting shieldwall. Chaos ensued as sword, axe, spear and hammer bore down on the untrained defenders; yet, to Tarek's great relief, the wall held. Shieldless, he fought from the second row, thrusting a spear into the mass of Mendari in front of him. He snarled with satisfaction sensing his spear tip penetrate soft tissue. Twisting the shaft, the unseen enemy warrior slumped to the ground. *One more soul to pass through the Veil by my hands.*

He came back to his senses when the defender next to him screamed, dropping to the ground with a black-feathered crossbow bolt pierced through his throat. Tarek grabbed the woman standing behind the fallen defender and pulled her forward to fill the gap. She stared at him, shaking. He thrust his spear into her hands and shouted, "Fight or die!" She blinked, nodded and turned to face the enemy, jabbing her weapon in front of her.

"Keep fighting, Nabayans! Think of your families!" Yet for all his encouragement and the valiant efforts of the defenders, it was clear to Tarek that it was only a matter of time before the superior strength of the Mendari would overpower them.

Dodging a spear thrust to his head, Tarek frowned, sure he heard someone call his name. He risked a brief glance to his side and realised he was right. Cerys' broken sentence stabbed dread into his heart. "Mendari...broken through...North Gate."

They'll head straight into them. He barged through the thinning line of defenders and gripped hold of her. "Where're Runa and Dagan?"

"I haven't seen them. W-What should we do?"

Unsheathing his sword, he locked eyes with the leader of the Village Watch. "Make peace with your gods and pray for a swift death."

4

RED MIST

Blood-spattered and breathless, Tarek sprinted for home. Every muscle burned and his ears rang from the din of battle, yet the thought of arriving too late spurred him on.

Ahead of him, house upon house burst into flames as the Mendari swept from the north. He veered onto the path leading to his house and gritted his teeth, hearing raised voices within. The door hung off its hinges and creaked in the chilly night-time breeze. He leapt through the doorway and roared, his sword poised over his head. He skidded to a stop and gawped at what he saw. On the floor, beside the fire pit, lay the lifeless body of a Mendari warrior, unrecognisable by the countless stab wounds inflicted to his face.

"Tarek! Help me!"

He spun on his heels, ready to strike, but lowered his sword, finding Runa and Dagan huddled at the far side of the roundhouse. She sat with her back pushed against the wall, her arms wrapped tight around Dagan. The boy growled like a caged animal. He flung his head back and caught his mother on the bridge of her nose. She yelped in pain, but kept her grip firm.

Rushing to them, Tarek dropped to the floor, prised the blood-drenched knife out of Dagan's hand and threw it across the room. He caught his breath, staring into his son's eyes. "By the goddess! It's worse than I thought."

"H-He saved us, Tarek. He jumped off the platform and took that boy down. But he kept stabbing him, over and over again, and when I tried to calm him down, he turned on me."

"That's what happens when they can't control it. You're lucky to be alive."

"How do we stop it?"

"He needs to vent all his rage. It'll tire him out. When I say *now*, let him go and get behind me."

"But he'll hurt you."

"Runa, more Mendari will come." He glanced over his shoulder towards the broken door. "I can't protect you if Dagan's like this. Please—I know what I'm doing.... Now!"

She released her grip, dodging her son's lunging arms, and scrambled behind Tarek. Free, Dagan flared his nostrils and bared his teeth. Then, with a furious growl, he pounced at Tarek, clawing, kicking and punching into his gambeson.

"That's right, son. Get all that anger out of you."

With one final half-hearted punch, Dagan slumped into Tarek's arms and sobbed. His son stared up at him, fear replacing the blind hatred from seconds earlier. "W-What happened to me?"

"It's known by many names, but Northern Taranians call it the Red Mist."

"L-Like the traitor's sword?"

Tarek glanced at Runa, widening his eyes.

She bit her lip, then shook her head.

"Yes, Dagan—like Grimbard's sword.... The Red Mist afflicts our descendants more than most. A curse of the mind. But if you learn to bend it to your will—"

Outside, a woman screamed. Then more voices. Voices with the distinctive southern accent of the Mendari.

Tarek gripped Dagan by the shoulders. "I know you're tired, but we need to leave. Can you walk?"

"I think so."

"Good lad." He crept to the entrance and peered outside. *Velak's balls!* A pair of well-armed warriors stepped out of a building at the top of their path. As tongues of fire leaped from the thatched roof of the dwelling, they turned towards his roundhouse, laughing and making crude gestures. Now he understood. The warrior lying on the floor was a youth, most likely taking part in his first battle. The veterans had sent him in on his own to make a man of him. Tarek spat on the floor. *You picked on the wrong family.* He turned back to Runa and noticed some empty dishes piled beside the fire pit.

"Get some hot ashes from the fire and bring them over here."

She kissed Dagan's cheek, then rushed to the fire pit and scooped a large, wooden bowl into the red-hot embers.

"Quick—they're almost here."

"I'm coming." She hurried across the room and crouched beside Tarek, her anxious face glowing from the searing heat.

"When I open the door—"

"Yes, I know what to do."

"Good. They're almost here. Ready?"

She nodded.

"Now!"

Runa jumped into the open doorway and hurled the red-hot embers into the face of the closest warrior. He shrieked as the scorching cinders burned deep into his unprotected eyes, blinding him. Tarek kicked him hard, sending him sprawling into the kitchen garden outside their house. The second warrior, startled, raised his shield to deflect Tarek's sword slash, aimed for his neck. The Mendari countered with his own vicious axe swing, forcing Tarek to step back to avoid it slicing through his gambeson and opening his chest. They circled, assessing each other.

"Where's my boy?"

"You mean the little shit lying on my floor with his face carved up? That's your son?"

The Mendari's face flushed with rage. He looked in through the doorway, then back at Tarek, sneering with unbridled hate. "By the whore goddess, I'll make you suffer for that. Then, as you fight for your last agonising breath, I'll show your bitch what a real man is like inside her."

Tarek raised his arms out wide. "Come and get me."

Enraged, the Mendari leapt forward, ramming his shield towards Tarek's exposed chest, swinging his axe to catch him just above the hips. Tarek stepped outside of the deadly arc, allowing the Mendari to hurtle past him, then spun in a half turn, slicing his sword across the warrior's exposed back. The warrior groaned as the blade severed mail, linen and flesh. He wavered for a few seconds before planting his face deep into the earth.

Without a second glance at the dying Mendari, Tarek called in through the open door, "Come on! We need to leave."

5
THE BWGAN

"Quick—into the shadows." Tarek grabbed Runa and Dagan by the wrists and pulled them up against the wall of the nearest roundhouse. He put his finger to his lips and nodded towards the track leading to the North Gate, as out of the choking fumes emerged the shadowy form of a large group of Mendari warriors. Two of the group approached the entrance to a house barely a stone's throw from their hiding place. They eased open the door and slipped inside.

Bastards. Tarek squeezed his son's hand, catching sight of a line of children tethered together within the mass of warriors. His stomach churned from the pitiful whimpers of the children piercing through the din of the ransacking of the village. Then, as Golanos peeked through a gap in the swirling layers of soot above them, he stifled a curse: the children wore identical robes, each bearing a sigil that filled him with dread—the Circle and the Cross of Velak.

From within the roundhouse, a man cried out, then a child screamed. A few moments later, the Mendari waiting outside laughed, watching the pair of warriors haul a thick-set boy out of the entrance.

"Lars! They've got—"

Tarek clasped his hand over Dagan's mouth and glared at him.

"Don't say another word or they'll find us. Do you understand?" His son blinked, then nodded. Tarek held his breath, waiting for a suspicious head to turn in their direction, but puffed out his cheeks in relief realising their presence remained undetected.

Lars craned his head back towards the entrance, wriggling and squirming to break free of the warriors' grip. "Da! What've you done to my da!" He stamped down hard on one of his captor's feet.

The Mendari snarled into his face. "You'll pay for that." He pulled his hand back to strike the lad.

"Hit him and he'll skewer you like a pig," said a Mendari within the group. "He wants them unharmed."

As the warrior lowered his hand, an icy chill shot down Tarek's spine. *Who wants them? And why?*

Then, from out of the opening, staggered Garin, his right arm dangling limp from a gash across his shoulder. "Please.... Don't take my boy. Take me instead, I-I beg you."

"By the whore goddess, do I have to do everything myself? Finish him."

"Yes, sir!" A warrior turned and approached Garin, raising her spear.

Runa gripped Tarek's arm. "Can't you help him?"

"No. It's too dangerous. I won't risk your lives." He buried Dagan into his chest and held him tight. "Put your hands over your ears."

Garin held up his hands to protect himself. "No! Plea—"

The spear thrust silenced him. As he slumped to the ground, Lars wailed in horror, thrashing, reaching out for his father's body.

A warrior stepped out of the group and raised a flaming torch to Lars' distraught and contorted face. "He's a bit beaten up, but he'll do. Get him warm and let's get back."

"Don't we need one more, sir?"

The warrior shook his head. "He's already got his eyes on the twelfth. Let's just take 'em to the gate and piss off back to our lot. I heard they've got a tavern and some barrels of that famous ale I keep hearing about."

"Red Renegade?"

"Yeah, that's the one. Is it as good as they say?"

"Better, sir."

"Then what're we waiting for? Move out."

As the group headed north, laughing and bragging about the night ahead, Tarek gripped Dagan tight and fixed his eyes on Runa. "Don't let him out of your sight." He scratched into his beard and considered his next move. The Mendari's words had given him the opportunity he needed. If most of the warband were congregating in the tavern, it was possible that only a few sentries remained at the North Gate. It was a risk, but one he had to take. "Come on—I know what to do."

He led his family around the back of the blacksmith's forge, through the healer's herb garden and along the thatcher's yard, until they reached the stretch of open ground that led to the North Gate and their way of escape. Squatting behind an upturned wagon, he scanned for sentries.

Runa tugged at his gambeson. "Can you see anything?"

"I can't see a damn thing through...wait. What's that?" As the billowing smoke and drifting ash cleared for a moment, eleven ghostly figures appeared in front of him.

"By all the gods, Tarek. Those poor children. What've they done to them?"

Ashen-faced, Tarek turned to his wife. "I-I don't know."

"We must help them."

"I want to, but it's too dangerous. I wouldn't put it past the Mendari to use the children as bait for people like us."

She grabbed his arm and glowered into his face. "You would leave them to their fates?"

He held her gaze. "Would you rather we all die?"

"How can—"

"Lars!" Before either of them could react, Dagan wrenched his hand free of his mother's grip and sprinted towards his friend.

"Dagan!" Runa leapt to her feet, but Tarek grasped for her hand and pulled her back.

"Don't be a fool." He drew his sword. "I'll go."

She stared out to where Dagan had disappeared into the night, her breathing shallow and erratic. "I-I can't lose another child."

"You won't. I'll bring our boy back."

"But I want to come with you."

Gently, he slid his hand inside the neckline of her dress, revealing the Circle and the Cross scarred over her heart. "What's the one thing the Mendari hate more than the Enorian religion of the North?"

"Those who take the Mark of Velak and turn their back on him." She placed her hand on his. "Have it your way... Find our son."

He kissed her, then edged out into the open, heading towards where he had last seen Dagan. Pushing deeper into the swirling tendrils of smoke, the ash singed his exposed skin and the acrid air stung his eyes and burned his throat. He stumbled on regardless, one faltering step after another, until he came upon the rigid shape of a boy.

Lars flicked his eyes to Tarek and then back to an indistinguishable point to the south. "T-Tarek.... They killed my da... and now—"

"I'm so sorry, Lars. But we can't stay here. You can come with us once I find Dagan."

Lars didn't answer.

"Come on, we need to find him."

"B-But the Bwgan's here."

"The Bwgan? No, Lars—it's just a story—but the Mendari *are* real and they'll kill us all if they catch us."

"It is real. Can't you see it moving in the dark?"

Tarek squinted to the south, into the inferno tearing through the thatched roofs of the village. "I can't see anything."

"I know it's there! It's got me."

"Got you?"

"Yes! It's got its long, scaly limbs around me. Feel it if you don't believe me."

Tarek stepped in front of Lars and flinched, bumping into something solid, yet saw nothing. He reached out his hand and recoiled from the cool, smooth texture of metal making contact with his skin. *What sorcery is this?*

Then, from out of the darkness, a thrumming vibration pulsed through the air. As it grew louder, throbbing in Tarek's ears, the hairs on his hands stood on end. With a great roar, a violent gust of wind ripped across the open space, dispersing the suffocating ash and smoke.

Three hooded figures strode towards him, their features silhouetted by the glare of the fires, the one in the middle head and shoulders above the two on either side. As they stopped, just within earshot, their features became distinct and his heart quickened.

Three became five.

6

KAINE

"By all the gods, Tarek, they've got Runa and Dagan."

Tarek ignored Lars and stepped towards the group.

"Dad!" Dagan pushed forward to run to his father, but the hulking figure behind him held him tight.

The warrior on Dagan's left held Tarek's scale armour and helmet that he had left back at the house, and the one on his far right clutched Runa by her hair. Blood flowed from her nose and her dress was torn down to her waist.

The darkness quickened within Tarek. He ground his teeth, willing himself to stay focused, to stay calm, to stay hidden.

"Oh, that's disappointing," said the figure in the centre. "I didn't go to all this trouble just for him to stand there and gawp at me."

"Are you sure this is him?" asked the one holding Runa. "Looks like he's been on that northern piss they call ale."

"It's him," said the shortest of the three, glancing down to Dagan. "Hard to hide when your eyes give you away."

"Well, if anyone knows who he is, it's you, Aderyn."

She laughed. "Oh yes, and he's got the tattoos to prove it." She looked over to the warrior holding Runa. "Once you see them, Rask, you'll want them for your book of skins."

"You've mistaken me for someone else. I'm just a farmer."

"And how would a farmer possess such a splendid coat of scale armour and a helmet emblazoned with the wren of the Nirasian clan?" asked the man holding Dagan.

"They're just cheap copies I bought from a travelling merchant."

The man chuckled from under his cowl. "And I suppose you bought that cheap imitation of a sword from them as well?"

"I did."

"Lies! This," he said, jabbing his finger at the armour, "is the armour presented to the Champion of Niras at the end of the Mendari war. And that sword you wield is Red Mist."

"Dad...what's he saying?"

The warrior patted Dagan's shoulder. "I'm sorry, Dagan, but your father's lied to you about many things."

"Don't listen to him, son."

"See how he squirms? Well, I won't lie to you. Your father is Grimbard, the disgraced Champion of Niras, sword brother to the tyrant King Rodric and to his scheming Master of War, Luis Ironfoot —better known as the Three Orphans of Treharne."

Inside Tarek, the darkness ascended, gaining in strength with every name uttered.

"I-Is it true, Dad? A-Are you the traitor?"

Runa twisted to face her son. "He's no traitor, Dagan. King Rodric accused him of a deed he—"

"Be silent, apostate!" Rask cuffed her with the back of his hand.

"Leave her alone, or—"

"Or what, Grimbard? You'll kill us all?"

"You have no idea what I'm capable of."

"Actually, I do." The man in the middle pulled back his hood to reveal his face.

Tarek's mouth dried. The face he looked upon had aged, yet he had no doubt who stood before him. "Kaine."

"I wondered if you'd recognise me after so many years."

"So you've finally come to take your revenge? Let my family go and I'll surrender peacefully."

The corners of Kaine's mouth twitched into a smile. "Oh no, Grimbard—I didn't just come for you." He raised his hand in the air, then flicked it down. From behind him, the rumbling thundered once more, rising in tone, until it crescendoed into an ear-splitting roar.

"Tarek, help me!"

He whirled to face Lars, just as the boy lurched up into the air, hurtling towards him. For a split second, he caught sight of the light of the fires streaking through a stream of shimmering air that hovered above his head. Launching off the ground, he struck the aberration with a mighty blow. The impact resonated through Red Mist's blade, through the hilt and through his body, hurling him onto his back. He scrambled to his feet, staring in dismay at his failed attempt, as Lars and the remaining ten children vanished into the flames rising into the night behind Kaine, their cries of terror fading into the tumult around them.

"Dagan," said Kaine, releasing his hold of the boy. "Go to your father and embrace him." Then, nodding to Rask, the warrior shoved Runa beside her son. "It's time for a family reunion."

As Kaine's companions laughed, Runa clasped Dagan's hand and rushed towards Tarek.

What's that bastard playing at? He racked his mind. Then, with a jolt of panic, he remembered what the warrior at Garin's house had said: *'He's already got his eyes on the twelfth'.* "Dagan!" He sprinted for them, just as two more rippling trails of air pierced a cloud of smoke behind Kaine. They plummeted to the ground, parting the grass, slithering towards his family.

With one last muscle-tearing effort, Tarek vaulted into the air, ready to shove his family away from the hidden terror. Yet as he landed, stretching his fingertips towards them, their eyes grew wide with terror. "No!"

The rippling tendrils of air lurched them up above the ground until they hovered halfway between Tarek and the Mendari. He stared at their writhing forms, helpless. "Please, Kaine.... Don't do this. They're innocent."

Kaine snorted. "Tell that to the dead you slaughtered when you marched into Mendaria."

"That was war."

"And so is this.... Take the boy."

Tarek and Runa screamed in unison as Kaine's hidden menace reeled Dagan into the distance, vanishing within the glare of the fires.

"My son!" cried Runa.

Tarek's blood boiled with unquenchable fury, sensing the darkness bubbling up from within. Only one thing held back his dark companion—Runa. He stared up into her distraught face. Once again, he had failed to save a child of hers.

"Can you feel it, Grimbard? Is your dark gift stirring?"

"Where's my son?"

"I'd be more worried about your apostate bitch," said Kaine, raising his hand once again.

"Is there nothing I can do to stop this madness?"

"Madness? How could you Northern Taranians and your despicable religion possibly understand our ways? Besides, it seems that your peaceful life in Nabaya has lulled your darkness into a state of torpor. Let's wake it up." He dropped his hand.

"No!"

The force holding Runa tossed her high into the air. Tarek ran underneath her, dropped his sword and held out his trembling hands. "I'll catch you, Runa!" She tumbled towards his open arms, then screamed. A tendril of shimmering air exploded out of her chest, her life-force descending to the floor as ruby-red droplets of rain. He dropped to his knees and stared up towards his wife's twitching body, his tears lost in the torrent of her blood washing over him. *I will avenge you. Wait for me on the other side of the Veil, my love— I won't be long.*

He gripped Red Mist and pulled at the leather strapping to expose the wren-shaped hilt. Then he stood to his feet and sliced the blade through his gambeson. The padded armour fell to the ground, revealing the soulless tattooed eyes of those silenced by Red Mist.

"Magnificent! They'll make a fine addition to my collection."

"Patience, Rask," said Kaine. "It's time to release your dark gift, Grimbard." He beckoned a group of warriors from out of the darkness. "Defeat him and you'll be greatly rewarded."

Tarek sneered at the approaching warriors, knowing that they stared fixated on his tattoos. "Yes. Look upon the eyes of the dead;

you'll soon find yourselves among them. Now come to me and embrace your death. For Runa and Dagan!"

The world blurred into a sea of red from his dance of death that he weaved between the shapeless forms of Mendari assailing him from all sides. And as Red Mist sliced, pierced and severed the flesh of his opponents, he found himself alone standing among the dead and the dying.

He ripped Red Mist out of the eye socket of the last warrior, grabbed the closest spear and hurled it at Kaine. It sped through the air, its aim true. "Die, you bastard!"

Yet Kaine remained standing. He held the spear tip barely a hand's breadth from his eyes. Stabbing it into the ground, he did the strangest thing—he clapped—and so did Aderyn and Rask. "Outstanding!"

Enraged, Tarek rushed forward. He sprung into the air and bore down on Kaine. He swung Red Mist over his head, ready to split the Mendari leader in two. As he brought his blade down, a flash of steel swept across his vision, parrying his swing. Their contact rang as a clear, high note, yet a moment later, only one blade remained. Tarek stared dumbfounded at the bladeless hilt held in his white-knuckled grip.

Two pairs of hands pushed him to his knees.

"H-How?"

Kaine sheathed his sword and unclasped his robe. "This is how."

Tarek reeled back, recognising Kaine's jet-black armour—armour he had not seen since the day he and his sword brothers killed Kaine's father, Banan the Giant. "All this time I thought I imagined it... But if it's all true, it fought for us, not for you?"

"You mean something that looked like this?" Kaine tapped his shoulder, and two sections around the neck lifted over his head to form a helmet.

"The wraith warrior."

Kaine laughed. His voice sounded unnatural behind the sleek, moulded helmet. "Is that what you call him? Isn't it ironic that this armour once saved your life but now heralds the end of the whore goddess' reign in the North and a united Tarania under the banner of the Circle and the Cross?"

Tarek spat at Kaine's feet. "By the goddess, get on with it and kill me. Anything's better than listening to your bollocks."

"Kill you? Now why would I do a stupid thing like that?"

"Y-You're not going to kill me?"

"No, Grimbard—you're going back home. Back to Northern Tarania. We're going to have so much fun!"

7

ESCAPE FROM VEDANA

Bathed in the bright mid-afternoon light of the Twins, the horses of the Taleni Elite Guard thundered along the Great North Road. At the head of the column, Amira rode in silence. She looked over her shoulder at the ashen clouds expanding in the South and closed her eyes. *So it begins.*

"Concentrate on the road ahead—more evacuees could still be ahead of us."

She snapped her attention onto the clansguard riding beside her, glowering at him from under the hood of her riding cloak. His scale armour jingled a melody with the rise and fall of his mount's gait, while the horsehair tail of his boar-crested helmet danced in the warm breeze. No-one could fail to recognise her father's champion: Alun Swordstorm.

"If I knew you were going to be like this, I'd have stayed back in Vedana."

"You should have. I only asked for Cai," she said, flicking her eyes to the warrior riding behind the Champion of Taleni. The young clansguard reddened at the mention of his name.

"I'm sure Cai's honoured that you'd consider him for such a task, but he's not yet named." He turned in the saddle and smiled at him. "Perhaps today is your day to perform a great deed, my son."

"Yes, Father."

"But this is madness," argued Amira. "The Mendari are at our walls. You should be there to protect him, not here with me."

"You know the answer to that. He treasures you more than anything else in the world—even his own life."

"Stubborn old man."

"Well, he's not called Aedan 'the Defiant' for nothing." A hint of a smirk crossed his lips. "One of many traits he shares with his daughters."

"I'm nothing like him, and neither is Yanna."

"That cuts deep, Amira."

"Damn his pride! Where's the wisdom in sending twenty of his greatest warriors to escort me, when one would have sufficed—even if he is unnamed."

"It was your father's wisdom that sent us with you. Of course, Cai could—"

"What's the matter?"

He did not answer, his expression darkening as he spotted something on the road ahead.

She frowned, then looked to the North. All along their journey, groups of refugees had littered the road, people of all castes sharing the same destination: the Fortress of Keld. Most of the lower castes trudged their way on foot, struggling with whatever possessions they could carry. Those of the higher castes rode on horseback or travelled by wagon. It was one such wagon, surrounded by a large group of grey-cloaked warriors, that held the champion's attention.

"Grey Cloaks," he cursed, digging his spurs into his horse's flanks. "As if we didn't have enough to worry about. Follow me, Named of the Taleni!"

"Stay close to me, my lady," said Cai, drawing beside her. "And please keep your hood up. Kaine's spies are everywhere."

She flashed him a smile. "I'm glad you're here to protect me, Cai." They set off at a canter, falling in behind the tail end of the Elite Guard.

Seeing more clearly as she neared the confrontation, a man, a woman and most probably their daughter stood in the back of the cart wielding pots and pans as weapons against the well-armed Grey Cloaks. The woman cried out in terror as a warrior bearing the triskelion of the goddess climbed onto the wagon and smacked the man with the hilt of her sword.

"Harm that man and you'll have me to answer to!" yelled Alun, pulling to a halt in front of the Grey Cloaks. The Named formed a wedge behind him, their shields covering their bodies and their spears levelled.

"Shield wall!" cried the Grey Cloak commander, poised with her sword at the man's throat. The forty-strong group shuffled together, locking their shields. "Stay out of this, clansguard. This is Communion business."

"I'll tell you one last time, Warden. Leave my friends alone, and you'll live to see another day."

"Friends?" she hissed. "Are you one of...them?"

Alun drew his sword. "This is Boar's Rage. I've never used it against another Northern Taranian, but today I'll make an exception for you," he said, pointing the blade's razor-sharp tip at the Grey Cloak commander.

"You dare threaten a Warden of the Communion?"

"I'll do more than—"

"Enough!" cried Amira, pushing her horse through to the front.

"Keep out of this, child, whoever you are."

Amira ripped off her hood and glowered at the Grey Cloaks. As her identity rippled through their ranks, they lowered their shields and fell to their knees—only the Grey Cloak commander remained standing. "Correct me if I'm wrong, Warden, but doesn't the rhyme say, 'The monarch, the noble, the clansguard and the priest, the skilled, the farmer, and all that dwell beneath'?"

"Yes," mumbled the Warden.

"Louder."

"Yes!"

"Yes, what?"

"Yes, my lady."

"Good. Now that I've established the order of things, get off that wagon before I order the Elite Guard to attack. And make no mistake,

Warden, they'll slaughter every last one of you without breaking into a sweat."

Reluctantly, the Warden sheathed her sword and, with a final sneer at the family, jumped off the wagon.

"What's your name?" asked Amira.

"I am Warden Elin of the Grove of the Goddess at Belanore."

"You're a long way from Belanore, Warden. Why is that?"

"Predina, Archwarden of Nirasia, sent us to reinforce the Grey Cloaks at Vedana, while your father rides out against the Mendari."

"You don't know, do you?"

"Don't know what?"

"The Mendari overwhelmed our army and now lay siege to Vedana. You'll be able to see the smoke from the fires over the next ridge."

"The Grove of the Goddess!"

"Indeed. So I suggest you stop harassing my people and make haste, or there'll be no Sacred Grove to protect."

The Warden nodded, then turned to her warriors. "To Vedana, Grey Cloaks, before it's too late."

As the soldiers of the Communion marched south, Alun cocked his head to the side and tapped his lips.

Amira narrowed her eyes. "What?"

"It seems as if little Lady Amira has finally grown up."

She rolled her eyes. "Well, if I hadn't intervened, who knows how much blood would have been spilled."

"I'm proud of you," he said, smiling. "Let me introduce you to my friends. I know one of them will be thrilled to meet you." He edged his horse towards the wagon. "Lady Amira, this is Dylan and his wife, Bethan. And this brave young lady," he said, nodding towards a young girl with long dark hair, "is their daughter, Keila."

Bethan stopped wrapping her husband's wound and curtseyed. Keila followed her example. "Thank the goddess you came when you did, my lady. Truly, I feared for our lives."

"What did you do to warrant such aggression?"

"Dylan argued with the Warden that it wasn't fair that we had to give way to them. The Warden wanted to teach him a lesson."

"Which caste are you?"

Bethan held up her right palm, revealing the anvil and the hammer brand of the Skilled Caste. Amira paled. Except for those born into the nobility, all children received their caste's brand on their thirteenth birthday. She looked at Keila and shuddered, imagining the red-hot branding iron searing the girl's soft, unblemished skin.

"It shouldn't matter what caste they are, Amira," said Alun. "They're Taleni, and that's all that matters."

"If only all the higher castes felt the same way, Alun," said Dylan, standing up with the help of Bethan.

Amira drew closer to the wagon, noticing that Keila held something in her hands that looked familiar to her. "May I see your doll, Keila?"

Handing over the doll, Keila reddened. "I-I don't play with dolls anymore. I'm almost twelve."

"I found it under Keila's bed when we were packing to leave," said Bethan. "She used to play with it for hours, pretending that she was your younger sister, my lady."

Amira smiled. "I'll tell Yanna that when I see her later. Mother loved listening to our stories when we were younger." She paused for a moment, lost in a bittersweet memory.

"It was such a tragedy what happened to your mother. She was a wonderful woman. Her people truly loved her."

"Thank you, Bethan. That means a lot to me."

She called Cai over to the wagon and held the doll out to him. "What do you think, clansguard? Is it a good resemblance?"

He examined the doll with its red wool for hair, a piece of thin copper wire for a torc, a scrap of blue and green plaid for a cloak, and a brown bead for one eye, and one of blue for the other. "Amazing likeness, my lady."

"Yes, it's like looking into a mirror," she said, handing the doll back to Keila.

"I just wish I could've found the other two dolls," said Bethan. "I think they were in Keila's clothes chest; but it was so dark, and we were in such a rush, I had to leave them there."

"One of Lady Yanna and the other of Keila?"

"Yes, my lady."

"That's a shame. I would've liked to have seen them."

"Never mind that, Amira," said Alun. He scanned the line of refugees. "I'm just glad you all got out alive... Although, Dylan, I wish you'd left last month after I warned you about what happened to Nabaya."

Dylan shrugged. "We were all taken by surprise at how quick the Mendari swept from the south. Besides, we thought we'd be safe in Vedana." He looked to the north. "I just hope the walls of Keld are as impregnable as you say."

"They won't get past those walls," said Alun, shaking his head. "Where will you go once you get to Keld?"

Dylan scratched an itch under his bandage. "We'll ask around to see if the fortress needs our services."

"Ask around?" said Alun, widening his eyes. "You won't get two minutes through the South Tunnel before you'll be swarmed by warriors begging you to make something for them."

"Why's that?" asked Amira.

"Well, we might have made a few well-known pieces in our time."

Alun roared with laughter. "By the goddess, man, just tell her. Lady Amira doesn't know one end of a sword from the other."

"As well as making your father's armour, I made the Armour of the Two Champions," said Dylan, pointing at Swordstorm's magnificent helmet and scale over mail armour.

"And I made Boar's Rage," added Bethan.

"Oh, I see...and who was the other champion?"

The couple glanced at each other. Bethan replied for them both. "I'm sorry, Alun. I know he was your friend, but I regret making Red Mist for him...after what he did."

Amira raised her brows. "Even I know who wielded that sword."

"Everyone in Tarania knows the story of the traitor—Tarek Grimbard."

"You're wrong, Beth," said Alun. "He's not a traitor."

"Tell that to King Rodric."

At Amira's insistence, the Elite Guard remained with the family for a couple of miles, just to make sure that the Grey Cloaks kept to their southerly direction. She spent the time talking to Bethan and Keila. It was rare for her to mingle with people from the lower castes. Not that the skilled were much lower than the nobility; yet caste precepts forbade social interaction unless sanctioned by the Communion. The lower the caste, the more stringent the rules.

Then, as it was time to say their farewells, she broke another rule; she leaned across in the saddle and hugged them. "I pray that the goddess will protect your family during these troubling times."

"Thank you, my lady," said Bethan. "And I pray that your father turns the tide against the Mendari, and drives them out of our land."

Amira pulled away from them and straightened her riding cloak. "Rest assured, Bethan, my father will triumph this day—I guarantee it."

8

DERWEDD FOREST

As a child, Amira had loved sitting beside her sister in Vedana's Great Hall, listening to the bards. Unforgettable stories like 'The Three Orphans of Treharne' and 'Enora and Galerius' reminded her of happier days. Yet there were some tales she would rather forget. As she flitted her gaze between the thick lines of ash, cedar, holly and oak looming over her from either side of the Great North Road, one story clawed at her mind: 'The Bwgan'.

A story as ancient as the Hen Rai, the Bwgan would crawl out of the depths of the forest as silent as a tomb, and would hide in the shadows, searching for the children it had seen from afar. Children that, once chosen, would never be seen again.

She flinched as a shadowy form darted to the right of her. "What was that?"

"A deer," said Alun. "Nothing more."

"Are you sure?"

"By the goddess, Amira, I swear that imagination of yours has a life of its own."

"I-I just want to get out of this place as soon as possible. Can't we go any faster?"

"No, it's too dangerous, Amira. It's highly unlikely that the king's engineers would've repaired the forest section of the road this early in spring."

"Why's that?"

"The spring rains would undo all their work in minutes. So no more looking into the forest for the Bwgan or whatever else it is you're imagining." He shot her a stern look that she knew well. "I don't know what unseen evil you expect to find in those trees, but believe me, the Mendari are real, and I want to get you as far away from them as possible."

"Can you at least tell me how long it'll take to get through this cursed place?"

"At a trot, we'll make the other side of the forest in a couple of hours."

"A couple of hours!"

"You'll be fine. Besides, I'm sure you can find a way to pass the time," he said, grinning at Cai, then winking at her.

"Alun Swordstorm, I find your teasing highly inappropriate considering the walls of Vedana may very well have fallen."

He softened his expression. "I'm trying to take your mind off it. You can't change what's happening at home, no matter how many times you look behind."

"I know.... Do you think the defences will hold long enough for all the townspeople to escape?"

"Honestly, I don't know. The Mendari I fought against yesterday were better organised and far more disciplined than during the war. It's Kaine. He's achieved what no other Mendari has done—he's unified the tribes. Goddess knows what else he's capable of."

Amira was about to question him further when he held up his hand. "Hold up!" As the Guard reared to a halt, Alun pressed his finger to his lips. "Shush. Listen," he said, pointing back the way they came. "Quick, get off the road."

The warhorses of the Elite Guard obeyed their riders instantly, but Amira's mount sensed her panic and reared on its hind legs. "Help me, please!" she cried, staring down the road, towards the rumbling of galloping hooves. Whatever was coming would hit her full on.

"Hold on, my lady, I've got you." She looked down to find Cai gripping her horse's bridle, whispering into its ear. How he calmed the horse was a mystery, but soon it whinnied and gently nuzzled the clansguard. "She's ready to listen."

"Thank you, Cai." As she pushed her hips forward in the saddle, the horse obeyed, moving off the road and into the trees. And not a moment too soon, as a cart and its hysterical team of horses hurtled towards them. As it sped past, the cart hit a bump in the road, tossing its load in all directions. Amira stiffened, her muscles tightening throughout her body. There on the floor, covered in blood, was Keila's doll.

"By the goddess!" She vaulted off her horse and ran to the figure. Falling to her knees, she pressed the little rag doll to her chest and wept.

A strong hand rested on her shoulder. Red-eyed, she glanced up to find Alun, ashen-faced, staring down at her. "W-what happened to them?"

"I don't know. Whatever it was, it put the horses in such a frenzy, you'd swear that Velak himself was pursuing them."

"And you say my imagination's vivid." Numb, she got to her feet, tucked the doll under her cloak and remounted her horse. "I need to go back. They could still be alive."

"You're not going anywhere."

"You can't stop me, Alun."

"Viperstrike, hold Lady Amira's reins," he commanded.

As the clansguard gripped the long leather straps, Amira resisted and hissed, "Let go of me!"

"I can't do that, my lady. Please stop, or I'll restrain you."

"You wouldn't dare," gasped Amira. Yet, the steely determination in the warrior's eyes was enough to know that she would stop her without a moment's hesitation. Defeated, she let go of the reins and rounded on Alun. "But we have to do something."

"Yes, we do. That's why I'm going back."

"But sir," said Viperstrike. "What about our orders?"

"Damn the orders." He beckoned Viperstrike towards him. "Lead them to Midway Bridge and wait for me there. If I'm not back within two hours, leave without me." He opened one of his leather saddlebags and pulled out two thin bamboo sticks. They were similar to the ones used at the Sacred Groves, apart from the uniform marks notched down each length. He held them out as Viperstrike struck steel on flint to light each one. Once lit, he handed one to her. "Remember, two hours, Catrin, and not a minute longer."

"Yes, sir."

Amira called over to the champion. "Please stay safe. I don't know what I'd do if something terrible happened to you."

Alun drew next to her and reached out for her hand. "I know you're scared, but remember who protects you. Oh, I almost forgot. I've got something for you."

"What is it?"

"It's from your father." He rummaged inside his saddlebag, retrieved an object wrapped in a leather pouch, and handed it to her.

She opened it. Inside, she found a scabbarded dagger with her clan's sigil of the boar carved into the handle. "Father's hunting knife?"

Alun nodded.

"Why do I need this? You said it yourself; I've no clue about such things. I'm not like Princess Seren or the other women who serve as clansguard. My father raised me in the ways of court. He knows that."

"I-I'm sorry, Amira, but he didn't give it to you as a weapon to fight with."

"I don't understand? If it's not for—" Amira stopped as she realised why her father had given her the blade. "No. How could he?"

"Your father's orders, Amira. If the Mendari capture you, goddess knows what they'll do to you. It would be a fate worse than death."

"No. I-I can't. I won't."

"I told him you'd be like this, but he insisted."

"I hate him!" she cried, "And I hate you too!" She dug her stirrups into her mount and galloped deeper into the forest.

"What are you waiting for?" said Alun, glowering at the Elite Guard. "Stop her before she breaks her neck."

All but one of the Guard thundered after the youngest daughter of Lord Aedan Taleni.

Cai drew beside his father. "You can't go on your own. Who knows what's waiting for you back there?"

"Not this time, Cai. You'll slow me down."

He knew his father was right, but all the same, he protested. "But—"

Alun narrowed his eyes. "Not another word. Besides, Viperstrike won't put up with Amira's stubbornness. I need you here to keep her out of trouble. Otherwise, Catrin's bound to gag her and tie her to her horse until they get to Keld."

"She wouldn't?"

"Yes, she would."

Cai sighed. "As you wish, Father."

"Good lad." He leaned forward and embraced him. "I thank the goddess every day for being on that beach and finding you in that shipwreck."

"I wouldn't be here if you hadn't."

"Nor would I."

9

WHATEVER THE COST

Amira shielded her eyes as she emerged out of the shade of the forest and into the glaring light of the Twins. The Guard had reached Midway Bridge.

Riding into the clearing, Viperstrike called the riders to a halt. She led Amira's horse to the crossing, tying the reins onto one of the stakes supporting the row of weather-worn planks stretching across the tributary of the River Valtara. Dismounting, she rolled her shoulders and stretched her back, sending a shimmering wave across the golden scales of her armour. "Can I trust you to stay here, or do I have to tie you up for your own safety?"

Amira shifted in the saddle. "T-that won't be necessary."

"Hmm.... Cai, get over here."

The young clansguard left his horse with a warrior and hurried over to the pair. "Yes, ma'am."

"Make sure Lady Amira stays out of trouble. I've got enough to worry about being stuck in this bloody clearing without keeping my eye on her." She examined the thin piece of bamboo sticking out of her belt. "Just over an hour left." She looked at Cai. "By the goddess, I hope your father knows what he's doing. I can't believe he's risking his life for..."

"Them?"

She spat on the ground. "Just make sure she stays put." Turning on her heels, she strode towards five clansguard arming themselves with crossbows. "I want every inch of the southern tree line patrolled. Stay within earshot."

"Yes, ma'am!"

As they headed towards the trees, she raised her voice to address the remaining warriors. "I want the horses corralled, fed and watered. Keep your shields and spears close at hand. Goddess knows how close the Mendari are to us."

"That woman's terrifying."

Cai nodded. "Father believes it won't be long until she's asked to become a champion to one of the other clan chieftains. She's one of the finest Named I've ever sparred with."

"Better than your father?"

"Now, that would be a contest to behold," he said, grinning. "But if he was honest, I think father would say there were only two warriors in Northern Tarania who surpassed him in skill: the king and, of course, Grimbard."

"And what about you, Cai? Do you think you'll ever be as good as them?"

"Well, I started my training a lot later than most novices."

"When was that?"

"Six years ago."

"So how old are you now?"

"In truth, I've no idea how old I am; but Alun said I looked like a boy of thirteen years when he found me—so that would make me nineteen."

"Oh, we're the same age." She chewed on her lip and shook her head. "It astounds me you've no memory of your life before the shipwreck—before Alun pulled you from the surf and saved your life."

"It's true. Everything before that is blank. I don't even remember my name."

"I wonder where your real family are?"

"Probably at the bottom of the Endless Sea."

"Oh, I'm sorry," she said, lowering her eyes. "I shouldn't have been so insensitive."

"No, it's fine. I can't mourn people I've no memory of. All I can remember is being found on that beach clutching this sword," he said, taking hold of the pommel of his weapon. "When he found me, he thought I was from the Warrior Caste, or even higher." He held up his right hand. "See? No branding. Not that Father cares about such things."

Amira grimaced. "Do you think the sword belonged to one of your family?"

"I'd like to think so. What matters is that the man who found me picked me up and gave me a new life. I owe him everything."

"That's something we have in common. Over the years, Alun has become so much more to Yanna and me. Especially after our mother died." She looked away from Cai and stared into the fast-flowing river, as the light of the Twins sparkled across its surface.

"I'll give you a moment to yourself."

"Thank you. And Cai?"

"Yes?"

"Thank you for saving my life on the road."

Cai smiled at her, then walked to the other side of the bridge to give her some privacy.

Alone, she ran her hands through her horse's mane as she did as a little girl. So many happy memories to choose from. Yet the events of the past few hours plagued her mind—no more so than the vivid image of the young girl and her mother huddled together in the back of the cart. She pulled the blood-stained doll from out of her cloak and played with the simple copper torc hung around its neck. *How many more innocent lives? I don't know if I can do this.* It was then that she remembered something that her father had taught her. 'In those times when your mind is full of doubt, take a moment to remember who you are and the reason you tread the path that has been chosen. Then all else will pale compared to fulfilling your destiny.' Reflecting on those words, she knelt beside the bank and refilled her waterskin. She drank deeply. The refreshing, ice-cold water flowed through her, reviving her, giving her clarity. *Forgive me, Father. I'll be the person you want me to be and follow my destiny, whatever the cost.*

She glanced down in front of her and frowned, wondering where she had placed the doll. It was not on the bank or in her robe. A glint of something metallic caught her eye, sinking into the watery depths. As the last few strands of red wool trailed downstream, she closed her eyes and sighed. "Whatever the cost."

10

THE SHIMMERING

"Any sign of him?"

"No, ma'am." Cai stabbed the butt of his spear into the ground and sagged onto his shield. He slapped his hand hard against the unpainted wooden surface. "He's running out of time."

"Worse," said Viperstrike, extinguishing the glowing tip of the bamboo clock. "His time's up."

"Can't we give him a few more minutes?"

"No. His orders were clear."

"But—"

"He'll be fine, Cai." She slapped him on the shoulder. "No-one knows these woods like your father. Ready your horse and stay close to Lady Amira. We're moving out."

He lingered for a moment, wondering whether to argue, but Viperstrike's tell-tale twitch at the corner of her mouth was all that was needed for him to wrench his spear out of the ground and head towards the bridge. His mind swirled with a multitude of dark possibilities of what could have happened to his father. He grimaced at his lack of faith. *No. He's the Champion of Taleni. He's just delayed.*

Amira sat cross-legged in the middle of the bridge, scratching into a plank with her father's blade. Catching sight of Cai, she sprung to her feet and hurried to meet him, but her face dropped as Viperstrike whistled a bird song, signalling back the patrols.

"We're leaving without him?"

He kicked into a clod of earth, sending a cloud of dust rising into the air. "He's run out of time."

"Then give him some more."

"I asked, but Viperstrike won't disobey Father's orders."

"We'll see about that." She stormed past Cai, heading towards the Elite Guard's second-in-command, who now stood by her horse, securing the saddle.

Cai spun around and chased after her. "Wait! You'll only make things worse."

Ignoring him, she planted her feet wide apart and jabbed her finger at the warrior. "You can't just leave him here."

Viperstrike glanced up, muttered something under her breath and returned to her task. "Your father commanded us to deliver you safely to your sister. He said nothing about tying you to a horse and gagging you." She yanked on a saddle strap.

"You wouldn't dare."

"Try me."

"It's not just me," said Amira, glancing back as Cai caught up with her. "Cai thinks it's a stupid decision, don't you, Cai?"

Cai remained silent. He squinted towards the southern entrance into the clearing and with a trembling hand pointed towards a lone figure staggering along the road. "Father?"

The others stopped what they were doing and cursed at what they saw.

Splatters of crimson blood covered his father's armour and Boar's Rage raked along the ground behind him. Reaching the centre of the clearing, he wavered to a halt, his breathing rasping in the unnatural silence that had descended over the forest.

Viperstrike ripped her shield off her back and tucked it in tight to her chest. "Clansguard! Form a shield wall around Lady Amira. Where're those bloody scouts?"

As the Taleni took up position, Cai took a faltering step forward, then another, and another until, before he knew it, he had rushed headlong towards his father.

From behind, Viperstrike bellowed his name. "Cai! Get back in formation! That's an order." But there was no stopping him. Only one thing mattered in the world—reaching his father.

Gritting his teeth, Alun pushed up on Boar's Rage and raised a hand to him. "D-don't come any closer. I-it's not safe."

Cai skidded to a halt. He scanned the clearing for any sign of danger. "I can't see anyone. Please, let me help you."

His father twisted his neck to look behind. "They're coming. Flee this place while you still can."

"Who's coming?" The trees behind his father blurred out of focus as a pocket of rippling air spread across the road. Shimmering, the phenomenon advanced towards them, gaining in substance each second it came closer to their position. "Father, what is it?" Trembling, Alun turned to him, with a look of outright terror in his eyes that shook Cai to his core.

"Too late. They're here."

"Who?" The answer to his question appeared before him: the rippling air solidified into the form of five warriors, each covered from head to toe in black plate armour over tunics tight as skin. Their helmets were no less incredible—smooth and featureless, they gave away nothing of the identity of the wearers within.

As they moved further into the clearing, one thing was obvious to Cai—they were Mendari. Emblazoned in blood red across each breastplate was the sigil of their religion: the Circle and the Cross.

"Save yourself."

"I don't want to leave you."

"Go. That's an order, clansguard."

Tears rolling down his cheeks, Cai backed away from his father, until a firm hand grabbed his cloak and hauled him inside the shield wall.

Viperstrike flared her nostrils and pulled him face to face. "Compose yourself, boy, or the last image he'll have of you is a snivelling wreck."

He wiped his eyes with the cuff of his gambeson and stood straight.

"Now stand by Lady Amira. She's your responsibility now. Your father gave us an order, and by the goddess I intend to get you all out of here alive."

"Yes, ma'am." As he pushed through the lines, the Elite Guard nodded to him, the distress and sadness as clear in their eyes as they were in his. But it was Amira's manic look of terror that took him by surprise.

She darted her eyes between Alun and Cai. "H-he's not supposed to get hurt."

"I can't believe it either; but Viperstrike's right: our duty is to get you out of here."

"We can't just leave him to whatever those things are," she said, staring at the five warriors. Her eyes widened, and the colour drained from her face. As a great clamour erupted from within the ranks of the Elite Guard, she screamed.

Cai snapped his sight back to the five and stared in horror as from around their backs each of them revealed the severed head of one of the Elite Guard sent to patrol the woods. "Bastards!"

The Elite Guard, famed for their unbreakable discipline, lost restraint. They broke formation, hurling challenges of single combat at the black-clad warriors.

"Get back in line," growled Viperstrike. "Or you'll wish you had died at the hands of one of those monsters."

"Oh, come now, clansguard. Monsters? Is that the best you can come up with?" Towering beside Cai's father, a sixth warrior materialised in black. He tapped the side of his shoulder and his helmet split into sections, disappearing into the armour around his neck. "We're not monsters. We are the Scions of the First."

The warrior's appearance took Cai by surprise. Unlike most Taranian males, Northern or Southern, he wore no beard or moustache, and his blond hair was cropped so short it was hardly visible against his sallow skin.

"I am known as Kaine, Son of Banan and Scion of the First. Chosen by

Lord Velak to cleanse the world of those who follow the false goddess." He looked over his shoulder at the five lifeless heads still dripping with blood. "I hope you'll choose more wisely than your foolish comrades."

"Brave words for a man who'll soon feel my steel slice through his neck," said Viperstrike, stepping out of the wall to face him.

"You have great spirit, just like this one." With one swift kick, Boar's Rage fell into the grass, and Alun slumped to his knees. "Your commander is one of the finest warriors I've ever faced; yet even he fell to my blade." He reached behind his back, retrieving his sword, and rested the magnificent double-edged blade across the champion's neck. "So believe me, Champion of Taleni, when I honour you by offering you the chance to use your skills for a nobler cause...a just cause. Renounce the whore goddess and embrace the love of Velak."

Alun laughed, coughing up blood and phlegm. He met the eyes of each clansguard until, after winking at Amira, he fixed his eyes on Cai and smiled.

Fighting the urge to cry out, Cai steeled himself and mouthed the words that every Taranian clansguard prayed before a battle. "For the glory of a warrior's death."

His father nodded, then craned his neck to face Kaine. "Mendari, my answer is this. I piss on your offer, I piss on you, and I piss on your god."

Kaine chuckled and patted the sword against Alun's shoulder. "Very well. You have made your decision."

"No!" cried Amira. "You can't do this."

Kaine straightened and locked eyes with her. "The offer was made, and he refused. I will not insult him or me with a second chance."

Amira buried her face into her hands. "I-I didn't ask for this."

Taking hold of her tremoring hand, Cai leaned in close to her. "It's not your fault." He glared at Kaine. "It's that bastard's fault and whatever dark magic he possesses."

She squeezed his hand tight. "I'm scared, Cai."

He pulled her in closer. "I won't let them harm you." *Or I'll die trying.*

"My sword," said Alun, reaching out to Boar's Rage. "Let me die as a warrior with my sword in my hand."

They held their breath as Kaine knelt beside Alun and placed Boar's Rage into the champion's hand.

Alun closed his eyes, sighed, then with his final reserve of energy and incredible acceleration, he thrust Boar's Rage up into a section of Kaine's tunic unprotected by his plate armour. The Mendari faltered backwards, holding his side where the blade had struck. He swayed for a few seconds before falling to the floor. With the cheers of the Elite Guard echoing around the clearing, the Champion of Taleni struggled onto his feet and staggered towards the fallen Mendari. As he stood over him, he grunted, hefting Boar's Rage above his head, ready to thrust the razor-sharp point into the Mendari leader's chest; but he hesitated, holding the blade closer to his bloodshot eyes and stared at it, frowning,

What's he doing? Cai strained to see what his father looked at. *Where's the blood? Where's Kaine's blood?*

His father knelt beside Kaine and removed the Mendari's hand from where his blade had struck. He turned to Cai and frowned. "Not a scratch; but how—"

In a dizzying blur, Kaine's hand drove deep into Alun's chest, pulsing a sickening rib-cracking snap through the air. The champion lurched forward as Kaine leered into his life-drawn face and mouthed something that even in the grip of death compelled Alun to stare wide-eyed at Amira and then at Cai. "Don't—"

That was the moment when one of the greatest warriors of Northern Tarania drew his last breath, as Kaine wrenched Alun's twitching heart out of his chest and squeezed it into a bloody pulp.

Cai's world spiralled down into despair. He looked on in utter disbelief as the Mendari leader lifted himself off the floor, gripped hold of his father's shoulder and shoved his corpse to his knees. He stood, holding his sword at the champion's neck. "Lord Velak, accept this blood sacrifice as a token of our devotion to you." He snarled into Alun's face. "This is for all the Mendari heads you took." In one swift stroke, he removed his head and kicked the body onto the grass, slick with the blood of the Champion of Taleni.

53

Time stood still. The remaining Elite gaped at the mutilated remains of their leader and friend, and Amira sobbed into Cai's chest. "He's gone, Cai."

He held her tight. "I-I know." He added his tears to hers.

Kaine reached down and retrieved Cai's father's head and held it up high for all to see. He levelled his sword at the Elite Guard. "So what will it be, Named of the Taleni? Submission to Velak, or death?"

Viperstrike spat in Kaine's direction. "Death. Ready yourselves, my brothers and sisters."

"Very well. You'll wish you changed your mind once you've met the Reaper." With Swordstorm's head in his hand, Kaine turned and marched towards the Scions. Vanishing within the rippling air, he said, "See you soon, Lady Amira."

At that moment, the surrounding air fizzed, as unseen Mendari bowmen released a hail of crossbow bolts. The Named braced for the onslaught, yet not one bolt hit their solid wall of shields, nor did any warrior cry out in pain. Not so for the Elite Guard's horses, corralled together in the clearing. They neighed in terror, rearing on their hind legs, thrashing on the floor, pulling at their tethered reins, desperate to escape the unbearable pain of the bolts.

"We have to save them, or we'll be trapped," cried a warrior, leaving his position, determined to protect his mount.

"Stay in formation!"

It was too late. The warrior screamed out as several black-feathered bolts punctured his body. He died before he hit the ground. In less than a minute, every horse in the corral lay dead or lame. Only Amira's horse, tethered to the bridge, remained unharmed.

Viperstrike called out from the front of the shield wall. "On three, we move back to the bridge. One, two, three!" Cai pulled Amira behind him as the remaining warriors provided cover. By the time they reached the bridge, another two warriors lay dead on the ground. Then, all at once, the attack ceased.

Cai held his breath, convinced that the Scions would return to finish them. Then he heard it. A sound like nothing he had witnessed before. Not even in his worst nightmares would such a sound have been imagined. It was unnatural—a guttural growl that undulated in tone. *What in the goddess' name is the Reaper?*

"Cai, get her on that horse!" barked Viperstrike.

"Yes, ma'am." He gripped Amira's hand and pulled her towards her mount.

"Ride as fast as you can towards Keld. Whatever you do, don't look back."

"But what about you?" asked Amira.

"Our orders are to get you to Keld. We know what we have to do. Now listen to me. Kaine knows who you are, which means he wants you for some unknown purpose." He eyed the knife pushed into Amira's belt. "You can't get captured."

"No! I won't use it on myself."

"You underestimate yourself, Lady Amira. It's time for you to be your father's daughter."

She flinched at his words and lowered her eyes.

"Don't look like that. There's no shame in fleeing."

"Come with me, Cai."

He shook his head. "I-I can't. It's my duty to fight for you."

She kissed him on the cheek. "I'm so sorry about your father, Cai."

"I will avenge him—I promise. Now get out of here, before I tie you on that bloody horse."

As she climbed up into the saddle, the unnerving sound grew closer to their position. The canopy shook and trunks snapped as the hidden terror powered its way towards them.

"What are you waiting for? Go."

Amira wavered. "I don't want to go without you."

"You have to."

Finally, she relented, turning her mare to face the bridge. Before she crossed, she looked back at Cai. With a trembling voice, she said, "It's not supposed to end like this."

11

THE REAPER

Oblivious to the threat of Kaine's oncoming menace, Cai knelt beside his father's corpse, laid Boar's Rage across his chest and placed his hands over the hilt. He stared at the fist-shaped hole and agonised over how a mere man could do such a thing. He played out his father's thrust in his mind, driven straight and with power into the chest of Kaine. What armour could withstand the point of one of the finest swords ever made? Cai had little time for superstition and folklore. Even the stories of the gods held little sway over his view of the world. Yet how could he deny what he had seen with his own eyes, and now heard, as the sound of Kaine's Reaper neared the edge of the clearing.

"Cai, we can't stay here any longer—we're burning the bridge."

"Yes, ma'am." He gripped his father's hands one last time. "What kind of power could do something like this to such a great warrior?"

"I don't know, Cai. All I know is that I'm not going down without a fight."

He stood and turned to face Viperstrike. "All I ever wanted was to fight alongside him and make him proud. So much so he'd recommend me to Lord Taleni to receive my name. And now..."

She gripped him by the shoulder and pressed her hand against his heart. "He's still with you, Cai. Fight alongside me and show him the man you've become."

"Thank you, ma'am. I won't let you down."

"For the glory of a warrior's death, Cai."

He stood to attention. "For the glory of a warrior's death."

They turned and hurried towards the rest of their group.

In all the stories his father had told him of the Named, never had the elite warriors of the Northern clans shrunk from adversity. No matter how hopeless the cause or insurmountable the odds, they never baulked. Yet as he neared the remaining Elite Guard, Cai saw the uncertainty and fear on every warrior's face, as it was on his own —for the world they thought they had mastered had changed. Changed to a world with a deadly new breed of enemy, changed to a world where their champion lay mutilated before them, changed to a world where a new level of fear existed. Fear had a new name, and its name was the Reaper.

Just as they reached the Named, an ear-splitting crash erupted from out of the tree line, as trunks splintered, branches snapped and leaves swirled into the clearing, leaving a yawning trail that disappeared into the southern depths of the forest.

Whatever the Reaper was, it had arrived.

The same shimmering apparition that preceded the Scions manifested itself before them—except this time the whole clearing rippled as if the air in front of them was alive. The non-stop thrumming of its low growl throbbed within Cai's ears. He wanted to drop his shield and spear, clasp his hands around the side of his head and run, but a sideways glance at Viperstrike reminded him of his promise. He darted his eyes around his comrades—he was not the only one in distress.

"Steady, clansguard. Remember your training. One step at a time, we edge back to the bridge. And keep those bloody shields tight."

Regaining their composure, they moved as one towards the crossing, and with a cacophonous, thundering growl that shook the ground under their feet, the Reaper followed. Cai gasped as a patch of grass flattened into a circle the size of a mature oak. Another appeared, then another, until he counted eight depressions within the clearing. *What in the goddess' name hunts us?*

Then, with just a few feet between them and Midway Bridge, a sliver of shimmering air extended out of the writhing mass and sped across the grass, towards the Elite Guard, and, to Cai's horror, directly to him. It rose until its tip shimmered a mere hand's breadth away from his face. Heart pounding, he tried to step back, but his leaden feet stayed rooted to the ground. His eyes grew wide as the shimmering form slid past his cheek, slipped under his armour and coiled itself around his petrified body. Constricted, he let out a whimper, sensing the tip tracing a snaking pattern from the small of his back right up to the top of his shoulder blades. The low droning surrounding him increased in pitch. He faltered as an image flashed into his mind of him standing on the prow of a ship heading out into the sea. A voice called to him. He turned to find a man and a woman, arm in arm, smiling proudly at him. His heart quickened, realising that he shared similar features with them. *Father? Mother?* Yet even as he came to terms with this revelation, what he saw next chilled him to the bone. Above his parents, the black sail of their boat unfurled and snapped taut in the wind. And embroidered in red was the Circle and the Cross.

"No, I'm not one of them. Get out of my head!"

The image vanished as a flash of polished steel sped past his eyes, striking the invisible force enveloping him. He flinched as metal struck metal. The Reaper roared in defiance, ripping away from the danger, but instead of retreating its limb, it stopped and coiled in the air, poised to strike at the owner of the sword—Viperstrike.

Even with his mind in a swirling fog, Cai thrust his shield out to protect Viperstrike, but the Reaper was quicker. It smashed through her shield, ripped through her scale armour and passed clean through her chest. Her head flopped around to Cai, eyes red and bulging, blood spurting out of her mouth. She tried to speak, but could only scream in agony as the Reaper wrenched her high into the air. It drew her close to its shimmering form as if it were a child examining an insect it had skewered with a needle.

With an anguished cry of defiance, the Elite Guard hurled their spears at the rippling form. The volley hurtled through the air, striking against whatever lay hidden within the shimmering; but as each spear fell to the ground, Cai accepted what he already knew in his heart: they were powerless against the Reaper.

They all stared up in horror, witnessing Viperstrike hovering above them, squirming as her life slowly drained away.

Cai pulled his eyes away from the scene. All he wanted to do was flee and find his way back to Amira, and to the safety of Keld. *Goddess!* The ground before him writhed with a mass of shimmering tendrils winding towards them. In a split second of deadly synchronicity, the invisible force lanced through the mail and plate of the Named and hauled them up to join Viperstrike.

Cai stood alone amongst shattered shields, shredded armour and the blood of his comrades. Then, in one final show of savagery, he witnessed the full wrath of the Reaper. Roaring in triumph, it whipped its tendrils high into the air, eviscerating every warrior. Their bodies exploded, showering Cai in flesh, blood and bone. He stiffened, ready for the inevitable. Yet the impaling thrust never came. "Come on, you bastard. Kill me. What are you waiting for?"

As he stood in the massacre's maelstrom, he was sure he could hear someone yelling at him, but his muffled hearing impeded his understanding. Was it the Reaper, taunting him? No. It was a person. *But I'm the only one left.* He heard it again—from behind. He turned in a daze to find a young woman on a dun-coloured mare, charging headlong over the bridge. "Amira?"

She reined in the horse, halting close to Cai. She screamed at him over the deafening rumble of the Reaper. "You swore to me I'd see my sister again. Take me to her, Cai, before it's too late. Don't let their deaths be in vain!"

Amira's words brought him back into the chaotic reality around him. There was nothing else he could do. He had to save her. He vaulted onto the back of her horse and smacked its rump with the flat of his sword, sending them hurtling across the bridge. He tensed, waiting for a tendril of pulsating air to rip him off the mare and drag him back to an excruciating death—but nothing came. He stole a glance over his shoulder. The Reaper's shimmering form towered motionless amidst the scattered remains of the Named and the Champion of Taleni. He wanted to gag, to cry, to scream; but she was with him. "Stay off the road. The trees will slow it down." *I hope.*

12

THE PLAINS OF KELD

Almost an hour had passed since fleeing the clearing. Cai had pushed Amira's riding skills to the limit, making her steer their horse hard through the dense forest undergrowth. The trees had blurred into streaks of green and brown as they snaked towards the edge of the forest, branches clawing out at them, cutting deep into their exposed skin. Even then, he had kept them moving until the forest had thinned out.

He slipped off the horse, crept to the edge of the northern tree line, and stared out onto the Plains of Keld. Hundreds of square miles of grassland stretched out before him. Satisfied that they were safe, he stepped out of the forest and collapsed onto the grass. As his bitter tears watered the ground, he did something that he had always considered futile and ritualistic—he prayed.

"Blessed Enora, I don't know why you spared me and not my comrades, but I ask you to give me the strength and the will to avenge them. I ask you to show me the meaning to the images the Reaper revealed to me and to the secret I bear. And I also swear on your holy name that I'll protect her with my life. I..." He grimaced and stood. *How could I ask for something so selfish on a day like today?*

He returned to where Amira waited for him. Even after all the trauma she had suffered, she smiled at him in a way that, were it not for the caked layer of grime, sweat and the remains of the Elite Guard covering his face, she would have seen him blush.

"We've strayed away from the road, but I reckon it's still around seven miles north to Keld," he said, stretching his aching arms. "There's a stream up ahead. I need to wash this filth off me before I go a step further."

"I'll join you. The stench is..."

"I know."

They found the stream and washed themselves in silence. He watched her out of the corner of his eye. Even in her bedraggled state, she mesmerised him. "Thank you."

She frowned. "What for?"

"You came back for me."

She stared into her reflection in the water and trailed her finger on the surface, distorting the image. "I couldn't bear the thought of losing you. These past few weeks have been the happiest I've been since before mother died. And now this..." She looked up, her eyes wide with fear. "Kaine said, 'See you later, Lady Amira'. What does he want with me?"

"We're not going to wait to find out," said Cai, stepping out of the stream. He mounted the horse and patted her flank. "Go easy on this one. She's gone through a lot today."

"She's not the only one," she said, joining him. She brushed Cai's hand with hers. "I don't know what I would've done without you." Their hands lingered together until they remembered what hunted them. She pressed her legs against her horse's flank and set off across the sea of grass, wavering in the wind.

Cai knew that at a walk they would arrive at Keld within two hours, but the endless expanse of green stretching before them had a way of tricking a traveller, as if time and distance lost all meaning. So it was not long before the plains lulled Amira into a fitful sleep. Noticing her slump in the saddle, he eased her back to lie against him and wrapped his arms around her to take hold of the reins. She murmured something under her breath and wriggled in closer to him. He listened to Amira's slow, rhythmic breathing as she slept and wondered whether he, an unnamed clansguard, twice orphaned, and the bearer of a secret that could cause his death, could find happiness with this woman. Cai cursed. *He lies dead with his heart ripped out and the Elite Guard torn to shreds. Am I that cold and selfish?*

He spurred the mare into a trot and wallowed for the next few miles in his self-loathing state.

"My lady. Wake up."

She rubbed her eyes and stretched, then leant back against Cai. "What is it?"

"Look, they're lighting the torches across the South Wall. We're nearly at the fortress."

She pulled Cai's arms tight around her. He dared not move in case it spoiled the moment. He yearned to kiss her soft, warm neck, so close to his lips. Yet Amira's breathing shallowed.

"Pull up!"

"Why? What's wrong?" He pushed up in the saddle to see what troubled her. "I can't see—" He froze mid-sentence, as a dark figure stood motionless in front of them. "It can't be. Not when we're so near."

The hairs on the backs of their necks stood tall, as something large distorted the waxing disc of Golanos high above in the Void. Then, as the unmistakable growl of Kaine's creature swept over their heads in an invisible storm, they knew they were trapped.

"You need to get to Keld and warn them," he said, unsheathing his sword. "I'll draw the Mendari away from you. Make a run for it."

"No! I won't let you face them. They'll kill you for sure."

"I don't care, as long as you're safe." He eyed the dagger. "But if they—"

She twisted to face him. "I can't...I don't have the courage."

Cai looked into her terrified eyes and realised he could not leave her. He gripped her hands. "T-then let's do it together."

"You would do that with me?"

"Yes, I would." He kissed her on the lips. "What's left to live for, if I lose you too?" He retrieved the blade from Amira's belt, placed it in her trembling hands and pressed it against his heart. "On the count of three," he said, pressing his sword against her breast. "One, two—"

A furious blur flashed before Cai's eyes, and an incredible force

63

knocked him flying off the back of the horse. The world spun around him. He crashed onto the ground, struggling to breathe. Sprawling to his feet, he realised that the mare had bolted into the gloom. *Goddess, let her live.* But as the Reaper roared and thudded across the plain, he beat his fists into the ground in anguish.

The dark figure of one of the Scions came into view above him. As the helmet slipped inside the armour, Kaine stared down at him. He tutted as if inspecting a piece of shoddy workmanship.

"Well, get on with it. Kill me, you murdering bastard."

Kaine chuckled. "Normally, I'd be more than happy to erase another Enorian from blighting the land, but Lord Velak wants you alive for some reason."

"No!" Cai reached for a dagger in his belt, but Kaine stamped on his chest, pinning him down.

"Really? After what happened to your father?"

"H-how do you know he's my father?"

Kaine moaned. "By the whore goddess, boy. Lord Velak knows everything."

Cai glared up at his father's killer. "I will avenge him."

"Of course you will. Sweet dreams." With a flick of Kaine's boot, Cai's head jolted back and smacked into the ground beneath him. As he descended into darkness, he swore he could hear a horse acting out its final death throes. *Amira.*

13

FACT OR FICTION

Tomos slouched in the chair beside his writing desk and traced his fingers across the letters embossed on the case of the codex placed in front of him. *A Collection of Tales of the Hen Rai.* Puffing out his cheeks, he opened the clasp, ready to read, but paused, as the contents of his pocket cried out for his attention. He slid his hand inside and smiled as he stroked the small, velvety parchment hidden within.

Since arriving at the fortress in the early hours of the morning, he had visited only one place outside of the Great Hall—the siege engine workshop. *It must have been her, but why?* The possibilities terrified him, but also excited him. So much so, that even with his uninvited guest hovering a few feet away, he slipped the note under the table, unfolded it and began to read. *Meet me at—*

"Stop fiddling around and show some interest in the gift I brought you."

Irritated, he stuffed the note back into his pocket and snapped his attention onto the man pacing beside the window. "You're in no position to give me orders, Madoc. Where in the goddess' name have you been? It's been over a month since I last saw you. You were supposed to accompany us on the journey south."

"I had business to attend to."

"Did you really? Well, Father's furious. I'm down to my last few doses of your infernal slop that you claim is an elixir."

Madoc shuffled over to the table and leered into Tomos' face. "You ungrateful boy. That infernal slop is saving your skinny, princely arse." He jutted his tangled, bushy beard at the silver amulet hanging around Tomos' neck. "At least you're not a complete imbecile."

"Superstitious nonsense. Just like this book."

"You'd be more appreciative if you had the decency to look inside."

"Ugh, very well. As long as you promise to stop your incessant whining?"

"Just open the damn case."

Tomos picked up the codex and thumbed through the pages, noticing that, every so often, a colourful illustration of a mythical beast or a magnificent warrior would accompany the text. He closed the book and grimaced. "Children's bedtime stories? I'm sixteen, not six."

Madoc chuckled. "So you remember them?"

"How could I forget? That's all you ever read to me whenever you came to visit. But why's this codex so special?"

"Read the inscription on the inside of the case and you'll understand."

"To our dearest child.
 May these stories remind you of the world that once was.
 Your loving parents,
 Enora and Gaius."

Tomos gaped at Madoc. "No. It can't be."

"What have I taught you about making assumptions without first assessing the evidence?"

"How could I ever forget?" Rolling his eyes, he returned his attention to the codex. He brushed his fingers across the pages, detecting some that had cockled and others where the pigments in the pictures had faded over time. "The ageing process seems to be genuine. And it's written in the language of the Hen Rai." He frowned. "B-but that would make this codex at least a thousand years old."

"Yes, it would."

"By the goddess, the Communion would give anything to add this codex to their collection at the Great Nemeton of Tremadon."

"They would—but not for the reason you're thinking."

"What other reason could there be?"

Madoc reached across the desk and flicked through the pages until, finding what he wanted, he prodded his gnarled finger on an illustration of a scene from one of the stories.

Tomos studied the picture. A young girl stood at the edge of a forest as Golanos bathed her in beams of milky-white light. Slithering in and out of the tree line were a dozen sinewy coils of silvery flesh, all but one dragging a terrified child into the shadowy depths. The last loomed over the little girl like a cobra ready to strike. "The Bwgan."

Madoc nodded. "The Communion believe that any form of evil that served Velak was destroyed when Enora and Gaius Galerius set fire to the Void. Anything that contradicts that belief would either be destroyed or locked away for all eternity."

Tomos tilted his head and narrowed his eyes at Madoc. "Then how did you get your decrepit hands on it?"

Madoc pulled up a chair and eased his aged frame into the seat. He fixed his gaze on Tomos, his bright eyes a sharp contrast to his ancient mottled skin. "I found it in the ruins of a Hen Rai settlement, two days' journey south of Vedana."

"You went into the Wildlands? I thought you were mad, but—"

"It was within the walls of Nabaya."

"Nabaya? Wasn't that one of the towns attacked by the Mendari?"

Madoc closed his eyes and nodded. "The Mendari call it 'The Cleansing', but no matter how they justify their holy cause, it's genocide."

Tomos closed the book and poured each of them a cup of wine.

He raised his cup and said, "To all that have perished at the hands of the Mendari and their dark god, Velak." They drank, then sat in silence for a while.

Tomos' mind ran riot with images of the Bwgan devouring the young and crazed Mendari zealots killing and raping the inhabitants of Nabaya. Then, from the edge of his consciousness, another image formed. He jolted upright and shivered.

"What's wrong? Are you having an episode?"

"N-no—it's nothing like that. I've just been remembering more of my weird dreams of late."

Madoc set his cup on the table and leaned forward. "Like what?"

"It's always the same—a shimmering form of a man, lingering in the shadows of my memories. And no matter how many times I try to make out who he is, I can't."

"That's just a side effect of your medicine. It's nothing to worry about."

"Easy for you to say." He drained his cup and looked out of the south-facing window. "Do you think Aedan Taleni can hold them off long enough for Father to reach Vedana?"

Madoc ignored Tomos' question, staring through him as if he wasn't there.

"Hey, old man. Don't fall asleep on me again."

The healer blinked several times and smiled. "Just trying to make sense of the mysterious visitor in your dreams. What did you say?"

"I said, do you think Lord Taleni can stop the Mendari?"

Madoc pressed his fingers together and tapped them on his lips. "No, I don't. I just hope your father thinks with his head and not with his heart. "

"What do you mean? "

"Keld is a formidable fortress, thanks to you. If your father has any sense, he'll stay here and fight the Mendari on his own terms."

"But what about the Taleni? We can't just leave them to fend for themselves."

"I'm sorry, Tomos. Sometimes a ruler has to make tough decisions for the greater good of the kingdom."

"Well, if I was king, I'd march to defend the Taleni...if I could fight."

Madoc gripped the edge of the table, stood, and walked around to him. He rested his hand on Tomos' shoulder and said, "I'm sorry, son. I wish I could give you what you want, but I'm afraid there's no cure for what happened to you. We'll talk more when I get back."

"Get back? You've only just arrived."

"I only stopped to give you the book. With the Mendari horde almost at Vedana's gates, I need to go home and gather extra medical supplies. Goddess knows how many wounded Taleni warriors and refugees there'll be crossing the plains. I need to prepare for them." He stepped over to where he had left his weather-worn leather satchel, opened it and rummaged inside. Hidden glass bottles clinked as he searched for one in particular. Finally, he retrieved what he was looking for and placed it on the desk. "That should be more than enough elixir for you while I'm away. And remember—"

"Yes, I know. Never take off my amulet."

"And no overdoing it at the feast. You were laid up in bed for days after the winter solstice festival."

"Oh, damn! I forgot all about the feast. I need to get ready." He paced to the door of the apartment and opened it wide, drumming his fingers on the frame.

"I can see I've overstayed my welcome." Madoc pulled his satchel over his shoulder, leant on his staff and lumbered over to him. "I hope that whatever's on that note is worth it." He winked at Tomos and left.

"You sneaky old fox." Tomos closed the door, pulled the parchment from out of his pocket and read it.

"Meet me at The Renegade tonight. There's a bard performing that you simply must come and see.
    Kaitlyn."

He blushed as his body quickened in a way that only happened when he thought about her. Whatever was happening to him, he wanted more. *So how do I avoid going to the feast and escape a fortress full of clansguard?*

14

THE GROVE OF THE GODDESS

Kurzon hammered at the large fortified gate of the Sacred Grove of the Goddess. "Hurry up! I haven't got all day." He glared over his shoulder at the sounds of revelry spilling out of Belanore's main street. Either side of the strip of churned-up mud ran a row of garishly painted buildings offering the clansguard of the nearby fortress of Keld many tempting ways to part with their earnings.

A warrior hurried down the centre of the road towards Kurzon. Emblazoned on his chest was the sigil of a golden hovering hawk, signifying his status as champion of the Zirani clan. "Did you find out which one she's in?"

The warrior nodded. "She's in The Renegade with about twenty other warriors."

Kurzon flared his nostrils and muttered an inaudible curse. "I'm sorry that you had to enter such a despicable place, Rory."

"I go where my lord commands." The champion spat on the floor. "It sickens me to see so many castes cavorting in that cesspool. And to think the princess—"

"Yes, she'll be the ruin of us all if she becomes queen."

"Unless you can guide her back to the goddess, lord?"

"Have I not tried? I wonder if she's beyond redemption?"

"Well, if you can't turn her back to the goddess, no-one can."

"No, Rory. I'm merely a servant. If it's Enora's will for Princess Seren to return to the Communion, then not even her infuriating stubbornness will stop that." He turned back to the gate and pounded hard on the wood. "Where in the goddess' name is the guard?"

A slat in the gate snapped open and a gruff female voice asked, "Who has business with the Communion of the Goddess?"

"It's Lord Zirani, here for a meeting with Warden Elgar."

"One moment, my lord."

Kurzon steadied his horse as a heavy, wooden beam scraped against the back of the gate. As it swung wide open on its strong, iron hinges, a grey-robed guard hurried out to meet him and bowed.

"Lord Zirani, they're waiting for you in the Grove of the Goddess."

"They?"

"Yes, my lord. The Archwarden of Nirasia has blessed us with a surprise visit."

"Has she indeed? Well, we'd best not keep her waiting," he said, handing over his horse's reins to the guard. "Make sure my clansguard have something to eat and drink while they wait."

"Of course, my lord. It'll be an honour to share an ale and break bread with the great Rory Swiftblade."

Kurzon raised a brow at his champion. "Not too much ale, Swiftblade. You know what your vision's like after a few pints."

Swiftblade grinned. "I don't know what you mean, lord."

Chuckling to himself, Kurzon made his way through the gate and proceeded into the outer court, where many of the temple's functional buildings were based. To his left, he passed the refectory, where a pair of acolytes knelt in the kitchen garden picking a selection of herbs for the evening meal. It was a wonder to Kurzon how anything could survive the harsh winters of Northern Tarania. Yet the unmistakable aromas of chives, mint, oregano, sage and thyme wafting towards him bore witness that life could flourish in the frost-covered ground.

Further along stood the temple dormitory, sleeping two hundred acolytes when full, and on the opposite side of a vast courtyard lay the stables and a well-equipped armoury. Beyond, set apart from the rest of the buildings, were the infirmary and blacksmith. Even further

71

away was a flour mill, powered by a large stream that passed through the temple grounds. Kurzon smiled with pride, knowing that it was his patronage that transformed the once-neglected Sacred Grove of Belanore into a true place of glory to the goddess.

In the centre of the courtyard, a group of acolytes practised hand-to-hand combat. Kurzon paused for a moment and scrutinised their progress. What were previously drunk, penniless warriors, thrown out of their warbands for all manner of misdemeanours, were now sober, goddess-fearing defenders of the faith: Grey Cloaks.

Nodding with satisfaction, he resumed his short walk, marching briskly to the other end of the courtyard, and entered a long colonnade of limestone monoliths that led to the most sacred part of the temple: the Grove of the Goddess. The ancient stones, protecting the grove from time immemorial, loomed either side of him, scrutinising his motives for entering the goddess' presence. Dense holly, ivy and mistletoe trailed across the soundless, weathered giants, grown for their ability to cleanse the living of any evil found lingering around them—for such abominations were unwelcome in the grove. Kurzon's heart quickened as he sensed the surrounding air become as still as the stones themselves. The goddess awaited.

At the end of the colonnade, two Grey Cloaks kept watch, crossing their spears, seeing someone approach. As soon as they recognised the Chieftain of the Zirani, they stood to attention, unblocking his way.

"At ease," he said, unsheathing his sword and handing it over to one of the pair. "Where are they?"

The guard slid Kurzon's sword into an empty slot in a nearby weapons rack. "Warden Elgar is taking the Archwarden on a tour of the grove, lord."

Kurzon nodded his thanks and headed inside.

The grove was comprised of the three most sacred trees in the Enorian religion: ash, oak and hawthorn. He was pleased to see new growth in their branches. Soon they would thicken into a canopy and shield the centrepiece of the grove, the breathtaking marble figure of Enora, from the elements above. The sculptor had exceeded Kurzon's highest expectations. Not only had he captured Enora's grief as she

72

stared up into the Void to witness the heroic, yet tragic death of her lover, but also her compassion and commitment for her people, and for her child. He stepped across the dressed flagstone terrace, crossing into the ring of flaming torches, and placed his hand reverently on the infant boy's head, cradled in the crook of his mother's left arm. "You never got to know your mother or your father." Then, kneeling before the goddess, he kissed her feet. "May your sacrifice never be forgotten." He wiped a tear from his eye, stood up and straightened his cloak.

"Anyone would think you were trying to eclipse the Great Nemeton of Tremadon."

Kurzon spun on his heels to find Warden Elgar and the Archwarden walking towards him. He knelt on one knee. "Archwarden Predina."

"If only all the nobility shared the same devotion as you, Lord Zirani," she said, holding out her aged yet elegant hand to him.

He kissed her golden bracelet of office. "You honour me with your words, Your Holiness."

"No, Lord Kurzon. It is you who honours me. Please stand. It does not sit well with me that a member of the Nobility Caste defer to me in such a way. I am merely a servant of the goddess."

He stood and smiled. "So what brings Your Holiness to our humble temple?"

"I felt it was high time that I came to see the progress you and Warden Elgar have made with one of the lesser-known shrines in Northern Tarania," she said, casting her eyes around the grove. "I'm impressed with what you have done."

"Thank you, Your Holiness," said Elgar. "That is high praise indeed."

Predina smiled thinly at the Warden, then made her way towards the statue. She trailed her fingers down Enora's right arm until she rested them on the short sword held in the goddess' hand. "Where are the flames?"

"That's what I asked, Archwarden," said Elgar, shooting a look of annoyance towards Kurzon.

"Oh, stop worrying, Warden. I'm merely curious."

"It was my decision," said Kurzon, drawing beside the Archwarden. "Forgive me, but as no-one knows what the weapons of the gods actually looked like, I felt it was inappropriate to add them."

She glanced over to the Warden, shuffling closer to listen in to their conversation. "Warden Elgar. Would you leave us for a moment? I need to speak to Lord Zirani in private."

"Oh...right. I'll...um, check on the guards."

"Excellent idea," she said, turning back to Kurzon. "Walk with me."

As they left the warmth of the ring of torches, Kurzon pulled his cloak tight around his body to keep out the chill of the spring evening air. After a short walk through a winding path between the ageless trees, they entered a circular seating area with a babbling granite obelisk positioned in the centre. "Shall we sit here, Archwarden?"

"Very well—but not for long. Otherwise, my bones will suffer for it. I'm not as young as you, Lord Zirani."

"Of course, I understand," he said, lowering onto the stone bench.

Predina gathered her robes of office and sat at a respectable distance from him and briefly closed her eyes. "This is truly a place of peace and holiness, Kurzon. The Communion is eternally grateful for your patronage."

"Thank you, Archwarden."

"As you have no doubt deduced, there is more to my visit than inspecting your progress."

"I assumed as much."

"Once again, we are in troubling times. The Mendari threaten everything that we hold dear. They know we are weak, and so do the People's Alliance—they'll make the most of this opportunity to cause dissension from within. Who knows? They may already be working with each other."

"That would be my assessment. I've also just received news that the Mendari have reached Vedana."

"By the goddess! I sent Warden Elin and forty Grey Cloaks to Vedana. I pray they got there in time." She shook her head. "It's hard to believe that Aedan would retreat behind his walls."

"That seems to be the case."

"Then we have little time. Tell me honestly, Kurzon. Is the king capable of rising to the challenge? I mean, he's not the man he used to be."

"Even after so many years, he struggles with the loss of dear Isabelle," he said, staring into the cascading water feature. "But there's no-one better suited to take on the Mendari. I just worry about what will happen if he were to fall in battle."

"Is that likely?"

"Not if I can convince him to stay at Keld. The loss of my wife's clan will be a terrible tragedy, but far better than the catastrophe of rushing to face an enemy embedded in Vedana."

"By the goddess, I hope you can. Otherwise, if he fell—"

"Seren would take the throne, if the Council of Clans endorses her claim."

"I know she's your niece, but from what you've told me, she's one step away from putting herself through the Veil."

"Sadly, you're correct. Nothing that Rodric or I say to her makes a difference."

"Then you'd better find a way to keep the king safe," she said, pointing a finger at him. "I think we should make our way back." With great effort, Predina struggled to stand. Her face paled as her bones clicked and creaked.

Kurzon sprung up and offered the Archwarden his support. "Please, let me help you."

As he lifted her up, she grasped hold of his wrist and leaned into his ear. "The Communion's dying, Kurzon. If the Mendari were to achieve a victory against the North during the Great Conjoining, the lower castes would see this as a sign of Enora's weakness and surely revolt." She pulled back and looked him in the eyes. "But with people like you, who'll do whatever needs to be done, there's still hope. Are you still that man?"

"Yes, Archwarden. I'm still that man."

As he escorted Predina back through the temple and to the main gate, he considered how best to approach deterring the king from his reckless plan. He stopped short of Rory and his clansguard, sitting around a brazier, sharing a drink with the Grey Cloak guards. As he bid Predina farewell, he said, "Rest assured, Archwarden, the king will listen to my advice."

"I do not doubt that, Lord Zirani," she said, turning towards a sullen Warden Elgar. "And tell your wife I'll pray to the goddess for the safety of her family and for the people of Vedana."

"Thank you, Archwarden."

"Lord Zirani," said Rory, rising from his seat.

"What is it?"

"It's the princess. She's still in the tavern and so pissed she can hardly speak."

"Her father will be furious with her."

"Sir! They're leaving the tavern!" called one of Kurzon's Elite Guard.

"Get the horses. She's gone too far this time."

15

THE FEAST OF CLANS

It had been years since Keld's Great Hall had hosted so many chieftains at one time. The clans coming together in such haste could only mean one thing: Northern Tarania was at war.

Servants scurried throughout the hall, supplying the chieftains, champions and the Named of each clan with a vast array of food and drink. Plates of steaming boiled pork and beef were greedily devoured by hungry clansguard, while others preferred the choicest cuts of venison and boar. Rodric was a man of simple tastes. He ignored the succulent meats on offer, opting for a fillet of baked salmon with honey and some slices of warm bread. He savoured the first morsel, as the tender pink flakes melted away in his mouth and he lost himself in a vision of happier days.

"Sire?"

He straightened in his chair and held his hand over his cup as a servant offered him mead. That night was one for clear heads, as he would meet with the chieftains at the Council of War. Decisions needed to be made.

He surveyed the scene before him. If he closed his eyes, the sounds and smells of the feast could have been from hundreds of years ago. Yet some things had changed. The derelict timber-framed hall was now clad in dressed stone; the leaky thatched roof had been replaced by regimented rows of cut slate; and the primitive earth floor was now arrayed in large flagstones of granite.

Six long lines of trestle boards were laid out, parallel to each other, with the King's Table positioned perpendicularly at the front of the hall. Six boards for six clans, with their banners and sigils hanging in splendour above them. To the far left sat his own clan, Niras, whose lands stretched out across the south of Northern Tarania. The long, rectangular banner of black and red plaid of his clan rippled in the warm air circulating throughout the hall. Above the banner, Rodric's chosen sigil for the clan stood resplendent in polished bronze. The wren had spiritual significance in Northern Taranian culture, but there was a more personal motive for Rodric choosing it; it reminded him of his sister, Eleri.

Next to Niras were the green and brown of the Belgar—the clan that lived to the east, within the borders of the Forest of Borgen. Then there were the Ovantae, in their distinctive black and yellow woollen braccae, who lived in the northern valley of Anree. To their right, sat his late wife's clan, the Zirani—the richest of all the clans, situated on a peninsula to the far northwest. Their exquisite four-colour plaid of blue, red, yellow and white was an example of their wealth. Next were the purple and black of the Galgari, where the Mines of Belith supplied the clans with iron ore, copper and tin. Finally, and noticeable for their absence, were the blue and green banners of the Taleni—the only clan that occupied land outside of the natural borders of Northern Tarania.

For hundreds of years, the Communion had kept the peace between the clans, ensuring that the Enorian religion and its caste traditions were preserved over progress or reforms. Rodric had changed all of that. Now, under his rule, the clans were highly organised regions of governance—wealthy, stable and progressive. Although they would never admit it publicly, he knew the Communion coveted his power and success, but were bound to show fealty, as were the teachings of Enora. Especially as he had achieved something that no other chieftain, archwarden, king or queen had accomplished: he had defeated the Mendari. Yet for that very reason, he had lost the one thing that gave him a reason to live

—his beloved Isabelle. And now, once again, the Mendari surged northward.

As soon as it was clear that the Mendari were planning to invade Northern Tarania, he had called for the muster to take place at the fortress. So far, only five thousand clansguard had travelled with their chieftains to make camp in the fields north of Keld. Twenty-six years ago, he had marched south with four times that number. But after heavy casualties and many veterans joining the Communion's Grey Cloaks, the Clansguard Caste had struggled to replenish its numbers. And now that he knew that Aedan Taleni had taken heavy losses against the Mendari, he fretted whether he should listen to Kurzon and make a stand behind the walls of Keld. The thought of abandoning the Taleni sickened him, but now that Aedan was sending his youngest daughter to Keld, escorted by the Taleni Elite Guard, he was sure the outcome of the siege was inevitable.

Immediately, Rodric had dispatched a detachment of mounted warriors to meet them on the Great North Road, but the Taleni party had failed to appear out of the border of Derwedd Forest. In fact, not one living soul had emerged onto the plains.

He turned towards the young woman sitting beside him. Like her late mother and younger sister, Lady Yanna Zirani's hair had been blessed by the Twins. It was as if Ulena had descended from the Void and burned her fiery breath into every strand of her hair. She wore it in the traditional way of the Zirani clan—three braids wrapped around her head, with a fourth trailing down her back. Yet it was her eyes that fascinated the king the most. Her blue and brown eyes were truly mesmerising—another characteristic she shared with her mother and younger sister. Kurzon had chosen well with Taleni's eldest daughter, much to the disappointment of every other eligible noble in Northern Tarania.

"Sire, has there been any word from the riders you sent out?"

"I'm afraid not, Lady Zirani."

"I shouldn't fret," she said, pushing her untouched plate away from her. "Alun Swordstorm has never failed my family. They must have made a detour to avoid detection."

Rodric nodded, then frowned, noting the empty seat beside her.

"It's not like Lord Zirani to be late. Do you have any idea where he is?"

"He was called away to the Grove of the Goddess in Belanore, sire."

"Even so, I'm surprised he's late. He knows how important this feast is."

"I'm sure he won't be long, s—"

Before Yanna could finish, the main doors to the hall flew open, as a furious Lord Zirani and half a dozen of his Elite Guard marched towards the King's Table. Benches scraped back as the Named of Nirasia rose to protect their king, but Rodric signalled them to sit. Even though weapons were banned at the feast, every one of them was skilled in unarmed combat. Whatever had angered Kurzon, Rodric would deal with it diplomatically, not with a drunken brawl and needless deaths with war on the horizon.

"Lord Zirani, you seem agitated. Come, sit and tell me what troubles you over a cup of mead." Yet it was clear to Rodric that the chieftain was in no mood for pleasantries. As he neared the table, Rodric realised that Kurzon's face was covered in cuts and bruises. His woollen cloak and sash were caked in mud, and his braccae were torn across his left knee. "What happened to you?"

"I'll tell you what happened to me, *sire*." He stopped in front of the king and glowered at him. "The princess assaulted me." The hall fell silent. Even the servants dared not move.

Rodric struggled to hide his irritation. "Lord Zirani, this is not the best place to discuss personal matters. Perhaps we should—"

Kurzon slammed his hands down onto the table, the boom echoing throughout the hall. "She's out of control. She attacked me without any provocation."

He dug deep. For a chieftain to behave this way towards him was an act of great disrespect. Kurzon knew it, and so did the hall. The clansguard became restless. He needed to resolve this before the hall descended into a riot, but it was Yanna who intervened.

"Husband, is this giving glory to the goddess? Disrespecting your king? The Book of Enora dictates that we should always show serenity, even when we have been wronged. Is this not so?"

"But—"

"Is this not so?"

"Y-yes...it does. But the princess—"

"And what does the goddess say you must do if you fail to show respect?"

"Damn you, woman," he said under his breath. "It says I must ask for forgiveness from the goddess and those that I've offended."

"It does indeed," she said, fixing her eyes on his.

"What? Now?"

"Yes, now."

Kurzon raised his hands in defeat and sighed. "If it pleases, my lady." He turned to Rodric, trying his best to remove the anger from his face. "King Rodric, I apologise for my behaviour. It was uncalled for."

Rodric stared at Yanna and then at Kurzon. "Your young wife is wise beyond her years, Zirani. If only all our conflicts could be resolved so quickly." He smiled at Kurzon. "I accept your apology. Now come and sit by your remarkable wife and explain to me what happened in Belanore." The hall collectively sighed in relief and returned to their feasting.

For the next few minutes, Kurzon explained how he met Princess Seren on Main Street, as he was returning to the fortress. Her entourage of young warriors had emptied out of a tavern and blocked his way out of the town. He admitted losing his temper with her, berating her about her behaviour and not being at the feast. According to Kurzon, Seren just stood there laughing at him, calling him a sanctimonious old fool who should mind his own business. Things got heated between them and punches were thrown.

Rodric rubbed his forehead to relieve the pressure building up within. As if he didn't have enough to worry about. "I know she's struggling with things at the moment. This is her way of numbing the pain she feels about Isabelle. Even now, after so many years, we all suffer from the loss. Every day's the same."

"I understand that, sire," said Kurzon, staring into the flickering flames of the fire in the hearth behind Rodric. "I also miss my sister... but Princess Seren is heir to the throne. What happens to Northern

Tarania if something were to happen to you? She's in no fit state to rule." He nodded towards the two seats left vacant at the King's Table. "And where's Prince Tomos tonight? Ill in bed? Such a clever lad in mind but so feeble in body."

"If anything should happen to me, then I would expect the Council of Clans to choose wisely for the sake of the kingdom," said Rodric, skewering another portion of salmon onto his knife. "In any case, Seren will find her way back to the light. I'm sure her stay in Belanore's jail will sober her up."

"The Communion and Warrior Caste won't like that move, sire. It goes against the precepts of inter-caste protocol. If only she'd turn to—"

Rodric waved his hand in dismissal. "Spare me the lecture, Kurzon. I've allowed you plenty of chances to preach to Seren. Now it's Ironfoot's turn to speak to her."

Kurzon tilted his head and frowned. "I'm surprised you're even speaking to him."

"Despite what you think, he's a good man; and in truth, I miss his blunt honesty and his grisly, chewed-up face."

"You're a better man than me. I can't forgive him for deserting you like he did."

"He had his reasons, as you well know."

"The man's a reformist. His sympathetic view of the lower castes clouded his judgement."

"Peace, Kurzon. I'm well aware of what needed to be done—even though it weighs heavy on my conscience." Losing his appetite, he sat in silence and reflected on the necessary but terrible events that had taken place four years before at the Mines of Belith. He reached into his tunic and took hold of Isabelle's ring hanging around his neck. *I know you disapprove of what I did; but what choice did I have?*

Breaking the silence, Yanna shifted in her seat to face Rodric and asked, "Sire, may I be bold and offer a suggestion regarding Princess Seren's welfare?"

He glanced across to her and smiled thinly. "I'm sure I've tried everything to get through to her. What do you suggest?"

"Perhaps I could speak to her as I also suffer from the loss of my mother? Since arriving here, we've enjoyed a few moments together and I believe she'll listen to me."

"Yes, I think she'd be receptive to that. Thank you, Lady Zirani."

"It would be my honour, sire. My father would expect nothing less of me and it would please him to know that I serve you in this way."

He reached across the table and held her hand. "And I promise you, Yanna, we'll find your sister."

"Thank you, sire. I just pray the Council of War agrees to march to Vedana."

Rodric glanced away from her.

"Sire? Surely, you're not considering Kurzon's strategy of leaving my people to the savagery of the Mendari?" She flashed her husband a withering glare.

"Northern Tarania is bigger than just one clan, Yanna," said Kurzon. "Your father knew the risks of remaining on the other side of the Valtara. Pray to the goddess that he dies a glorious death and takes his place of honour with the children of Enora."

Yanna's lip trembled, but she remained silent.

A while later, as the feast drew to its raucous end, Rodric stood and raised his hands for silence. Even at fifty, he was still the embodiment of the Taranian heroes that the bards would tell tales of. A physical match for the mightiest of warriors within the hall, he trained with his Elite Guard, pushing himself to higher standards. His long greying hair was swept back behind his shoulders, allowing his heavy gold torc to be admired by all. Although it was more fashionable to wear a full beard, he preferred to wear only a moustache, as was the tradition of the clans.

"Thirty-four years ago, in the village of Treharne, Banan and his Mendari warband killed my mother and left me and my dear sister to burn to death, trapped inside our home." He held out his palms to them. "I carry these scars as a testament to my desperate but futile attempts to get through to Eleri as she lay unconscious within the flames." He stared up at the Nirasian banner as tears crisscrossed his face, glistening in the light of the waning fires of the Great Hall.

Unlacing his tunic, he pulled it over his head to reveal the collage of gruesome faces inked over his body and jabbed his finger at the largest face tattooed across his chest. "But you know how the story ends."

Every clansguard in the hall stood to their feet and slammed their hands onto the wooden trestle boards.

He waited for the noise to die down. "And now his son, Kaine, threatens the North. I will not lie to you, my brothers and sisters. It is highly likely that Vedana has fallen."

The hall growled their response.

Rodric nodded to each clan. "I know each and every one of you would march to Vedana in an instant, but we must be cautious. You have my word that the Council of War will make the best decision based on what we know. The security and safety of you and your loved ones matters to me the most."

The warriors hammered the boards in approval.

"And when the time is right, we will join as one. Not as separate clans, but as free Northern Taranians, standing side by side in the shield wall. You will strike your enemies down and cover your own skin with the faces of the slain. And when they flee from our blades, we'll drive them back into the south and then send them over the cliffs to meet their false god in the Netherplain—every last one of them!"

A tumultuous roar of defiance rang through the hall as the Named jumped on their stools and onto the boards, holding their arms aloft. Rodric pumped his fists into the air. *We may not have the numbers, but we have something Kaine will never have—the Named.* He turned and walked towards a door behind the King's Table. The chieftains and their champions left their clans and followed him.

The Council of War was about to begin.

16

THE RENEGADE TAVERN

Tomos licked his lips in nervous expectation as the landlady of The Renegade set two frothy pints of Keld's most famous ale before him. He stood in front of the worn, wooden bar, surrounded by people from all walks of life, and grimaced, as he realised that his gloves were bonded to the surface of the bar. His mind conjured up all manner of disgusting substances that had combined to create such a potent adhesive. *Goddess! Do they ever clean this place? If Father doesn't kill me after this, surely the blight living in this stinking place will do the job.*

"There you go. Two pints of Red. That'll be six darns, love."

"Ah...I've only got a sofran," said Tomos, handing over the gold coin.

The wiry, imposing woman leaned across the bar and set her eyes on him. "A sofran, you say? That's a load of money for a young lad like you to carry around," she said, lowering her voice. "You didn't steal it, did you?"

Tomos paled. "N-no. It's mine. I swear."

"Hmm...I'm not so sure about that." She sniffed twice and frowned. "You smell like a common labourer. So how would you be holding such a fine amount of money?"

Tomos took a step away from the bar, but the wall of people

behind pushed him back. "I'm of the Skilled Caste. An engineer. I-I mean an apprentice engineer."

The landlady cackled and grinned, exposing a set of teeth that had seen better days. "Oh, that's a good one, love." Without warning, she grabbed his right hand and pulled off his glove. "That's strange. Your hands are as soft as a newborn's skin." She glanced at his clothes then narrowed her eyes. "There's something not right with you, boy. Let's see what branding you have."

"No. Please, I beg you."

"Huh!" She flinched and pulled away as if his hands were red hot. "I-I beg your pardon, my lord. If I'd known that you were of the Nobility Caste, I would never have dared to be so rude."

"Please, I-I don't want any trouble. I just want to watch the bard with my friend."

"Of course you do, my lord. I'll get Dai to clear a space at the best table for you."

"That won't be necessary," he said, looking over his shoulder. "I think she's already found us a place."

"As you wish, my lord. Oh, your change."

"Keep it—in exchange for your discretion?"

"Oh, I understand," she said, winking. "Your secret's safe with me. Mari never gossips." She placed the gold sofran into her money belt. "Especially when she makes more money in one minute than she'd make all night."

As Tomos nervously laughed at the joke, he took hold of the drinks and turned to find his companion. He scanned the sea of revellers until he spotted her, surrounded by a group of boys. He tensed, clenching his jaw, as her face lit up from something that the boys said. Seeing Tomos, she pushed her way through the crowd to meet him. "You took your time."

"Never mind that, Kaitlyn. Who are those boys?"

"Just some local lads who should know better than to pester me."

"You looked like you were enjoying yourself."

She bit her lip. "Are you jealous?"

"N-no."

She beamed. "Good. Now come on. I spotted a space on the way in." She turned and pressed deeper into the packed tavern.

Tomos took a deep breath, lifted the cups over his head and followed her into the mass of people. *Too late to back out now.*

"Told you it was free," she said, pointing to a bench a few tables away from the stage. She slid onto the seat and patted the smallest of spaces remaining on it.

Tomos wavered.

"Well, aren't you going to sit down? He'll be starting the second part soon."

"I-is it clean?"

"Oh, for the love of the goddess." She took hold of his arm and pulled him almost onto her lap. "That's cosier," she said, snuggling into him, teasing him with her bright blue eyes.

Tomos shifted, reddening by the second. It was his first time in The Renegade. In fact, it was his first time in any tavern. The smells, the sounds, the faces, were all alien to him. This was by far the most adventurous thing he had ever done in his restricted and cocooned life. If Madoc or, goddess forbid, his father, found out about his escapade to Belanore, he would be locked away in his room forever.

It was uncanny. The old healer seemed to know exactly where he was, day or night. Even with Madoc away from the fortress, Tomos was sure the old scoundrel had someone spying for him. That night was different—he didn't care if he was found out. The stakes were worth the risk. He was with her.

"I didn't think you were going to show up. You know there're plenty of lads who'd love to be where you are, Tomos."

He looked over to the boys who had been talking to Kaitlyn. They stared at the pair, smirking. Six pairs of hungry eyes lusted over his companion. "W-well, it's not that easy to slip out of the royal quarters and evade everyone else between here and Keld—even if all the warriors have been called back to the fortress."

She laughed, drawing close to whisper in his ear. "I'm joking. Do you really think I'd choose one of those idiots over Prince Tomos Niras?"

Tomos glanced at the crowd swamping the bar. "The tavern

owner saw through my disguise. She called me 'Lord', but I'm sure she knew more than she was letting on. I had to pay her off." He turned back to Kaitlin. "Why do I even need to hide my identity? Seren doesn't."

"Even though your father keeps you hidden from the wider world, you could still be recognised by an off-duty clansguard. And if you were caught here with me, a girl from a lower caste..."

"I don't care what they think. It's my life and I should be allowed to live it as I want."

"Maybe—but when you've been brought up to know your place, disobeying caste precepts will get you and those around you into trouble. You'd get nothing more than a telling off from your father, but my caste would be shamed by my behaviour." She turned over her right hand and stared at the anvil and the hammer. "My family would be branded casteless," she said, sliding her finger across her palm to make a cross, "And we'd be forced to live in one of those terrifying camps or flee south to find work in the mines and quarries of the Wildlands."

"I've heard of those despicable institutions. When Seren's queen, I'll—"

"Shhh. Not so loud." She frowned at him. "Are you sure you're only sixteen? You speak in words I've only heard the bards use."

Tomos shrugged. "I enjoy reading. There's not much else for me to do."

"Well, keep your voice down or, no matter how good your disguise is, it won't just be Mari who'll recognise you." She assessed the threadbare woollen cloak and cap she had given him. "I just wish you'd left that strange necklace back at the fortress."

"What, this?" he asked, holding the silver locket up to show her.

"Goddess, Tomos. You can get your throat cut for a few darns in a place like this. Put it away. Do you never take it off?"

"No, I'm not allowed. Madoc says that it enhances the strength of my medicine. Without it, my condition will worsen and I could even die."

"That's awful. How does it work?"

"Healers like Madoc never share their knowledge."

"Sounds like magic to me. Maybe he put a charm inside?"

Tomos chuckled. "He certainly has the look of a sorcerer, and the bad habits."

"Well, just make sure you keep it hidden," said Kaitlyn, pulling Tomos' robe tight around his chest.

"Hey! What—" Tomos paused, catching his sister's name being used in a conversation near him.

"I'm tellin' you, it's true. She's up to her neck in shit this time," said a harsh-sounding voice behind them. "Keep well away from that one. I reckon she'd slit your throat for looking at her the wrong way."

They both looked up to find a sour-faced, rotund bar hand looming over them. The man struggled to catch his breath as he laboured through his night's work. His balding head glistened in the light of the open fire, and dark patches of sweat seeped through his filthy, woollen tunic. He leaned forward to collect some empty ale mugs left on the table, his sizeable frame rubbing up against them. Tomos froze, not daring to draw in another breath in case he inhaled the stench that invaded the surrounding air. To their relief, the bar hand moved away from them and walked towards another table.

What did he mean? Tomos needed to know. "Excuse me."

The man stopped and turned towards Tomos. "Yeah? What do you want? Them benches won't clean themselves, you know."

Clean isn't the word I'd use. "Sorry. Did you say the princess is in trouble?"

The bar hand screwed up his face and snorted. "Have you just crawled from under a rock? It's all the talk on Main Street, boy. She only went and picked a fight with that uncle of hers. You know? The blond-haired chieftain who wears the fancy plaid."

"Lord Zirani?"

"Yeah, that's him. Thinks he can put us out of business with his bloody temple? Piss off back to Zirani, I say, and leave us ordinary folk alone."

"Yes, but what happened to Princess Seren?"

"Velak's balls! Can't an honest man get back to work?"

I doubt there's an honest bone in your sizeable body. "Please, good sir?"

The bar hand shrugged and sighed. "Some folk say that Ironfoot hauled her off to the town jail. Now piss off and leave me be."

The town jail...Father will be furious. I can't wait to see his face.

As the bar hand stomped off, Kaitlyn slipped her leg over the bench and slid up close to Tomos. "That was very bold of you, Tomos I like it...I like it a lot."

He shivered. "You do?"

"Oh yes," she said, sliding her hand between his thighs. "Look— the bard's about to begin."

Tomos widened his eyes. His body tingled from her touch. He focused his attention on the stage in front of him, hoping the lack of light hid his flushed face and any other signs of his excitement. *That's odd.* He frowned, thinking that a drunk vagrant had wandered onto the raised platform. Yet everyone fell silent at the sight of him. "What? He's the famous bard everyone's talking about?"

A shrill voice hissed behind him. "Shhh!"

"Sorry," he said, unable to take his eyes off the bard. Even in the light of the lanterns lit to illuminate the stage, the bard's face remained obscured by a tangle of ropy hair and a bushy, unkempt beard. His oversized, full-length tunic gave nothing away of the physique of the man within.

A young serving girl hurried onto the stage and placed a stool next to the storyteller. "Ah, thank you, young lady. I'm not as steady as I used to be...especially after a few pints of Keld's finest," he said, lowering onto the stool.

The room erupted with laughter.

"A toast to Mari, queen of The Renegade and brewer of the finest ale in all of Northern Tarania." He held up a pint of Red Renegade and drank deeply, allowing the dark red liquid to run down his beard. The audience cheered and followed his example.

"Ah, that's better. Before the interval, we left our heroes as they had just been rescued by Lord Govannon's warband, after the Mendari had razed the town of Treharne to the ground. Now orphaned, the three boys found themselves at the mercy of the Nirasian chieftain in Hythe's Great Hall.

"Fortunately for the boys, they bore the brand of the Clansguard

Caste, although the eldest of them, Rodric, winced as the chieftain inspected the burns inflicted to his hands. When the chieftain grew suspicious, Luis and Tarek swore to Govannon that their friend received the burns after trying to free his sister from their blazing home. The chieftain took pity on Rodric, and knowing that he had lost many clansguard in the fight against Banan, welcomed the boys into his service.

"It was a wise decision, as the boys quickly became skilled in war, growing in favour with their comrades and the people of Nirasia. And although they were inseparable, they gained reputations that set them apart: Luis grew as a commander, excelling in strategy, and Tarek learned how to control the Red Mist, becoming the most feared warrior in Nirasia; yet with all their greatness, both deferred to Rodric. And soon enough, his reputation exceeded that of Govannon's. The chieftain seethed inside until, believing that Rodric planned to overthrow him, he sent the three to rescue the son of a minor noble from brigands. Unknown to them, the chieftain had arranged a deadly surprise.

"They found the boy in a glade at the edge of the Forest of Borgen, close to the Dunree Marshes. His throat had been cut, and the brigands were nowhere to be seen. Then, from out of the tree line swarmed Banan and his warband, greatly outnumbering the Three Orphans of Treharne and their small group of warriors."

The bard paused and drained his cup. "I'll not offer any wild speculation of what happened during the battle as some bards will do—for as we know, friends, the three boys entered a pact never to speak of it. And our great king frowns upon such gossip. All we know is that on that day the Three Orphans of Treharne defeated Banan and became known as Luis Ironfoot, Tarek Grimbard and Rodric Shieldbane."

The crowd applauded and cheered as the bard lowered his head in gratitude. Assuming that he had finished, the audience got up to leave.

"One moment, my friends," said the bard. He stood and walked to the front of the stage.

The crowd settled back into their seats.

"For too long, you've been told stories of the heroes of Northern Tarania and accepted them as the honest folk that you are. You see, my friends, for all of these years, you've been told lies—lies about the castes, lies about the Mendari god and lies about the king."

Tomos nudged Kaitlyn. "I don't like where this is going. We need to leave."

"Shhh...I'm listening."

"Your leaders tell you they can win the war against the Mendari. They lie: I've seen the power of Velak and none can stand against it."

Every fibre in Tomos' body implored him to get out and find the nearest clansguard; but like everyone else in the room, he sat rooted to his seat, mesmerised by the grizzly old man before him.

"The Communion of the Goddess tells you it's Enora's will that you're bound to your caste and can never, ever question it. They lie. And, my friends, if that was not enough, your king would have you believe he is a true and just ruler. He lies."

Gasps of shock and shouts of anger reverberated across the room. It was clear to Tomos that the bard's words fell on receptive ears. Something stirred within him. He stood to his feet. "How dare you spread lies about the king. He's made Northern Tarania into a place where people can live in peace. Why would you say these things?"

"Shut up, boy, and sit down. What do you know? Let the bard speak," said an unknown figure among the crowd. Many joined in with the rebuke.

Tomos remained standing, locking eyes with the bard. *I can't let him get away with this.*

The bard stared directly at Tomos, then looked across to Mari, who nodded.

"But, there's hope, my friends. I come with a message from the South—a message of peace and hope for the people of the North, no matter which caste, no matter which clan. A chance to be renewed by the unfathomable love that only the one true god can give."

"Kaitlyn, we can't stay here. He's crazy. He'll get us all killed."

"B-but he's right, isn't he? The Mendari don't believe in the caste system. All are equal in the eyes of Velak."

Before Tomos could reply, the trouble started.

The doors to the tavern burst open and a detachment of clansguard pushed their way through the throng to get to the stage, clubbing anyone who refused to move. The patrons, angry and drunk, retaliated.

"Rise up, my friends! For your day of salvation comes at the Great Conjoining of the Twins and Golanos." The bard raised his hand towards Tomos, who stood motionless amid the ensuing chaos. "He's coming for you, Tomos Niras. Listen for his voice."

"You're the son of the king?" growled someone behind Tomos. The next thing he knew, a pair of rough hands hauled him into the brawl spreading throughout the tavern.

"Tomos!" Kaitlyn lunged towards him, desperately gripping hold of his robe. Cursing as it slipped over his head, she sprung onto the back of a rioter leering over Tomos, clawing at him with her nails. He shouted out in pain, grabbed hold of her and slammed her into the floor. Tomos' anger welled up from within. He scrambled off the floor and threw a punch at the man; but even before his fist connected with the man's face, Tomos' strength ebbed out of him and his legs buckled. He crumpled face down onto the floor, defenceless.

"Come on, lads. Let's give the prince what he deserves."

Surrounded by faceless assailants, Tomos curled up into a tight ball, as kick after vicious kick struck flesh and bone. He whimpered in agony, terrified that the Veil awaited him. Then, as quickly as the attack started, it stopped. He didn't need to see the clansguard—the sound of their chainmail was unmistakable. They made light work of his attackers, clubbing them senseless, dragging them off to the town jail to be dealt with severely. *Serves you right, you bastards. Oh goddess! Kaitlyn.*

"I've got you, your highness. You're safe now."

Even with the deafening ringing in his ears, Tomos managed a wry smile, as the owner of the familiar voice lifted him gently onto his broad, powerful back. "Ironfoot—I haven't seen you in years."

"It's been a while, your highness."

"You've gone to look old," said Tomos, casting his gaze around the tangle of bodies surrounding him.

"I see you've gained your mother's sarcasm."

Tomos swayed, struggling to keep his eyes open. "W-what?"

"You're worse than I thought. No more talking—I need to get you to Madoc," said the sheriff, turning towards the tavern's entrance.

"H-he's not in Keld. W-wait.... I-I can't find her, Ironfoot."

"Who?"

"G-Gwen's daughter, Kaitlyn—she's hurt."

Ironfoot's expression darkened. "Now listen to me, Tomos. As far as your father is concerned, you came here alone. If you care for her, you'll keep your mouth shut. Do you understand?"

"Y-yes, I-I understand."

The sheriff glanced over to the other side of the room as a pair of warriors hauled the bard off to a cell to sober up. "He'll think twice about performing drunk once my clansguard have had some time with him."

"That's all? A beating and a night in a cell? He's a traitor."

"I'd be more concerned about what punishment you'll get for this little escapade. You're lucky to get away with only a few bumps and bruises. What were you thinking? You know what happens when you get overexcited."

"I-I couldn't help myself, and I failed her. I hate this bloody illness." He snatched for the amulet around his neck, then paled. "No. It can't be." His eyes grew wide with panic.

"What's the matter?"

"My amulet. I had it around my neck and then...oh, goddess, she was right. I've been robbed."

17

THE COUNCIL OF WAR

Rodric stifled a yawn. It was well past midnight and, try as he might to stay focused on the endless bickering, his eyes drifted aimlessly around the room holding the Council of War until they fell on the flickering, incandescent flame of a wall sconce. He marvelled at the simple elegance of it—a thing of such beauty. Yet as he traced a finger over the ridges of scars moulded across his hand and drew in the smoke wafting across the room, he found himself back in Treharne, back inside the inferno of the roundhouse and back to the moment he lost her. He heard her scream within the suffocating fumes swirling throughout the house and called out to her. *Eleri, I'm coming.* He recoiled as a heavy beam from the roof collapsed to the floor, cascading a myriad of sparks into his eyes, blocking his way to her. "Eleri!"

"Sire?"

He bolted upright in the chair. "What?" he asked, spluttering.

"Are you feeling unwell, sire? We can reconvene in the morning, if you prefer?"

Rodric blinked a few times to focus his blurry eyes on the owner of the voice—Sorcha, Chieftain of the Galgari. "No, I'm fine. We need to decide tonight."

"I'm afraid that might not be possible, sire. We're still in deadlock."

Kurzon glared red-faced towards Sorcha. "Why, after all the time spent repairing and improving Keld, would you want to give that advantage away? Let them come to us."

"So says the man whose lands are furthest away from the threat. What if it were your lands fouled by the Mendari horde or your family butchered before your eyes?"

"Are you calling me a coward, Galgari? I was fighting in my father's warband long before you killed your first Mendari."

The room fell silent, as all eyes focused on Kurzon.

Sorcha gripped the edge of the table. "You know perfectly well when that was."

Kurzon softened his expression. "Your loss at the hands of the Mendari assassins was a vile act of savagery. I still mourn the loss of your parents, as well as my sister and all the other victims of the Day of Sorrows. We all lost loved ones during that dark time," he said, looking around the table. "I understand your eagerness to take revenge on those that committed the deed. I'd love nothing more than to plunge my knife into that scheming traitor, Tarek Grimbard; but heading straight into a battle with an enemy whose strength is unknown is reckless."

Sorcha nodded. "What you say is true, but would our dead kin not cry out for justice for the people of Taleni? How many will die or be forced into their dark religion while we wait behind the walls of Keld?"

Mayhem resumed as the room erupted into yet another round of arguing. Rodric's face twitched in annoyance, but knew he had to let the chieftains hammer it out between themselves—such were the conventions of the Council of War.

Lord Belgar raised his hand to speak, but the others, so absorbed in their fiery exchange, ignored him. Rodric grinned, knowing that Kilien Belgar was not a man to irritate. And right on cue, the chieftain slammed his hands onto the table and brought every eye in the room on him. He crossed his arms and sent a withering glare around the table—even Rodric, desperate not to let a chuckle escape from his lips, did not escape the wrath of the Belgar chieftain. Fergus, Kilien's brother, champion and interpreter coughed. "I believe my dear brother would like to speak."

Rodric found their exchanges both fascinating and a clear reminder of the bravery and loyalty of this man to him. The Mendari War was far from one-sided. The Southerners had fought the Northern Taranians for every foot of land, and it was the Belgar clan that had paid the highest price. One fateful morning, the Mendari launched a ferocious counter-attack against the Belgar. They would have been annihilated if it were not for the bravery of the legendary Woodland Warriors covering their retreat. However, during the carnage, Kilien was captured and had his tongue cut out during his torturous ordeal.

Although it was possible for Kilien to form a limited number of sounds, he preferred to sign. So, as he wove a tapestry of signs to his brother, Fergus interpreted. "Sire, you know I sacrificed much to remain loyal to you...But many of my kin died during the war...We are still brave but have learned to be cautious...I agree with Lord Zirani. Let them come to us."

"How can you say that?"

Rodric snapped his attention to Manon, Chieftain of the Ovantae.

"Who was it that rescued you from the Mendari? Was it him?" she asked, pointing at Kurzon. "Or was it the man whose chair is empty at this table? Aedan Taleni? He saved your life. Is this how you'll repay him?"

As Kilien's face burned red with anger, he unleashed a tirade of signed unpleasantries towards the Ovantae leader.

Furious, Fergus turned on his brother. "How dare you say such things about her."

The Belgar chieftain stood abruptly, hands on hips, and jutted his chin towards Manon.

"For the sake of the goddess, Fergus, stop protecting my honour and just say the damn words."

"H-he's just angry, that's all, my lady. He doesn't mean it."

"Mean what?"

"T-that perhaps the same madness that clouded your mother's judgement is now clouding yours."

The room gasped. Manon flared her nostrils, scraped her seat back and stormed towards Kilien.

Fergus jumped to his feet and stepped in front of her. "Please, Manon. He didn't mean it."

"If you have any feelings for me, then you'll move aside."

Fergus' mouth dropped. "That's not fair, Manon. You can't use that against me—he's my brother."

She shouldered passed him and scowled at the Belgar chieftain. "I've great respect for you, Kilien, and your love-struck brother and his futile attempts to gain my affection; but if you ever bring up my mother's illness again, I'll deprive you of another part of your flesh and eat it for breakfast."

"Sit down and compose yourselves," commanded Rodric. "The only person who gains from this is Kaine." A knock at the door distracted him for a moment. He nodded to a guard to open the door. "Lady Zirani?"

"Your majesty," she said, bowing her head. "I apologise for the interruption; but as my father is unable to represent the Taleni, I humbly request you allow me to speak on his behalf."

Rodric shook his head. "I'm afraid only a chieftain can vote at the Council of War...but I see no reason why you cannot sit at the table." He glanced around the room. "Any objections?"

"But she's part of my clan now," said Kurzon. "She's Zirani, not Taleni."

"You're correct, of course; but in dire circumstances as these, is there anyone more qualified to speak for the Taleni than she?" He didn't wait for a response. "Please, Lady Zirani. Take your father's place at the table."

"Thank you, sire," she said, sitting between the two other women present.

After her demonstration of wisdom at the feast, Rodric wondered if she could provide an alternative perspective to their dilemma. Her softer, feminine features seemed out of place, compared to the battle-hardened, commanding pair of chieftains sat either side of her.

Deputising for her mother, who had fallen ill at the end of the Mendari War, Manon commanded the Ovantae heroically. It was said that, despite overwhelming odds, she led the successful charge of a key Mendari hillfort. The eye patch she wore was evidence of her unwavering bravery, even with a Mendari crossbow bolt lodged deep into her eye socket. It was of no surprise to Rodric that 'Fearless' was the name that first came to him when he considered what Manon's warrior name should be. After all, she had done all of this by the tender age of eighteen.

Sorcha was only a couple of years older than Yanna, yet her eyes revealed a woman who had witnessed great trauma—the kind that permanently scars the soul. At thirteen, she was the youngest person to receive her warrior name from King Rodric. The name he chose encapsulated how she was found amidst the remains of the ambushed column on the Carran Pass, covered head to toe in blood, hacking the head off a wailing attacker with her father's long sword. Around her were the lifeless bodies of her family and the Galgari Elite Guards, as well as the headless corpses of two other Mendari assassins sent to kill them. It took four warriors to subdue her raging bloodlust on that fateful night—for the Red Mist had descended upon her. That was why Rodric named her 'Bloodrage'.

The formidable chieftain kept her hair short in the way of her clan, using a lime mixture to create fierce spikes to put fear into the hearts of the enemy. She scrutinised Yanna, then shook her head at Rodric. "Sire, while I agree with your reasoning for allowing Lady Zirani to sit in her father's seat, surely her lack of understanding of military strategy will be a hindrance to her?"

"A good point, Lady Galgari." Rodric smiled at Yanna and stood to his feet. "Let me explain the situation." Making sure he showed no bias, he presented both sides of the argument, using the large map of Tarania rolled out on the table before them.

"So, as there's deadlock between the chieftains, the burden of decision rests on my shoulders." He levelled his gaze at Yanna. "Even though it pains me to say it aloud, I believe the Mendari have already taken Vedana."

"Then lay siege to it and force Kaine to negotiate the release of my father."

"You assume your father would allow himself to be taken alive. That's not Aedan the Defiant's way."

Yanna's face paled. "B-but even if there's the slightest chance, surely we must take it?"

"What if that's what Kaine wants us to think, and we take unnecessary risks to free him? We could be walking straight into a trap."

"That's what I've been saying all along," said Kurzon, slapping his hand onto the table.

"If you had your way," said Sorcha, "You'd let Kaine walk right into Northern Tarania, so long as he left the lands of the Zirani alone."

"How dare—"

"This is hard enough for me as it is, without you at each other's throats," said Yanna. She turned to Rodric. "Sire, is there no way the army can be divided, so that a compromise can be made?"

"By the goddess. This is what you get when you try to explain military strategy to a civilian. No offence, Lady Zirani."

"None taken, Lady Ovantae." Yanna stood and studied the map. "But surely if you used all of your combined mounted warriors to reach Vedana first...what's that called?"

"A vanguard," said Manon.

"Yes, a vanguard...they could spring Kaine's trap and be fast enough to pull back to...where is it? Ah, there it is," she said, pointing to Midway Bridge. "Where even a modest shield wall could stand against the whole of the Mendari horde."

Rodric stroked his moustache. "It would be a bottleneck for sure. We'd have at least a thousand Named to send."

"Hmm...it would be worth the ruse, just to see what we're up against," said Sorcha. "That's if they can disengage the Mendari with minimal casualties. And then there's the difficult task of riding through a forest—especially Derwedd, with those treacherous tar pits around every corner." She glanced over to Kilien. "Perhaps the Woodland Warriors could provide cover?"

Kilien nodded his agreement. "They could hide in the trees and pick off any Mendari that give chase."

Kurzon got to his feet and leaned over the section of the map showing Midway Bridge. "So they get through to the clearing," he said, prodding his finger on the icon of the bridge. "What happens once they engage? Stalemate? I mean, what will it achieve?"

"Well, we either hold the crossing long enough to bring the main bulk of the army to the fight, or we make it look like the Named have had enough. They retreat and draw the Mendari out onto the plain," said Rodric. "Kaine may have brought some order to their chaos, but I'll wager once they smell blood and the Red Mist takes them, no amount of discipline will hold them back. If we're lucky, they'll come into range of our new siege weapons and be obliterated before they get anywhere near the walls."

Yanna looked around the table. "I realise that there'll be a lot of casualties among the Named, but at least it wouldn't be the entire army walking into a trap...and it could force Kaine to bargain."

Rodric smiled warmly at Yanna. "Once again, I'm awed by your insight."

Yanna blushed. "If I'm honest, sire, my father and Alun would talk of military matters constantly. I must have remembered more than I thought."

"I've no doubt about that," said Rodric, rising to his feet. The other council members followed his example. "So, has this third course of action changed any of your stances?" They all shook their heads. "I see." His mind flashed back to the night he held Isabelle rasping for her final breath. Before that moment, he would not have hesitated to mobilise the army and march on Vedana. That man no longer existed. He met Yanna's look of expectancy. "I'm sorry, Yanna. The risk's too great. We make our stand here."

18

THE PRINCESS OF BELANORE JAIL

Seren knew she was awake, but she dared not open her eyes. She had often heard Galgari sailors recall their first time sailing on the Endless Sea—how the serpent would test their strength by rolling under their boat and curse them with the sickness of the waves. As her whole body whirled in the darkness, it would have been easy to believe that she also travelled across that endless expanse of water. Yet she knew where she lay, gripping hold of the worn wooden bench: Belanore Jail.

She vowed to herself that last night would never happen again, but her body knew better than to trust her empty promises. A familiar sensation of discomfort rose from the pit of her stomach. A watery mouth, excessive sweating and deep breaths could only mean one thing. Unable to hold off the inevitable, she grabbed the piss pot beside the bench, pushed her face into the foul-smelling container and retched until her muscles ached and there was nothing left inside her stomach. With the little strength she still possessed, she eased onto the bench and returned to her semi-conscious state.

For the remaining hours of the night, the vicious cycle of disorientation, vomiting and paralysis continued, until finally, weak and dehydrated, she sat up. *Velak's balls. I stink.* She winced as she examined her bloodied and bruised knuckles. *Was I in a fight? Who with?* She racked her fuzzy memories until the image of a man formed inside her mind. He wore his long, blond hair loose over his shoulders, with his moustache plaited past his neck, fastened with ornate gold discs on each end. His gold-plated scale armour, emblazoned with a hawk with its wings outstretched, complimented the four-colour plaid cloak hanging over his shoulders. She cringed as she relived the moment she swung a left hook into his face. *Oh shit. He'll never forgive me for this. Nor will Father.* She spat on the floor. *As if I care what they think.* Nevertheless, she had one regret. She thought of her unexpected new friendship with Yanna. *Will she ever talk to me again?*

Pulling out of her self-absorbed thoughts, she took in her surroundings. As her father's representative to Keld, she had often visited Belanore, sometimes on official matters but mostly by the lure of its vices. Yet this was a first—thrown into a stinking cell as if she were one of the lower castes. The act had not gone unnoticed by the jail's other residents. *Looks like the sheriff's been busy tonight.*

Belanore's primary income was serving the needs of the fortress, so there had been little evidence of the trouble brewing in other parts of Northern Tarania. There was a begrudging acceptance of each other. The town needed the warriors, and the warriors needed the town. Yet as a dozen pairs of eyes, reflecting the dancing flames of the wall sconces, stared coldly at their royal inmate, she realised that the lower castes were more agitated than usual.

She tried to recite the rhyme that the castes taught to their children. "The monarch, the noble, the clansguard and the priest, the...what's next? I can never remember the next bloody line. Oh well, who gives a shit.... I doubt that any of you lot are found in the first four verses." Still, they had one thing in common—she also hated the rhyme, but for a different reason. If her mother had accepted the caste system, if she had stayed away from the Council of Clans, if she had not been betrayed by a trusted friend, then she would still be alive.

She had forgotten how many times she had asked her father why her mother had been murdered. He always replied with, 'What does it matter? She's dead.' And that was on his good days. It was only when Tomos' healer saw her running out of her father's study, upset, that she finally received an explanation. Madoc sat her down and explained that the Mendari were angry that Northern Tarania had invaded their country, and in retaliation, they sent groups of assassins out to murder each clan chieftain's family. Although most of the assassins were stopped before achieving their goal, a few completed their mission. The Galgari family were wiped out, apart from the youngest daughter, Sorcha, and Seren knew only too well the extent of the attack against her family. Even though she accepted what Madoc had told her, she still believed, deep down, that her mother's obsession with reforming the caste system had made her vulnerable.

From the far end of the jail, someone approached. Seren cursed under her breath as the unusual rhythm of their walk gave away their identity. She got up off the bench and struggled across the cell, determined to vent her fury at the person approaching; but after a few unsteady steps, a fresh round of nausea hit her. "Oh, shit!" She collapsed face first onto the unforgiving flagstone floor, howling as her nose crunched sideways.

The jail erupted as the inmates hurled their scornful laughter at her.

"Yeah, wait till you're outside of this shit hole and I'll show you real pain, you bunch of spineless scum."

The prisoners hushed and slipped into the darkest recesses of their cells. Seren might not have been Named, but only a fool would challenge her. Many considered her to be as good as any champion in Northern Tarania, but Seren cared only about being a match for one warrior—the warrior who betrayed her family and still lived to tell the tale: Tarek Grimbard.

She ignored the blood flowing from her broken nose and leered through the bars of her cell at the man now sitting at his desk opposite. "Ironfoot, you interfering bastard. I don't care if you were my father's Master of War. I'll have you thrown into the deepest, darkest dungeon in Caerniras when I get out of this maggot-infested dump."

Ironfoot ignored her; he was busy concentrating on lighting his pipe. After a couple of unsuccessful attempts, a warm glow finally appeared within the bowl. He sat back in his chair, closed his eyes and drew in a draft of smoke.

"Don't you dare ignore me."

Ironfoot released the contents of his lungs into the air and sat up to face her. "If only I could, Seren."

"Princess Seren."

"Oh, of course. Please forgive me, your highness. It's good to see you, Princess Piss Pot," he said, nodding towards the toppled container beside the wooden bench.

"Piss off, Luis. Between my uncle's preaching and your constant snooping, can you blame me if I want to enjoy a quiet drink with some of the other warriors?"

"A quiet drink? If it weren't for the amount of money you spent in the town, you'd have been barred months ago. You're labelled a troublemaker, your highness."

"As if I give a shit about what they think." She smirked, nodding towards the occupied cells. "And there was me thinking you sympathised with the lower castes."

"I do, but even I draw the line at dissension against your father."

"It must be hard for you."

"What is?"

"Fleeing to Belanore, only to find your old life catching up with you after so many years."

"What's done is done. I refuse to let the past control the future, and neither should you." He leaned towards her. "The pain and anger you carry will destroy you if you don't let go of them."

"And I thought Kurzon was the preacher. Save your breath. I didn't listen to him, and by Velak's balls, I won't listen to you."

"Well, you should listen because one day you'll be queen," said Ironfoot. "You're making too many enemies. And this incident last night. You need to tread carefully with your uncle. He's not a man to cross."

"He's an idealistic fool who still believes in his archaic religion."

"He's no fool, Seren; and don't underestimate the power of the Communion. Your father may be king, but remember who influenced the clans before he united them."

"What? So that stupid rhyme is wrong? The priest should be above the king?"

"If you'd been listening to your tutors, then you'd know the rhyme is hundreds of years old. And in that time, how many accomplished what your father has achieved?"

"Oh, I don't bloody know...a few?"

"Two that we know of."

"So?"

"So," he said, jabbing his pipe towards her. "The Communion endures through it all. It's all about influence, Seren. Which is why you need to stay on the right side of your uncle...even if it pains me to say so."

"But he condemned me in front of my friends. I couldn't allow him to disrespect me like that."

"Not all fights are won by brute strength. You must find other ways to deal with conflict."

"He damn well deserved it!"

Ironfoot sighed. "Which is why I had to put you in here for the night."

"Maybe for the lower castes, but when was it permitted to throw a princess into a common jail?"

"Since your father told me to teach you a lesson, princess. That's when."

"My father? Why?"

"It's not my place to question the king."

"Listen to me, Luis. There are far more pressing issues at hand. I need to prepare for the Mendari." She smiled at him through the bars. "I'm sure my father will understand."

"Really? Your father would understand if I disobeyed a direct command?" He took another deep inhale of his pipe and allowed the smoke to vent slowly out of his mouth. "Preparation, you say. If I was still Master of War, you'd be the last person I'd want standing in a shield wall, let alone commanding the Named. You need to discipline your mind, Seren."

She snapped. "Well, you're not. I never understood why you abandoned my father during the caste uprising. I guess it must be true what they say—that you're just a washed-up, bitter cripple, who showed disloyalty to the higher castes."

"Ouch. That must cut deep," said an unfamiliar voice, coming from the adjacent cell. "She's certainly got her father's temper."

Seren spun towards the voice, trying to locate the owner. As her eyes adapted to the lack of light, she could just make out the shape of a man sitting on a bed at the back of the cell. "Whoever you are, you'd better shut your foul-smelling mouth before I do it for you."

A throaty, raucous laugh burst out from the man. "I'm afraid you'll have to join the back of the queue. Isn't that right, sheriff?"

"Who is he?"

"He's the bard who's been performing in The Renegade. He drank too much last night and said some things he shouldn't have."

"What things?"

The bard pushed off the bench, staggered across the cell and shoved his grisly face between the bars. "Would you like me to tell you, your highness?"

"Oh, yes...I've seen you around. Looks like they've worked you over. So what did you say to get Ironfoot all flustered?"

Through his matted veil of hair, the bard's mouth curled up into a smile. "Just the truth, your highness. Just the truth."

"Bollocks," said Ironfoot. "You're full of shit, bard."

Seren narrowed her eyes at him. "If I thought you were stirring up trouble with the lower castes, I'd run you through myself."

"Perhaps I could change your mind by telling you things that no-one else knows about your father?"

"Piss off, bard. Save it for those stupid enough to fall for your lies."

"Lies? I only ever speak the truth," said the bard. "It's just that some would prefer I kept the truth a secret...like secrets from the day the Three Orphans of Treharne met."

"W-what did you say?"

"You heard me, sheriff," said the bard, pulling his greying locks behind his head to reveal his face. "Perhaps the princess would like to know what really happened the day her aunt Eleri died?"

Ironfoot's pipe fell to the floor, cascading hundreds of sparks into the air. He clambered out of his seat and hobbled towards Seren's cell as fast as his false leg would allow. He fumbled through a large set of keys attached to his belt and unlocked the door.

"What are you doing?"

"I'm letting you go, your highness. You need to leave."

The bard laughed. "Can't she stay a bit longer? We're having so much fun."

"Not a chance." Ironfoot pulled her out of her cell and marched her down the corridor, towards the jail's exit.

"Get your hands off me."

"Promise to behave?"

She glared at him but relented. "Yes...Velak's balls! You're strong."

"Not bad for a washed-up, bitter cripple."

Seren lowered her eyes. "I-I shouldn't have called you that...but you angered me."

"Forget it. I've been called worse. Remember, Seren—your enemies will attack your weaknesses. Control your emotions, or they'll be the end of you."

She nodded respectfully, knowing that he spoke the truth. Whether she had the strength to tame the demons within her was another thing entirely. She changed the subject. "What happened back there? Why did a creature like that get under your skin?"

"Let's just say he's not welcome in these parts."

"I can believe it. Look at what he achieved in one night. The last thing we need is trouble from the lower castes when the Mendari are so close."

"I'm surprised it didn't happen sooner with all the tension out there."

"Well, I suppose you know them better than you know your own people."

Ironfoot refused to bite. "Perhaps you should ask your father who was their greatest champion? You might be surprised by his answer."

Seren cursed under her breath. "He always clams up when the subject brings back memories of 'You Know Who'."

"Perhaps he'll be more open if you show that you can be the daughter he needs you to be?"

"Not much chance of that happening."

"Well, you might not think you can change, but I believe you can."

Staring at the floor, she wound a braid of flaxen hair around her finger. After a moment, she looked at him and asked, "You really think I can change, after everything?"

"The bard's right about you having your father's temper, but you've also got your mother's fierce passion and determination. Use them to sort yourself out."

"Thank you, Luis. That means a lot to me."

Ironfoot grinned. "Come on, I'll let you out."

As she neared the entrance, Seren glanced back to the bard's cell. "Should I inform my father of this bard's presence?"

"Leave that to me. I'll send him a message explaining what happened and why I let you out early."

"If you insist," she said, as Ironfoot unlocked the entrance. The chill of the night lingered, as winter refused to submit to the oncoming appearance of the warmer summer months. As she slipped into the courtyard, she paused. "And Ironfoot, I never want to spend another night in this shit hole."

"It's a shit hole, for sure, but it's my shit hole. Fine. Just try to stay out of trouble. You're supposed to be a bloody princess."

She chuckled, realising how ridiculous she must look. "I'll try to remember that."

Luis waved goodbye to the princess, producing the most genuine smile he could summon. As soon as she was out of sight, his smile faded. He locked the jailhouse door and returned to his desk, choosing to lean on the edge. His stump ached—it always did. Rolling up his left trouser leg, he unfastened the iron-plated limb and placed it on the desk. The skin around the exposed stump appeared swollen and cracked. All he wanted to do was scratch the damn thing, but he knew better. He opened a small bottle of ointment that he retrieved from his pocket and poured a few drops onto the affected area, gently applying the sweet-smelling liquid.

The bard stood by the bars, his bright amber eyes burning fiercely in the light of the sconces.

"I remember begging you both to put me out of my misery," said Ironfoot, lowering his voice not to be overheard. "Not because of the pain, but of the shame I felt. How could I be a clansguard with only one leg? Just like the princess said—a cripple."

"Maybe we should've left you in that glen. One less grumpy bastard in the world."

"And you're still an arrogant, smart-arsed bastard," growled Ironfoot, tightening the last strap of his false limb.

"Why change the habit of a lifetime?"

"Fifteen years, Grimbard...fifteen bloody years," he said through gritted teeth. "Why now? You swore an oath to leave and never come back."

"I have my reasons."

"Not even our blood oath will stop him killing you if he sees you again—especially as you're stirring up trouble with the townspeople."

"Oh, that's just me getting your attention. You know what I'm like."

"Unfortunately, I do."

"I'm surprised you didn't work it out earlier. How many other people do you know with eyes of my colour? You're losing your touch."

"Bollocks to that. It didn't even cross my mind that you'd show up, let alone be dressed like...that," said Ironfoot, screwing up his nose. "So now that you've got my attention, what do you want?"

"I wasn't lying in the tavern when I said I come with a message from the South. It's for Rodric."

"A message? Who from?"

"Kaine."

"Velak's balls, Grimbard. Do you despise us so much that you'll side with the Mendari?"

"Just send for him. He needs to hear what Kaine has to say—even if it costs me my life."

"I gave up any influence with the king when I resigned as Master of War. I'm just a sheriff now—nothing more, nothing less."

"You mean that nasty business at the mines? From what I hear, that was Zirani's plan, not yours."

"I could've begged the king to reconsider, but I chose to walk away."

"Maybe, but I don't believe that the king would deny you a meeting now that he's in Keld. Just send for him. Please."

"Fine. On your own head be it." He walked to his desk, sat down and composed a note to the king. He read it back, cursed and scrunched the parchment into a tight ball. Trying again, he took his time on every word he wrote.

Grimbard grinned through the bars. "Having problems, Luis?"

"Piss off. If I say this wrong, it'll be my head on a spike as well as yours." He sealed the note in a plain envelope and called a guard from the other end of the jail. "For the king's eyes only, clansguard."

"Yes, sir."

As the guard marched off to carry out his order, Ironfoot relit his pipe and slumped into his chair. "Well, whatever you've got to tell him, it had better be the best story you've ever told, Grimbard."

For a moment, Tarek let his guard down, revealing the grim determination that Ironfoot remembered so vividly. "Believe me. He'll want to know."

19

NIGHTMARES AND DAYMARES

Tomos awoke, disoriented. As much as he tried, the horrors of his recurring dream remained frustratingly hidden from his conscious memory. All that linked each sweat-stained, restless night was waking up abruptly and shivering as if he had slept in a tomb. But this time was different—he experienced a new sensation. The brawl in the tavern had left him bruised and aching from head to toe. He cursed as he recalled his misadventure at The Renegade. As his eyes gradually grew accustomed to the lack of light inside his bedchamber, the familiar figure of his father sharpened into view beside him.

"The adventurer awakes."

"What time is it?" he asked, rubbing the sleep mucus out of his eyes.

"Early. It's still dark outside."

"Goddess, you look worse than me. Have you had any sleep?"

"Sleep? Sleep is a luxury that parents with obedient children can afford. Something I can only imagine now that you've joined your sister in tormenting me."

Tomos fought back his tears. "I-I'm sorry."

"Sorry that you disobeyed me or sorry that you got caught? Do you know how irresponsible and dangerous your actions were?"

"I only went there to meet a friend and listen to the bard. I didn't know a fight was going to break out. What's so bad about that? Seren does far worse."

"This isn't about Seren. You deliberately lied to me, slipped out of the fortress to go to a *tavern* and lost your amulet."

Tomos clenched his fists in frustration. "I knew it. It's all because of this blasted illness. Am I to live the rest of my life cooped up like a prisoner? I'd rather die than live like that."

"Don't say that, Tomos.... And what about Gwen's daughter? What if something terrible had happened to her?"

"You know." He blinked and looked away. "W-what will happen to her?"

"Nothing. It's a good job your uncle or one of his over-zealous Grey Cloaks from the Grove didn't find you together. You risked a lot just to spend some time with a pretty girl."

Tomos fiddled with the edge of the blanket. "It's not like that. She's a friend."

Softening his expression, Rodric said, "I realise that you're getting to an age where you want more independence, but last night wasn't the way to go about it. You know the rules. You're not allowed to socialise with people from the lower castes, unless it's one of the permitted festivals."

"Why do you allow the Communion to dictate to you like this? You're the king."

Rodric stared at his son, wide-eyed.

"What's the matter?"

"Y-you reminded me of someone else for a moment."

"Who?"

"It doesn't matter. What matters is you keep your opinions about the Communion to yourself."

"It's not fair," he said, punching the mattress, regretting it as his muscles ached from his beating. "What else do you know about last night?"

"The clansguard told me everything."

"Everything?"

"Yes, everything. Do you feel any worse without the amulet?"

"I'm still alive, if that's what you mean."

"Don't jest, Tomos. Madoc gave you the amulet for a reason. Trust you to pick a day to be a rebel when Madoc's on one of his trips." He leant in close to Tomos and rested his hand on his shoulder. "That aside, I'm proud of you for standing up and defending me—but I'm the king, and there'll always be people who resent me."

"Some defender I was. I couldn't even throw one punch before taking a beating in full view of everyone. So much for Tomos Niras, son of Rodric Shieldbane." He flopped into the bed. "I'm a failure."

"No, you're not. I don't care if you're not a warrior. You're my son and that's all that matters to me."

"If it wasn't for this damn illness, I could be so much more." Agitated, he flung off his blankets and paced to the bedchamber window. He unlocked the shutters, opening them wide, allowing the cool morning breeze to envelop him.

"Goddess, Tomos, you'll let all the heat escape."

"Doesn't feel cold to me."

"Really? You must be coming down with a fever."

"No...I always feel like this after one of my dreams." He slouched onto the windowsill and rubbed an itch on the back of his neck. "Do you think dreams are important to understand?"

"I'm sure Uncle Kurzon or Madoc would have better answers for you."

"They've got an answer for everything. I want to know what you think."

His father stroked his moustache. "Mostly, it's like my memories have been shaken together inside my mind and then played out as a series of bizarre tableaus. Then, once in a while, my dreams make sense, and I relive moments from the past as clear as the day they happened."

"Lucid dreams. So you remember all the details?"

"Oh, yes. Cruel recollections of days I'd rather forget," he said, looking away from Tomos. "So no, I wouldn't take *any* solace from my dreams."

"I wish I could remember mine."

"It's probably a side effect of the elixir."

"You mean that disgusting slop I shove down my throat every day?"

"That 'disgusting slop' is keeping you alive, my boy."

"I know," groaned Tomos. "But I get so frustrated.... I-it's like I'm barely existing. Anything overly energetic and, well, last night happens."

"I understand your anxiety, but would you prefer death?"

"Of course, not. I just wish there was another way." He turned and stared out of the window. The fire braziers that lined the South Wall floated in the blackness of the night. In the light of day, from his elevated, south-facing bedchamber, Tomos could see for miles, over the Plains of Keld and almost as far as the northern border of Derwedd Forest. "During the next few days, you'll fight Kaine and his horde, standing side by side with the Named in the shield wall. That's where I want to be, but I can't even throw a punch without fainting. I'm useless."

"Here you go again. Think of all the incredible discoveries you've found from the books of the Hen Rai and how you've helped the Skilled Caste improve so many things in Northern Tarania."

"But I want to be like those brave warriors in the stories. Like you —Rodric Shieldbane, King of Northern Tarania and slayer of Banan the Giant." The floorboards creaked as his father walked to the table next to the window and poured a drink of wine. Tomos frowned, watching his father swallow the contents of the cup in one long, thirsty gulp. *Father drinking so early in the day?*

"I believe the bard at the tavern told you the tale of the Three Orphans of Treharne. Did he tell you I defended my family with great honour and bravery, but couldn't save my mother and sister?"

"I-I didn't hear the first part, but I've heard other bards tell that tale. Why?"

"Because it's not what really happened."

Tomos turned to his father and frowned. "There's a different version?"

The king nodded. "Yes, there's the truth. What I tell you now is between the two of us. Understand?"

"Yes, Father." It was rare for his father to open up and reveal something private about his past. Life's events had turned him into someone who struggled to show affection, especially to his children. Yet Tomos knew with no doubt that his father loved him.

"I was sixteen, with not a care in the world, and had just returned from collecting mushrooms with Eleri when my father burst into our home and thrust a sword into my hand. He said to me, 'Mendari raiders. Protect them, son. Don't let them get captured.' The look of despair carved into his face told me so much more of what he wanted me to do. He embraced us all and turned to join the rest of the defenders.

"I watched in horror as the Mendari smashed down the gate and swarmed into the town. They surrounded Treharne's brave but outnumbered clansguard veterans and slaughtered every last one of them. When I saw my father impaled by a Mendari spear, I spewed my guts, fainted and collapsed to the floor. I've no idea how long I was unconscious, but as I came around, I heard my sister scream as a Mendari warrior dragged her off the blood-smeared, lifeless body of our dear mother. Her dress had been ripped off and unspeakable things done to her. The same fate awaited my little sister unless I could overcome my fears and defend her.

"And so, trembling with a mix of rage and terror, I took hold of my sword and charged at the Mendari, slashing wildly at his face. I remember his look of amusement as he swatted the sword out of my hand. The next thing I knew, he rammed me up against the wall with his giant hand crushing my windpipe. I was helpless. I thought I was going to die.

"The Mendari sneered into my face, tightening his grip around my neck. But then his expression changed—his arrogance and ferocity replaced by painful confusion. Releasing his grip, the warrior reached over his shoulder and pulled my blood-soaked sword from out of his back. Behind him stood my sister, quivering, her hands covered in Mendari blood.

"The warrior roared in anger. He spun around to face Eleri and slashed down with my sword, carving a vicious gash across her face. She screamed in agony, crumpling to the floor. I watched, frozen to the spot, as the Mendari staggered towards her, lifting the weapon above his head, ready to deliver the decisive thrust. Then, with my father's words sending a surge of strength through me, I jumped on the Mendari's back and dug my fingers deep inside his open wound. He reeled back, grasping at my tunic to throw me off, but I held on and opened that wound up wide with my bare hands. As the sawdust floor became a blood-saturated pulp, he collapsed on top of me and fell silent. That was the first time I'd killed another person."

Rodric faced Tomos—his eyes stinging from the bitter tears that rolled steadily down his face. "Do you know what it's like to feel helpless? You asked me about my dreams—I don't need to be asleep to relive this nightmare, or what happened to your mother. They haunt me constantly."

"What happened next?"

His father pushed off the windowsill, sat on the edge of the bed, and invited Tomos to join him. "I honestly believed that I was going to die trapped under that bastard—but do you know what made me fight to survive?"

"Eleri?"

"Yes, she was still alive...barely. I could hear her whimpering, so close to me, calling my name, begging me to help her." He rubbed the palm of his hand with his thumb. "And that's when I saw the flames spreading across the thatched roof. The Mendari love nothing more than a 'cleansing' fire of purification."

"Is that how you got those burns?"

Rodric nodded. "Between the searing heat, the fumes and the sheer weight of his corpse, I could hardly breathe; but as Eleri's cries turned to screams of terror, I heaved with all my might and pushed the Mendari off me. In that instant, a beam from the roof plummeted towards me. I scrambled to the side just as it crashed onto the floor, but as it splintered; casting red-hot embers and shards in all directions, I shielded my eyes with my hands. And well, you can see the results."

"Goddess. The pain must've been excruciating."

Rodric closed his eyes and nodded. "But at least that pain faded over time. I don't know how I kept going, but I found my way around the flaming debris and followed my sister's voice until, with one final gut-wrenching scream, she fell silent."

"She died alone?"

"Yes, and I would've shared her fate if it weren't for Luis and Tarek pulling me out of the roundhouse. I owe them my life."

"So that's why you couldn't execute him?"

"That, and they vouched for me when Govannon grew suspicious about my burns. After that, we swore a sword brother oath to each other."

"Can I touch them?"

Rodric nodded and held his hands out.

Gently, Tomos trailed his fingers over the scarred skin of each palm. He noticed on the right hand an indistinct patch of faded black skin that was all that was left of the Clansguard Caste brand his father received when he was thirteen. "What did it feel like when you received your branding?"

Rodric pulled his hands away. "I've said enough."

"I-I'm sorry, Father."

"Never mind about that. The reason I shared this with you is that all the stories of brave warriors winning honour and glory are just that—stories. Stories to stir up the courage of the young so they won't realise how horrific war really is until it's too late to turn and run." His father swallowed, then shook his head. "I nearly lost you once. I won't let that happen again." He stood up, his expression stern. "You're my son, and I'll not have you throw your life away just because some drunk bard weaves a tale that you want to believe to be true. If you want to be honourable, do as I say and stay out of trouble. There's more than one way to be of service to your king."

"Service to your king?" The words cut deep. "And there was me thinking that you'd finally brought down your wall."

"That's not fair, Tomos. You know how difficult it is for me to—"

They turned to the door as someone knocked.

"Enter," commanded his father.

"Sire, I've a message from the Sheriff of Belanore," said a guard, handing over a plain envelope.

The king opened it and pulled out a small parchment. Tomos strained to read what was written, but it was too far away.

"What's he playing at?" said his father, frowning. "Tell him I'm on my way."

"Should I inform the Elite Guard to accompany you?"

"That won't be necessary; I'll come alone."

"Yes, my king," said the warrior, spinning on his heels, disappearing through the door.

Before leaving, Rodric returned his attention to Tomos. "Don't leave your chamber until Madoc returns."

"What? Not even down to Gwen's workshop?"

"Especially not there. It won't bode well for Kaitlyn's family if you pursue her affection any further. Even I'll struggle to protect them from the Communion—there'll be consequences. Besides, I've already found a match for you."

"Who?"

"Lady Amira Taleni...if she survived Vedana."

20

THE VOID

The warm caress of the stream of tranquillity enfolded Amira, carrying her deeper into the darkness. Guided only by the whim of the strangely familiar current, she drifted until time lost all meaning. Within the blackness, she perceived a myriad of bright shards of light floating as far as her eyes could see, filled with defining memories from her young, bittersweet life. As one such memory passed by, she gasped in astonishment. Within the light she recognised a familiar figure. *Mother. Is it really you?* She reached towards the light, desperate to run her fingers through her mother's fiery red locks; yet the moment she touched the image it disintegrated into a cloud of silvery smoke, forever lost to her. Time and time again, she reached out for other precious memories, only to witness them disappear before her eyes. *Is this really the Void? Or...no.* She squeezed her eyes tight, unwilling to allow herself further heartache. *Are you punishing me, Enora? Have you sent me to the Netherplain? Am I paying for...* She paused, as she breathed in a scent that she knew so well, prompting her to rub her finger and thumb together. *That smell, that texture. I'd recognise them anywhere.* Timidly, she opened her eyes and beamed with delight. In front of her, a shard had settled between her hands, and within it a small brown book revealed itself to her. It opened, falling to a page written by a hand that brought joy to her heart

—*Yanna*. The words called to her, inviting her in. She accepted and opened her mind to the power of the words contained within.

Amira wrapped her blanket tight around her body as she stared up into the vast expanse of the Void. Enthralled with the darkness above her, she failed to notice the balcony door edge open and the shadowy figure creep out towards her on all fours.

"Boo!"

"Ahh!" she screamed, cowering under the blanket.

"Shhh. You'll wake them up," said Yanna, pulling the blanket off Amira's face. "There's a surprise. My little sister's sleeping out on the balcony again."

"I'll get you back for that." Amira frowned. "What're you doing up at this time of night? Are you ill?"

"No, I'm fine. Just woke up and couldn't get back to sleep." Her sister eyed her blanket. "Room for one more under there?"

Amira giggled. "Yes. If it's not too childish for you?"

"Goddess, I'm only seventeen. Although, if Father had his way, he'd have me married off before the end of the year." She slipped inside the blanket, linked her arm with Amira's and kissed her cheek.

"Why'd you do that?"

"Do I need a reason to show my little sister some affection?"

Amira stayed silent for a moment and then turned to Yanna, biting her lip.

"I know that look. What's wrong?"

"I-I just wish we could stay like this forever.... Why do we have to grow old and die?"

"Oh, Amira," said Yanna, hugging her tight. "What brought this on?"

She pointed up into the air. "I don't want to go up there when I die, alone in the dark."

Yanna wrinkled her nose and fixed her eyes on Amira. "Have you been reading the Book of Enora?"

Amira nodded. "Is it true?"

"Well, that's what it says in the book...but I think there's something else after that."

"What do you mean?"

Yanna gave her that know-it-all look that she used far too many times.

"Ugh. I hate it when you do that. Tell me?"

"I don't know, Amira."

"Oh, please, Yanna. I'm ten years old. I'm not a baby."

"Fine; but you must keep it a secret—not a word to anyone." Yanna cupped her hands around Amira's ear and whispered, "You see those lights in the darkness? I know what they are."

"Of course, you do. We all do. They're the Children of Enora."

"So the Communion tells us...but what if they're wrong?"

Amira gasped. "That's blasphemy."

"Do you want to know or not?"

She thought for a moment, picturing the colour of her father's face if he found out about their conversation; but her curious nature overcame her fear. "I-I suppose so."

Yanna grinned. "I'll be right back." She got up, went inside and returned with a small leather-bound book.

"Is that yours? I've never seen it before."

"No-one has. You can't tell anyone. Not even mother or father."

She nodded.

"I mean it, Amira. It's our secret. You can't tell a soul."

"I *promise.*"

Yanna scanned the surrounding area. Satisfied they were alone, she knelt beside Amira. "This is a book of long-lost secrets from the old world."

"The Hen Rai?"

"Shhh...keep your voice down."

"Did you steal it from Mother's library?"

"No, I didn't. I found it among the presents at my sixteenth birthday celebration."

"Really? From whom?"

"I've no idea. When I opened it, I found pages of notes written in a language that I'd never seen before. See for yourself."

Amira studied the text. "How strange. The letters are the same as ours, but I can't read any of the words."

"There aren't many who can. I remember mother telling me that hundreds of years ago the North and South had two different languages, but over time they merged into what we speak today. I think this is old Mendari."

"Can you read it?"

Yanna's eyes lit up. "Yes, I can. Whoever wanted me to have this book translated some of the writing. I think it was passed to me to finish the rest—like they're testing me. It's taken me ages."

"Tested? Why?"

"I don't know."

Amira yawned, struggling to keep her eyes open. "I really need to go back to bed—but first, tell me what your mysterious book says about the Void?"

Yanna nodded, thumbing through the pages. "Ah, here it is."

Eagerly, Amira sat cross-legged opposite her sister. "Can I read it?"

"Certainly, but don't crumple the pages." She placed the book onto Amira's lap and showed her where to read. "Here's my translation in the common tongue." Then she stretched out on the balcony floor and closed her eyes.

Amira couldn't help herself. She rubbed the parchment between her fingers. "What a peculiar texture." Curiosity piqued, she pushed her nose into the smooth page and breathed in the odour. "It doesn't smell like any book I've read."

"Are you going to read the passage or just spend all night smelling the thing?"

She poked her tongue out at Yanna, then began to read.

"And the chosen will arise within the bowels of the Beasts of Light and journey through the Void unto the place where all life began."

"Well?"

"I don't get it. Bowels of the Beasts of Light?"

'Well, I'm not entirely sure I've got that right...but look at the lights," said Yanna, pointing up to the Void. "They move."

"Do they?"

"Yes. Don't take my word for it. Pick one of the brighter ones and notice where it is every hour. Then you'll see."

"And you think that they're the Beasts of Light taking the dead to...where was it?"

"Where all life began," said Yanna.

"I wonder what that means?"

"Just watch and see."

Amira settled down beside Yanna and focused her attention on a bright light directly above her. She frowned as a thought popped into her mind. "Why doesn't the Book of Enora speak of these Beasts of Light?"

"Now who's the smart one? Perhaps there's more to this world than the Communion tells us? Maybe they don't know themselves?"

A deafening crack of thunder pulsated throughout the darkness above them, as the blackness of the Void was torn asunder by a shaft of brilliant white light. Amira shielded her eyes from the blinding rays, expecting her body to burst into flames at any moment.

───

"Lady Amira?"

Lowering her arm, she squinted and noticed a silhouetted figure standing over her.

"Don't be alarmed. Your body will be weak and disoriented. Let me help you out."

"W-where am I?"

"You're in Vedana."

"Vedana? And what's this thing I'm in?" She stretched her arms out, sliding her hands across the padded walls and ceiling of her tiny chamber. As she moved her body, the bed she lay on moulded itself to keep her comfortable. "I-I thought I was dead and travelling through the Void."

"You're not the first to think that."

Not the first? She stared at the man above her, realising that he wasn't silhouetted, but clothed entirely in black. "I-I think I've seen you before, but my head hurts when I try to think about it."

"Don't worry, all your memories will come back to you—one tiny piece at a time."

"But why do I feel like this?"

"I don't know the answer to that. I just know it happens."

"Who are you?"

"I'm Scion Juran and Lord Kaine has entrusted me with your protection."

"Lord Kaine? I-I feel I should know who that is."

"You'll remember, soon enough," he said, offering her his black-clad hand. "I'll take you to your apartment in the Great Hall so you can rest."

Overcome with exhaustion, she clutched his arm, allowing him to lift her out into the dawn morning light and carry her towards the Great Hall. She glanced over his shoulder and shuddered as the open space in the courtyard shimmered. *I've seen that before somewhere.* Other Mendari warriors walked away from the rippling air, each one carrying a child. One word emerged from the fog of her memory. One word that sent a sharp pang of guilt into her stomach. *Keila.* "Where're they taking those children?"

"Somewhere safe, Lady Amira. They've been chosen by Velak."

21

THE UNWELCOME REUNION

Hooded and alone, Rodric slipped through the Great Hall. He doubted that any of the servants clearing the feast would notice him —just one more warrior suffering from overindulgence from the night before.

Unlatching the main door, he eased it open and stepped into the welcome embrace of the fresh, early morning air—a sharp contrast to the stale, sweaty stink of the feasting hall. To the east, Ulena's light dispelled the blackness of the Void, as she once again ascended from the depths of the Netherplain.

He remembered another time standing there, looking off to the south. A young and inexperienced king of an unstable alliance of clans, he made the bold decision to take the fight to the Mendari—a move that could have been catastrophic or be the beginning of a golden era for Northern Tarania. Based on the evidence of the improvements made to Keld, he was confident that he would leave an enduring legacy.

Many years ago, Keld had been a hillfort of strategic importance to the Nirasian clan. From its meandering course in the Northern Belith Range to its wide estuary to the west, the River Valtara made travelling to and from Northern Tarania an almost impossible challenge. Even the Galgari, with their knowledge and skills of boatbuilding, would rather take their chances on the open sea than tackle the unpredictable nature of the Valtara. Yet there was one place where the bedrock had resisted the eroding power of the mighty river. The small series of islands that were formed allowed his Nirasian ancestors to build a bridge across the river and construct a hillfort to protect it, but Govannon had neglected the strategic importance of Keld, and allowed raiders from the south to enter Northern Tarania without being challenged.

Once returning north, Rodric commissioned the rebuilding of the ancient hillfort. A sturdy stone bridge was built over the dilapidated wooden remains of the former crossing, with a formidable drawbridge replacing the final section in recent years. The long-forgotten ramparts were repaired, and an intimidating stone wall was erected on top of the massive ring of earth. Within the fortress, an additional plateaued mound was raised, to allow a clear view of the south and act as the central administrative area for the stronghold. Since that time, Keld had been maintained by one hundred clansguard, but with the imminent threat of a new Mendari attack, the full might of the Northern Taranian army blanketed the fields to the north.

Keeping to the shadows, Rodric made his way towards the North Gate, which remained open to allow the constant flow of supplies to pass through it. Bored into the packed earth of the rampart, the tunnel leading to the entrance reminded him of the adits driven into the Belith Mountain range, where its miners toiled to extract various ores from the rock. Although far shorter, the design principles were the same. The tunnel was excavated with a rectangular profile and at a slight upward angle to allow efficient drainage of rainwater. Timber posts and caps, installed at regular intervals, supported the sheer weight of the packed earth surrounding the tunnel. Raised at each end was a pair of ironclad portcullis gates, twenty feet tall and two feet thick. In the event of a siege, these massive guardians of the fortress could be sent crashing to the ground in seconds.

As Rodric slipped underneath the inner gate, he winced, imagining what ten tons of wood and iron would do to a person trapped underneath. Yet it was the tunnel itself that troubled him.

Rodric was a warrior, not an engineer. He understood the rudiments of what the builders had explained to him, but walking under all of that earth unnerved him. Tomos had no such reservations; he understood it all.

Over the years, Madoc had provided Tomos with enough books of the Hen Rai to rival the collections of the University of Northern Tarania and the Communion. This in itself was an astonishing achievement, but Madoc's finds were exceptional in other ways. Not only were the texts in excellent condition, but it was the information contained within the pages that fascinated Rodric, and it was Tomos who ignited this passion.

After reading one particular book, Tomos had rushed into his father's private office at their home in Caerniras, requesting an audience with Callum and Gwen, his master engineers. He had designed several improvements to the capital's defences he was sure they would want to consider. Rodric dismissed them at first, putting it down to Tomos' youthful enthusiasm. Then one day, as he walked towards the workshops, he noticed several engineers gathered together in a circle discussing something that excited them. As he neared the group, he realised that in the centre of the ring of engineers stood a young boy holding various pieces of parchment. It was Tomos. Rodric remembered being angry with the boy for taking up the valuable time of his engineers. However, when Callum saw him, he beamed with delight, congratulating him for having such a clever son. With the knowledge and understanding of a master engineer, Tomos had calculated and designed structural improvements to the Northern Taranian capital that even the renowned husband-and-wife duo would have struggled to conceive. From that day, Rodric had Madoc teach him the language of the Hen Rai, but even though he learned to decode the words, he could never truly comprehend their meaning like Tomos could.

Over time, Rodric realised that Tomos differed from the other children. Could he truly have been touched by the gods? After nearly losing him on that fateful night, Rodric thanked the goddess for sending Madoc to his aid just as his infant son drew close to the Veil. Still, as he hurried through the torch-lit tunnel, even the knowledge that the beams that loomed above his head had been reinforced based on his son's designs did not stop the ice-cold chill running down his back. He quickened his pace.

"Fresh air." Rodric breathed in deeply, relieved to be out of the claustrophobic underpass. He walked beneath the outer portcullis and emerged on the Great North Road that stretched all the way to Caerniras. Before leaving, he had considered riding to his destination, but he felt like walking—a welcome opportunity to enjoy his own company for once. Although the town of Belanore, which lay just over a mile to the northeast, was a place he would prefer to avoid.

He spat on the floor in disgust. Like a parasite that feeds off the living, Belanore leeched the hard-earned wages of the garrison, in a never-ending cycle of drinking, gambling and whoring. He should never have sent Seren as his representative to the fortress. Like a starved, ravenous wolf finding an unprotected flock of sheep, Seren gorged herself on every vice found in that festering abscess on the landscape. If it hadn't been for the surprising intervention of Ironfoot, he would have never discovered the full extent of her demise. Between Tomos' illness and Seren's path of self-destruction, he felt helpless. It was at times like this when he missed her the most. *You were so wise—how I could use your wisdom now.* He gripped the delicate ring hanging from his neck and took strength from the love of his life.

Approaching the military encampment, he heard the usual clamour of an army waking up: officers barking orders, swords clashing against shields and countless field kitchens preparing a hearty breakfast for five thousand hungry mouths. The aroma of freshly baked bread made his stomach rumble. He wondered what else the clansguard would be offered. Perhaps some bacon and honey, or even a hot, steaming bowl of salted porridge. His mouth watered, but he knew he had no time to stop, so he continued north —Ironfoot's message perplexed him.

The sounds of the camp faded, leaving only nature's orchestra to accompany him on his short journey. Treading on the grass verge to stifle his footsteps, he listened to their song. The pre-dawn chorus of blackbirds, robins and skylarks had been in full verse for over an hour. Now that Ulena rose over the eastern horizon, wrens and warblers had joined their melodies to the ensemble. The avian choir took him back to a simpler time. He cherished those early years, sitting on the hill above their house with his mother and sister, learning to whistle each birdsong. His mother could mimic them all. It was magical—leaning on the soft, dew-covered grass of a dawn morning, in total awe of her. The first song she taught them was the wren. She said it was an easy melody to start with, as it was loud and repetitive. Rodric chuckled to himself, recalling the hours spent striving to perfect the whistle. Not so for Eleri. Just like her mother, she learned them all with ease and enjoyed tormenting her older brother with her faultless repertoire. He smiled, then added his wren whistle to the dawn chorus.

Rodric's spirits lifted. Spring showed its favour to the northern lands, as the lines of ancient oak that ran the course of the road bloomed green with new life. Farmers ploughed their fields in preparation for sowing cereal crops. Golden fields filled with barley, wheat and oats would be ready for harvest in the autumn. Twenty-three years of peace had allowed the people of Northern Tarania to prosper. Even the lower castes, who constantly complained about the unfairness of the social order, were far better off than in those dark years of the Mendari raids.

A short time later, he left the Great North Road and headed towards the town. A small ditch and wooden palisade encircled the settlement, providing protection from the world outside.

Passing through the unguarded wooden gatehouse, he stepped onto Main Street. Taverns of all shapes and sizes flanked him, bearing all manner of gaudy signs to entice an off-duty clansguard into their seedy establishments. Rodric fixed his eyes on the far end of the street and marched down the middle, ignoring the temptations. If he had his way, the whole town would be razed to the ground. Kurzon, on the other hand, saw an opportunity to rekindle the love for the goddess, and—more concerning to Rodric—to increase the numbers of Grey Cloaks at the Sacred Grove of the Goddess. As he reached the end of the street, the Grove loomed in front of him.

Although smaller compared to the places of worship of the larger settlements, the Grove buildings dwarfed the other structures of the town—its prominent silhouette cast a long, dark shadow down Main Street.

On the corner, the town's blacksmith tended to his furnace, ready for the day ahead. The short, robust man gave the king the briefest of glances before returning his attention to working his bellows. Even through his heavy cloak, Rodric sweated from the intensity of the waves of heat radiating from the furnace. He lingered for a few moments before turning into a side street that led to a long stone building—the town jail.

As he neared, a guard posted at the main entrance challenged him. Rodric lowered his hood, and the guard blanched, apologising for not recognising him. "At ease, clansguard."

The guard quickly turned towards the main door, unlocked it and opened it wide for the king. "Your majesty," she said, bowing her head towards Rodric. The king smiled and stepped inside.

The jailhouse was very simple in design. A long, wide corridor ran the whole length of the right-hand side of the jail. To the left, a dozen box-shaped cells faced inward. Vertical iron bars enclosed the cells, denying the occupants any privacy; not that the usual visitor to the jail was in any state to consider such notions.

As he made his way down the corridor, the hatred pouring from the packed cells was palpable—more than usual for Belanore.

"King Rodric."

It was Ironfoot. The sheriff made his way towards him, stopping and bowing awkwardly in front of him. "How long has it been, Luis?"

"Four years, sire."

"I see you've lost all of your hair."

"I had little to start with."

At that, Rodric placed his hand on Ironfoot's shoulder. "I've missed you, my friend."

"I've missed you too, sire."

Rodric frowned. "I hate you calling me that. We're sword brothers, or have you forgotten?"

"Of, course not, Rodric."

"That's more like it," he said, smiling. "Still, I'm not happy that you let Seren out without asking me first. What's this all about, Luis?"

"I'll explain everything, but not here. Follow me."

Ironfoot led him to his private quarters at the other end of the jail. He paused for a moment and turned back to Rodric. "Before we go in, you need to promise me you'll stay calm and let me explain the situation."

"Luis, I don't like the way you're acting. There's something amiss here."

"You'll just have to trust me."

Following Ironfoot inside, Rodric's first impression was that it was undoubtedly Ironfoot's room. The few pieces of furniture he owned were utilitarian by design and function—perfectly reflecting his modest lifestyle. Rodric smiled. *Some things never change.* But something was different. He scrunched his nose. "What in the goddess' name is that awful smell?"

Ironfoot gave his answer by nodding over to one of the high-backed chairs facing away from them.

"Will you stop playing games with me, Ironfoot? What's this all about?"

"You haven't changed a bit, Rodric. Still as impatient as the first day we met."

Rodric's eyes narrowed. His hand twitched around the pommel of his sword. "Grimbard."

Grimbard stood and turned to face him. "Please excuse my dishevelled appearance. Luis refused my request for a bath and a shave."

Rodric snarled, pulling his sword out of its scabbard until Ironfoot's hand gripped the pommel.

"This is why I wanted you to stay calm. He asked me to bring you here. You need to hear him out."

Full of rage, Rodric wrenched the pommel away from Ironfoot and in one swift movement levelled the razor-sharp blade against Grimbard's neck. The traitor kept his eyes on Rodric, not flinching.

"Please, Rodric. You know our pact."

"How can you say that? He doesn't deserve to live when she's rotting in the ground."

"Please. I beg you not to do it. I know you. You'll regret it."

"What do you know of my pain?"

Ironfoot laid his hand on Rodric's shoulder. "Her absence is like a spear through my heart. She was like a sister to me...and to him."

Rodric hesitated, then lowered his sword. "I warned you never to come back. Yet fifteen years later, here you are."

"You know, brother, I wish you'd have run me through with your sword. It would've been far less painful than the torture of knowing that you believe that I betrayed you."

"So even after all these years, you still show no remorse for your crimes?"

"Oh, I'm full of remorse, brother. I regret many things about that night, but I didn't betray you. I was set up."

"Ah, yes. The *Great Conspiracy*."

"Brothers," said Ironfoot. "This is something that'll never be settled. Let Grimbard speak and then do with him as you wish."

"Very well," said Rodric, sheathing his sword. "But if you're playing one of your mind games with me, Grimbard, I will cut you down. And clean yourself up, man—you stink."

"I'd be pleased to do so."

"So tell me, *brother*. What's so important that it's worth your life?"

"I have a message for you. A message from Kaine."

22

THE BARE NAKED TRUTH

Cai quaked in the corner of the prisoner enclosure, scrunching his eyes tight as yet another Taleni paid the blood price for rejecting the love of Velak. Even with his hands clasped over his ears, he quailed as blood gurgled and innards piled into a bowl below the poor wretch's feet. Then, as with every other victim, the Mendari untethered their body from the side of the cart and tossed it onto the grotesque crescent of corpses that stretched around Vedana's Great Hall courtyard. He braced himself, knowing what would follow. Risking the briefest of glances, he fought back the bile in his throat as a Mendari tossed the overflowing bowl of human entrails into the bonfire set between the line of blood-smeared carts. Blood hissed, and intestines sizzled. Wafts of cooked offal and coppery traces of Taleni blood drifted into the enclosure. He gagged.

"It seems as if our time of tribulation has arrived, my brothers and sisters. Pray to her for the strength to endure what is to come."

Cai looked up, recognising the voice. "Y-you're Warden Elin from Belanore?"

"I am. And who are you?"

"Cai."

She scrutinised him for a moment and then allowed the faintest of smiles to cross her bruised face. "You were with that meddlesome noblewoman and her champion."

"I was, until those bastards caught up with us," he said, eyeing the three black-clad warriors standing in the courtyard.

"And you're the only survivor?"

Cai wiped away the tears forming in his eyes. "Yes."

The Warden nodded and waved her hand at the handful of Grey Cloaks imprisoned with them. "And we're what's left of our relief force. But we rejoice knowing that the goddess has honoured us with martyrdom for her glorious name." She stood, straightening her cloak, and brushed off the dried blood and grime from the image of the triskelion embroidered on her gambeson. "It's time."

"Come on, you filthy whore goddess loving scum. Your salvation awaits."

Cai shuddered as the gate to the enclosure creaked open, allowing a group of warriors to pile in and herd the prisoners out into the courtyard. He tried to stand, but his legs gave way. He yelped as a Mendari grabbed his hair and yanked him towards the gate.

"Not him," commanded a deep, booming voice from outside the enclosure.

Cai stared out at the Scions of the First, each standing beside a cart, wielding vicious curved ceremonial daggers. His eyes fell on the tallest of the three—a rugged, blond-haired warrior who would not have been out of place in the Taleni Elite Guard, if it were not for the armour of black he wore.

"You don't want the boy, Scion Alvar?"

"No—leave him."

"Yes, Scion."

"Wait. Why not him?"

"Don't start, Rask," said Alvar. "You know Kaine wants him alive."

"Exactly; alive. Doesn't mean I can't have some fun with him."

"Do you dare—"

"Leave him, Alvar," said a young woman leaning against the adjacent cart. "He won't kill him. He's not that stupid...I think."

"Piss off, Okita, or I'll wipe that grin off your face."

She flicked her blade out towards a terrified Grey Cloak being dragged towards her, splattering him with blood. "Any time you're ready."

"Enough! Have the boy, but don't expect me to back you when Kaine hears about it."

"I can deal with Kaine."

Alvar shrugged. "Very well. Bring out the boy."

Cai's heart pounded inside his chest as a warrior shoved him out of the gate towards Rask. The Mendari flipped his dagger into the air and sneered at him. He grabbed him by the arm and pushed him up against the blood-slick cart. There was no doubt in Cai's mind that Rask could snap his bones in an instant.

Rask traced the dagger around Cai's face and frowned. "Why would Kaine care what happened to a pathetic creature like you?"

"I-I don't know," said Cai, petrified to look the Scion in the eyes.

"Ah, it can speak...barely. What's your name, creature?"

"C-Cai."

"What kind of name is Cai? And look at me when I'm speaking to you, boy."

"It's the name Swordstorm gave me," he said, gritting his teeth. He forced himself to lock onto Rask's deep-set, wolf-like eyes, but found his attention pulled to the Scion's bald head covered in tattooed writing that looked familiar, yet he could not read.

"Just Cai? I thought you rode with the Elite Named?"

"What? I-I can't hear you."

Rask snapped his attention onto Alvar's stripped and tethered prisoner. "Can't you shut her up?"

Despite Alvar's threats, Warden Elin bellowed a hymn of praise to the goddess. "Stop that wailing, or I'll let Rask burn you alive."

She sang louder.

Alvar cursed, then looked over to Rask. "Do you want to cleanse her?"

"Tempting; but I'll keep my creature," said Rask, smirking at Cai. He forced his head around to watch as Alvar smacked Warden Elin across her head with the hilt of his dagger. As her head flopped forward, a pair of guards prised open her mouth and pulled out her tongue.

Rask's face lit up in gleeful expectation. "This is what we do to wardens of the goddess who insist on spewing out their heresies."

In one final act of defiance, Warden Elin struggled to sound out the melody of the hymn, but as Alvar severed her tongue, her hymn of praise descended into a pitiful groan of gurgling agony.

"Will you renounce the whore goddess and turn to Lord Velak?"

She spat blood into Alvar's face as her answer.

Wiping his face with his hand, he said, "Then be cleansed from this land, Enorian." The blade slid across her exposed stomach.

Cai shut his eyes in revulsion.

"Open your eyes, boy," said Rask. "Because when Kaine's finished with you, I'll make you suffer so much more that you'll beg me to end your miserable life." He scratched his beard with his blade. "You're a strange creature. You ride with the Elite Named of the Taleni, but you cower at the sight of blood being shed. Hmm...I wonder?" He leaned in close to Cai and smirked. His breath smelled rancid, as if he was rotting from the inside. He gripped hold of Cai's right hand and turned it over. "No branding.... You're a noble?"

"I-I don't know."

"You don't know? Are you witless?"

"N-no...I-I just can't remember."

"Let's see if you're tattooed." With a flick of his wrist, Rask sliced through Cai's bloodied and torn tunic. "Take it off."

"N-no, I can't."

"Take it off or by the whore goddess, I'll flay you alive."

"Don't even think about it," warned Alvar.

Rask scowled at his comrade. "A little cut won't kill him." He swept his eyes back on Cai and flared his nostrils. "Take, it, off."

Trembling, he pulled the severed tunic off his shoulders and dropped it to the floor.

"Now turn around."

Cai hesitated.

"I said turn around." Rask cuffed him across his mouth.

He winced as droplets of blood slithered down his chin.

"The next one'll break your jaw. Now do as I say."

Cai shuffled around and closed his eyes in shame as the secret that he had kept hidden from all but his father was now revealed to the Scion.

"By the whore goddess."

"What's wrong?" asked Alvar.

"Come and see for yourself."

Cai heard Alvar and Okita rush across to join their comrade. They gasped as they discovered what had excited Rask.

"Have you ever seen tattoos like this before?" asked Okita.

"No...but they're remarkable." Rask ran his finger over the faded text that lay on the small of Cai's back and gasped. "How in the whore goddess' name have you got ancient Mendari on your back, boy?"

"I-I don't know."

Alvar and Okita's breath wafted over Cai's skin as they huddled in close to read the writing.

"It's incredible."

Mustering enough courage, Cai asked, "W-what does it say?"

"I'll not speak the language of the First to a piece of Enorian scum like you," hissed Rask.

The Scion's ice-cold touch projected a pulse of revulsion throughout Cai's body, tracing the same pattern that the Reaper had done. Finally, reaching the base of Cai's neck, Rask stopped. "There's something under all this filth," he said, spitting onto Cai's skin and rubbing the dirt away. "What's that?"

"A hill or a mound?" suggested Alvar.

"Well, whatever it is, the rest of the tattoos make a path towards it."

"It's a map," said Okita.

"Yes." Rask ran the tip of his blade across Cai's shoulders. "And it'll look perfect as the next page in my book of skins."

"Don't be a fool," said Alvar. "Don't you think that's why the boy's important to Kaine?"

"What in the name of Velak are you doing with that boy?"

Cai froze, recognising Kaine's voice.

"I-I told him to leave him, but he wouldn't listen to reason."

"Is that so? Come here, Rask."

As Rask withdrew his grip, Cai grabbed his torn tunic and turned to find Kaine and one of the other Scions standing a few feet away from them. Kaine's companion reminded him of the time he met Manon of the Ovantae. This woman held herself with the same air of authority, even though he could see little of her features, as her long brunette hair, streaked with grey, swept across her face.

Rask stood in front of Kaine.

"I gave instructions for the boy to be kept alive."

"I wasn't going to—"

Like lightning, the woman struck him across his face. Rask wavered but remained standing. His hands edged towards his pair of short swords strapped to his back.

"Move any closer to those blades and I'll slice your head off."

Cai frowned. The woman's voice seemed more melodic than the harsher southern accents of her fellow Scions.

Rask dropped his arms to his side. "Now why would I be foolish enough to fight Kaine's sister and champion?"

A smile appeared from under her fringe. "One day, Rask, we'll find out how good you really are."

"That's enough, Aderyn," said Kaine. "You've made your point."

She stepped back to allow Kaine to move close to Rask.

"You know how much I love you, brother, but cross me again and I'll feed your guts to your dogs while you still breathe. Is that clear?"

"Yes, brother."

"Good." He patted Rask on the shoulder and walked towards Cai. "Don't be afraid, Cai. If you show me the markings, I'll allow you to go to see someone who's very keen to know you're alive."

Cai widened his eyes. "Amira? I thought your beast killed her."

"Now why would I want to hurt a lovely young lady like that?"

"And what about Lord Taleni? Is he still alive?"

The Scions chuckled.

"Where is he?"

"I assume his body lies in there somewhere," said Kaine, sweeping his hand across the pile of corpses. "But his head sits on a spike above the Southern Gatehouse, alongside your father.

Cai wanted to scream, but the thought of seeing Amira kept him silent.

"Now turn around."

He did as he was told.

"So that's why he wanted him alive."

"Do you recognise any of the landmarks?" asked Okita.

"No." Kaine tore something off his shoulder. Cai twisted to see what it was, but the Mendari leader eased him back. "Stay still." A short single note rang from the object. "I'll need to commune with Lord Velak. Let's hope he's in a sharing mood."

"And the boy?" asked Alvar.

"Give him some food and clean him up. Then take him to Lady Amira's apartment. I'll come for him once I know more about his tattoos." At that, Kaine and Aderyn set off towards the Southern Gatehouse.

Cai glanced guiltily over to the drooped corpses of Warden Elin and the other Grey Cloaks. Once again, he had been spared from a horrendous death. Why? He stared up at the line of heads arrayed on the Southern Gatehouse and swallowed hard. Yet knowing that Amira lived cast a shard of light into the darkness wrapped around his mind.

"Let's go," said Alvar.

A hand gripped his shoulder. He did not need to turn to know it was Rask.

"This isn't over, boy. Once Velak's finished with you, there'll be no-one to protect you."

Alvar ripped his hand off him. "Will you never learn?"

Rask laughed and turned away, whistling.

If ever there was a man who represented pure evil, it's him.

23

BANAN THE GIANT

Luis stretched his arms above his head and yawned. "Well, at least we know he's not an imposter. Only Grimbard could take this long to preen himself." He scooped the last spoonful of salted porridge into his mouth and wondered if he should have a third portion. He reached over to a large pot on his desk, ready to refill his bowl when he caught Rodric staring at him. "What?"

"I forgot how much you love your food."

"Well," he said between swallows, "A man could die of hunger waiting for Grimbard."

"I've had enough of this," said Rodric. He stomped over to Luis' private quarters and hammered on the door. "For the love of the goddess, hurry up or I'll leave you in a cell to rot your miserable life away."

"If he takes any more time, I'll throw him in myself...if I can stay awake."

Rodric nodded towards the corridor of cells. "Not that you've got a lot of room to spare. You've had a busy night, Luis."

"Our friend's drunken performance struck a chord with the locals. He never considers the consequences of his actions on others —just as long as it gets him what he wants."

"Even after so many years, his treachery continues to leave its mark." Rodric drew up a seat opposite him. "There's something I need to say to you."

"You know I wouldn't have left unless—"

"No, it's not about that. It's about Seren."

Luis pushed his bowl to one side and placed his elbows on the table. "What about her?"

"Did you wonder why I sent Seren away from Caerniras?"

"I assumed you wanted to give her some responsibility."

"Yes...but there's more to it than that."

"Like what?"

"She never forgave me for sparing Grimbard's life and demanded to leave the capital and go south to kill him. We argued and harsh words were said. In the end, we came to a compromise—she could represent me in Keld, but I forbade her to set a foot further south."

"And you believed that she'd honour that?"

"She's too much like her mother," said Rodric, shaking his head. "But if I refused, I might have lost her forever."

"Seren certainly shares Isabelle's stubbornness, but she's also a lot like you, my friend."

Rodric laughed. "She's got a temper, for sure."

"I meant she hasn't come to terms with Isabelle's death."

"Can you blame her?"

"No."

"What I didn't foresee was her anger and grief fuelling her appetite for self-destruction. I'm sure she came to Belanore to find leads on Grimbard, but, well, you know the rest."

"Unfortunately, I do."

Setting his eyes on him, Rodric leant forward and clasped hold of Luis' arms. "If it wasn't for you, she'd have been found dead in some stinking alleyway months ago. I can't thank you enough, my friend."

"You know I wouldn't let anything happen to her—despite what took place between us."

"I know, but it still needs to be said." Rodric released his grip and sat back in his chair. "There's also something else I'd—"

The door to Luis' quarters flew open. Tarek stood in the doorway in nothing but a pair of braccae with his ochre-coloured tattooed skin on display. "Goddess, Luis. None of your tunics fit me. Have you been hoarding them from your twenties?"

"No," said Luis, glowering. "I bought them just over a month ago."

"Velak's balls. I *have* been drinking too much Red," he said, rubbing his stomach. He gathered the knotted cords of jet-black hair into a tight ponytail and fastened them with a thin strip of cloth.

"Oh, stop whining," said Luis, eyeing the streaks of grey running through Tarek's hair. "You're just getting old—we all are."

"You looked old the day we first met, my friend."

Rodric slammed his hands onto the table. "Enough of this. You might be able to pretend that things were as they once were, but I can't." He scraped the chair back and strode towards the doorway. "The sooner we get this over with, the better." He barged past Tarek and disappeared into the room.

Luis followed his sword brothers into his quarters and closed the door behind him. He pulled up a seat next to the others, now sitting beside the glowing embers of the previous night's fire.

Rodric clutched his hands on his knees and glared at Tarek. "Well? What does that bastard want to say to me?"

"Here," said Luis, offering Rodric a glass of wine.

"I don't need that."

"Oh, I think you do."

Rodric sighed and accepted the drink. "You never let up, do you?"

"No, never." He poured another glass. "I'm a fool for a lost cause."

"Speaking of lost causes, is that one for me?" asked Tarek.

"Not a chance—you're way past redemption."

"You're no fun at all." Ever the bard, Tarek got up and paced in front of the fireplace. "Before I relay my message, I wanted to ask you both about Banan's ambush."

"I didn't come here to reminisce about the past. Say what you need to say."

"Please, hear me out, Rodric. After that, do what you want with me."

Rodric let out a long sigh. "Fine. Get on with your story."

"There must've been at least forty warriors with him, pouring out from the trees. How we missed them, I'll never know." He stopped in front of the smouldering fire, resting his hands on the stone mantle, and peered into the glowing charcoal. "I saw you fall, Luis, at the hands of that giant—his war hammer pulverising your lower leg. I tried to get to you, but there were too many."

Luis rubbed his iron limb and grimaced. "Sometimes in the night, I wake up screaming with that bone-crunching crack tormenting my ears. As clear and as painful as the day it happened."

"I watched him stride over to you as you heaved your broken body across the blood-smeared ground to find your axe," said Rodric, with eyes full of sadness. "He stepped over you, smirked, and kicked the axe deep into the undergrowth. And then the bastard hefted his hammer over his head to smash your face into a pulp. I screamed every curse I knew to turn his attention onto me, but that's when I got hit on the back of the head."

"Yes, we were well and truly up to our necks in shit," said Tarek. "But then something happened that I've never really thought about until a month ago."

"What happened a month ago?" asked Luis.

"I'll get to that in a minute. What I want to know from you both is, did you see anything strange during the fight? Something that in the heat of battle you put down to the effect of the Red Mist or your senses playing tricks on you?"

"I don't know what you think was there, but the last thing I remember before passing out was Banan leering down at me." Luis turned to Rodric. "What about you?"

Rodric stayed silent. He stared into the fire until Luis called his name.

He rubbed his forehead and shrugged. "N-no...I saw nothing."

"But in all that time, you've never described how you defeated Banan," said Tarek. "You said it yourself—you were struck on your head."

"I don't need to explain myself to you," said Rodric, glowering.

"Then tell me, brother," asked Luis.

"I can't remember."

Tarek shook his head. "So that's it? You can't remember one of the most important moments of your life? The day you took Banan's head and claimed Shieldbane?"

"For the third time, I can't remember," said Rodric, through gritted teeth. "Unlike some people, I don't lie."

Tarek ignored the slur. "Well, someone else remembered."

Rodric narrowed his eyes. "Who?"

"Kaine."

"He's lying."

"No, he's not, because he saw what I'd always thought was a figment of my imagination."

"What?" asked Luis.

"The Wraith Warrior."

Rodric threw his hands into the air and turned to Luis. "This is ridiculous. You don't actually believe any of this?"

Luis frowned. "Describe it to me?"

"What I remember is hazy, but you must remember I was stuck under a pile of Mendari, suffocating."

"Clearly a reliable account," said Rodric, raising his eyes to the roof.

"As I drifted towards the Veil, I glimpsed something strange approaching through the tree line—shimmering ripples in the air that moved between Banan and his warriors. The last thing I remember was my attackers' screams of terror, as each of them was torn away from above me by a warrior clothed completely in black. When I regained consciousness, I saw you kneeling over Banan's body, with the Mendari's war hammer in one hand and his head in the other."

Rodric snorted. "Merely your mind playing tricks on you due to a lack of air."

"And so I thought until a month ago."

"What happened?" asked Luis.

"That was when the Mendari razed Nabaya to the ground."

"You were there? Why?"

"That's a long story, Luis; all you need to know is that Kaine found me."

"So what's this got to do with his message?"

"He wants you to know that he remembers every detail of how his father died." He stepped closer to Rodric. "And he knows what happened at Treharne."

Rodric lurched up and glared into Tarek's face, grabbing him by the shoulders. "What did you tell him?"

"Nothing. We swore an oath never to tell a soul."

"Then how would he know of that day?"

Luis scratched his nose in thought. "Are you sure he knows? He could be bluffing?"

"No," said Tarek, glancing at Rodric. "He knew about *everything*."

Rodric flopped into the chair, his breathing hard and fast. "What does he want?"

"He's got an offer for you."

"What kind of offer?"

"He knows your army's nowhere near as strong as the one that invaded Mendaria. And with the thousands at his command, he offers you the chance to negotiate Northern Tarania's surrender and avoid the needless massacre of your people...if they turn to Velak."

"What do I have to do?"

"Meet him at the Stones of Valtara when the Great Conjoining of Golanos and the Twins take place."

"And I assume that refusal will cause a full-scale war and my secrets shared with my enemies within Northern Tarania?"

Tarek nodded.

"Of course, this could just be another one of your mind games?"

"I'm not lying."

"I find that hard to believe—just like the lies you spun the day she died."

"Look into my eyes, Rodric, and tell me if you can honestly believe that I'd do anything to hurt Isabelle and the children."

"Oh, yes, the Great Conspiracy. Only you could make up such absurd notions of Mendari spies drugging you and setting you up to take the blame. All lies—just like the ones you spread about me in the tavern. Even to my son."

"The propaganda about Velak?"

"So you knew, Luis?"

"Yes, but I thought it was just him raving, fuelled by too many Red Renegades."

Tarek squared up to Rodric, eyes burning bright with anger. "At least I admit that my past is littered with mistakes, but I know, with all of my heart, that I never betrayed you on that fateful night. I begged you to believe me as you had me dragged out of the brothel, beaten and banished from Northern Tarania."

"Enough of this. She was murdered because of your selfish, lustful desires. I'll not listen to another deceitful word uttered from your mouth."

"Heed my words, Shieldbane. If you ignore Kaine's demands, he'll wipe Northern Tarania off the map."

"We beat them once, we'll beat them again."

"No, you won't." He sat down and rubbed his face with his hands. "Like I said, I'd forgotten about the Wraith Warrior...until the night Nabaya burned. I saw the same black armour again—on Kaine and the Scions of the First."

Rodric shook his head. "A warband of wraiths? Only you could conjure up such fantasies."

"It's the truth."

Jabbing his finger into Tarek's chest, Rodric said, "Since when has the truth ever left your lips?" He spun around and marched to the door. "Make sure he stays locked up."

As Rodric disappeared from view, Tarek looked up to Luis, tears streaming down his eyes. "They'll be massacred...and he'll still stand before Kaine at the Stones."

"How're you so sure?"

"I've witnessed the power of Kaine and his Bwgan. They murdered my family."

24

A PAIR OF SWANS

Seren slid under the steaming hot water inside her wooden bathtub and held her breath. Every bruise and cut from her fight stung intensely as the natural antiseptic solution of the bathwater took effect. Seconds turned to minutes as she refused to be controlled by her fragile anatomy and gripped the sides of the tub in defiance. Then, as her head pounded and every cell in her body demanded oxygen, she burst up through the surface, sending a tidal wave of soapy water over the edge of the bath, submerging the tiled floor of her chamber. She flung her head back and inhaled a deep intake of air, coughing as it burned her chest. Pressing her back against the side of the tub, she giggled, knowing that the longer she stayed under, the closer she got to the Veil and the more alive she became.

Her thoughts returned to the surreal events that took place at the jail. Out of all the questions that churned within her mind, one perplexed her the most: what had the bard known about Luis and his sword brothers to make the sheriff react like he did? A knock at the door interrupted her thoughts.

"Princess Seren?"

"Yes, Carys?"

"I'm sorry to disturb you, your highness, but Lady Zirani is here and wishes to see you. Should I tell her you're busy?"

Shit! She must be furious with me. "No. Show her in, Carys. Then leave us."

"As you wish, your highness."

Seren climbed out of the bath, dried her long, blonde hair roughly and wrapped her robe around her body. She took a deep breath, opened the bath chamber door and walked into the room. "Lady Yanna, I'm so sorry—" She froze. Her visitor stood facing away from her, looking out of the bedchamber window. The bright early afternoon light of the Twins pierced the sheer fabric of her white cotton dress, highlighting every curve of her body.

On hearing the door open, Yanna turned to face Seren. Her movements were slow and graceful, and she paused in full profile, smiling warmly at the princess. The effect was immediate on Seren. She consumed the exquisite view, as the light accentuated the profile of Yanna's breasts, rising and falling in an intoxicating rhythm that fell in sync with the beating of her own heart.

"Is something wrong, your highness? You look flustered."

"Oh...umm...I think I spent too long soaking in the bath. My mind's still a bit fuzzy from all the heat."

"I can come back later if you prefer?"

"No. Please, stay. I've got something to discuss with you."

"And I with you, your highness."

Velak's balls. She hates me.

Trying her best to remain calm, Seren led Yanna to a raised platform in one corner of her room that served as a seating area. Scattered across the dark, hardwood couch were a rich assortment of comfortable, feather-filled pillows and soft cotton sheets. Ignoring the option of comfort, Yanna lowered her delicate frame onto the hard wooden surface and sat upright. Seren hesitated, then sat beside her.

"What did you want to discuss with me, your highness?"

"I've no doubt that you're furious with my conduct with your husband," she said, struggling to make eye contact with Yanna. "I wouldn't blame you if you never wanted to speak to me again, but..."

"But you want to explain why it happened? Is that it?"

"Y-yes. If you'd permit me to do so?"

"There's nothing to explain," said Yanna. "I know my husband. He looks at your lifestyle and judges you for it. If he had any shred of empathy, he'd realise that it's your way of dealing with a lifetime of anger and grief." She picked up a cushion and cradled it in her lap. "I'm sure you're aware that I also lost my mother in tragic circumstances." She glanced up at Seren. "So truly I understand your pain, how it tears at your soul and how you're never, ever whole again."

"I-I didn't realise you felt that way. You always seem so serene and in control."

Yanna grimaced. "Not at all. I'm like a swan—graceful above the water, but paddling frantically beneath."

"I'd never have guessed."

"It's the truth. I hide my true emotions from the rest of the world, whereas you use yours as a well-crafted weapon, there for everyone to see and fear."

Seren shrugged. "A great warrior embraces their pain and uses it to make them stronger."

"And how's that working out for you?" Yanna shifted closer to Seren. She lifted her hand to her face, trailing her fingers gently over the sore wound visible across the bridge of her nose. "Look at you. You're slowly killing yourself, both physically and emotionally."

"I'm not a wallflower, Lady Zirani," said Seren, pulling away from Yanna's touch.

Undeterred, Yanna continued. "What about all the emotions you suppress? When was the last time you had joy in your life? Allowed someone past your defences? Loved someone?"

"I don't need any of those things." Seren stood abruptly. "I've plenty of friends and enjoy my life."

"You mean the ones in the taverns?" asked Yanna, rising to confront her. "How many of those just hang around to take advantage of you? Can you remember which ones you slept with the morning after? Is that your definition of enjoying life?"

"Stop it. I'm warning you, Lady Zirani. You're overstepping the mark."

"Good. Then maybe you'll understand what everyone else sees

when they look at you: the princess who tortures herself because she couldn't save her mother."

"How dare you!" She slapped Yanna hard across the face.

Yanna rubbed the reddening patch of skin. "I know the story. How you fought like a wild animal to protect your dear mother and baby brother, how you saved your father's life and how your mother died in your father's arms, as your brother fought for his tiny life."

Seren flopped to the floor, sobbing. "I couldn't save her. I was too weak to protect my mother. It should've been me, not her."

"How can you say that? You saved your father's life. Any other five-year-old would've clung to their dying mother, shaking in terror. *You* turned, faced evil head-on and survived."

"I-it doesn't feel like that to me," said Seren, drawing her knees up tight to her chest. "The guilt inside me rages constantly, and the only way I know how to quell it is to drink myself numb." She raised her head and looked Yanna directly in the eyes. "How do you cope with your loss?"

"I won't lie to you—I struggle daily. In the still of the night, when I'm alone with my own thoughts, I agonise over the death of my mother. They say it was an accident caused by too much wine and a misplaced step on the bedchamber stairs. I don't accept that." She knelt in front of Seren and smiled. "But every morning, before I leave my chamber, I put all of that anger, grief and suspicion inside a box and lock it away, so I can cope with what the day has in store."

Seren frowned. "A real box?"

"Oh, yes. A real box, with a real key," said Yanna. She reached out and took Seren's hands in hers. "Stop drinking, Seren, before it's too late to stop."

"I know...it's what everyone tells me, but I feel so alone and lack the strength to change." She ran her fingers over the bruise on Yanna's cheek. "You're the only one who seems to understand what I'm going through and I repay you by striking your delicate face. I lost control. I'm sorry."

Yanna closed her eyes and brushed her lips across Seren's fingertips. She looked up, focusing her magical eyes on hers. "There're other ways to lose control that are far more enjoyable."

Seren's heart raced. Was the moment she had fantasised about in the privacy of her dreams about to become a reality? Her hands trembled. "L-like what?"

"Like this." Yanna leant forward and kissed her tenderly on the lips.

Seren panicked, pulling back. "B-but you're my uncle's wife."

"So? I saw how you looked at me earlier." She took Seren's hand and drew it up against her breast. "Tell me you don't want me and I'll leave." She got ready to stand, but Seren gripped her hand.

"Please don't go...but—"

She pressed a finger to Seren's lips. "Shhh. Don't say another word." Slipping her arms around her neck, she parted her lips and kissed her.

This time, Seren held her nerve, matching Yanna's passion until, with the taste of honey flavoured beeswax and oil lip balm intoxicating her senses, she submitted to the desires of her heart. She moaned and flicked her tongue across Yanna's full, moist lips, eager to taste more of her.

Yanna eased away and smiled. Her widened pupils held Seren with a power that drew her in deeper, bewitching her. Standing, she pulled her to her feet with surprising ease for one so delicate. Seren had little time to catch her breath as Yanna gripped her shoulders firmly and turned her.

"Oh, Yanna." She tried to turn, but the red-headed beauty forced her back around. The loss of control excited her. She bit her lip and curved her back as Yanna trailed her teeth along her neck and up to her earlobe, tearing at it playfully. Then she stopped, breathing softly into her ear.

"Take off your robe."

Barely controlling her trembling hands, Seren did as she was told and shivered as the robe slid off her shoulders and fell in a pile around her feet.

"Put your trust in me and I'll give you a reason to live. You never have to feel alone again."

"Promise?"

"Like a pair of swans—once joined, never parted."

Yanna's dress dropped to the floor. She pressed her body tight into Seren's and caressed the contours of her sinewy, battle-hardened body until, with a cry of delight, she discovered her breasts for the first time. "Are you ready to submit to me, your highness?"

"I was ready the moment I first laid eyes on you."

"Good," said Yanna, stepping past her, allowing her nails to rake against Seren's flushed skin. She made her way to the bed at the far side of the room and turned to face her. "Lie down."

With a warm, moist sensation throbbing between her thighs, Seren crossed the floor, climbed onto the bed and rolled onto her back.

Yanna crawled onto the bottom of the bed, her red, tousled hair tickling Seren's skin as she moved up. She stared into her eyes, pushing her knees in between her thighs to spread her legs. "Do you trust me?"

Seren, her voice barely a whisper, replied, "Yes."

"Then close your eyes...you're mine now."

Then, as Yanna slid down between her legs, Seren gripped the sheets and willingly gave herself over to Yanna.

Later that afternoon, as Yanna kissed her farewell and slipped out of her chamber, Seren beamed with pleasure. She felt as though her heart could burst open with a feeling that she had long forgotten was possible. Then the thought that she had pushed deep down in the depths of her mind resurfaced. *If he ever found out about this, he'd kill me.*

25

THE HOPE OF AN UNNAMED CLANSGUARD

Cai raised his hand to Amira's apartment door but hesitated.

"I don't know what you're worried about. All she's done since arriving here is worry about you."

Cai glanced at the Scion leaning against the passageway wall, expecting to find a look of scorn on his face. But as the Mendari looked up and brushed a dark, curly lock away from his eyes, he smiled.

"Surely she's in mourning for her father?" he asked, frowning.

"I'm sure she would be—if she knew."

He slumped into the door, as the sudden weight of responsibility crushed his hopes of a happier reunion. *Goddess, give me the right words to say.* He took a deep breath and knocked on the door.

"There's no need to wait. She's expecting you. Good luck."

I'll need more than luck. He opened the door and walked inside, recognising a familiar fragrance that lightened his heaviness. *Amira.*

As he expected, the layout of Amira's apartment was like that of the one he had lived in with his father. As Champion to the Clan, Swordstorm had risen to the highest position a clansguard could ascend to without being accepted into the Nobility Caste. And with the position came considerable wealth and an apartment within the Great Hall. That was where the similarities ended; where their apartment had been warm, welcoming but understated, Amira's furnishings were opulent, a statement of her position—and that was only her reception.

"Is that you, Cai?"

"Y-yes, my lady."

"Come in...and Cai?"

"Yes, my lady."

"Considering all we've been through, I think we can dispense with the formalities of caste status. Call me Amira."

"Yes, my—I mean, Amira."

Hearing her giggle at his clumsiness left a bittersweet taste in his mouth. Apprehensively, he stepped into the main living area of the apartment and gasped as his eyes consumed the explosion of colour throughout the room. It was as though a rainbow had fallen from the sky and cascaded its colours on every item of soft furnishing contained within. Upon every inch of the wall hung the most elaborate tapestries he had ever seen. Many of the scenes he recognised from the famous stories of the North as told by the bards.

He stepped onto a vibrant rug covering the hardwood floor but stopped to look over his shoulder, grimacing at the muddy footprints his boots had left behind. He panicked, rubbing each boot against the back of his braccae.

"It's a bit late for that."

He glanced up and gawped at Amira entering the room from her bedchamber, floating across the floor in a fur-trimmed purple dress that rippled lightly in her wake. Her curly locks trailed down her neck in a simple yet elegant ponytail. Flashing him a smile, she walked to a writing desk positioned beside a large shuttered window that overlooked the courtyard and unlocked a drawer with a key she kept around her neck. She opened it, placed a small leather-bound book inside and locked it.

"Must be precious to lock it away like that?"

"You have no idea." She turned to face him, smiling, yet Cai's serious expression flattened the corners of her mouth. "I-I thought you'd be pleased to see me?"

"I'm so sorry, Amira, but I've news concerning your father." He lowered his eyes and shuffled his feet. "I regret to inform you, Lord Taleni is dead."

Amira blinked and reached out for the chair next to her desk to steady her faltering stance. She closed her eyes, and with a trembling voice, asked, "H-how do you know?"

"Kaine told me."

"B-but surely he'd want to keep him alive to bargain with King Rodric?"

"That's what I thought; but he's dead."

"W-where is he?"

Cai gulped as his mouth dried. "I'd rather not tell you."

"Tell me, damn it. I've a right to know."

With tears welling up in his eyes, he said, "His head's displayed above the Southern Gatehouse next to Father's."

"A-and his body?"

Cai walked to the window, opened the shutters and looked down into the courtyard. The light of the Twins was fading but he could still see the faces contained within the crescent of the dead. "Down there, among the rest of our people." Behind him, Amira let out a whimper.

"Cai?"

He spun around to her.

She trembled as the warmth drained from her face. "Help me. I-I feel—"

He sprang forward as Amira's legs gave way, catching her in his arms. His whole body ached from the punishment it had received from the Mendari, but he ignored it. If he could take her pain and add it to his, he would have done so without a second thought. Gently, he carried her across to a couch in the middle of the room, laid her down and knelt beside her. "I'm here for you," he said, taking hold of her hand.

She stirred and opened her eyes, full of fear, sadness and uncertainty. "To think I was so angry with my father for giving me the knife. Yet now I know it was my only way of ending this nightmare. I should've used it."

"Don't lose hope, Amira. I don't think Kaine would've allowed you to stay in your apartment if he wanted to do you harm."

"But why?"

"I don't know, but I might be able to find out."

"How?"

"Kaine needs me and I think I know why." He turned away from her and lifted his tunic to expose his tattooed back.

Amira gasped. "By the goddess, Cai. Who did this to you?"

"I-I can't remember. I just know Kaine's—" He stiffened and held his breath as Amira's soft caress traced a familiar pattern across his reddish-brown skin. The sensation was a total opposite to Rask's icy-cold, skin-crawling touch or the constricting embrace of the Reaper; each movement sent a pulse of pure delight through his body.

"Who are you, Cai the Unnamed?" she asked, sitting up beside him.

He turned, his face almost touching hers. "Right now, I'm the luckiest clansguard in Northern Tarania." He kissed her on the lips.

She responded, but as each kiss increased in intensity, she pulled away.

"What have I done wrong?"

"I-it's not you, it's me. "

Cai closed his eyes and silently cursed. "No, it's not. You've just found out about Lord Taleni and I take advantage of your grief. I'm a disgrace."

She shook her head. "No, you're not. If anyone's a disgrace, it's me." She flicked her eyes towards the door, then brought them back on Cai. "I-I can't do this anymore."

"You can, if you let me help you."

"You don't understand, Cai."

"Then make me understand."

She opened her mouth to speak, but the door to her apartment opened. Kaine strode into the living area, accompanied by Aderyn and Okita.

He glowered at Amira. "Get her ready."

As the pair of Scions approached Amira, Cai jumped up to shield her, but Aderyn shoved him down onto the couch. "Stay down, lover boy, or you'll regret it." They hauled her up and escorted her out of the room.

"Where are you taking her?"

"Don't worry, Cai," said Kaine. "You'll be reunited, soon enough. Now come with me. We've much to discuss."

26

HONOUR HER MEMORY

Within his private chamber, Rodric slouched in his chair, exhausted. Between his children's behaviour, the Council of War, and confronting Grimbard, he had not slept for the best part of two days. Nevertheless, with war looming, he insisted that they should share a meal as a family to honour Isabelle's memory. Seren and Tomos sat either side of him, facing each other, their body language clearly showing that they would prefer to be anywhere than sharing a late evening meal with him. *The things I do for you, my love. One day, maybe sooner than you think, we'll all be together again, up in the Void. Then you can deal with their disobedience and tantrums.* He laughed.

"Are you even listening to me, Father?"

"Oh, I'm sorry, Seren. What did you say?"

She groaned. "Sometimes I wonder if you do that on purpose."

"I've no idea what you mean," he said, gulping down the contents of his cup, leaving white froth all over his moustache.

"Are you drinking ale?" asked Tomos. "I didn't think you liked the taste."

"Well, since the two of you are so fond of Red Renegade, I thought I'd try it myself."

"I only tried one cup, and that was smashed out of my hands during the brawl." He glanced sideways at Seren, a sly grin appearing on his face. "I hear Seren is the expert with Keld's finest—and any other vice there is in Belanore."

"Bollocks. At least I can throw a punch without fainting."

Rodric shot Seren a disapproving glare. "Where did you learn language like that?"

Tomos grinned. "From the tavern, obviously."

"Wrong answer, little brother. You can blame Ironfoot for that delightful new addition to my vocabulary."

Rodric shook his head. "I love that man, but he's got a mouth like a sewer."

"And that sewer was overflowing last night."

He frowned. "Why was that?"

"That despicable bard got under his skin."

Rodric narrowed his eyes at her. "I don't want you going anywhere near that man—he's poison."

"So Luis told you? Don't worry. I've no intention of stepping near him or the bloody jail again. Which brings me back to my question you so skilfully avoided."

"Which was?"

"Goddess!" She gripped the table in frustration. "Now that I've learned my lesson and Luis has lectured me, will you let me fight?"

"No."

"But why not? You need me."

"Another relaxing meal for the Niras family," said Tomos, throwing his chicken thigh onto his plate.

"You can shut your smug, know-it-all mouth. Where will you be when the fighting starts? Hiding in your room, you spineless little shit?"

Tomos narrowed his eyes at his sister and then nodded. "I agree with you, Father. After the fight with Uncle Kurzon, I don't think Seren knows who the enemy is any more. She's out of control."

She shoved her seat back, stood up and leered across the table at her brother. "At least I can finish a fight, not crumple onto the floor like some defenceless animal, cowering in fear."

Rodric slammed the table with his cup, spilling the ruby contents over the various dishes laid out on the table. "Behave yourselves. You're not little children any more. Seren, sit down."

"But he—"

"Sit down, now." He fixed her with a stare that could chill the fiercest of opponents to the bone. She glared back at him, but then relented, grabbing hold of her chair and scraping it across the wooden floor. She slumped onto it and folded her arms in disgust.

Tomos opened his mouth to make a comment but realised the stare was now focused on him. He sat up, retrieved his discarded chicken and nibbled nervously on the meat.

"Your mother would be appalled if she could see you like this. You dishonour her memory."

"Father, you say that, but every time we ask about her you shut us out," said Tomos. "How can we dishonour her when we know so little about her?"

He stared at them, so different yet consumed by the same hunger to know more about the one thing that could bring peace between them: Isabelle. His thoughts turned to the impending battle and the possibility that he might not return. Maybe it was time to share? As he had told them, they were no longer children. "What do you want to know?"

Both siblings sat up, attentive, unused to their father being so open with them.

"All we know is what the rest of the kingdom knows. Tell us about the Isabelle Niras that only you knew. What were her mannerisms? Am I like her?" asked Seren.

"Did she enjoy reading?" asked Tomos.

"Yes, she loved reading. She read every night to you," he said, looking at Seren. "She would try to introduce new stories, but you would beg her for the same two every night—"

"Oh, yes, I remember: the Bwgan and...umm...the story of Enora and Gaius Galerius?"

Rodric smiled and nodded.

"Who would've thought you'd be interested in a love story?" said Tomos.

"Seren was more interested in the fighting and the magic than the romance, Tomos."

"Why am I not surprised?"

Seren glared at Tomos, then stifled a giggle. "What else can you tell us?"

"She was a wonderfully sensitive and generous person. And astute —it was as if she could read your mind," he said, beaming, remembering a private memory. "Her stubbornness was legendary. When she wanted to win an argument, it didn't matter who you were, she'd win." He smiled, watching the pair stare at each other and laugh. *Oh, yes—you've got that trait in abundance.* "She doted on both of you and was determined to give you a normal childhood, to let you experience things first hand. In fact, that's why we took you everywhere with us. I remember, one time, visiting Glanmorden. Once all the formal engagements were over, we took you into the Forest of Borgen." He smiled at Seren. "You wouldn't stop asking questions, continually pulling at your poor mother's hand to look at some strange fungus or an insect you'd never seen before. It was magical watching you together."

Seren's eyes glistened. "Thank you for sharing that with me."

"What about me?"

Rodric chuckled. "You were only a baby, but I can recall you trying to eat anything you could get your hands on. Dead or alive, it didn't matter. We had to watch you like a hawk."

"Ugh! Really? That doesn't sound like something I'd do."

"Well, you did." Rodric smiled sympathetically at his son. "It's hard to believe you've changed so much."

Frustrated, Tomos scratched an itch at the back of his neck. "I guess my illness had something to do with that."

"I don't know, Tomos. Maybe you could ask—?"

"By the goddess! He was talking about Mother," said Seren, shifting to face Rodric. "She was the champion."

"Champion?"

"It's just something that Ironfoot said to me this morning. He suggested I should ask you about the champion of the lower castes; but it's obvious—it was Mother."

Rodric nodded. "We both detested the caste system; but she wanted to do more, and persuaded me to call a Council of the Clans to discuss reforming it. Of course, her stance was highly controversial with the Communion. She even lost favour with her own family. Kurzon almost disowned her."

"That's terrible," said Seren.

Rodric stayed silent and drifted off into thoughts of those final dark days of his beloved's life.

"It sounds like you were both heavily involved in our upbringing," said Tomos. "I thought it was traditional to have a servant or a wet-nurse to do all of that?"

Rodric brought his attention back to the room. "Your mother was adamant that if we were to bring life into this world, then we'd take responsibility for it. Of course, you had servants, but your mother did as much as she could for you until—well, you know."

Tomos played with the food on his plate and muttered something under his breath.

"What did you say?" asked Rodric.

Staring down at his plate, he asked, "Why would someone want to kill her?"

Reaching for the ring hanging around his neck, Rodric said, "I ask myself that question every day."

Seren snorted. "Well, whatever the reason, if it wasn't for that traitor, Tarek Grimbard, she'd still be alive."

Rodric shifted uneasily in his seat. He still had to decide what to do with Grimbard. Goddess forbid that Seren discover the real identity of the bard in the jail. "Now listen to me, both of you. Clearly, you have issues with each other, but if I don't make it back tomorrow, you'll need each other more than ever. When a ruler dies, a kingdom can become a treacherous place for their children."

"That's why I want to be there to protect you, Father. It'll kill me to sit here and wait, not knowing if you'll return."

"But that's what you'll do. Your fiery, unstable behaviour makes you too unpredictable to command the Named. You'll stay here in the fortress, and I'll say no more on the matter." He stood and walked around the table to where Seren sat. "Are you too old to hug your father?"

"Never," she said, rising to her feet and embracing him.

"You're so much like your mother. I wonder how you'd have turned out if it were her standing here and not me."

"Don't say that," she said, wiping a tear from her eye. "I'm your daughter as well. I long for the day when you'll honour me with my warrior name. So come back alive, old man."

He kissed her on the forehead and made his way to Tomos.

"And what should I do?"

"Like I told you before. Stay in the Great Hall until Madoc returns."

"I should be fighting with you in the shield wall, not sitting in my room waiting for Madoc."

Rodric sighed. "I told you this morning, Tomos. You must forget any thoughts of becoming a warrior. It'll never happen."

"It's not fair," he said, scratching the same patch of skin again. "I hate my life."

"Show me any person who doesn't want to change something in their lives, and I'll prove they're a liar," said Rodric. "You're who you were meant to be, Tomos, never forget that." He hugged his son. "You'll have to excuse me. I need to attend to a few things before I get some much-needed sleep."

"Father?"

"Yes, Tomos?"

"What happens if Madoc doesn't return?"

"Why? Are you feeling the effects of losing the amulet?"

"I-I'm not sure.... I've just got a patch of itchy skin and it's driving me mad."

"Do you have any salve to rub on it?"

"I don't know. The old man leaves all sorts of weird concoctions in my room."

Rodric gripped Tomos' shoulder. "He'll not let you die after he saved your life so many years ago. I'm sure he'll be back soon."

Alone with his thoughts, Rodric fretted over Grimbard's message. If the Communion discovered his secret, not even he could protect his children from their wrath. He smacked his fist onto the table. *I'll bury Kaine and my secret with him on the battlefield.* He called to a warrior standing guard outside the room. "Inform the chieftains I've decided to follow Lady Zirani's plan. Muster the Named. We're riding to war."

27

IN THE LAIR OF THE WOLF

Cai drummed his fingers on the arm of the chair and puffed out his cheeks. After the blurring events of the past two days, waiting in the lavish surroundings of the man who had destroyed his life gnawed at his conscience, but what else could he do? They had her.

He agonised over Amira's fate. His stomach churned as a flood of terrifying scenarios invaded his mind. What were they getting her ready for? An interrogation? Or something even worse? He wanted to demand answers, but he could not risk angering the Mendari leader. For now, he decided to go along with whatever game Kaine wanted to play. The next round had taken him inside the Wolf's Lair—Kaine's palatial tent.

For a while, Cai had wondered whether the Mendari leader had forgotten about him, but hearing voices approaching, he snapped his eyes to a set of curtains just as they parted, revealing a troop of white-robed servants. They swarmed all around him, lighting sconces, refuelling the fires and arranging a long table with the most exotic and colourful food he had ever seen. Then, as Kaine entered the room, they stood to attention until he sat opposite Cai.

"Wine."

A servant scurried over to the pair and poured two glasses of wine, setting them on a low table dividing Cai and his host. "Do you require anything else, Lord Kaine?"

"No. Just leave the jug."

"Yes, lord." He clapped his hands twice, signalling to his fellow servants to leave the room.

Kaine leaned forward and offered Cai one of the glasses of wine. "This'll help to take away the chill of the night."

Cai eyed the container warily.

Kaine chuckled. "Oh, of course. You think it's some kind of drug or poison. I'll be happy to drink some if you like?"

"No. It's fine. You obviously want me alive for some reason," said Cai, stretching over to take the drink.

"Besides, why would I waste my finest vintage just to kill you? This is Mendarian wine from the vineyards of the south coast. Not that piss you Northerners call wine."

"I wouldn't know. I prefer ale."

Kaine peered down his nose at Cai and sniffed. "Of course you would. You're an uncivilised Taleni clansguard."

Cai shrugged, then brought the glass up to his mouth to take his first sip.

"What in the name of the whore goddess are you doing, boy? Wine should be assessed for its quality before drinking. Observe." Kaine raised the glass to his nose and drew in the aroma of its contents. "Ah, perfection," he said, prompting Cai to do the same. "Tell me, boy. What does that uncultured nose of yours detect?"

Cai frowned.

"Go on, smell the damn thing."

Confused, he pushed his nose over the rim and inhaled a lungful of air.

"Well?" asked Kaine, leaning forward in his seat. "What can you smell?"

Smells like a horse after it's been in the rain. "I-I can smell fruit."

"Of course it smells of fruit, you dullard. Which one?"

"Umm...redcurrant?"

Kaine's face twitched. "And there was me thinking that you were smarter than most. Do you honestly think that such a wine as this could be made from..." He struggled to get the word out of his mouth. "Redcurrants?"

"I-I don't know. Blackcurrants?"

"No. Nothing in your godforsaken climate would make something that even the gods themselves would fight over. "This," he said, swirling the ruby red liquid inside the glass. "This was made from Velak's gift to the Mendari—the grape."

All that to tell me it was made from a bloody grape. "That's fascinating. Can I drink it now?"

"I might just as well give it to my dogs," said Kaine, sulking. "They'd appreciate it more." He waved his hand at Cai's glass. "Go ahead."

This had better be worth the wait. He took a tentative sip and swallowed. The first thing he noticed was the wine's intense but pleasant warmth sliding down his throat—just what was needed for a cold spring night. As the heat lessened, the unfamiliar but refreshing fruity flavours teased his taste buds. He drank some more, and did not stop until he had drained the glass. Glancing up, he realised Kaine was smiling.

"I told you it was perfect for a night like this." He kicked his feet up on the table and drained his cup. "Another?"

Cai nodded and held out his glass.

Refilling his cup, Kaine said, "A few more of these and you'll be as bold as one of your famous Northern Taranian heroes."

"I don't think there's enough wine in all Mendaria to make me as bold as those mighty men and women."

Kaine laughed. "Believe me, Cai, you'll need all the boldness you can muster once you discover what Lord Velak has in store for you." With his glass in one hand and the jug in the other, he stood and walked across the room until he came to a curtained-off section. "It's time you found out about your destiny."

Swallowing hard, Cai gripped his glass tight and followed the Mendari leader into the adjoining room. He could not help but be impressed by the splendour and sheer size of the tent, dwarfing many of the chieftain's great halls in Northern Tarania. If he had not seen it from the outside, he would never have guessed it was a temporary structure. "I was going to ask you why you didn't use Lord Taleni's private rooms, but now I understand."

"Why would I suffer a slum when I can enjoy the luxury of my home?" He walked on a few steps, then stopped and faced Cai. "But it's more than that. This is where I feel closest to Lord Velak—where he speaks to me. It's truly a sacred place."

"He actually speaks to you?"

"Yes. Doesn't the whore goddess speak to you?"

"Not to me. How do you hear him?"

"In ways that would confound your tiny primitive mind." He turned and clapped his hands. Out of the shadows appeared several white-robed servants who busied themselves brightening the many lamps scattered throughout the room.

As the light improved, Cai scanned the features of the room. A large oval table and six chairs dominated the centre and along the walls stood an array of desks and shelves packed with various plans, charts and documents; a map, hanging from one wall, caught Cai's attention. He recognised the familiar shape of Tarania, surrounded by the Endless Sea, but it was several land masses surrounding it that astonished him.

Kaine stood beside him. "Impressive, isn't it?"

"But how could anyone know what lies across the Endless Sea? As far as I'm aware, there are no ships capable of travelling such a distance, and the ones that tried never returned."

"Who said anything about travelling across the sea?"

Cai wrinkled his nose. "But that would mean the mapmaker would've had to sprout wings and look down from the Void to see what to paint."

The Mendari leader widened his eyes. "That's more like it, Cai."

"But that's impossible."

"Nothing's impossible, especially not for the First."

"What? You're telling me this is a relic from over a thousand years ago?"

Kaine nodded.

"But how could it be from—"

"That's the wrong question, Cai." Kaine walked to a chair

positioned at the head of the table and sat down. "You should ask why you've got a tattoo on your back showing landmarks from over the Endless Sea. Sit down."

Stunned, Cai pulled one of the chairs from under the table and sank into it. He gulped down the rest of his wine and thrust the glass out to Kaine. "Can I have another?"

The Mendari leader's brows arched. "I knew you'd want more."

"I'm going to need it." As he drank, he considered the Armour of the First and the Reaper. Two days before, he would have scoffed at even the notion of such things. Yet he knew all too well how real they were—so why not the existence of other lands? His mind flashed to the visions awakened by the Reaper. Then, staring up at the map, he said, "I'm not from Tarania."

Kaine cocked his head to the side. "So you know?"

"Yes. At Midway Bridge, when the Reaper touched my tattoos—it awakened memories from my past."

Kaine leaned forward. "What things?"

For the next few minutes, Cai closed his eyes and explained what he had seen in as much detail as he could remember. When he finished, he reopened them and found Kaine gazing at him in wonder.

"Remarkable.... So there're others who worship the Circle and the Cross? People like you, Cai."

He shivered at Kaine's deduction.

"It seems as if Lord Velak has kept us both in the dark about your worth to him." Kaine stood, walked over to the far side of the room and picked up an item from a table.

Cai straightened in his seat as the object began to glow. "What's that?"

"Behold the power of the First," said Kaine, stroking his hand across the object.

Startled, Cai rocked back on his chair as, appearing above the centre of the table, clearer than a reflection in a mirror, hovered his tattooed back. Tentatively, he stood and stretched out his hand to the image, gasping as his fingers slid through his russet-coloured skin. "I-it's just air. How—"

"Never mind how," said Kaine, returning the object to the table. He paced around the room to stand beside Cai and raised both hands towards the image, pulling them apart to focus on the writing stretching across the small of his back. "This text is known by all who follow the teachings of Lord Velak. Would you like me to read it to you?"

"Yes."

"'And the Pathfinder will travel to the place where His spirit lies imprisoned and deliver unto Him that which was lost. Then He will break forth from His shackles and rise again to journey over land and sea to where the Leviathan of the First slumbers, waiting to be reunited with its master'."

Beaming, Kaine faced Cai and gripped his shoulder. "You are the Pathfinder."

Cai stared with unfocused eyes at the Mendari leader. "T-they were bringing me to Velak?"

"Yes. Until Enora sent the storm to shipwreck you and muddle your mind."

"But why would she do that?"

"Because you symbolise everything that she and her foul Communion detest about our faith—you're the harbinger of Lord Velak's ascension and the completion of his great plan."

No. You're wrong. I'd never betray my people. He pointed at the remaining tattoos. "So what does the rest of it mean?"

"The only person who can work that out is you, Cai. Lord Velak will show you how to unlock your memories as you journey to search for him."

I'd rather kill myself. "And what about this thing that was lost?"

Kaine stood and paced over to the map. "The one who is lost is from Northern Tarania. We want you to find this person."

"Northern Tarania is vast," said Cai, looking up to the map. "Who is this person, and where do they live?"

"He's a boy of sixteen years, and currently, he's living in Keld with his family."

"Currently?"

"He's only visiting Keld. He comes from Caerniras."

"Well," considered Cai. "Only certain castes are permitted within the fortress. Is his father a warrior?"

"Oh, yes. An exceptional one."

"Exceptional? Then he must be one of the Nirasian Named."

"He certainly is," said Kaine, his mouth curling up into a sickly smile. "He's their leader."

Cai fell silent, as the identity of the boy sent a shock wave of impending doom throughout his mind.

"Yes. The boy is King Rodric's son, Tomos Niras," said Kaine. "You are to infiltrate Keld, find the boy and get him out of the fortress."

"You want me to enter a fortress packed with hundreds of clansguard and abduct the Prince of Northern Tarania? Not to mention, avoiding his fiery sister and his father—the greatest warrior king this land has ever seen."

"Not abduct, extract. Believe me when I say that the boy will be a willing volunteer," said Kaine. "I assure you, King Rodric will be nowhere near his son when you arrive at Keld. You'll encounter little opposition."

And I thought my life couldn't get any worse. "Why would Tomos simply get up and follow me out of the fortress? And where would I take him?"

"One step at a time, Cai," replied Kaine. "This is your chance to prove yourself to Lord Velak. You've witnessed the unmatched skill of the Scions of the First and the terrifying power of the Reaper. Do you really think Rodric can stop us?"

"I-I don't know.... But Prince Tomos? It's an impossible task."

"All I'll say is that the fates of many are in your hands. Do what he's asked, and you not only earn your freedom, but Lady Amira's as well."

Lady Amira. Kaine had played his patient game and now showed his unbeatable hand. He knew how Cai felt about her. The only prize that could turn Cai into a traitor: love. Every logical fibre within his mind implored him to agree with the Mendari leader. Yet deep down, he remembered the oath that he swore as a clansguard, that tied him to his lord and his king. How could he break that oath? He'd be sucked into the Netherplain if he committed such a grave betrayal of those he served. He had to ask the question, even though it would no doubt anger Kaine. "And what if I refuse?"

"Oh Cai, you know I can't take no for an answer. Perhaps you require a different form of persuasion?" Once again, Kaine clapped his hands. This time, two Mendari warriors entered the room where they sat. "Remember Cai, everything taking place is moving you closer to your destiny, but I never said it would be painless. Ensure our guest gets an excellent view of the proceedings."

The guards hauled Cai out of his seat and dragged him kicking and screaming across the room. Behind him, Kaine said, "I think you're going to love what we've got planned for you. It's quite literally to die for."

28

DREAMS OF THE LUCID KIND

Candle in hand, Rodric opened the door to his privy, stumbled across the worn wooden floorboards and gripped the side of the stone wash basin. He leant towards the silver-coated mirror hanging from the wall and cursed at the reflection staring back at him. Even in the dim light of the solitary flame, the dark shadowy rings framing his lacklustre eyes confirmed what his foggy mind and aching muscles already told him: he needed to sleep.

Ever since Isabelle had died, his sleep had been brief, fitful and, as he had told Tomos, an unwelcome reminder of the horrors of his past. Yet the many sleepless nights that had plagued him since learning of the new threat from the south troubled him—so much so that he reached across to a shelf and retrieved a small bottle that Madoc had given to him. He pulled out the cork stopper and tipped two identical round white discs onto his palm.

"Goddess only knows what you've put into these things, Madoc." He chuckled, knowing that he had long since given up asking the enigmatic old man about his unconventional practices. "But if it helps me to get some sleep, I don't bloody care." He popped them into his mouth and swallowed. Then, trudging into his bedchamber, he placed the candle onto the table beside his bed, and without undressing, flopped onto the mattress.

For a while, he stared at the ceiling and considered the torrent of worries flooding through his mind. Then, as promised by the old healer, he felt his body grow heavy, as if it were sinking into the mattress. As his eyes drooped and he drifted towards unconsciousness, he mouthed, "For once, please let my dreams be kind to me."

"How many times do we have to go through this? There's no point prolonging the agony. Open your eyes and let's get on with it."

Rodric groaned. "Easy for you to say—you're just a voice inside my dream."

"That's just downright hurtful. Anyone would think you resented me."

"You reckon?"

"How rude. And to think I was going to praise you for opening up to your children."

"They're not children anymore."

"True. And if it weren't for you, they'd have died along with their mother on that terrible night."

"It doesn't make it any easier." Reluctantly, Rodric opened his eyes, finding himself inside a dimly lit room, with no windows or furnishings, apart from his bed and a plain wooden door positioned in front of him. "I suppose you're right. No point prolonging the inevitable."

"Good man. I'll get things ready on the other side."

Rodric rolled out of bed and traipsed to the door. He reached out his hand and turned the handle. Within, numerous mechanisms creaked, rolled and rumbled until, finally, the door unlocked with a click. He took a deep breath and pushed the door open. "And so it begins."

He stood at the top of a staircase holding a cup of ale. *Poor bastard. It must be killing him to be on guard duty tonight.* Below him, he could hear the revelrous din of the Elite Guard enjoying the hospitality of the innkeeper. He wished he could stay with them for a few more rounds, but he knew it was his turn to be with the children. Also,

Isabelle needed her rest for her address to the Council of Clans. He had no doubt in his mind that she would achieve her goal of reforming the caste system, after all the deals and promises she had made with each clan. Even her own family were receptive to her proposals—apart from Kurzon, of course.

He turned into the corridor leading to his family's room. "Here you are, you miserable sod. Let it never be said that Rodric Shieldbane doesn't think of his—" He stopped mid-step. "Oh, great. I knew he couldn't resist spending some time with the children. If he's winding up Seren, he can stay up with her all night." Chuckling, he crept down the corridor and stood in front of the door leading to the room. Not that he needed to creep, with all the racket coming from downstairs. He counted to three and then flung open the door to surprise them all.

"Aha! Caught—" What he saw inside ripped his heart in two. There, lying face down on a blood-soaked bed, was Isabelle. She was alive, but her life ebbed with every strained breath she took.

"Daddy!"

Rodric spun around just in time to see a masked man lunge for him with a curved blade. Reeling back to avoid the knife slash aimed for his chest, he threw the ale into his attacker's face and grabbed his arms, slamming him into the wall. The man winced but dodged Rodric's punch aimed for his head. As he smacked his fist into the wall, the attacker lunged out with his elbow, ramming it hard into Rodric's cheek. Blood erupted out of his mouth and into his eyes, impairing his vision, but he saw enough of the flash of steel aimed at his face to duck away before it slashed across his throat. The man swept the blade back for another strike, but this time Rodric caught hold of his knife-wielding hand, pushing it down to meet his upcoming knee, and crunched the intruder's thumb out of its joint. The force of impact catapulted the weapon to the other side of the room where Seren sat trembling, gripping hold of an iron poker from the grate. Beside her lay the tiny body of Tomos. *He's not moving!*

The attacker took advantage of Rodric's moment of distraction, launching his head into the bridge of his nose, blinding him in an explosion of blood and cartilage. Reeling away, Rodric swung wildly in all directions, desperately hoping to land a lucky punch on the man. Then, just as he risked the briefest of moments to wipe the blood from his eyes, the attacker struck. Rodric groaned as the man kicked him hard from behind, sending him crashing through the door and hurtling into the corridor. He slumped against the wall, winded and disorientated.

The next thing he knew, the intruder pounced on top of him, his hands wrapped like a vice around his throat. Rodric tried to tear his grip away from his neck, but he failed. As his last reserve of air expired within his lungs, he prayed to the goddess that she would spare his children from the terrifying fate that awaited them. Then, the attacker's eyes bulged and reddened as the tip of his curved blade tore out of his throat. He tried to scream, but all that came out was a sickly bubbling gurgle of blood and air. Heaving the dying man off his battered and bruised body, Rodric gasped. Seren stood over him, eyes full of terror and shaking. He struggled off the floor and wrapped his arms around his daughter. "What a brave little girl you are," he whispered in her ear.

"H-he didn't see me sitting in the corner, so I hit him with the poker when he tried to hurt them. Will they get better, Daddy?"

"I hope so, Seren. Go downstairs and raise the alarm. I think there's a healer staying here. Bring him to me." Just before she left, he asked, "Where's Tarek?"

"I-I don't know, Daddy."

Rodric seethed. *Where are you, Grimbard?*

As Seren ran down the corridor, Rodric rushed into the room and picked Tomos up off the floor. He ground his teeth, discovering the nasty gash of the assassin's blade cut across his son's thigh. He pressed his ear to his chest. Tomos' fragile lungs rattled every time he took a tiny breath, but at least he was alive.

"Rodric.... Are the ch-children safe?"

"Isabelle!" he cried, rushing over to her. He laid Tomos beside her and gently rolled her over onto her back, but blanched discovering multiple stab wounds inflicted to her chest. He grabbed a pillow, desperate to slow the blood pumping from her wounds, but she gripped his hand and stared up at him through listless eyes.

"No. It's too late for me, my love."

"No! There's a healer downstairs. He'll help you."

"T-the Veil calls to me. I-I can see it." She raised her trembling hand in front of her. "You need to let me go."

"B-but I can't live without you. You're everything to me."

"You'll find a way, Rodric Shieldbane. Now kiss me, one last time."

Sobbing, Rodric pressed his lips to Isabelle's as she let out one final laboured breath. He pulled back and stared into her vacant eyes. It was over. She had passed through the Veil.

The scene paused.

"You've never stopped loving her, have you?"

"You know the answer to that," he said, wiping the tears from his eyes. "No-one will ever replace my beloved."

"At least you saved the children. Thank the goddess that Madoc was visiting the tavern."

Rodric nodded. "If he hadn't intervened, I would've lost Tomos as well."

The scene faded as another wooden door appeared in front of him.

"Where next?"

"Isn't it obvious?"

"Nothing's obvious with you."

Upon opening the door, Rodric stood alone within a forest. Madoc's instructions had been clear: 'In ten days, meet me at the Leaning Stone of Borgen as Ulena reaches her highest point in the Void and I will return your son, alive and well.'

So just as the eldest of the Twins reached her zenith and peered between the treetops, Madoc emerged out of the shade on horseback. His eyes gleamed, as if Golanos herself lived within him. Yet as bright as they were, Rodric recognised the same emotion that he saw when he gazed into his own reflection—loss. Perhaps that was why he trusted the old man.

He strained to see Tomos. "Where is he, Madoc? Did you save him?"

"I did," said Madoc, unfolding his robe to reveal Tomos cradled in the crook of his arm. "But I must warn you, King Rodric, Tomos will never fully recover from his wound." He opened the woollen blanket covering Tomos to reveal the scar from the assassin's blade.

Rodric paled. "What do you mean, never?"

Lowering Tomos into his arms, Madoc said, "He must take the medicine I've made for him every day." He rummaged inside a bag hanging over his shoulder, pulled out a large bottle of green medicine and handed it to Rodric.

He pushed the bottle into his cloak pocket and gently opened the blanket to get a better look at his son. He frowned. "And what's this necklace for?"

"It increases the potency of the medicine. He must never take it off—not even for a minute."

"Or?"

"Or he'll become extremely ill and may even die."

"Then I'll make sure he never takes it off."

Madoc nodded.

Within his arms, Tomos sneezed and wrinkled his nose. "Poor little mite. You've been through so much, for one so young." He kissed Tomos on the forehead and closed the blanket. "He looks so pale…. A result of his treatment?"

"Yes, your majesty. Powerful medicine leaves its mark, especially when someone has been so close to death as your son. I'm sure other side effects will manifest themselves as time goes on."

"Like what?"

"He could suffer from fits, mood swings and even a loss of strength if he overexerts himself."

Rodric's mouth grew dry. "But that would mean he'd never be able to become a warrior?"

"I'm afraid so, your majesty. But what he loses in physical strength, he'll gain in other areas."

"What other areas?"

"Like intelligence, King Rodric. The medicine I've made could increase Tomos' aptitude for learning and retaining information."

"And who'll teach him all of this knowledge now that dear Isabelle has passed through the Veil? I've got barely enough energy to

179

rule a kingdom and deal with the rising tensions within Northern Tarania, let alone the treachery of the Mendari."

Madoc smiled at him sympathetically. "As I must resupply your son's medicine every few months, it would be no trouble for me to assist you in Prince Tomos' education."

Rodric's eyes narrowed. "And what do you get out of this, Madoc?"

"I'll be honest with you, sire. I've grown fond of your son and want to give him the very best chance of surviving this terrible act."

"Very well. I'll make arrangements for a room to be made available for you. Thank you, Madoc. I don't know what I'd have done if he died."

"Father! Help me, please. I can't take the pain anymore."

The scene froze.

"I can't remember that happening? He was just a baby. Are you playing games with me?"

"Don't blame this one on me. I think it's coming from outside."

"Father, wake up! I need you."

Sweating, Rodric shot up out of bed and stared at the blurred image in front of him. As his sight cleared, he discovered Tomos, staggering towards him. "What's wrong?"

His son scratched wildly at the back of his neck. "The pain's excruciating! I-I can't take it anymore." He screamed and collapsed in a writhing heap on the floor.

"Tomos!"

29

AN ACT OF DEVOTION

It was close to midnight, yet every surviving soul inhabiting Vedana had been herded out of their homes and forced to stand outside the town's South Gatehouse. Ranks upon ranks of Mendari warriors stood silent, boxing them in at spear-point.

Cai winced as another bout of cramp gripped hold of his calf. He pushed down on the affected leg and rubbed his muscle gently to relieve the pain.

"Stop fidgeting, you worm."

Cai glowered at the guard standing beside him. "I would if I could sit on the ground."

"Lord Kaine said stand, so that's what you'll do, or you get my boot up your arse like the last time."

The other guard sniggered and cuffed Cai across the head. "Toughest warriors in Tarania?" She spat into the dirt. "What a load of bollocks."

He cursed under his breath and looked up at the waxing disc peering down at his misery from the Void. Golanos had moved far enough to know that minutes had passed into hours since the pair of warriors had dragged him out of Kaine's tent to wait in front of a tall timber platform, illuminated by a dozen flickering torches.

Risking the briefest of glances behind, he stared with trepidation up at the gatehouse in search of the heads of his father and Lord Taleni, but it was no use. Where eyes once burned brightly, now only soulless, gaping holes remained. The crows had feasted well that day. *You deserved better than that.* He turned to the front and anguished over the possibilities awaiting him.

Not long after, a warrior made her way onto the platform, carrying the traditional war-trumpet of the Mendari. The crowd hushed as she lifted the elongated instrument to her lips, allowing the animal-shaped bell to be seen by all. A single, haunting note droned across the assembled host. As she stopped, the Mendari warriors stood to attention.

Silent anticipation hovered over the crowd. Then, as one, the Mendari smacked their spears against their shields in a slow, steady rhythm that led to gasps of wonder rippling through the townsfolk behind him. Looking over his shoulder, Cai discovered the source of their astonishment: a flaming sword, floating down a corridor of Mendari warriors. As the Taleni gawped at the mystical display of incomprehensible power, Cai knew that many of them would wake up the following morning believing in a new god.

He watched in trepidation as it neared his position, until it slowed beside him, sending a shiver through his body. A shimmering form of a Scion leaned in close, their ice-cold breath pluming out into his face.

Barely audible above the roaring flames of the blade and the bone-jarring clashing of shields, Kaine said, "It's nearly time, Cai."

Light-headed, he steadied himself. *Time for what?*

The sword reached the front of the gathering and ascended a set of steps positioned at the centre of the platform. With the Mendari's beating rhythm reaching a deafening crescendo, it stopped, hovering above a wooden dais.

Then a second gasp of surprise escaped from the mouths of the Taleni. Kaine and the five Scions of the First appeared out of the darkness and lowered their helmets. The Mendari leader stepped up to the dais, held the sword aloft, and addressed the crowd.

"I am Kaine, son of Banan and Scion of the First. I have been anointed by Lord Velak to bring light to this dark world and cleanse it of those who follow the whore goddess." He swept the sword across the captive Taleni. "You are summoned here tonight to bear witness to a great sacrifice to our lord. And I hope that once you have seen what happens to those who reject Lord Velak, you will accept the Circle and the Cross with grateful hearts." He levelled the sword at Cai. "Bring me the boy."

Cai's bowels loosened as a new level of fear enslaved his mind. Two pairs of rough hands pulled him out of the crowd and dragged him towards the platform. His eyes darted around, desperately trying to find a way to flee his nightmare, but there was no escape. The Mendari warriors threw him at the feet of their leader and then left the platform.

"You may know this boy," said Kaine, sliding the point of the flaming sword into a raised iron stand in front of the dais. "His name is Cai, son of Alun Swordstorm, whose head sits on a spike above us." He pointed towards the gatehouse. "And it is time for him to understand the great burden of responsibility he now carries." In one stride, he towered over Cai, yanked him onto his feet and turned him to face Vedana. "Bring them down."

Terrified, Cai stared towards the gatehouse, straining to recognise who had been summoned. He heard them before he saw them—the clanging and jangling of chains heralding the arrival of a pair of escorted prisoners, wearing hooded, full-length cloaks. As they laboured down the aisle of warriors, it was clear from their shrouded forms that one of them bore the well-built frame of a warrior and the other, shorter and slighter of build, sent a wave of panic through Cai's mind. *Amira? No, it can't be her. He said he had no reason to hurt her.*

The pair were shepherded up the steps and each made to stand behind a large bronze bowl resting on a wooden altar. Okita stood behind the smaller of the two and Alvar behind the warrior.

Kaine nodded to Okita. She unclasped the robe and slid it off the slighter figure's shoulders. The Taleni cried out in horror. Amira, dressed in a plain white robe adorned with the Circle and the Cross, stood with her mouth gagged. Rough iron manacles were chained around her ankles and wrists.

Anger replacing his fear, Cai rounded on Kaine. "You said you wouldn't hurt her."

Kaine threw his hands in the air. "Oh, Cai, are you really that naive? I said 'I' wouldn't hurt her, but you, on the other hand—what better way to show your devotion to Lord Velak than to sacrifice the one closest to your heart?"

"You're sick. I-I could never hurt her."

"I'm sick?" Kaine drew close to Cai, his lip quivering. "That's clever coming from you, boy. You who convinced her into a suicide pact on the Plains of Keld."

Cai willed himself to stand his ground. "And by the goddess, I wish we'd done it. So no, I'm not playing your twisted game anymore."

Kaine twitched his brows and spun away from him. "Cai dares to defy me. Very well. You leave me no choice." He waved towards the crowd. The Mendari roared and jabbed their spears into the hysterical townsfolk, crushing their friends, neighbours and family to escape the vicious iron tips of death. As dozens dropped to the ground, the screaming and wailing for the dead tore deep inside Cai's mind.

"Stop! You've made your point."

Kaine raised his hand, and the Mendari disengaged. "Good, because the next time I signal, they won't stop until every Taleni, young or old, lies dead in front of you." He fixed Cai with a look that burned away any defiance left within him. "Understand?"

"Y-yes."

"Louder!"

"Yes!"

Kaine beamed and rubbed his hands together. "I'm so glad you do, Cai, because I've left the best surprise until last." He nodded to Alvar. "Remove his cloak."

As Alvar removed the cloak from off the warrior, an even louder gasp of shock reverberated throughout the surviving townsfolk. Lord Aedan Taleni jutted out his battered and bruised chin and pushed out his barrelled chest.

You bastard. Cai balled his fists, but one flick of the Mendari leader's eyes at the Taleni kept him compliant. "You said you killed him and put his head on a stake." He held his hand out to Amira. "A-and I told her."

"Well, I lied. Besides, I love a family reunion, don't you? Oh, of course you don't. They're all dead."

"Please, stop."

"I haven't even got started yet. Bring me the knife."

Aderyn approached and handed Kaine a knife bearing the sigil of the boar carved into the handle. He held it up. "I believe you're all familiar with this blade. Ironic that a blade belonging to the Taleni family will shed their own blood."

"Wait, Kaine. You don't have to do this. I'll do whatever Velak asks."

"I know you will," he said, handing him the dagger. "And you can start by sacrificing one of these to him."

Cai blinked. "One of them?"

"He's a merciful god, Cai," said Kaine, patting him on the shoulder. "But it's up to you which one lives and which one dies."

You call that mercy? He stared at Amira and then at Lord Taleni. "But how can I choose between them?"

"Don't press my patience, boy, or you'll have even more innocent blood on your hands." Kaine glanced at each of the prisoners. "Hmm...perhaps we should hear what father and daughter have to say on the matter. Ungag them."

As Okita untied her, Amira coughed and rubbed her throat. "D-don't listen to him, Cai. He's manipulating you to get what he wants."

"Mind your tongue," growled Okita, striking Amira across the back of her head. She fell to the floor with a yelp.

Cai rushed to her side and sat her up. "I'm so sorry, Amira."

"It's not your fault," she said, rubbing the back of her head. "We never stood a chance." She leaned in and kissed him, the bitter taste of her tears moistening his lips. "No matter what my father commands you to do, you kill me. Remember your oath to him and what'll happen to you if you—"

"Cai," boomed a familiar voice from behind him.

He touched her forehead with his, then got to his feet and stood to attention in front of his chieftain. "Yes, lord?"

Taleni smiled with approval. "At ease, clansguard. What I'd give to spend a few more seconds with your father." He stared up at the gatehouse. "I mourn his loss. Alun was so much more than a champion. I loved that man."

"We all did, lord."

"No, Cai, I mean I truly loved him. And he loved me."

"I didn't know, Lord."

"After Lady Zorana died, he comforted me like a brother until our feelings for each other could no longer stay hidden." He glared at Kaine. "And it kills me to know that his murderer still lives."

Smirking, Kaine bowed towards him.

"Now listen to me, Cai. One way or the other, that villainous bastard'll have my head on a spike next to your father's before the night's over. So I beg you—give me the chance to die on my own terms."

"But Lord—my oath?"

"Some oaths are worth breaking. But if it weighs on your soul..." Taleni lifted his head to face the townsfolk. "Hear me, my people. On this dark, terrible night, when this boy chooses between the lesser of two evils, I hereby release him of his clansguard oath and command him to sacrifice me and save my daughter."

Kaine raised his hands and slow clapped. "Very touching. Now, for the very last time, Cai, make your decision."

The blade in his trembling hand weighed heavier than any war hammer or axe. He wavered, pacing between father and daughter, his hands knitted behind his head. *If I kill her, I'd never forgive myself, but would she ever forgive me if I chose her father? Goddess help me.* In the end, his heart overruled his head. "I'm so sorry, Amira." He stepped in front of Lord Taleni. "As you command, my lord."

Amira buried her hands into her face and sobbed.

"Good," said Kaine, scruffing Cai's corded locks. "Now one more thing. You must slit his throat so that the blood pours into the bowl."

Cai closed his eyes, unable to breathe, until he felt a pair of battle-hardened hands clasp around his own.

"It's all right, Cai," said Taleni, "We'll do this together."

He straightened, nodded to his chieftain, then stepped behind him. Hesitantly, he reached around and placed the blade against Lord Taleni's neck.

Clasping the blade, Taleni cricked his neck and said in his booming voice, "For the glory of a warrior's death, Cai, son of Swordstorm."

In barely a whisper, Cai replied, "For the glory of a warrior's death."

"Do it."

Hands quivering, he drew the blade across his lord's neck and unleashed a flood of crimson blood that oozed out of the wound and into the bowl.

The townsfolk cried out in dismay. Amira stayed silent.

Taleni released the dagger and gripped the sides of the altar. Then, as his strength left him, he slumped into Cai's arms. He strained his head to face his daughter one last time. "I-I can't see her, Cai."

"Quick, Amira, comfort him before he dies."

She shook her head, stepping back until Okita stopped her.

"Is she near?"

Cai frowned at Amira, then turned back to Lord Taleni. "Yes, lord, she's right beside you."

He smiled up at where he thought she was, and then exhaling his final, gurgling breath, Aedan 'the Defiant' Taleni died.

Kaine gripped his shoulder. "Amira only lives because it binds her fate to yours. So make sure you stay on Velak's path. Get some rest, for tomorrow you travel to Keld."

30

DUTY CALLS

Rodric leaned over the bed and dabbed the blood, sweat and mucus from Tomos' face. His son whimpered, then stirred, twisting his head away from him, revealing the crisscross patch of scratches that he had gouged out with his bloodied nails. With great care, he lifted Tomos' head, removed the bloodstained linen cloth from under the wound, and slid a clean one in its place. Then, resting him onto the pillow, he smoothed his sweat-soaked hair away from his face and kissed him on his forehead. "If I could change places with you, my son, I'd do so in an instant."

"Don't you think it's time to send for a healer?"

Rodric glanced at the man sitting in the armchair next to the bed. "There's only one healer who can help him, and he's likely to be miles away from here."

Kurzon snorted and pushed out of his seat to stand opposite Rodric. He stared down at his nephew and pulled on his moustache. "If you won't send for anyone, let me summon a warden to pray for him?"

"Pray? Was it Enora who delivered him from certain death fifteen years ago? Besides, I don't want anyone seeing him like this."

"Do you despise the goddess that much? Have you no faith left in your heart?"

"I lost my faith the day Isabelle died in my arms."

Kurzon sniffed, then broke away from Rodric's glare to look at the smouldering bamboo clock placed on the bedside table. "It's nearly time." He cricked his neck and rolled his shoulders. "I've no wish to argue with you, Rodric, but if you don't act soon, he won't survive many more seizures."

"Don't you think I know that? Look at what he's endured already." He rolled up his sleeve and rubbed a red hand-sized mark imprinted across his wrist. "There's a strength in him I never knew existed. If we can get him to swallow some of Madoc's elixir, then maybe there's a chance he'll make it."

"You put too much faith in that charlatan and his ungodly practices. And now, when you need him the most, he's nowhere to be found. Don't you find that suspicious?"

"He's always drifted in and out of our lives; but he always made sure Tomos had enough elixir until the next visit. No," he said, peering down at his son. "If that damn amulet was still around his neck, none of this would've happened."

Kurzon screwed up his face. "Listen to yourself. Amulets and elixirs. He's made a fool out of you, Rodric. You accepted him into your home with no knowledge of his past. He could be from the Wildlands or even Mendaria for all you know. Or worse still, casteless."

Rodric planted his hands onto the mattress and leaned across the bed. "I wouldn't care if he was casteless. He saved Tomos, and that's all that matters to me."

Kurzon jabbed his finger at him. "Dangerous words, even for a king."

"Shhh. He's stirring."

Tomos moaned and clenched his teeth, twisting to reach behind and bury his nails into the wound at the back of his neck.

"Keep his hands down."

"I'm trying to. By the goddess, you're right. He's strong."

Tomos' terror-filled eyes flew open. Then, as his body lurched into a deformed arch, a torturous scream erupted from his lip-curled mouth.

"We've got you, son." Yet Rodric knew they were mere words. He watched in horror as Tomos' eyes rolled up into his eyelids, and his mouth foamed white with spittle. With one final spine-breaking convulsion, he let out an agonising groan and flopped onto the mattress, as still as the dead. A reddish-yellow patch of urine seeped through his tunic, and dark smears of runny faeces soiled the bedclothes underneath him.

Kurzon's face drained of colour. "Rodric...he's gone."

"No!" He sprung onto the bed, put his ear to Tomos' face and listened. Every desperate second of silence assaulted Rodric's mind, dragging him further into despair, but he would not give up. "Come on, son! Fight." He felt a hand rest on his back.

"It's too late—he's passed through the Veil."

"Be quiet. I think I can hear something.... It's very weak, but..." He looked at Kurzon, then exhaled. "He's alive."

Kurzon made the sign of the triskelion. "Thank you, goddess."

After turning Tomos onto his side to stop him from choking, they both slumped into the nearest chairs and waited in silence for him to recover.

In the lull, Rodric rubbed his face as a fresh wave of exhaustion hit him. His mind would not rest, as the only issue that could override his concern over his son resurfaced: Grimbard's message. He snatched a sideways glance at Kurzon, sat with his head back and his eyes closed. If his over-zealous brother-in-law and the Communion found out what Kaine had over him, the consequences would be severe. Which was why, even with his son teetering on the threshold of the Veil, he knew what needed to be done—silence Kaine. It was the only way to keep his family safe. Not that Tomos would see it that way.

Tomos stirred. He stretched his legs out and rolled onto his back. "W-where am I?"

"You're in my bedchamber." Rodric slid onto the bed and lifted Tomos into a sitting position.

"Ah. Careful. Everything hurts."

"No wonder, after all you've been through," said Kurzon,

propping some pillows behind his nephew. He retrieved a cup off the table and held it to Tomos' lips. "Drink this."

He took a sip and eased back to face Kurzon. "How long have you been here?"

"Your father called me when you collapsed, over six hours ago."

"Six hours?" He lowered his eyes and stared at the space around his neck. "It's the amulet, isn't it?"

"Yes. It's too much of a coincidence to be anything else," said Rodric. "At least we know your fits are coming every half hour, so we'll be ready for them."

Tomos sniffed, then pulled a face as he discovered the source of the stench. "By the goddess. I really am up to my neck in shit."

Kurzon's mouth twitched into a smile. "I'm pleased to see your ordeal hasn't blunted your sense of humour. What's the last thing you remember?"

"I know I got out of bed unable to bear this intense throbbing in my neck and must've wandered into Father's room. The next thing I remember is waking up here."

"And how do you feel now?" asked Rodric.

"It's like every part of my body's on fire. And this blasted throbbing in my neck never stops. I wish I could dig my hands inside and give it a good scratch."

"And you would've done just that if we hadn't stopped you," said Kurzon. "You're stronger than you look, dear nephew."

"Am I?"

"Oh, yes," said Rodric, showing him the mark across his wrist.

"Humph. Next you'll be telling me I can throw a punch without fainting." He looked around the room. "Speaking of tavern brawls, I'm surprised Seren's not here. She'd love nothing better than to see me squirm in my own faeces."

"Actually, she was here. And she was very concerned about you."

"Really? I should put myself near to the Veil more often."

Rodric raised his eyes and tutted. "Only you could make a joke at a time like this."

"Oh, you know me, Father. I never let an opportunity go to waste."

He chuckled and regretted it immediately, as a muscle-wracking coughing fit doubled him up.

"Be careful."

"It was worth it," he said, between wheezes. "So, where is she now?"

"Seren offered to keep Yanna company in her vigil of prayer for you," said Kurzon.

Tomos gawped at Rodric. "Seren...praying?"

"I know. I'm as surprised as you are." He walked over to his closet and rummaged through his clothes until he found a clean robe. Returning to the bed, he placed it over Tomos' shoulders. "You have little time before the next bout. Uncle Kurzon will take you back to your room and get you cleaned up." He faced his brother-in-law. "Make sure he takes his elixir and is never left alone."

Kurzon frowned at him. "Surely you're not thinking of continuing this foolish charge south after this?"

"You're leaving me?" asked Tomos, pushing up onto his elbow.

Rodric flinched inside. He turned away from his son's downcast face and walked over to the window, opened the shutters and stared out into the gloom just before dawn.

"Father, answer me. Are you leaving with the Vanguard?"

He closed his eyes, drew in a deep breath, then exhaled. Tugging onto the ring around his neck, he begged Isabelle to forgive him as what he would say next would hurt their son. "I have to put my duty as king before my duty as a father. I'm sorry, Tomos, but that's the way it has to be."

"Nonsense, Rodric. If you're still determined to send the Vanguard, let me command the Nirasian Named and Rory Swiftblade can lead my own."

"Please, Father, listen to Uncle Kurzon. Or let Seren go instead."

"No, she's unfit to lead. And it's my responsibility to protect the kingdom."

"Even if it means abandoning me?"

"I don't expect you to understand," he said, turning to face his son. "Perhaps one day, if you become king, you'll also experience the profound decisions a ruler has to make."

"If I become king? I could be dead and buried in our family's tomb by the time you return."

"And if I stay and Kaine defeats us, how many other parents will bury their sons and daughters when the Mendari swarm across Northern Tarania?"

"Surely you don't think that your presence alone will be the difference between victory or defeat?"

"Save your breath, uncle. Father's already made his decision."

"Please, Tomos. This is not a decision I take lightly. I need you to understand that." He neared the bed and stretched out his hand to his son.

Tomos recoiled. "Don't touch me."

"Please, don't be like that. I've always been there for you and your sister. Don't you know how dear you are to me?"

"I thought so, especially over the past few days. But when it comes down to it, Father, duty trumps family every time."

"That's enough, Tomos. I'm going whether you like it or not. Kurzon will stay here to supervise your recovery until Madoc returns."

"Is that a command, your majesty?"

"Yes, it's a bloody command, Lord Zirani. I'll send word to Swiftblade to lead the Zirani Named."

"So that's it?" said Tomos, struggling to get up onto his feet. "Put me back in my room and fight your damn war?"

Kurzon eased him onto his feet. "All this stress isn't good for you, Tomos. You need to save your strength."

"Can you blame me? Let the blasted illness take me." He glared at Rodric. "You hear me, Father? I don't care anymore. Come on, uncle. There's a foul stench in here and it's not from my shit."

As Kurzon opened the door, Rodric rushed towards Tomos, reaching out for his son, knowing that this could be the last time they would ever see each other.

Handing Tomos over to a pair of guards, Kurzon spun on his heels and held up his hand to stop him. "I may not have any children, but if I did, I'd never leave them in the state that you leave yours in. So fight your war. I pray to the goddess that, should you return, you'll have the sense to grovel at their feet—if they still breathe." The door slammed shut.

Rodric roared in frustration and hammered his fist into the wood. *Perhaps it would be better for everyone if I never came back?* But he knew that if Kurzon learned of his secret, his children would never be safe.

With that ominous thought burned into his mind, he straightened, strode across the room and flung open his war closet. Dawn was approaching. It was time to prepare for war.

31

KEEP YOUR WITS SHARPER

Cadarn swivelled his ears and jerked his tail from side to side. Leaning forward, Rodric smoothed the chestnut stallion's flank to calm him, sensing the tension building in the horse's muscles. "Not much further, boy. You're not the only one who hates going through this blasted place." He scratched him behind his ear and was rewarded with a whinny. "That's more like the Cadarn I know. Can't have you setting a bad example to the other horses." He turned in the saddle to glance at the line of two hundred mounted warriors stretching back through the South Tunnel. The Nirasian Named were going to war.

Even though the tunnel unnerved him, Rodric's thoughts drifted back to the events in his bedchamber. Tormented, he relived the moment he reached out his hand in desperation for Tomos' acceptance, only to receive a shattering display of disgust and rejection from his son. Perhaps it was his tired mind playing tricks on him, but it felt as if the weight of Isabelle's ring grew heavier around his neck with every step he took away from Tomos.

Please don't judge me. I thought you of all people would understand why I have to do this. If he hates me for the rest of his life, so be it. At least he'll have a life. He sagged in the saddle and sighed. "It is what it is."

From somewhere along the column of riders, a woman's

haunting, melodic voice swept over the heads of her comrades and enticed his attention back into the present. He smiled, recognising the song that every clansguard sang on their way to battle: 'The Song of Enora and Galerius'.

***

Far in the past when the world was young,
The gods came down from the Void above.
They spun their lies, and they promised us hope,
Of a home in heaven, with lives full of love.

Yet all they brought was sadness and pain,
As they stole from us our children of light.
And all was lost, till one of their own,
Turned from the darkness and took up the fight.

***

As she released the final word of the second verse, she paused, allowing the echo to diminish into the blackness. The hairs on the back of Rodric's head stood tall, as one by one, the drums of the North thundered into life. He straightened in the saddle, as wave after wave of the thumping rhythm shook every bone until, with a single blast of the dremon horn, they drew to a thunderous climax and entered the chorus.

The Named added their voices and smacked their shields in a steady beat. With an iron will, Rodric forced all of his pent-up grief, suffering and troubles out of his heart and expelled them through his song. No amount of sleep or medicine could make him feel as alive as he did at that moment.

***

Enora
Galerius
Saved us all
From Velak

So now we fight,
To honour their names,
For the glory
Of a warrior's death
For the glory
Of a warrior's death

Lost in the moment, Rodric squinted as he exited the outer gate and emerged onto the plain, just as Ulena appeared from the Netherplain, gracing the living with her warmth and light.

As his sigil of the wren appeared majestically out of the tunnel, he realised that all the other clans were singing. Beaming with pleasure, he surveyed the mounted contingents of the other clans, formed in an orderly column, stretching out into the distance.

At the rear were the Galgari, with their purple, black and white plaid banners fluttering proudly in the breeze. Fixed to the top of each pole was the fearsome emblem of the clan: a bronze coiled sea serpent with the words 'Life and Death' carved underneath. A reminder that as much as the Galgari relied on the sea, they also feared it.

Next in line waited the Ovantae Named, with their pair of salmon in their endless circular pursuit of each other. Each mirrored scale of the salmon was hinged separately, allowing the wind and light to perform an intricate iridescent dance across their bodies. As well as their reputation for being ferocious in battle, the Ovantae prided themselves on their thirst for knowledge and wisdom. Ask any Ovantae, and they would boast that it was their love for the taste of the salmon that had granted them their great knowledge and understanding of the world.

Further on, with its wings fully extended, the hawk of the Zirani clan soared high above the heads of the Named. Displayed on a bronze plaque below the bird of prey was the clan's motto, 'Keep your weapons sharp and your wits sharper'. Kurzon was the embodiment of that saying. He was a skilful commander and warrior who could hold his own with most. Yet the quality that set Kurzon apart from his peers was his ability to assess a situation and get the best out of it—whatever the cost.

When Ironfoot had resigned as Master of War, during the Mines of Belith incident, Rodric had no choice but to turn to Kurzon and his strict religious, authoritarian policies to strengthen the security of the throne. Although Kurzon never attempted a coup during Rodric's dark years of depression, he hoped that his brother-in-law would be as loyal to Seren. Only time would tell if the rift between them would heal enough for Kurzon to consider Seren to be a credible heir to the throne.

Rodric winced, remembering the confrontation of a few hours earlier. With so much at stake, he could not afford to make an enemy out of his brother-in-law. That was why he had reluctantly agreed with Kurzon's demand for him to remain at Midway Bridge to oversee the defence of the crossing. Manon would take command of the Vanguard and face Kaine at the northern edge of Derwedd Forest.

Finally, at the front of the column, stood the Named of the Belgar, including a large contingent of their legendary Woodland Warriors. Rodric considered the Tree of Life to be the most beautiful of all the Northern Taranian sigils. Carved out of a single block of yew, found only in the Forest of Borgen, the tree was designed using an eternal knot that represented the endless cycle of life. Flowing up from the roots to the highest of looped branches and then back down again, it was awe-inspiring to behold.

Unlike the heavily armoured horsemen of the other clans, the Woodland Warriors wore lighter, camouflaged armour that enabled them to blend into the forest. For a sword, they preferred the shorter-bladed kladimos that many warriors used in a shield wall. The weapon was just as effective when fighting in the confined space of a dense forest. But by far the most effective armament used by the Belgar was the forest bow.

Almost as tall as the warrior using it, the circular-shaped bow was also constructed using wood from the yew tree. The Belgar were fiercely secretive about how the weapon was constructed and how archers were trained to use the most powerful bow in Tarania—for in the hands of a skilled archer its range, power and firing rate were unmatched. Even more devastating was unleashing a volley of a few hundred arrows towards an advancing force. Rodric had witnessed the lethal results of a hail of Belgar arrows many times on the battlefield. Fortunately for him, he had always been with them, never against them.

The Belgar had been eager to join his quest to march south during the Mendari War. They had suffered greatly from the Mendari incursions, and their hatred for the Southerners outweighed any rivalries with the other clans. He wondered what would have been the outcome if they had refused to join him. What he knew for sure was that the Woodland Warriors would play a crucial role in the battle to follow. He was counting on it.

Relieved to have left the confines of the tunnel, Cadarn needed little encouragement to trot over the drawbridge, tack and chainmail jangling in time with his increased gait. Rodric loved the sound—even more so when in full gallop. "Just keep it at a trot, boy. You'll get your chance to gallop later on," he said, patting him on his neck.

As he returned to the firm ground of the plains stretching out before him, he noticed Kilien, Sorcha and Manon locked in conversation with a warrior from the Zirani clan. It was Rory Swiftblade, Kurzon's champion.

He had a good idea of why the chieftains were worked up. As he neared the group, Manon's voice could be clearly heard above the others.

"No, Swiftblade. I'm not saying that you're unable to lead the Zirani Named. I'd be honoured to fight alongside Zirani's champion; but I'll ask one more time—where is he?"

"I don't know, Lady Ovantae," said Rory, struggling to keep his composure. "Like I've already told you, I was given my orders from the king, commanding me to lead the Zirani Named. That's all I know."

"Even so, it concerns me that your lord isn't here, especially as he voted against this course of action."

Sorcha spat onto the ground. "I told you he'd end up scheming his way out of this."

Rory edged his mount closer to the Galgari chieftain. "I would speak better of the man who saved you from financial ruin and put down your miners' rebellion."

"How dare you speak to me like that? I am a chieftain, and you will show me respect."

Rory's hand slid down to the pommel of his sword. "I'll show your heart the tip of my blade if you disrespect my lord again."

With a flash of steel, Sorcha pulled her sword out of its sheath and swept it towards Rory's neck. He parried the swing and their hilts locked together with a ringing clang. The Named turned and faced the commotion.

They bared their teeth at each other, the veins in their necks bulging. Rodric knew the signs well. The Red Mist would soon be upon them and blood would surely be shed. "That's enough!" he commanded, pulling up on Cadarn's reins. "I've already ordered my daughter to sit out of the battle. Don't think for a minute that I'll delay sending you both back to the fortress. Is that clear?"

They hesitated.

"Bloodrage, Swiftblade, stand down, or I'll smash your heads together with Shieldbane. I won't tell you again."

This time, they blinked, glanced at the king, then looked back at each other.

"We will finish this, Swiftblade," said Sorcha. "But not today. There's enough Mendari blood to quench both our rages."

Rory nodded and sheathed his sword. "I look forward to it, Lady Galgari."

Rodric glared at his chieftains. "We might just as well surrender to Kaine if this is how we'll be with each other." He faced Sorcha.

"You are Chieftain of the Galgari, not some outlaw who kills just because someone looks at them the wrong way."

"Yes, sire," said Sorcha, unable to look him in the eyes.

"Good."

"With respect, sire," said Manon. "As your chieftains, surely we have a right to know why Lord Zirani is not riding out with us?"

Rodric sighed, then nodded. "You're right, Lady Ovantae. You deserve to know." He explained to the group what had happened to Tomos since the misadventure in the Renegade Tavern. "So, in Madoc's absence, I've asked Lord Zirani to supervise Tomos' care and recovery while I'm away. To his credit, he offered to lead the Nirasian Named and his own, but I declined. It is my duty as king to command our forces into battle."

"So who will command the fortress if Kurzon sits with your son?" asked Fergus, on behalf of Kilien.

As Rodric urged Cadarn towards the front of the column, he shouted back, "An old friend owes me a favour, and I'm calling it in."

32

LOVER OF ALL WOMEN

Layered in armour, Luis stepped out of his room and paced to his desk. He raised his shoulders a couple of times, then screwed up his face. "Velak's balls, I forgot how heavy this damn mail is."

"That's not the same old piece of junk you've had since before the war?"

Luis glanced at Tarek staring at him through the bars of the cell with a hint of amusement on his face. "So what if it is?"

"I'm surprised it hasn't fallen apart. You should've got Dylan to make you some scale armour."

"And what sigil would I have on my chest? A leg of iron? A stump? Bollocks to that."

Tarek's smile faded. "I hate it when you belittle yourself. Everyone knows we would never have beaten the Mendari without you."

"Humph." He pulled the belt fastened to his mail tight around his waist and tied it in a loop. "And I live with the consequences of my actions every day."

"It was war, Luis. You did what you had to do to bring Rodric victory." Tarek leant through the bars. "And now you're doing it again."

"What was I supposed to do? Leave Keld in the hands of Zirani who was too young to command during the war, or some untested noble?"

"Kurzon Zirani is more than capable of commanding. Admit it. You love the fact Rodric picked you and not him."

"Bollocks. Besides, who are you to lecture me about defending Northern Tarania?" He neared the cell. "Why *are* you helping Kaine when he killed your family?"

Tarek gripped the bars and drooped his head. "I have my reasons. And believe me, if I had a choice, Northern Tarania would be the last place in the world I'd be right now."

"Why?"

Tarek snorted, then looked up to stare Luis straight in the eyes. "Because they'll win."

Luis slammed his hands against the bars. "By the goddess, man. Do you want them to win?"

"It doesn't matter what I want," he said, pushing up off the bars. "But there're people in the North who would welcome them."

"Who?"

"The People's Alliance."

"Why would they want to ally themselves with those fanatics?"

"And what is the Communion?" Tarek paused and wagged his finger at Luis. "I thought you of all people would understand?"

"I do; but spend a lifetime being ruled by Kaine? Never."

"You won't have a choice, my friend."

Luis sighed and slumped against his desk. *What am I going to do with you?* He watched as Tarek retrieved a wooden cup of ale from the untouched breakfast tray and took a sip. He pulled a sour face and glared at Luis. "Goddess, man. Lock me up by all means, but do you have to torture me with this watered-down piss? Haven't you made me suffer enough?" He tipped the ale onto the flagstone floor and tossed the cup onto the tray. "And by the way, you owe me a free punch after your guards gave me that beating."

"You deserved it," said Luis, snorting. "Here. Give me that bloody cup, or you'll never stop your incessant whining."

Tarek picked it up and passed it through the bars. "I thought you'd never ask."

"Don't go anywhere," said Luis, with the faintest hint of a smirk appearing on his face.

"A joke, from Luis 'stone-faced' Ironfoot? I *have* been away a long time."

"Not long enough." Luis entered his quarters and searched across a shelf full of sealed jugs until he found the one he was looking for. "I can't believe I'm opening this for *him*." He returned to the desk, dragged his chair in front of Tarek's cell and sat down. Pouring two drinks, he offered one to his captive. "You won't taste anything better."

Tarek took it, sniffed the contents and grinned. "Velak's balls. Is this what I think it is?"

Luis nodded.

"Where in Northern Tarania did you get Mendarian wine from?"

"I have my sources. They might be a bunch of crazed religious fanatics, but they make the most delicious wine in all Tarania."

"I might've been living in Nabaya, but didn't Rodric ban any trading with Mendaria?"

Luis flicked his brows.

"You should be behind these bloody bars, not me."

They both laughed at that. And for a while, they sat and enjoyed the luxurious flavour of the wine.

Luis drained the remaining dregs of his cup and sighed. "I should really be heading for Keld."

"Oh, don't be so hasty. I doubt we'll see each other again after today."

"If I'd be so lucky." He scratched an itch at the back of his hairless head and nodded. "One more, and then I'm off."

Half an hour later, Luis tipped the jug upside down, shaking the wooden container to get the last few drops of the potent wine into his cup. "It's been a long time since we sat down together and had a drink like this."

"Years and years," said Tarek. "I remember some nights when the three of us were so pissed we thought we could fight the entire tavern."

"I'm sure we did. I think we're still banned from The Safe Haven in Carran."

"Bloody hell, I think you're right. We were lucky to get out alive. Those Galgari sailors were tough bastards."

"I know. I've got the scar to prove it," said Luis, feeling across his cheek. "So many great times...and then you had to ruin it all."

Tarek's smile vanished. "It wasn't like that. I was set up. Do you honestly believe I'd leave my post without a good reason?"

"I wasn't there, remember? Like Swordstorm, I never believed you could do such a thing, but you can't argue with the evidence, Tarek. You were found in a room at a brothel with a pair of whores lying beside you in bed and a satchel full of Mendari gold hanging on the bedpost."

"Y-yes, I know; but I went to that place after being tipped off that the Mendari had commissioned assassins from the Sept of Shadows to kill senior members of the Council of Clans."

"So why didn't you tell anyone else about this plot?"

"I did. I told Isabelle the day she took Seren to the Stones of Valtara."

"I remember you telling me about the trip, just before I left for Vedana; but you failed to mention any plot."

"That's because she begged me not to breathe a word to anyone— not even to you or Rodric."

Luis nodded. "No doubt fearful we'd postpone the gathering?"

"Yes. Not even a death threat would stop Isabelle from attending that meeting," said Tarek. "Besides, my informant said that I could trust no-one, that the Mendari had spies everywhere. She even warned me that the Mendari had infiltrated the higher castes."

"Now that is something I can believe." Luis took a sip of wine and swished it around his mouth before swallowing. "So your informant was a woman?"

"Oh, I know where you're going with this. I'm sorry to disappoint you, but she wasn't my type."

"Not your type? I thought you were the lover of all women?"

Tarek glared at him. "This isn't funny, Luis. And to be honest, the only thing I remember about her was the unusual way she wore her hair—all swept over her face as if she was hiding something."

"I'm sure she was. Like her identity."

Tarek shrugged. "Well, whatever it was, the sneaky bitch obviously slipped something into my drink and, well, you know the rest."

"Did you see her put something in?"

"No, but she must have."

Luis sighed. "I don't know, Tarek. It's all so unbelievable. And let's be honest, it wasn't the first time a woman turned your head from your duties."

"I know my past exploits, damn me, but I'm telling you the truth." Tarek's eyes glistened, reflecting the torchlight of the jail. "I loved that woman. She was like a sister to me." He lowered his eyes. "Rodric's right. It's an injustice that she lies in the ground. Believe me, brother, when I say I'd do anything to go back to that night and change what happened."

"I do not doubt that, Tarek." Luis raised his cup. "To Isabelle Niras —our sister. The purest and wisest of people that ever did walk this world."

They drained their cups and lamented the loss of the Queen of Northern Tarania.

After a while, Luis broke the silence. "So, tell me. How does Tarek Grimbard, lover of all women, end up having a wife and son?"

"You believe me?"

"Yes, I do. I can see the pain of your loss in your eyes."

Tarek tipped his cup upside down. "It's a long story. Better get another jug."

After returning with a second jug of Mendari wine, Luis refilled their cups and sat down, as Tarek stood to tell his tale.

"After Rodric banished me, I spent two years in the Wildlands selling my sword to whoever could afford me. Warlords, merchants, anyone who would give me some coin for a drink and a roof over my head. It was then, after a slight misunderstanding with a particularly unpleasant warlord, that I decided to keep my head down for a while."

"Did this slight misunderstanding have anything to do with his wife or daughter?"

"Hmm...I think on that occasion it was both."

"Goddess, Tarek."

"What?" he said, flinging his hands up in the air. "It's not my fault they found my long, dark locks irresistible."

"I'll wager that wasn't the only thing they found irresistible."

"I have no idea what you mean," said Tarek. "As I was saying, I needed to find somewhere away from the Wildlands. So I headed south and found myself in the employment of a young landowner in Northern Mendaria. He and his family farmed a few acres away from all the squabbling tribes in the South. I think they knew I was from the North, but they still welcomed me, and I began to help around the farm."

"That must have been a strange experience for you?"

"To be honest, I loved it. There was no-one to fight, no scores to settle and no more caste system. I knew I'd never be whole after losing Isabelle, but at least it made life bearable."

"I'm guessing that it didn't last?"

"It did for a few months. I grew fond of the family. They treated me with kindness, and for a short time, even the pain of losing Isabelle lessened."

"What happened?"

"Kaine started to swallow up the other tribes. Anyone who managed to escape from his sweeping horde fled north. I'm not sure how they found the isolated farmstead, but an armed group turned up looking for trouble. I was in the stable helping Runa, the mistress, when I heard the screaming and shouting coming from the fields. Troubled, I ran as fast as I could to see what was happening."

"Some things never change, do they?" said Luis, shaking his head. "In the stable helping Runa, the mistress? After all they did for you?"

"It wasn't like that," said Tarek. "When I got there, I found Runa's husband, Mikkel, dead in the field, and their terrified young son, Nils, running towards the family's farmhouse. A crossbow bolt whistled past the boy, narrowly missing him. He had a chance. I yelled at him, telling him to run in a zigzag pattern, but he was so scared he just changed direction and ran straight towards me. Behind him, I could hear one of the bastards cranking a crossbow ready for another shot. He was so close. A few more seconds and I could've deflected the bolt. He didn't have a few seconds. The crossbow spat out its deadly black bolt and an instant later, Nils lay dead, a few feet from where I stood. The bolt had split his head in two."

Luis gnashed his teeth. "It's bad enough when the innocent are caught up in the heat of a battle, but what you've described is cold-blooded murder. What happened next?"

"I'd buried my armour and weapons in a nearby wood before I started to work for the family, so all I had for a weapon was the pitchfork I'd been using in the barn. When I ran towards the crossbowman, as he prepared for another shot, I could hear his comrades laughing, making wagers on where the bolt would hit me. They soon shut their mouths when they saw how fast I could run, realising that I'd reach their friend before he'd get off his shot. They tried to intercept me, but it was too late. I launched my makeshift weapon as soon as I felt confident that it would hit its mark. It did. I skewered that bastard, just as he levelled the crossbow at my chest. As he squealed like a pig, pitchfork buried deep into his neck, I ripped the crossbow from his hands and fired it at the nearest attacker. She went down an instant later, the bolt ripping through her chainmail and plunging into her heart. Three remained. By now, they'd realised that I was no simple farmhand, and that I had some combat skills. So they circled me to limit my options. I wrenched out the pitchfork and decided to try a different approach."

"What did you do?"

"I spoke to them and said that if they left immediately, they would live to see another day. I could tell that my calm manner spooked them—that even though they outnumbered me, they feared me. That was when I played my winning card. I ripped off my tunic, revealing the countless tattoos of the eyes of the dead. It worked. For the legend of Tarek Grimbard, Champion of Niras and one of the Three Orphans of Treharne, was known as far south as Gol Zaram. The bastards paled as they realised who they faced. Then they ran. They ran as if death itself pursued them."

208

"You allowed them to live?"

"Of course not. After I helped Runa bury Mikkel and Nils, I offered to take her to her family in the north of the Wildlands. She accepted my help, but, now knowing who I was, insisted that I track and kill the last three, so her husband and son could rest in peace. I agreed."

"So you ended up using your gift even when you tried to find a different way?"

"Yes...but using it to exact judgement on those bastards felt right."

Luis rubbed his head, feeling the effects of the wine. "Thank you for sharing this with me, but I really do need to leave soon. Am I right that you settled down with this woman and she gave birth to a son?"

"Yes. We settled in Nabaya and not long after our son was born. We called him Dagan, and he'd be twelve years old this summer."

"You were married for that long? If you can bear it, can you tell me what happened on the day they died?"

Tarek returned to his stool and recounted what happened the night the Mendari attacked Nabaya. He told him about how the Red Mist took hold of Dagan, how his friend, Garin, was killed and how he led his family through the chaos of the slaughter until they reached the open ground before the North Gate. He described in detail the encounter with the invisible force that poor Lars had called the Bwgan and the arrival of the three hooded warriors holding his family. When he came to the part about the incomprehensible disappearance of the children and the horrific death of Runa, his voice dropped to a whisper; every word seemed to take a heavy toll on his soul. "I was a fool to think that I could hide away and pretend to be someone else. They died because of me...because of Grimbard."

"I'm so sorry, Tarek. No-one deserves that kind of pain."

"But that's what they wanted, Luis. They wanted my pain to force Grimbard to resurface, to witness his wrath and bloodlust. He didn't disappoint them. The tall one set a dozen warriors on me, but I killed them all, laughing as Red Mist sang its deadly song of death. And as I pulled my blade out of the remaining warrior's eye socket, I took hold of her spear and launched it at the tall one."

"Did you kill him?"

Tarek shook his head. "The bastard caught it mere inches from his head, struck it into the ground and did something that angered me even more than I already was."

"What did he do?"

"He clapped."

"He did what?"

"He tested me, Luis—to see if I still had the gift."

"What happened after that?"

"Enraged, I ran at him, launching myself into the air with Red Mist ready to cleave into his skull."

"And?"

"In a dizzying blur, I found myself kneeling before him with Red Mist's blade sliced off at the hilt."

"How is that possible?"

"I don't know. It was then that Kaine finally revealed himself to me."

"I assumed as much."

"Listen to me, Luis. He was wearing the same black armour that I saw the day Banan died. I always thought I'd imagined it, but now I know—the Wraith Warrior really does exist."

"Are you sure, Tarek? Traumatic events can affect the mind in many ways."

"No. I swear to you that's the truth."

Luis shook his head. "I've no doubt that these terrible things happened to you, but Bwgans and Wraith Warriors?" He frowned. "And another thing I don't understand is that you said your son died, but didn't you say the Mendari wanted the children unharmed?"

Tarek whispered something inaudible.

"I can't hear you. Speak up."

Tears in his eyes, Tarek beckoned him to come closer to the bars.

"What are you trying to say?"

"I'm sorry."

"Sorry for what?"

"This." With the speed of a snake strike, Tarek grabbed hold of the back of Luis' head and slammed it into the bars of the cell.

As Luis blacked out, he mumbled, "Treacherous bastard."

Luis slumped forward against the rough iron bars of the cell, allowing Tarek to retrieve the keys from his friend's belt. He slid the key inside the lock until it clicked open, then passed them on to the prisoner in the adjoining cell. He fixed the man with an unambiguous stare. "If the sheriff or any of his clansguard end up dead, I'll come for every one of you. Is that clear?"

The man nervously smiled, then nodded. "Then what?"

"Go to The Renegade. Mari knows what to do next."

As the man turned away, Tarek waited until the rioting started. He did not have to wait for long. As the sound of the prisoners and clansguard clashing filled the jail, Tarek opened his cell and pulled Luis inside. He patted him on his bald head. "Now we're even, old friend."

He closed the door behind him, edged around the prisoners throwing the clansguard inside the cells and slipped out of the jail, into the early morning air.

33

A BITTERSWEET FAREWELL

Cai pulled his hood over his head, wrapped his heavy plaid cloak around his body and made his way out into the deluge. The late spring rains had arrived. He trudged down the street, every step taking him closer to the pair of figures waiting for him under the cover of the North Gatehouse. He fought the urge to turn and run from their gaze, but the two Mendari guards would likely drag him back through the stinking mud if he tried to flee. So, reluctantly, he pushed through the filthy sludge, weighed down by guilt, until he faced the survivor of the horror of the previous night.

Pulling his hood down, he trembled as he stared into the magical, bi-coloured eyes of the one he chose to save. A great fear welled up from within. *She must detest me for what I've done.* Before he could agonise over her thoughts a moment longer, Amira threw herself at Cai.

She wrapped her arms around him. Trembling, she said, "It's not your fault, Cai. You did what my father commanded you to do. You saved me."

"It doesn't make it any easier." He held her tight as they mourned the loss of her father.

"Well, this is all very touching, but I'm afraid destiny calls—you've got a job to do."

Cai turned to face Kaine. He hated him with every fibre in his body, yet he knew no matter where he went, he was bound to the course the Mendari leader and his god had set him on.

The guards stepped behind them and prised them apart.

"Remember, Cai, her life hangs in the balance. It's down to you to ensure that the scales fall on life, not death."

"How do I know if you'll keep your side of the bargain?"

"You don't; but what choice do you have?"

"You have a choice, Cai," said Amira. "You can leave and never come back."

Kaine nodded to the guard holding Amira. The warrior struck her from behind with the back of his hand. She yelped, reeling into the mud, face first.

"You bastard!" Cai lunged towards her, but the warrior behind him gripped him tight. "Is this how you'll treat her when I'm gone?"

"Not if she learns to hold her tongue." Kaine stepped over to the dazed girl and folded his arms. "Are you going to behave, Lady Amira?"

Amira twisted her head to the side, wiped the filth from her face and spat blood from the cut on her lips.

"For the love of the goddess, say nothing else to anger him."

"I'd listen to Cai, if I were you."

Quivering, she squinted up at Kaine. "Yes, I'll behave."

"That wasn't so hard, was it?" He reached down and pulled her onto her feet. "It's time for you to leave, Cai. Do you have the letter?"

Cai nodded, touching the letter inside his gambeson pocket.

"For Lady Yanna Zirani's eyes only, Cai. What else did I tell you?"

"To keep well away from the Great North Road."

"Yes. Rodric's marching south, but you should be able to cross Midway Bridge before he gets there." A sneer formed on Kaine's face. "Don't even entertain revealing your mission to him, or I promise things'll get a lot worse for her," he said, stroking his hand through Amira's hair. She flinched, but kept silent.

The act brought bile into Cai's mouth. He swallowed it down and held Kaine's gaze.

"My operative in Keld knows you're coming and will make arrangements for you to gain access to the prince."

"How do you know these things?"

"Oh, Cai. I thought you would've worked out by now that nothing is impossible for Lord Velak. They'll make themselves known to you as soon as it's safe to do so."

"They'd better make it sooner rather than later," said Cai, mounting the horse Kaine had provided him.

"I've already told you. Your destiny is not to die in Keld. Lord Velak has much bigger plans for you."

Easy for you to say. Cai forced out a smile. Yet inside, a pang of remorse gripped his heart. "I'll come back for you...I promise."

"Just stay safe. That's all I ask."

"One more thing." Kaine nodded to a warrior who retrieved two scabbarded swords that Cai recognised instantly. "I believe this magnificent blade belongs to you. And I'm sure you know who owned the other one."

Cai held back his tears as the warrior held his own sword and Boar's Rage out to him. "I'm not worthy to wield such a blade."

"That's up to you; but I'm certain presenting such a famous weapon will give you more credibility when you enter Keld."

"I knew there'd be a reason," said Cai, snatching the swords out of the Mendari's hand.

Kaine chuckled, then drew the Circle and the Cross in the air with his gloved hand. "For the Glory of Velak, Cai the Unnamed."

Cai blinked as the ritual brought back the image of his parents into his mind, wondering if they too had blessed him on his journey across the Endless Sea. *Do I really want to know the truth?* He puffed out his cheeks, then pushed his hips forward in the saddle and walked the horse through the North Gate. He was tempted to look back one last time, but he resisted. *No. The next time I see her, it'll be to free her from these barbaric monsters and their sick god...or die trying.*

Amira watched Cai disappear into the gloom of the rain. A tear rolled down her face.

"Bring her."

She flinched, wiping her eyes with her sleeve, and spun around to see Kaine marching away from the North Gate.

The guards stood either side of her, remaining still, until she stepped out into the rain to follow the Mendari leader.

As she wound her way through Vedana's streets, the remaining townsfolk acknowledged her presence with a bow or a curtsy, their faces full of sadness from the horrific events of the past few days. Passing through the Great Hall courtyard, she gagged as the stench of the wall of rotting corpses invaded her nostrils. She stared straight ahead and quickened her pace.

Almost at the South Gate, she stopped and stared at a sign above a large rectangular building. *Bethan and Dylan of Vedana. Weaponsmith and Armourer.* She walked towards the front door.

"My lady. Lord Kaine wants you—"

"He can wait. There's something I need to do." Not waiting for the guard's response, she pushed open the door and stepped inside. It was obvious from the state of the main room that the house had been looted and anything of value had been taken; but what she searched for had a value of a different kind. She navigated through the destruction until she found a room that she was sure belonged to Keila. She breathed in the cold musty air of the abandoned room and surveyed its contents. *There it is.* Amira knelt beside the child's old wooden chest that had been overturned in the madness of the looting. Tipping it back onto its base, she rummaged through Keila's clothes and pulled out a dress that incorporated the blue and green plaid of the Taleni Clan—a dress that Keila would have worn on her branding day. Amira grimaced and threw it onto the bed. Finding nothing else in the chest, she stood and bit her lip in frustration. *They have to be in here, somewhere.* Then, as she turned, she caught sight of two glints of bronze from above the lintel of the door. She pushed up on tip-toes and reached her hands to the back, praying that no spiders were lurking in the shadows. *Got you!* In her hands were two dust-covered dolls—one with red wavy hair and the other straight and black. She tucked the dolls into the belt of her dress and cast her mind back to the foggy memory of her leaving the shimmering form that she now realised was the Reaper. If Keila was among the children led away from the terrifying beast, she would find a way to give the dolls to her. It was the least she could do for the poor girl.

After a short rain-sodden walk out of the South Gate and through the Mendari camp, she arrived at Kaine's palatial tent. Seeing her approach, the guards stationed outside snapped to attention and drew open the outer flaps. Inside, she unclasped her soaking cloak and threw it to a white-robed servant hurrying towards her. "My lady. Lord Kaine's not a patient—"

"Where *have* you been, child?" Kaine rounded on the guards escorting her. "I told you to bring her to me. We can't take any chances, not with the boy so close."

"Yes, lord. B-but she wanted to go into a smithy's workshop. And being who she is…"

"Get out of my sight—all of you."

The guards spun on their heels and the white-robed servant disappeared behind a split in one of the curtains.

Kaine eyed the dolls. "What in the whore goddess' name are you doing with those?"

"They belong to a girl I met on the Great North Road. She left them behind and I want to give them to her." Amira stared down at her feet. "That's if she's still alive."

Kaine lifted her head to make her look at him. "Did I not teach you that sentimentality is for the weak? It distracts you from your purpose, from fulfilling your destiny."

"But I thought I'd completed it? What else do I have to do?"

"Fooling the boy was just the start. There's so much you need to learn about our ways, and of course, there's the ceremony."

Amira frowned "Ceremony?"

"All in good time, my child. And then, once the North is taken, everyone will know who you are."

"Yes, Father."

34

DOUBLE OR NOTHING

Kaitlyn loved the rain. When everyone in the fortress would rush indoors, taking shelter from the frequent rainstorms, she would run outside, barefoot, spinning around with her mouth open wide, catching as much rain as she could. It summed up her life. She lived for the moment. It was just a pity that those moments were few, being so far away from the excitement of their home in Caerniras. So when she had been told to meet her mysterious employer beside the River Valtara, in the middle of the first downpour of the season, she took the time to enjoy every minute of the walk out of the fortress and down to the riverbank. That part of the river, east of the fortress, ran past a small pebble beach and a copse of willow trees, with their trunks stretching out above the fast-flowing channels and their branches playfully skirting their feather-veined leaves across the surface of the water. She was pleased that this was the place of the meeting. It was her haven of solitude, away from the busy fortress and her mother's constant nagging.

She spent a few minutes searching the beach for some flat stones and, when she had collected enough, found her favourite branch to lean on. She was soaked through, but she didn't care. Soon she would have enough money to leave Northern Tarania; she would be free.

"Do you have it?"

Kaitlyn flinched, steadying herself on her precarious perch. "Goddess! Don't sneak up on someone like that. If I fell in there, I'd be swept into the Valtara Estuary before anyone knew I'd gone missing."

The figure, clothed in a black leather hooded overcoat that covered them from head to toe, stepped closer to her. "I asked you a question. Do you have it?"

It had been just a few days ago when Kaitlyn had been approached by one of the barkeepers in The Renegade, explaining that someone wanted to speak to her. The tavern was packed, as there was a new bard in town, who spun the most amazing tales and sung with a passion that could bring the toughest of warriors to tears. Kaitlyn loved all the tales. It took her out of her mundane life to places that she could only dream about. She didn't want to miss any of the next performance, but her curiosity got the better of her.

The stranger had rented one of the tavern's private booths, which were used for more intimate meetings. The barkeeper opened the door and Kaitlyn stepped inside. It was dark and the figure inside the booth covered their face with the hood of their cloak. When the stranger finally spoke, Kaitlyn was surprised to discover that she was in the presence of a woman. She was well-spoken, just like that oaf, Prince Tomos, who often visited her mother's workshop. The silly woman thought it was because the young prince enjoyed discussing new ways to build; but she knew better. She tried to place the woman's accent. It was more southern than the Nirasian accent of the prince. She thought it might have been Taleni, or even further south than that. Wherever she was from, she said she had noticed Kaitlyn's awe-filled expression when the bard was describing the world beyond Keld and Belanore. She asked her if she had ever travelled out of Northern Tarania. Kaitlyn had laughed, saying that Keld's southern battlements were the furthest she had ever been south. So when the stranger offered her the chance to earn enough money to travel to wherever she wanted in Tarania, she agreed without any hesitation.

"Do...you...have it?"

"Goddess, yes, I've got it." Kaitlyn reached inside her dress and pulled out a chain that had a silver locket attached to it. "Prince Tomos' so-called magical amulet." The woman reached across to take the chain, but Kaitlyn snatched it away from her. "Not so fast. I want my reward first."

The woman stepped back and pulled off her hood. "I'd be careful how you speak to me, child."

Unfazed at discovering the woman's identity, Kaitlyn skimmed another stone across the water. "So what does Lady Yanna Zirani want with Prince Tomos' amulet?"

"You should mind your own business, child."

"Well, if you pay me double, I'll be sure to mind my own business and keep my mouth shut."

Yanna chuckled. "You sneaky little bitch."

"I am that," said Kaitlyn, grinning. "So, do we have a deal, Lady Zirani?"

"Tell you what," said Yanna, looking out across the river. "As you love tavern life so much, I'll wager you for it."

Kaitlyn sat up straight on the branch. "What kind of wager?"

"If you can skim a stone to hit that rock in the middle of the river before I do, I'll give you triple the amount."

"Sixty sofrans! And if I lose?"

"I take the necklace and you leave Keld today with nothing."

"You're on. Here. I'll even give you my best skimmers."

Yanna reached out and took the pebbles. "Aren't you going to stand and throw?"

"Nah. I'm fine sitting up here," said Kaitlyn, full of confidence. "Ready?"

Yanna nodded. She planted her feet firmly on the bank and let loose. The stone skipped across the fast-flowing water until it ran out of energy almost halfway across the width of the river.

Kaitlyn's stone veered off to the left, but could have easily hit its mark. She grinned at the noblewoman, knowing that the money was as good as hers.

They both unleashed another volley of skimmers. Above the loud rumbling of the river, one pebble hit the stone with a crack.

Yanna faced Kaitlyn. "Looks like you've won your wager, child."

219

"Fancy your chances again? Double or nothing?"

"No, I know when I'm beaten," said Yanna, retrieving three bags of coins from her leather overcoat. "Here." She threw one of the bags over to her.

Kaitlyn opened the bag and inspected the contents. She whistled softly. "I've never seen so much money."

Yanna threw over a second bag. "Now throw me the amulet and I'll throw the last bag over to you."

Kaitlyn nodded, lifting the necklace over her head.

"Ready? Three, two, one, throw."

Kaitlyn tossed the amulet; but Yanna threw the money bag high into the air, making Kaitlyn look up and track its upward arc. As she followed the bag down, she caught a flash of movement in the corner of her eye. The next moment, she screamed out in pain—a pebble hit her hard on the side of her head, blurring her vision. She lost her balance and slid off her perch, just managing to grab on to the branch. Her feet dangled mere inches away from the deadly torrent below. Desperately, she tried to pull herself up, but the branch was wet from the rain. She cried out as her grip failed her, sending her towards her watery death. With great speed, Yanna crouched beside Kaitlyn and grabbed hold of her wrists, dangling her perilously over the water.

"Please! I'm sorry. Just pull me up and I'll leave Keld and never come back. I-I don't care about the money. Just help me...Please!"

"And if I do, you'll never say a word to anyone?"

"I swear on the goddess."

"Let me spell it out for you, you pathetic little wretch. Who do you think King Rodric would believe? You? A girl who took his son to a tavern and almost got him killed, or his wise, supportive sister-in-law? You'd be thrown into Belanore's jail or even worse, branded casteless and sent to one of those horrifying camps."

"Y-you're right. Which is why I'll swear allegiance to you and do anything you want. Just pull me up."

Yanna widened her eyes and dropped Kaitlyn lower, submerging her feet into the torrent below.

"Wait! I beg you! There must be something I can do for you?"

"Hmm...well, there might be one small task that your miserable soul could be useful for."

"I'll do it! Whatever you want."

"Very well, you can live...for now." Yanna hauled her out of the water and threw her onto the bank.

"T-thank you, my lady," said Kaitlyn, panting and shaking with relief. "You won't regret it. I promise."

"Remember, child, there are far worse ways to die than drowning in the depths of the Valtara. Betray me and I swear to you, your family will suffer greatly." Yanna turned away from her and walked towards the fortress. "Pick up your money and come with me. It's time to earn your life."

35

THE VOICE WITHIN

Tomos struggled to his feet and staggered over to his bedchamber window. Breathless, he grasped on to the wooden shutters and thrust his fever-ridden body out into the deluge. Every muscle within his ailing frame burned white-hot in protest of the slightest movement. Defeated, he slumped against the window ledge and drooped listlessly into the swirling springtime storm.

Within seconds, the crusted accumulation of bile, phlegm and sweat dissolved into the torrent of rainwater flooding over him. He shook his hair and swept it back over his forehead, inhaling the fresh air—a welcome relief from the stale, pungent odour that had lingered around him since the middle of the night.

Steadying his breathing, he peered down into the murky, grey mist rising from the saturated ground. Those unfortunate enough to be out in the rain scurried frantically in all directions, desperate to be out of the elements and drying themselves beside a warm, cosy fire. Deep down, he envied them, for there was no shelter from the storm that raged throughout his body and mind. Neither would there be any refuge for the thousand clansguard marching towards Vedana.

Like his father, he had little time for the Communion or the goddess, but even so, he mouthed a silent prayer for the Named heading south to fight for everything they held dear. Grudgingly, he included his father in his half-hearted invocation.

His thoughts turned to the events of the early hours of the morning. Never before had he experienced such betrayal by someone so close to him. What made it worse was that he understood his father's logic. The presence of the king would obviously bolster the Vanguard's morale. He knew that; yet the growing resentment he had for his father burrowed deep into his troubled heart. Perhaps his heated declaration of hate was closer to the truth than he cared to admit?

He cursed, realising that he had lost track of time. Pushing off the ledge, he studied the bamboo clock on the table beside the window. *Only a couple of minutes left before the cycle begins again.*

For the briefest of moments, the cooling effects of the rainwater had soothed the self-inflicted wound at the back of his neck, but to his dismay, the severe itching increased in intensity until, unable to bear it, he smashed his fist into the wall. "I can't live like this anymore."

In that split second of clarity, he made up his mind. He turned from the window, checking to make sure his uncle was still sleeping in the armchair beside his bed. *So much for your vigil of prayer, Uncle.* Kurzon's infamous snoring reverberated throughout the room.

Quietly, Tomos lifted the table under the window. He placed the tray of half-eaten food and the bamboo clock onto the floor and steadied himself. His body tremored. *It's now or never.* Gripping hold of the window frame, he climbed onto the table and then stepped onto the ledge. His heart pounded like a hammer inside his chest.

"Go on, Tomos. Choose the easy way out. It's what they'll all expect you to do."

Tomos froze. "Uncle?"

Kurzon snorted and shifted position in the chair, oblivious to the events taking place in front of him.

I-I must be hallucinating.

"Yes, you're losing your mind, Tomos. All the more reason for you to end it all."

"Ah! Get out of my head." He leaned further forward, trembling, rocking back and forth, trying to draw up enough courage to let go. A violent convulsion pulsed through his body. He lost his footing on the slippery wooden surface and toppled forward. With a desperate lunge with his arm, he caught hold of a swinging shutter and pulled with all his strength to get back on his feet. He pressed his head against the wet, wooden surface and sobbed.

"Hmm…It seems to me you're not that committed to your cause, young Tomos."

What's wrong with me?

"You've lost all hope, Tomos. Why else would a boy of sixteen throw his life away?"

Just shut up and leave me alone.

"But if I shut up, you won't know the real reason you're in such a mess."

W-what do you mean?

"Something that I've been trying to tell you for many, many years."

Impossible. I've never heard your voice before. You're just a symptom of my disease.

The mysterious voice inside his head chuckled. *"I'm so much more than that. Now step away from the window and lie on your bed. It's pointless me telling you what you need to know when you've smashed your head into a pulp."*

Tomos hesitated.

"Everything you ever wanted to know about yourself, Tomos.... Tantalising thought, isn't it?"

"I must be crazy." He struggled onto the floor and flopped onto the bed, as another spasm wracked his body. *This had better be worth it.*

"Oh, it is, Tomos. Now close your eyes and give in to the pain. I'll be waiting."

As Tomos gave up his fight, he rasped through gritted teeth, "Waiting where?"

The world faded to black.

"Wake up, Tomos."

Startled and confused, Tomos opened his eyes. His stomach knotted, recognising the voice that had spoken to him earlier. As his eyes grew more accustomed to the dimly lit room where he found himself, he could just make out a spectral form residing in the shadows. *I think I've been here before.* His memories were muddled, but he was sure this was a place of oppression and imprisonment. To confirm his fears, he looked down to discover that his ankles were bound by rough, iron manacles that were chained securely to an enormous stone wall. He pulled hard against the cold, metal rings, and winced in pain for his efforts. His calloused skin was evidence enough that his previous efforts to break free were in vain. "I don't know how, but I know this place. I've been here before."

"That would imply that you left."

"W-what do you mean?"

"This has been your prison since he stole you away from me."

Tomos snapped towards the voice in the shadows. "I don't understand. How can I be in prison? Who stole me away from you?"

"This prison is within your mind," said the ghostly figure, emerging from the shadows. Dressed in a tight-fitting garment that shimmered with a legion of vibrant colours, the figure crossed the stone floor and placed his hands on Tomos' shoulders.

Tomos gasped as a surge of energy pulsed through his body. "Who are you?"

"Someone you can trust, Tomos." Tears trickled down the figure's translucent skin—an effect that made it impossible for Tomos to recognise any distinguishable features of his face. "For sixteen years, he locked you in here, to keep you away from me. But today is the day you begin your journey to freedom."

"Are you telling me that my father did this to me?"

The figure paused for a moment, then said, "Rodric did not do this to you."

"Then who?"

"The old healer—he's your jailor."

"Madoc?"

The man snorted. "So that's what he calls himself these days."

The room shook as if it was in the grip of a violent earthquake.

"We have little time—your cycle is resetting. I promised you answers, and you'll get them soon. You'll just have to trust me."

Tomos' flesh prickled and his feet rose off the floor as something he could not see tugged at his body from above.

"I can't keep you here much longer," said the figure, pushing him back down to the floor.

"Wait! I don't even know who you are."

"Who else would have the power to speak to you inside your head? The whore goddess?"

"W-what? No. You can't be him. The gods don't exist."

"Yet here I am, standing before you." The figure held his hand out to Tomos. "You've nothing to fear from me. All I want is for you to be free and to hear my side of the story."

Tomos edged away. He pushed his back against the cold, hard wall of his prison. "I don't want to know any more. Leave me alone."

"As you wish; but know this—your illness is a ploy to stop you from realising your potential. All those things you desire to be: a mighty warrior, respected among your peers, feared or even loved. I can give you all those things and more."

"W-why me?"

"Because you have been chosen, Tomos."

As the rumbling of the foundations of his prison intensified, Tomos strained to listen to the words leaving the incorporeal mouth of the ghost within his mind.

"Wait for the Pathfinder. Follow him, and he will lead you to me."

Once again, the world faded to black.

"Ah!" Tomos bolted out of bed, sweat pouring out of him. His vision was blurred, and his head throbbed in agony.

"Be careful, Tomos. You had another episode," said Uncle Kurzon, easing him down. "It sounds like you had a terrible nightmare."

"W-why? What was I saying?"

"I couldn't make much sense of it, but you kept repeating one name—a name that chills me to my marrow."

"W-who's name?"

"Velak."

36

A QUESTION OF SUPERSTITION

Throughout his many years as a warrior, Rodric had fought battles in every kind of weather. From dodging hail as thick as his wrist to battling through thigh-deep drifts of snow up in the Garron Peaks, nothing fazed him. Yet the fog that had formed during the early morning deluge was a different matter entirely.

Frustrated and soaked to the skin, he walked Cadarn through the unbroken cloud of suspended droplets of ice-cold water, gritting his teeth in a futile attempt to stop them chattering. He pulled his cloak tight over his scale armour and glowered at the woman riding beside him. "Is it me, or is this fog getting thicker?"

Manon didn't reply. She remained rigid, staring straight ahead.

"What's the matter?"

"Something's wrong here."

"I know what you mean. It's the fog—it's unsettling." He peered up into the rain, trying to locate Ulena or Kilena. "I thought the Twins would've cleared this soup by now. I've never seen it so thick and so cold."

"No, it's not the fog that's bothering me. It's the forest."

"What do you mean?"

"It's hard to describe—like it's in shock. No, it's more than that; deeper, more profound." She pressed her lips together. "It's grieving."

Rodric tilted his head in surprise. "I thought the Ovantae dismissed such superstitious notions?"

"Not everything in the world can be explained by the books of the Hen Rai, Rodric. The Ovantae study the world around them and learn to discern meaning from all living things. It's not about whether you believe in superstition—it's about having an open mind." She turned and met his stare. "Something that I thought you of all people would understand."

Rodric blanched, avoiding her gaze. After a few moments of thought, he asked, "And why do you think the forest is grieving?"

She scratched underneath her leather eye patch. "I suppose the best way I can explain it is to compare the forest to any other living thing—it's in pain."

"I sense nothing." He swept his hand through the expanse of suffocating cloud in front of him. "All I know is that this damned fog is slowing us down." Manon nodded at his words, but Rodric could read the uncertainty written across her face. "The scouts are due to report back soon. Hopefully, they'll allay your fears."

"I hope so. I really do."

They rode on in silence, into the eerie greyness enveloping them. Raindrops descended through the gaps of the late spring canopy, impacting as tiny splashes in the numerous puddles covering the Great North Road. The slightest breeze wound its way through boughs of ash, elm, juniper and pine, casting spectral trails of swirling grey clouds, as if the dead, as well as the living, made their way through the forest.

Manon's unsettling behaviour refused to leave Rodric's thoughts. The last thing he needed was one of his chieftains casting doubt into his own mind—it wouldn't be the first time an Ovantae chieftain had lost their grip on reality. He glanced across to Manon. "Can I ask you something?"

She chuckled wryly. "I wondered how long it would take for you to bring her up."

"I'm sorry, but when you talk of forests grieving, I see her in you."

"Is that a good thing?"

Rodric paused, trying to phrase what he wanted to say without causing offence. "No-one can deny that Branwen restored peace to the Ovantae Clan after your father ravaged it with his tyrannical rule; but—"

"But what? Her descent into madness is what everyone remembers about her life? That she believed that the goddess spoke to her?"

"Regrettably, yes. I remember staring deep into your mother's intense, unquestionable eyes. She believed it all. Now, after all the years of despair I felt after dear Isabelle's death, I understand how powerful emotions affect the mind. I rue how I handled your mother's removal, but we were at war."

"You did what you had to do for the kingdom," said Manon, unable to look him in the eyes. "Are you worried that I'll succumb to the same darkness that took her?"

"If I thought that, you wouldn't be leading the Vanguard out against the Mendari."

Manon smiled briefly, then turned to stare down the road.

Rodric winced, wondering if he had gone too far. She was right about one thing—he had an open mind. Otherwise, he would never have trusted Madoc with his son's life.

"King Rodric!" Barely a few feet away, the ghostly form of a figure sat upon a horse emerged out of the fog.

"Report."

"We've secured Midway Bridge, sire," said the scout, reining his horse to ride beside the king. "But...there's something else."

"Speak plainly, man."

"We've found the remains of Lady Amira's escort."

Rodric stiffened in the saddle. He met Manon's grave expression and returned his attention to the shaken scout. "Remains? How do you know it's them?"

The scout pulled a heavy coat of mail and scale armour from under his cloak. He lifted it up to show the king.

"Goddess," mouthed Rodric, recognising the armour immediately. Where the head of a boar once proudly raised its tusks, a fist-sized gaping hole had taken its place. "Swordstorm."

"So that's what you witnessed," said Manon, looking out into the forest.

Rodric clenched his jaw, forcing himself to look at the scout. "Did you find her? Did you find Lady Amira's body?"

"No, sire, but the fog hindered our search."

"Then there's still hope. Rejoin the other scouts and find anything that may help us find Lady Amira."

"Yes, sire."

As the scout vanished into the fog, Rodric sighed deeply and rubbed his weary, bloodshot eyes. "Manon, I understand that there are things in this world that cannot be simply explained by what's written in a book, but you must understand that I cannot have one of my chieftains casting omens of doom before a battle."

"But, sire—"

"No more, Manon. That's enough."

"As you wish, sire." She wheeled her mount around and stared at him through troubled eyes. "Just because you choose not to believe, doesn't make it disappear."

37

THE FIRST DAY OF THE REST OF YOUR LIFE

As the last of the white-robed servants disappeared through the curtained partition, Amira leapt off her bed, dashed across the room and stood in front of the full-length mirror, admiring her reflection.

The soft, pale blue silks of her Mendari gown caressed her skin in a way that not even the finest of her old Taleni dresses could achieve. She closed her eyes tight and counted to ten. *Am I dreaming, or has this day truly arrived?* She drew in a deep breath and hesitantly peeked at the mirror. *It has!* Giggling with delight, she whirled in a circle until she dizzily collapsed onto the carpeted floor. "Welcome to the first day of the rest of your life," she said, staring into the sparkling, bi-coloured eyes gazing back at her. "There's no going back, even if you wanted to."

Her smile faded as she recalled the events of Derwedd Forest. While their deaths were part of Lord Velak's great plan, she genuinely regretted the fate of the Taleni who had died at the hands of the Mendari—one more than any other.

Swordstorm's last look of affection for the girl that he treated like his own daughter struck a blow to her jubilant state of mind. *I tried. I really tried; but you let your Taleni honour get in the way of saving your life.* Her face creased as she noticed the tears welling up in her reflection. *No. You don't get to spoil my day. Not even you.*

Annoyed, she wondered how her sister could close herself off from such conflicting emotions; how she could lie with a man like Zirani, an enemy of the Mendari.

At least her father had intervened just as she thought she would have to lie with Cai. That's what she kept telling herself; but why did her lips tingle every time she lingered on their kiss in her room? Her face flushed red, warming her skin and drying her mouth. Flustered, she stood, walked over to her bed and sat next to her bedside table. She poured a drink of water and slaked her thirst. *It's times like this that I wish I could talk to you, dear sister.*

As always, whenever she pined for Yanna, she gained solace between the pages of her sister's journal. To her delight, her father had brought it over from her chambers, along with some of her other possessions.

After Yanna had revealed the language of the First, Amira had begged her sister to teach it to her. It became their secret language—a language that years later they realised they shared with their true father and the original owner of the book. When Yanna had left to marry Zirani, she entrusted the safekeeping of the journal to Amira. 'It's yours for the time being,' her sister had told her. 'Until I return.'

She took the book from the bedside table, stretched out on the bed and began her ritual. Carefully, she opened it and found the next blank page. She rubbed the parchment between her fingers, then held it up to her face and inhaled deeply. "Yanna."

Ritual complete, she rose from her bed and made her way to the writing desk she had requested from one of the servants. She made herself comfortable on a cushioned stool, picked up a writing quill and submerged the nib into the inkwell provided. As the rain padded against the stitched quilt of animal hides high above her head, she prepared to write. After the events of the previous night, she knew exactly what she wanted to document.

I write this in memory of Zorana of Kelaris.

Our mother was the daughter of the most powerful warlord in The Wildlands: Vasska the Shrewd. It was during the final years of the Mendari raids when she first met the man who for years we thought was our father. Aedan Taleni had just become chieftain after his father had been killed in a Mendari ambush. Determined not to fall to the same fate, the young Taleni lord proposed a treaty with the warlord, who, true to his name, could see the tide turning, now that a new hero in the North had defeated the mighty Banan—our grandfather. Knowing this, Vasska offered his eldest daughter, Zorana, to the young chieftain. She was a tall, red-headed beauty who stole Aedan's heart the minute he laid eyes on her. They wedded without delay and then travelled back to Vedana where they lived happily for a few years until Rodric marched south.

Aedan instantly warmed to the charismatic King of Northern Tarania and his two companions, Luis Ironfoot and Tarek Grimbard. He agreed to march south with him to put an end to the Mendari threat, once and for all. After much pleading, Zorana convinced Aedan to allow her to travel with the army so that she could visit her family. Although still in love, the couple's inability to conceive put a strain on their relationship. Our mother believed that the healers of her tribe had the power to cure her barrenness.

After three long, bloody years of fighting, the Mendari tribes were finally defeated. Aedan returned to Vasska's stronghold, Kelaris, a changed man—scarred from the brutality he had witnessed, and to his shame, committed. But he was not the only one who had been transformed—for his wife had now become a mother. Holding Zorana's hand was a little girl, no older than three years. That was the day when Zorana introduced Aedan to my sister, Yanna. It is said that Aedan collapsed onto his knees and wept at the sight of such pure innocence. Yanna was the very image of our mother with her trailing locks of coral red hair and the magical bi-coloured eyes that favour our family. She was indeed her mother's child. And for that reason, no-one questioned if Yanna was Aedan Taleni's daughter. Seven years later, in similar circumstances, I was born into this world, and for a while, our little family lived a life of perfect bliss—or so we thought. For the more our mother travelled to the Wildlands, the greater were Taleni's suspicions that she was there to meet a lover.

I remember the night, vividly. I was lying outside in my usual place on the balcony when I heard raised voices from inside my parents' bedchamber. Frightened, I called to Yanna, but she was fast asleep, and I couldn't wake her. The voices got louder. I couldn't hear everything they said, but one word has stayed with me to this very day: whore. Taleni called our mother a whore! Although I didn't understand the meaning of such a word, I realised Taleni was full of rage. There is nothing more deadly than a warrior who has lost control and sees the world through the Red Mist. In the morning, a serving girl discovered our mother's body at the bottom of the steps leading to our parents' bedchamber. They said it was a tragic accident—that she slipped after drinking too much wine in the night. They are wrong. My mother died at the hands of Aedan Taleni, after discovering the truth of why our mother travelled so many times to the Wildlands. It was for our real father—her only true love—Kaine of the Mendari, son of Banan and protected by Vasska, who loved him like a son. I have always found it strange that even though the knowledge of Mother's double life cast doubt on us belonging to him, Taleni treated us no differently than before. Regardless of that, we secretly planned his demise and all that he held dear. Let me tell you something that will please you, my dear mother. Last night, Aedan Taleni's throat was cut by one of his own in front of the people of Vedana.

You are avenged. May you now rest in peace, my beautiful mother.

Amira's eyes glistened with tears that she had held back for many years. As she waited for the ink on the parchment to dry, she stood and stretched her aching back.

"Excuse me for the intrusion, my lady," said a servant, hovering at the entrance to her living area. "Your father has requested that you join him for lunch."

Amira nodded and followed the servant out towards the centre of her father's tent. She had so many questions for him to answer, including why he had spared the children. *Is it possible that she's still alive?*

"How do you feel about the ceremony, my lady? Excited?"

Amira frowned. "I'm sorry. Which ceremony?"

"The Taking of the Mark, my lady," said the servant, stopping and turning to face her. "I thought your father would have told you about it? We're all so very pleased that you'll become one of us."

"I can't recall him telling me. What kind of mark?"

The servant smiled and tapped his hand over his heart. "We belong to him through obedience, pain and sacrifice. We are branded with his mark."

Amira paled. "You mean like the Enorian castes?"

Screwing up his face, the servant said, "We have but one brand: the Circle and the Cross."

"You mean everyone must have it? Even the nobility?"

"Of course, my lady. All must undergo the ceremony as we are all equal in the eyes of Lord Velak."

"I see."

"I suggest we hurry. Your father does not like to be kept waiting— even by his daughter."

38

AN UNHOLY DEPARTURE

Devastated, Rodric and his chieftains stood before what remained of Lord Taleni's Elite Guard.

After viewing the extent of the carnage, Rodric had reluctantly ordered the scouts to amass the remains of the escort, including the carcasses of their horses, into a sickening line of flesh, bone, leather and metal. To avoid panic, he instructed Swiftblade to organise the preparation of the defence of the crossing, insisting that no-one was to stray over the bridge, hoping that the fog was thick enough to hide what lay within.

"I will avenge you, Swordstorm," said Rodric, laying the champion's armour across his headless corpse.

"So say us all," echoed the others gathered around the bodies.

For several disquieting minutes, the chieftains kept to their own counsel, unwilling to be the first to break the silence—unwilling to voice what everyone else was probably thinking.

Rodric sensed the uncertainty growing within each of them. *I should say something, but what?*

To his relief, Sorcha broke the silence. She signalled to the commander of the scouting party to join the group. "Are you certain there are no Mendari among the dead?"

"Yes, my lady. Apart from their black-feathered bolts, there's no trace of them."

"So the Elite Guard are slaughtered without putting up a fight?" The Galgari chieftain held her palms out and looked around the group. "Am I the only one who finds that strange?"

"Perhaps they took their wounded and dead when they left, my lady," said the scout commander.

"You assume they had casualties. And what about that?" asked Manon, pointing at an uprooted tree barely a few feet from where they stood. "You think the Mendari had the strength to rip that out of the ground and throw it all the way over here?"

Rodric rounded on her. "And what? Some unseen supernatural force did it, causing the forest to grieve?"

The others avoided Rodric's aggressive stare, unwilling to intervene. Only Manon matched him.

"Well, go on. What else has your Ovantae intuition deduced? Enlighten me."

She looked at the evidence before her. "Are all the bodies of the fallen torn to shreds?" she asked the scout commander.

"No, my lady. Several of the Named are intact—their only wounds from crossbow bolts."

"Wouldn't the wild animals of the forest ravage all the bodies?" asked Sorcha, walking next to her.

"Are you sure wild animals did it? Can't you sense it? The uneasiness of the forest?"

Rodric snorted, stamping on a Mendari bolt lodged into the ground. "We're wasting time. Enough of this nonsense."

Kilien grunted at Rodric and wagged his finger at him. "No."

"Kilien, if it weren't for your unquestioning loyalty and personal sacrifice, I swear I'd knock you flat on your back for less."

"Wait," mouthed Kilien, holding his hands up in an attempt to placate Rodric. Turning towards the dead, he stepped slowly through the line of bodies until he found one that was covered by a leather hide. He knelt beside the remains, lifted the cover and looked underneath. The Belgaran chieftain was a hard, uncompromising warrior, used to the horrors of warfare; yet he paled at the sight of the grotesque fusion of bone, sinew and armour—all that remained of a once-proud clansguard. Spitting in disgust, he waved Fergus to come closer and signed to him.

"That's what you want me to say?"

Kilien nodded.

Rodric glared at Fergus. "Well?"

"My brother agrees with Lady Ovantae. This is not the work of any animal that lives within this forest."

Kilien narrowed his eyes at Fergus and prodded him hard in his side.

"You want me to say *that*?"

A second, harder prod answered his question.

"Just get on with it," said Rodric.

Fergus cleared his throat. "Please forgive my manner, sire. It's just that my brother believes that...umm...this is the work of the Fae."

"The Hidden Ones?" asked the scout commander. "That's just old folklore to keep children from straying into the forests...isn't it?"

"Of course it is," said Rodric, spitting out each word.

Kilien crossed his arms and glowered at Rodric.

Fergus began, "He—"

"I don't need an interpreter to know what that means." Rodric gawked at the chieftain in disbelief. "First Manon spouts off about the forest being alive, and now you want me to believe that this is the work of...the Fae? By the goddess, is there none among you who will show their king a shred of common sense?" He turned to Sorcha. "And what about you? Do you believe in such ridiculous notions?"

Sorcha creased her brows in thought, then gave him her answer. "The Galgari may not give much credence to the beliefs of those that dwell within the forest, but we know the Endless Sea. When you're out there, at the mercy of the waves, it's commonplace to witness things that cannot be explained by the knowledge of this world." The young chieftain ran her hand through her short, spiky hair. "So if the Belgar and Ovantae believe that something of the Netherplain killed the Elite Guard, then I'll take heed, sire—and so should you."

"I see. So it falls to me to be the voice of reason." Seething, Rodric spun away from the group. From out of the fog, he could hear the sounds of the Nirasian Named making ready for war while the rest of the Vanguard waited patiently for the order to advance. In his mind, he envisioned squads of warriors completing their allotted duties. Some would be corralling the horses, ready for a swift, organised retreat, while others would be unloading vicious tetrahedron caltrops and other deadly obstacles off wagons.

"Can you hear them, the mighty men and women of Northern Tarania? They go to their tasks confident in the knowledge that they have no equal on the battlefield." He turned and strode over to Swordstorm's body. "But even they would fear an unknown enemy that can take the head of one of the greatest clansguard in all Tarania." He crouched beside the Champion of Taleni and laid his hand on the punctured armour. "Please forgive me, old friend." Stony-faced, he pushed off the ground and fixed his ice-cold stare on each of the chieftains. "We carry on as planned. And if I hear of any one of you spreading a word of what we've discussed here, I'll have you in chains and will find someone more loyal to rule your clan."

No-one, not even Kilien, dared to test Rodric's patience. They all nodded obediently.

"Sire. What do you want me to do with the Taleni dead?" asked the scout commander.

"Burn them. No warrior is to pass over the bridge until nothing remains of what went on here."

"Burn the bodies, sire? What about their right of an Enorian blessing?"

"Damn the Communion and damn the goddess! Burn them."

Without another word, Rodric stormed towards the bridge. He spat out one curse after another, disgusted at his lack of self-control; but how could he hope to win the battle with the Named looking over their shoulders in fear of the Fae or even one of Grimbard's Wraith Warriors dragging them towards the Netherplain? Yet in his heart, he could not shake the feeling that his chieftains' theories held more truth than he dared admit.

It's just like before, when Banan ambushed us. Not that he would ever admit it to that traitorous bastard, Grimbard. He would take the truth about what happened on that fateful day to his grave.

Grave. He stopped and forced himself to watch as the scouts lit the tar that had been poured over the corpses of the Taleni Elite Guard. "Go well, Alun Swordstorm, and take your place of honour up in the Void."

.

39

THE SPEAKING-GLASS

"Your father apologises for the delay, my lady," said the servant, slipping inside her father's War Room. "Would you like me to light some lamps? It's hard to believe that it's only just past midday. You'd be forgiven in thinking that it was dusk already."

"W-what did you say?"

"I asked if you'd like me to light the lamps." He narrowed his eyes. "Are you feeling unwell, Lady Amira? I can call for a healer?"

"No, I'm fine," she said, lying. "I'm just tired from everything that's taken place."

The servant nodded. "As long as you're sure," he said, turning and walking towards a heavy set of drapes at the far side of the room. "Oh, and one more thing. You're more than welcome to look around the War Room, but for your own sake, touch nothing. Your father would be most displeased."

Amira stayed silent. Her facade of confidence withered as soon as the white-robed Mendari disappeared into the adjoining room.

Ever since the servant had mentioned the ceremony, her overactive imagination had conjured images of the white-hot brand searing her young, unblemished skin over her racing heart: the blistering heat, the repulsive stench of burnt flesh and the overwhelming, trauma-inducing pain. It was all too much for her.

Clasping her hands over her mouth, she gagged as vomit welled up into her mouth. Her legs buckled and the world around her spun at a dizzying pace, forcing her to collapse into the nearest chair. She pushed her head between her knees, closed her eyes and breathed in slowly—just like her sister had taught her to do. Yanna had explained to her it was her fear of pain, not the experience, that brought about her panic attacks. *Tell that to my body.*

Even in the darkness, her world reeled, relentlessly thrusting her deeper into her despair. *I just want it to stop.* She sobbed as everything that had taken place over the past few days took its toll on her—so much anger, so much deceit, so much death.

Time crawled agonisingly for her, but eventually she built up enough courage to raise her head and open her eyes. She licked her lips and swallowed, scrunching her face in disgust from the taste.

She flinched as someone coughed behind the heavy drapes. Holding her breath, she eyed the opening, expecting her father to walk in. To her relief, no-one entered.

He can't see me like this; he'll think I'm weak. What else did Yanna tell me to do? She scoured her mind until she plucked the words from the countless conversations that had taken place between her and her sister. She mouthed it under her breath. "'Try to distract yourself from your fears.'" *How do I do that?*

Looking around the darkened room, the only feature that stood out was the towering map of Tarania, hung on the walled partition in front of her. So for the next few minutes, Amira studied every inch of the map, memorising as many features as she could. *I've never seen such a detailed map. Is this what the Twins see when they look down upon us? How*—She paused and chuckled. *Who would've thought it? Yanna's method works.* Not that it helped her get out of the ceremony; but for now, at least, her sister's strategies would help her face the imminent arrival of her father.

A thought occurred to her. *Yanna couldn't have taken the mark. How could she lie with Zirani with the Mark of Velak scarred above her breast? So maybe there's a way for me to avoid it?*

As her father had yet to appear, and she needed to stretch her legs, she decided to make the most of her time by exploring the War

Room. As well as the map of Tarania, numerous plans, charts and documents, stored in leather cases, were stacked into neat piles on various desks and shelves around the perimeter of the room. Some were bound similarly to the secret journal, stood on end with their spines facing out. Amira hoped that, in the future, she would be allowed to spend time with the fascinating array of records and literature. She wistfully fantasised about the wonders she would discover within each.

Pulling away, she moved towards the drapes, lightly trailing her fingers along the polished surface of the large table beside her. *So this is where the Scions of the First meet.* Amira shivered as she evoked the memory of experiencing utter dread when she encountered them for the first time at Midway Bridge. *And I was on their side.*

A bright shaft of light pierced the gloom from an opening high above her head, prompting her to shield her eyes from the glare. *Must be a break in the clouds.* She craned her head up as far as she could and squinted to find the light's source. She had not noticed it in the gloom, but fixed in place at the top of the tent was a large sheet of glass. *Why would such a luxury be placed so high?* Intrigued, Amira followed the shaft of light downwards until she found the area of the room that it illuminated. *An empty desk? No, wait. There's something on it.* She stepped around the edge of the table, stopping in front of the ray of light. There, laid out on the desk, was a collection of objects that aroused Amira's curiosity.

The first item to grab her attention was a row of highly polished sheets, set inside a leather-bound frame. The material held the faintest of reflections, as if most of the light had drained into the depths of the blackness of the surface. *I've seen something like this before; but where? Surely, it wouldn't hurt if I took a closer look?* She scanned the room to make sure she was alone. Satisfied that nobody was near, she gently placed her hand on one of the sheets. *It's warm.* She bent over and took a sniff. Apart from the unpleasant concoction of smoke, food odour and sweat absorbed into the leather frame, she discerned little else.

That's interesting. Attached to the side of the frame, Amira spied a thin black cord that wound its way across the desk. She ran her fingers along the length until she found the end fixed to another unfamiliar object. *What's this?* It was just like the slate tablets she used to draw on when she was young, except that this was a lot smaller, easily able to fit into her palm. Unlike her childhood slate, the unusual material was highly reflective, like a thick sheet of opaque glass. She studied her reflection and cringed, noticing her puffy, bloodshot eyes—not that she could do much about that standing in her father's War Room.

Fastened to the longer parallel sides of the rectangular object was a loop of black, stretchy material that Amira assumed was a strap. *Hmm...* She positioned her arm beside the unusual mirrored glass and twisted it back and forth. *Perhaps you wear it like a warrior's arm guard?* Returning her attention to the glass face, she indulged her senses by lightly brushing the smooth, mirrored surface. "Goddess!" She reeled away from the desk, as a bright light broke forth from the once dark piece of glass. She panicked, thinking that someone must have heard her, but nobody came into the room. Edging closer, she peered into the bright illumination and gasped. An unnervingly lifelike image of her sister stared up at her. "Yanna?"

Just as she spoke her sister's name, the bright white light of the glass turned black, with a smaller image of her sister positioned at the top. Beneath, two words were displayed. *That's the language of the First.* It read, 'Call Yanna?' *Call Yanna?* Her face creased. *What does that mean? I can't call her—she's all the way in Keld.* She shrugged. *I suppose it wouldn't hurt to try.* "Yanna," she whispered. Nothing happened. Trying again, she spoke louder. "Yanna." She waited a few seconds, then huffed. *Useless.*

Defeated, she turned from the desk to continue exploring when she stopped and groaned. *I'm such an idiot. It's asking me the question.* She returned to the desk, leaned in close to the glass, and in the language of the First, said, "Yes."

Immediately, in response to her answer, the words displayed on the screen flashed. *Now what's it doing?* Amira's eyes grew wide, her jaw dropped, and her pulse quickened as the impossible became possible. Yanna's image filled the glass, and this time she moved. Her sister, flushed in the face, peered over her shoulder.

"Father?" she asked, staring up out of the glass. "Why are you calling me now? This isn't our usual time. I could be discovered and —" She frowned. "Why is it so dark in there?"

Bewildered, Amira gawped into the wondrous object. She picked it up and turned it over. *What kind of magic is this?*

"What in the whore goddess' name are you doing? Are you drunk on Mendarian wine again?"

Quickly turning the glass upright, Amira gasped. "Yanna, is that really you?"

"Amira? Come into the light so I can see you properly."

"Oh, of course." She moved into the shaft of light beside her. "Is that better?"

"Never mind that. What are you doing with father's speaking-glass?"

"Speaking-glass? So that's what it's called."

Yanna rubbed her forehead. "Concentrate, Amira. Father will be furious when he finds out you've used it. He's executed people for less."

"But I didn't know."

"Did you have one of your little urges to touch and smell everything?"

"Maybe," said Amira, feeling foolish in front of her sister.

"How many times have I told you to think first?"

Amira lowered her eyes. "Too many."

Yanna moved closer to the speaking-glass and examined her sister's eyes. "You've been crying. What happened?"

Amira's bottom lip quivered as her newfound resolve wilted.

"Tell me, and do it quickly, before one of us gets caught."

"I-it's the ceremony."

"Oh, I see. Well, the Mark will be the last of your worries if he finds you talking to me."

"I don't care. The thought of the brand burning into my skin..." She steadied herself against the desk. "I-I don't know if I can do it."

Yanna softened her harsh expression. "I know you don't want to hear this, dear sister, but you don't have a choice."

"But you haven't got it."

"And for a very good reason—my mission."

"Well, what if I said no?"

"Then you'd see the side of father that only the enemies of Mendaria see."

Amira's mind reeled as she recalled the moment Cai slit Aedan Taleni's throat. "He wouldn't do that to me, his own daughter?"

"Listen carefully, Amira. If you force Father to choose between his god and you, it'll always be Lord Velak who wins. So be careful, little sister. Do as you're told."

Amira sighed. "And I thought the worst was over."

"It is, and from what Father's told me, you played your part perfectly."

Amira bit her lip. "There were times when I doubted. All those deaths...I hope it was worth it?"

Yanna frowned. "Surely, you don't regret the death of Taleni?"

"Of course not. He deserved everything that happened to him."

"Good, because that's what we've been dreaming of ever since we found out the truth. Remember that, dear sister."

"I know. It's just I thought that once my mission was over, I'd find it easy to adjust to Mendari ways. I wish you were here to guide me."

"Once Keld falls, we can all be together." Yanna glanced over her shoulder, then grinned at Amira. "Before you go, swipe your hand from the bottom to the top of my face."

Amira did as she was instructed. In an instant, Yanna's face leapt out of the glass and hovered in front of her. It was as if she stood in the War Room with her. "Goddess. H-how is that possible?" She reached out to touch Yanna's face and marvelled as her hand cut through the vivid representation of her sister, causing her image to ripple in the stillness of the air.

"Now that's what I call magic, dear sister."

"It's like you're a spirit from the Netherplain."

"Except I'm very much real and sitting in my private chamber in Keld, looking at my beautiful little sister." Yanna beamed. "You're all grown up. A young woman."

"Stop it. You're embarrassing me."

"It's what I love to do." Yanna's smile vanished as she snapped around to look at the chamber door. "I think someone's outside. We've spent far too long on here. Remember what I told you about Father. Don't give him any reason to doubt your loyalty to him or Lord Velak." She blew a kiss towards Amira and then disappeared.

Amira traced her fingers around the space where the form of her sister had just stood. "I miss you already."

"What in the name of the whore goddess are you doing?"

Amira spun around, still holding the speaking-glass.

Her father glared at her. He bared his teeth, grinding them hard into each other, and clenched his fists into tight balls, turning his knuckles white.

"I-I didn't mean to—"

"Put...it...back," he said, seething.

"Y-yes, Father." Amira quickly did as she was told. As she turned back to him, she flinched. He was barely an arm's length away from her. "I'm so sorry, Father."

"I've told you before—I don't give many a second chance."

"But Father, I didn't know—"

He thrust his face forward, snarling. "If the Enorians discover your sister's true intentions, they'll torture and execute her. The years of planning for Lord Velak's return will be ruined. All because you couldn't keep your hands to yourself."

Amira blinked rapidly and tensed her body, ready for the impending blow to her face. But instead, Kaine stepped back, slowing his breathing, then held out his hands towards her.

"You must understand, Amira, that even though you're my daughter, I cannot shield you from Lord Velak's wrath should our plans be discovered. I'm certain that he'll have seen your indiscretion and will expect you to atone for it."

"Atone?"

"Yes, to pay for your foolishness. Although," he folded his arms and paced in a circle. "Perhaps taking his mark will be enough to appease him?"

"The Mark of Velak?"

"Yes. I was going to carry out the ceremony after we took Keld, but

I wonder if he'll be satisfied and accept you as one of his own if we do it today?"

"Today?"

Kaine nodded. He stopped pacing and wagged his finger at her. "Disobey me again, and I'll deal with you severely. Do you understand?"

"Yes, Father."

"Good." He straightened his cloak and smiled. "Well, after all this unpleasantness, you must be absolutely starving." He clapped his hands, and a host of servants entered the War Room bearing various trays of food and drink. "Sit with me, daughter. There is much to discuss."

Numbly, Amira sat next to him. She cast a nervous glance at the man who now sat happily pouring a glass of his beloved Mendarian wine. *I don't know who scares me the most: you or Velak.*

40

GO TAME THE BEAST

"Are you going to finish that?"

I think you've had quite enough for both of us. "I'm just savouring the flavour, Father."

Kaine chuckled. "You should've seen the look on that boy's face when he tasted Mendarian wine for the first time."

Amira's stomach knotted at the mention of Cai. "What will become of him?"

Her father drained his cup and signalled to a servant to refill it. A thin-lipped smile crossed his face. "Don't tell me you actually care for him?"

She blushed. "It's just that I found it hard to deceive him when he was so kind to me, and..." She hesitated, reliving the terror of Keila's runaway wagon. "He saved my life."

"Your deceit was necessary for the plan to work."

"Even so, it didn't make it any easier. I'm not a natural liar. Not like..."

"Not like me, or your sister?"

"I-I didn't mean it like that. It's just difficult for me to hide my true emotions."

"Obviously, judging by the colour of your face," said Kaine, thrusting his overflowing cup towards her. "It's a good job he spent most of his time staring at your chest and not your face."

She shifted in the chair and took a sip of wine, unable to look her father in the eye.

His mouth curled into a smirk. "I'm teasing you, child. You need to relax, Amira," he said, waving his finger at her. "Your sister was the same until she learned to separate her true feelings from the mask she wears for the Northern Taranians."

"Her box with a lock?"

"Yes, her box." He eyed her cup. "You can start by drinking the rest of your wine."

She put the cup to her lips and didn't stop gulping until it was empty. "I just hope the cost was worth it?" she mumbled, dabbing her lips dry with a napkin.

"Of course, it was. Regardless of your misgivings, you succeeded in binding the boy's fate to yours, compelling him to turn against his lord and his king—just as we planned. However, the inking on his back was a twist that none of us had anticipated." He stifled a laugh. "Apart from Lord Velak, of course."

"Do you know where Cai's tattoos lead to?"

He flashed her a look of frustration. Scratching his ear as if an insect had bitten him, he said, "That's something yet to be revealed to me. You'll learn that our lord can be somewhat cryptic when he speaks. But I'm sure whatever secrets lay hidden in the mountain at the top of Cai's tattoos is of great importance to Lord Velak." His expression lightened. "I still can't believe the boy comes from a land that shares our beliefs."

"Does that mean you'll keep him alive once he's completed his mission?"

Her father narrowed his eyes. "Amira?"

"What? You think I've got feelings for him?"

"As you said, you're a useless liar—which is why your paths will never cross again."

She paled but nodded in understanding. "I know, Father. Just don't kill him. Please."

"He might have a Mendari past, but he's Northern Taranian through and through."

"What harm can he do once you subdue the North?"

"If he learns about what you've done to him, made him do for a lie and who you really are, do you think he'll still look at you in the same way? And believe me, that boy is clever and cunning. Add his unbridled hatred of me to that list, and he becomes a great threat to me."

"But your armour makes you invincible. You can do anything with that on."

"Apart from being without it." He fell silent for a moment, then fixed his eyes on hers. "The reason Cai is a threat to me is that he'll hurt me by hurting you."

"He wouldn't...would he?"

"I'm not going to wait to find out."

"But Father?"

"No. The matter's settled."

She closed her eyes, fighting back the tears. "I hate how I feel."

Her father looked away and drank his wine.

Amira waved the servant across and pointed at her cup. "Fill it up and leave the jug."

Within a few minutes, she called once more for the servant, who replaced the empty container with a full one. Aimlessly, she twisted her cup between her fingers and thumb and stared at the shaft of light piercing the shade. "Why hasn't it moved?" she asked herself, noticing that the beam still shone on the unusual leather frame. She rubbed her forehead. *Must be the wine.* Returning her attention to her father, she gathered her wine-fuelled courage and caught his gaze. "Father?"

"If you think I've changed my mind after a couple more cups, you're greatly mistaken, dear daughter."

"No. I can see you've made your mind up. I wanted to ask you about the Reaper." She hesitated, wondering if she should continue.

"Well, what about it?"

"Why is it taking children?"

Kaine paused in his efforts to chew into a juicy tomato and cocked his head to the side.

Oh, no. I've said too much.

He swallowed the contents of his mouth and wiped his hairless chin with a napkin. "By the whore goddess, you're a curious one, aren't you?"

"It's that girl I met on the Great North Road. I wondered if the Reaper took her and she's—"

"Still alive?"

"Yes."

He leaned back in his seat and rested his hands behind his neck. "It's possible. If the girl met the requirements to be selected for the Chosen, then the Reaper would've taken her."

"The Chosen?"

He raised his brows, exhaling noisily between pursed lips. "Don't you know anything about our religion?"

"Not as much as I thought I did," she said, dropping her gaze to her half-eaten plate of food.

"Hmm...well, as you brought up the Reaper, I may as well tell you how I found it."

Amira sat up, attentive.

"It was in 1176—six years after you were born. As you know, your grandfather gave me shelter at Kelaris after my father died. Over the years, I explored every inch of that fortress—or so I thought. One night, after everyone else had left the feasting hall and was fast asleep, your grandfather enticed me to stay longer with the lure of a cup of his famous barley wine." Kaine screwed up his face in revulsion.

"What's wrong?"

"Tasted more like an ale than wine, but I didn't dare say so. I'll tell you one thing, it was incredibly strong—so strong that, after a few cups, we were as pissed as two Northern clansguard sitting in one of their filthy taverns. Vasska was spinning stories of the men he'd killed and the women he'd bedded." He stroked his chin. "Or was it the women he'd killed and the men he'd bedded? Perhaps it was both? In any case, that's when it happened."

"What happened?" she asked, leaning in closer.

"From under our feet, the flagstones vibrated with a sound so deep it was like a roll of distant thunder. I started to speak, but Vasska put his finger to his lips, staggered onto his feet and gestured that I should follow him. So I did.

"He led me through the ancient corridors that I'd grown to know so well until we arrived at a locked door I had always believed led to a disused cellar. Vasska fiddled with the bunch of keys attached to his belt and retrieved one, which he used to unlock the door. As he pulled it open, the stale, uncirculated air fled out of the opening as if death itself pursued it."

Kaine paused, staring up at a random section of his roof. "I might have been drunk, but I can tell you that the hairs on my neck stood on end as I looked into the blackness."

"Peering inside, your grandfather drew close and told me that, hundreds of years ago, his ancestors had erected Kelaris on the ruins of a structure built by the Hen Rai. It is said that as they laid the foundations to the fortress, the builders could hear the growl of a fearsome beast resonating from the depths of the ruins: a creature, so the legends tell, that could only be tamed by a descendant of the First —a Scion. Once he'd finished, he handed me a torch from one of the nearby braziers and explained that beyond the door was the only way into the ruins. I laughed at him, saying that no amount of barley wine could make me go into that room."

Again, Kaine paused. He closed his eyes and shook his head. "Now, looking back, I can understand why the old fox did what he did next; but back then, I could've thrown him off his own battlements."

"Why? What did he do?"

"He shoved me through the doorway, slammed the door shut and locked it."

"Grandfather did that to you?"

He nodded. "He should have been called Vasska the Devious Bastard, not Vasska the Shrewd."

Amira nervously laughed.

"I hammered at that door, cursing, threatening and even begging him to open it. He refused. All he said to me before he walked away was, 'This is your destiny, Son of Banan, Scion of the First. Go tame the beast.'"

"That would be one of my worst nightmares."

Kaine agreed. "As a Northerner would say: I was shitting myself."

"What happened next?"

"So, trapped inside, I fought the urge to crumple to the floor and succumb to my fears. Not because of the darkness, but because of that sound, amplified through the narrow corridor where I now stood. Whatever made that wretched, primal growl waited for me within the gloom. I thought of my father's disapproving glare, relieved that he wasn't there to witness my shame. If it were him, he would stand tall, jut out his chin, grip Shieldbane in his hands and stride into the darkness.

"It must infuriate you that King Rodric took not only grandfather's head but also his war hammer for his own?"

"*Rodric Shieldbane*," he said, through gritted teeth, "is nothing more than a coward, a liar and a thief."

"What do you mean?"

Kaine shoved his chair back and stood, pacing around the table. "I'll say no more about that man in my home, except that he'll soon pay for his shameful deeds in the most heartrending of ways."

"As you wish, Father," said Amira, craning her neck back to see him as he passed behind her.

"Well, Banan wasn't there, but his son was. I wrapped his courage around me like a coat of mail, gripped hold of the torch to stop my hand from trembling and stepped into the oblivion."

For the next few minutes, Kaine described edging along the cramped passageway until he came to a steep, spiralling stairway and how he perilously descended hundreds of steps until he came to the bottom and found himself in front of an impenetrable rockfall.

Amira frowned. "How did you get through?"

"When I said impenetrable, I didn't mean for me," he said, flexing his arm muscles. "As the last embers of my torch faded into the darkness, I hefted the final rock blocking my way, tossed it to the side and spied through the gap."

"What did you see?"

"Total darkness; yet the sound was more distinct than before. I knew I was getting close. So with no clue about what lay beyond, I wriggled my way through the gap in the rocks and rolled onto a smooth, hard surface. Then, as I stood in the darkness, something astonishing happened."

"Astonishing? In what way?"

"The place where I stood burst into light as if Ulena and Kilena had found themselves trapped in the depths alongside me."

"How is that possible?"

"You've witnessed the power of the First: the Reaper, the armour, the speaking-glass. Isn't it possible that the Hen Rai also possessed great power—especially as they could defeat the First?"

Amira shrugged. "So now that you had light, what did it reveal?"

"Even now, after all this time, I remember vividly what appeared out of the darkness. All around me, stretching far into the distance of a cavernous hall, stood statuesque creatures wrought in many forms of metal that not even the most skilled smiths would be able to identify. Some stretched high above me like enormous, iron towers, and others spawned many arms that resembled the branches of the mighty oak found in the Northern forests. I was a mere insect in the company of giants."

"But the Reaper wasn't among them?"

"No. The sound originated further into the vast structure. So I dusted myself down and pushed onwards, ever closer to the sound of the beast.

"I must have counted over thirty metal giants by the time I reached the other end of the structure, so mesmerised by their presence that I almost forgot my purpose for being there...almost. For I now knew where the beast lay. Stretching out across the enclosing wall was the largest pair of doors I'd ever seen. They were high enough and wide enough to allow the most enormous of the giants to pass through unhindered. And it was from within those doors that I sensed the beast's presence."

He stopped pacing and stared into Amira's eyes. "I don't need to explain to you what that felt like."

She shuddered in response. "No. You don't."

"I crept up to the doors, placing my hands onto the smooth, metallic surface, and leaned in to listen. It was there. And do you know what? It sensed me. With a deafening crack, the beast rammed the enormous doors, the collision so powerful it threw me across the floor. Totally disorientated, I got up on my hands and knees, expecting the doors to be smashed to pieces with the beast lunging towards me, ready to rip me to shreds."

"And?" asked Amira, breathless.

"The doors held fast."

"But I thought you said nothing could withstand the might of the Reaper?"

"Nothing in this world can," said Kaine, shaking his head. "But those doors were made by the Hen Rai. The old stories were true— they'd trapped it; and it had been stuck there for over a thousand years."

"No wonder it was enraged."

Kaine nodded. "My mind implored me to turn and run, but another force compelled me to move forward. Of course, I now know that to be the Will of Velak. It gave me strength when I had none. So, pulse racing, head swirling, I got up and staggered over to the doors."

"I don't think I could have done that," said Amira.

"Perhaps you'll think otherwise once you take his mark?"

She groaned silently. *I almost forgot about the damn mark.* "So how did you release the Reaper?"

"Even though everything in that cavernous chamber was beyond my comprehension, I was sure that, like any door, there must have been a way to open it. I searched everywhere: on the doors, on the walls, and even on the floor. Nothing. It was just as I was ready to admit defeat that I noticed a pile of rags half-hidden by the feet of the closest giant to the door. As I drew closer to inspect it, I realised that something was concealed in the heap."

"What was it?"

"A corpse."

"A corpse?"

"Yes; but I'd never seen one like this before, and I've seen my fair share of dead bodies. It was as if the flesh and skin had shrivelled tight around the skeleton."

"But how did the corpse help you open the doors?"

"It wasn't the corpse itself, but what it clutched in its withered hand—a small, metal box, with lots of tiny sticks attached to it. With no other ideas, I pulled it free from the corpse's grip and examined it. From what I could see, the little sticks moved back and forth, like a wooden brake on a cart. Guessing that they must have something to do with the Hen Rai structure, I flicked every one of those little sticks without success until I came to the last one. As I pushed it forward, I held my breath and watched the doors. After a few heart-stopping seconds of waiting, I cursed in frustration, about to toss the useless metal box back onto the corpse. Then, with a sound that reminded me of the hiss of a viper ready to strike, the doors began to slide apart.

"The beast within roared and slammed its body into the widening gap. Immediately regretting my decision, I panicked and flicked the stick down to close the doors, but it was too late. The shimmering beast had wedged itself into the gap and used its snake-like arms to prise the doors further apart. Scared out of my wits, I turned and fled towards the rockslide. I've always been quick on my feet, but I barely made a few feet before a tendril of rippling air wrapped tight around my body and hauled me off my feet. From behind, the beast's presence loomed over me. It turned me around, and I finally came face to face with its menacing, vibrating form."

Kaine closed his eyes and bowed his head. "Only one other time have I experienced total helplessness as I did at that moment."

"When was that?"

"The day I witnessed the shimmering for the first time. The day my father died."

"I thought only the Scions of the First and the Reaper possessed the power to shimmer?"

He shook his head. "No. There is another—the Thief who stole the Vessel."

"I don't understand."

258

"It doesn't matter. What I'm trying to say is that I truly believed I was going to die."

"So why didn't it kill you?"

Kaine drew up a chair beside Amira, slipped his hand into his tunic and pulled out a pair of metallic discs attached to a chain hanging around his neck. "These saved me."

"How?"

"As the beast poised itself, ready to send me through the Veil, my chain fell out of my tunic, revealing the same two discs I'm holding in my hands. When the beast spotted them, it immediately lowered me to the floor and backed away."

"Why? What's on them?"

Kaine pulled the chain over his head and passed them to her.

Both discs were identical in shape and material, as what was engraved on each one. The last three lines made no sense to her, but the first stood out. "Conan Lynch. Where've I heard that name before?"

"Really? It's—"

"No. Don't tell me. It's..." *Think, Amira, think.* "The journal—you wrote about him in your journal—he's your ancestor."

"Oh, you were paying attention," said Kaine, twitching his brows. "So there I was, standing in front of the beast, wondering why it had spared me. Then a harrowing thought occurred to me. What if it had something far worse in store? In that moment of dread, I sank to my knees, and with my head bowed, I prayed aloud to Velak to give strength to my trembling body and allow me to die with honour. And do you know what happened next?"

"No. Tell me."

"Lord Velak heard my prayer."

"How do you know that?"

"Because he spoke to me through the beast."

"The Reaper can speak? Well, what did he say?"

"Apart from a handful of words, I had no idea what he said."

"Like your ancestor's name?"

He nodded. "You must understand that the common Taranian tongue has evolved from the languages of the Hen Rai and of the

First—over a thousand years to blend and mutate into what we speak today. So yes, certain words have stayed with us."

"So now knowing the language like you do, can you tell me what he said to you?"

Kaine nodded. "He said, 'Scion of Praetorian Lynch, I need your help'."

"By the whore goddess."

"I'm sure I said something on the same lines when I heard it," said Kaine, chuckling. "On hearing the name of my ancestor, I raised my head and gasped in awe of what now stood before me. Gone was the shimmering pattern, and in its place was a creature unlike any other I'd witnessed in that underground expanse."

"What did it look like?"

Kaine widened his eyes and said, "Absolutely terrifying."

"In what way?"

"You really want to know?"

"Yes."

"It's not easy to describe, so I'll show something that looks just like it."

"Show me?"

Kaine didn't respond. Standing, he made his way to one of the shelves positioned next to the map of Tarania and retrieved a cylindrical leather case. He returned to his original seat, opened it and pulled out a single roll of parchment.

"What's on there?"

With an impish look in his eye, he asked, "Are you still scared of spiders?"

Amira flinched, half-expecting to find one on her back. "Where?"

"Calm down," he said, laughing. He turned the parchment around. "Whoever created the Reaper drew their inspiration from this."

Repulsed, Amira hid her eyes from the skin-crawling image sketched onto the smooth, faded material. "Get that away from me."

"What? It's just a common wolf spider." He pointed around the room. "I dare say there's a few lurking in here after all the rain we had earlier."

"Stop it," she said, standing abruptly. "I-I need to go. I can't stay in here. Not when one of those is near."

Kaine slammed his hands onto the table. "Sit down and control yourself, child."

"You don't understand. They make my flesh creep."

"Stop whining. You wanted to know what it looked like."

She glanced at the drawing out of the corner of her eye. "W-what's that thing on its back, with all the white balls around it?"

"That's where a wolf spider carries its eggs."

"Urgh. Does the Reaper have one of those?"

Kaine grinned at her. "You should know—you were inside one."

Amira's colour drained from her face.

"The Reaper wouldn't hurt you—it saves the young; it doesn't kill them. Not like that bedtime story the North tell their children of the Reaper...what's that name they gave it?"

"The Bwgan?"

"Yes, that's the one."

"But still. The thought of lying inside one of those...eggs—" She rubbed her head, as the effects of the wine shifted from a pleasant, numbing sensation to that of nausea. "I-I need to lie down. I think I'm going to throw up."

"Good idea. You'll need a clear head for the ceremony."

"Yes, Father."

"And don't forget, Amira. He'll expect you to atone for your transgression from earlier," he said, tilting his head towards the speaking-glass. "I just hope he's in a forgiving mood and doesn't make you suffer."

"Suffer? How?"

"Hmm...for your sake, I hope it doesn't involve spiders."

41

THERE'S HOPE FOR HER YET

The sweat-saturated inner layers of Luis' gambeson clung to the prickly hairs that covered his back. Even protected by his braccae, his iron limb absorbed the combined heat of the Twins, blistering the sensitive skin around his stump. To make things worse, the egg-shaped lump on his forehead throbbed, reminding Luis of the treachery inflicted on him barely a few hours earlier.

He said, 'I'm sorry.' He'll be bloody sorry when my clansguard catch up with him. There'll be no mercy for him this time.

Once Luis had regained consciousness, Grimbard and all the prisoners had escaped the jail, leaving a trail of destruction in their wake. Luckily, there had been no deaths, but with the unrest spreading throughout the town, Luis knew it was unlikely to stay that way.

So was that your plan all along? Incite a caste uprising? All that bollocks about Wraith Warriors and Kaine's proposal? Did you even have a wife and son? Or was that just another one of your lies?

Snapping out of his introspection, he reined his horse to a walk as Keld's North Gate loomed in front of him.

"Halt! State your name and business."

Squinting, Luis craned his neck towards the gatehouse battlements, where a pair of young warriors stood guard. One, he warily noted, aimed a crossbow at him. "Afternoon, lads. I'd appreciate it if you'd lower the weapon. The triggers on those models are sensitive little buggers," he said, smiling up at the pair.

"I asked you a question, old man," said the warrior beside the crossbowman.

Old man. Luis gripped his reins tight and bit his tongue. "My name is Luis Ironfoot, and I'm on the king's business."

"Goddess. The old fool must be losing his mind."

"Why'd you say that, Finn?" asked the warrior holding the crossbow.

"Because he says he's Luis *bloody* Ironfoot, you idiot. He can't be Ironfoot—he's dead."

Luis simmered. "I'm not dead or old. I *am* Luis Ironfoot and King Rodric has commanded me to take charge of the fortress."

"Velak's balls. The poor bastard really believes he's Ironfoot."

"Maybe I should shoot him to put him out of his misery?"

"Go away, old man, or I'll let Ellis use you as target practice."

This day just keeps getting shittier by the second. For once, he regretted not accepting Rodric's offer to commission a coat of armour in thanks for his service during the Mendari War. *At least these fools would know who I am.* He closed his eyes and groaned in frustration. "Wait, I can prove who I am." *This is so demeaning.* He rolled up his braccae to reveal his iron leg. "Look."

A crossbow trigger release, followed by the crack of rawhide against a lathe of yew, propelled the bowman's deadly response to his action.

"Oh, shit!" The bolt whizzed past his mount's head and slammed hard into his iron-plated leg. As if conjured by a bard's vivid imagination, the projectile spun up and hovered just in front of Luis. He snatched the bolt out of the air and stared at it in disbelief.

Finn howled with laughter, patting Ellis on the back for his marksmanship. "Well, if you're Luis Ironfoot, then I'm Tarek Grimbard. Now piss off before the next bolt splits your head in two."

Incensed, Luis gnashed his teeth. "So far today, I've had my head smashed into an iron bar, survived a jail riot, and now I have you two arseholes to contend with. Now I intend to kill only Mendari today, but I can make an exception and throw a pair of useless guards off their gatehouse if they keep me waiting for a second longer."

Finn's grin disappeared. "Don't say we didn't warn you: kill him."

"Hold your fire!" commanded a warrior, running onto the battlements. The guards stood to attention as Princess Seren unleashed a tirade of obscenities, pointing down towards Luis. She stared down at him. "I'm sorry, War Master Ironfoot. Lord Zirani and I have been so busy with Prince Tomos that we assumed Father had given word to the gatehouse that you were arriving."

"Apparently not," said Luis, holding the bolt up to her. "Seems as if the younger generation don't know who I am."

Furious, Seren rounded on the ashen-faced clansguard. "Not only did you fail to recognise the greatest general Northern Tarania has ever had, but you actually discharged a bolt at him?"

"I-it was an accident, your highness. W-we didn't know," spluttered Finn.

"Didn't know? How many other warriors do you know that have a leg of iron and call themselves Luis Ironfoot? Get out of my sight before I allow the Master of War to shove that bolt so far up your arses you'll be shitting through your mouths for the rest of your worthless lives. Go."

Even in his discomfort, Luis managed a wide grin as he recognised in Seren the embodiment of both her parents. *You may have the makings of a great leader after all.*

The immense portcullis gate groaned open to allow Luis into Keld, and he coaxed his mount into the North Gate Tunnel. After a few minutes, Seren emerged on foot out of the darkness.

"I can't believe they shot at you," she said, shaking her head. "Do you want them disciplined?"

"No. They're clearly inexperienced, and..." he paused, mulling over a thought. "Actually, they can join my personal guard and see if they can stay alive longer than a *mad old man* can. Besides, that lad's a crack shot with the crossbow. He's wasted on the North Wall."

Seren snorted. "Just for a moment, I thought you'd gone soft."

"Rumours, princess, mere rumours."

They both laughed, then continued into the tunnel.

"Speaking of rumours, is it true that your insane bard started the riot in the jail?"

"Oh, yes," he said, rubbing his swollen head. "I've got this to prove it. Treacherous bastard."

"Well, his neck will soon be on the block. I knew there was something suspicious about him."

More than you know. "How's Tomos?"

"Not good. I've never seen him as bad as this. What makes things worse is what Father did to him—he's heartbroken. I actually feel pity for my irritating little brother."

"I hope I'm not keeping you away from him?"

"No, it's fine. Uncle Kurzon, Yanna and I are taking turns to watch over him."

"Really? Have you and your uncle made peace?"

"Hmm...I don't know about that; but we're trying our best, under the circumstances."

Luis nodded. "I'm pleased about that. Goddess forbid something bad happens to your father, but if it did, your uncle's vote at the Council of Clans would be vital for you to become queen."

"That's what Father said."

"He's right. He might not seem it, with all his pious words and deeds, but Kurzon can be ruthless when he needs to be—ask the children of the miners who were massacred at Belith. Don't underestimate him."

"I won't." She patted the horse's flank, reassuring it as they pushed deeper into the tunnel. "So," she said, looking up at him. "Now that you're here, where will you go first?"

Chuckling, he said, "I think I'd like to stay in here."

"What, stay in the tunnel?"

"Anything's better than riding in that accursed heat. The air's so cool down here."

"You can thank my brother for that."

"Indeed." He stared at the huge timber cap of yew supporting the weight of the earth above their heads. "I knew Tomos was clever, but if half of what I've heard is true, he's a bloody genius."

"It's all true, and the little runt knows it."

"Jealous, princess?"

"Of him? No; but I think he is of me. He'd give anything to become a warrior."

"It must be devastating for him to know that it'll never happen."

"He needs to stop whinging and get on with his life—something I need to do too."

Luis turned to her and arched his eyebrows. "It sounds like you're coming to your senses."

"Well," she said, shrugging. "After Father made me stay behind, I've had plenty of time to think about things."

"And he said nothing about your role here at the fortress, did he?"

Seren frowned. "What are you getting at, you wily old fox?"

"Less of the *old*. I doubt your father would mind if you were to act as my guide around the fortress. A lot has changed since I was here last. Perhaps you could advise me on how best to defend Keld?"

She scrunched her nose and cocked her head to the side. "Advise you? I thought you said you wouldn't even have me beside you in a shield wall?"

Luis winced. "I did, didn't I? So prove me wrong, your highness."

"Well, it is Yanna's turn to watch Tomos after Uncle Kurzon, so I suppose I could help."

"Excellent."

Seren stared straight ahead, but Luis knew she was grinning. He stifled a laugh.

"What's got into you?"

"Oh, I'm just wondering what you've done with Princess Piss Pot? Something's changed, and for the better."

"I-I don't know what you mean."

"Despite the fact that everyone thinks I'm either ancient or dead, I can still tell when someone's in love."

"I'm not in love, Master of War," she said, glaring up at him.

"What's the poor wretch's name? Do they know what they're letting themselves in for?"

"Any more impertinent questions about my personal life and I'll get those two numbskulls to shoot you in your good leg," she said, slapping his mount's rump.

As his horse set off at a gallop towards the light of the exit, Luis allowed himself a moment of reflection. *I promised you, Isabelle, that I'd look out for her. She's had a rough ride, but I think she's going to make it. She'll make you proud.*

Not long after, they emerged out of the tunnel and veered to the left of the Great Hall. As they passed between the largest building in Keld and the drill field, where rows of unoccupied shelters blanketed the ground, Luis recalled what Grimbard had revealed about the attack on Nabaya. He pulled on the reins, steering his horse to face the camp, and listened. Nothing he had said could be considered trustworthy; yet the silence within the refugee camp declared to Luis that Grimbard's belief that the Mendari pursued and killed all that tried to escape north was the truth. "I was so sorry to hear about Lady Amira and her escort."

Seren did not reply. She crouched to the ground and stabbed her knife repeatedly into a tuft of grass until it finally pulled away from the soil. She rotated her blade to examine the roots, before casually flicking it away. "You know, I'd do anything to bring Amira back to Yanna. Anything."

"It's been two days," he said, beginning to piece together Seren's newfound optimism. "It seems more likely that they shared the same fate as the poor souls who would've occupied those tents." He swept his arm across the drill field.

"For dear Yanna's sake," she said, standing up. "I hope you're wrong."

"I hope I'm wrong for the thousand Named heading towards Vedana."

"Yes, of course.... What are your thoughts on the plan?"

"I'll be honest with you, Seren," he said, gently digging his heels into his horse's flank, guiding it back onto the path. "I'm inclined to agree with your uncle; but don't tell him I said so."

"What makes you think that?" she asked, catching him up.

"Why are there no survivors? It's as if the Mendari are doing everything they can to keep us in the dark about their strength and strategy."

"But surely the plan of using the Vanguard will draw Kaine out, revealing his numbers?"

"It could work; but it worries me how stretched they're making themselves. The plan relies on assuming that the Mendari are distracted with the siege, but what if Kaine's already taken Vedana? Derwedd Forest could be crawling with Mendari."

"Well, at least Yanna's plan brought the clans together. I agree it's risky, but surely you of all people know that any battle has an element of uncertainty—and we're talking about the Named. Nothing is a match for them."

"True...but that's not the only thing I'm worried about."

She caught hold of the reins and brought the horse to a stop. "What do you mean?"

"Your father's so determined to rush to Vedana and kill Kaine that I believe he'd stop at nothing to achieve that goal—even if it cost him his life and that of the Vanguard."

"Why would he do that?"

Luis reached down and gripped her arm. "Because he wants to protect his children."

"What aren't you telling me, Luis?"

He hesitated, remembering the sword-brother oath the three of them had sworn thirty-four years ago. "All I can tell you is that there are things hidden in your Father's past that if revealed could put Tomos and you in grave danger."

"What things?"

"I swore an oath to your father never to tell a soul, and I mean to keep that promise."

Seren fell silent. She pressed her feet into a patch of mud, leaving behind a perfect footprint that would harden in the afternoon heat of the Twins. "When we had dinner last night, I knew something worried him."

"Yes—and that's why he had no choice but to leave Tomos. I just hope his determination to meet Kaine doesn't turn into blind rage."

"The Red Mist?"

"Yes. Did he ever tell you about the time the Red Mist took him?"

She rolled her eyes at him. "As if he'd open up to me about something like that."

"It happened at the Battle of Lake Grimlin. The water turned thick with blood that day, as the Mendari bodies piled up around Shieldbane. I, myself, have never experienced the Red Mist, but watching your father carve through countless enemies, I understood what the bards meant when they spoke of a warrior weaving their deadly dance of death."

Seren lowered her eyes. "I think I've lived my whole life in a red mist, so I wouldn't know if I've ever truly experienced it."

"Believe me, Seren, you'd know."

"Is it true that the Red Mist steals a part of the soul each time it takes hold of you?"

Luis nodded. "And each part is replaced by an insatiable yearning to delve deeper into the dance until only darkness remains."

"Like you become a slave to it?"

"It seems most likely with your father. Even after all the Mendari lay slain around him, he begged for more. He even begged his own men to dance with him."

"That's terrible. Is there no way to control it?"

"Even the Named, who train for years to control it, are mere amateurs compared to the one man living who bends the dance to his will."

"Grimbard?"

"Yes, Grimbard. There'll never be a more skilful artist of combat to stand on the battlefields of Tarania."

"I would still face him after what he did to my family," said Seren, sneering into the distance. "I dream of it often."

I hope you never find out how close you were to fulfilling your dreams.

Nearing the far end of the drill field, the pair turned right and joined the road that ran through the central area of the fortress. To their right, the clansguard barracks had been supplemented with enough tents to house the thousand warriors now stationed within the walls. With the same number of Named with the king, the remaining three thousand clansguard waited at the camp to the north of the fortress, ready to be deployed should the need arise. Laid out in a line on the opposite side of the road were the administrative buildings. Beyond them, the armoury, smiths, stables and equipment stores could be found.

At one such store, a group of engineers loaded several large spherical objects onto a cart. Luis paused to watch them, fascinated by the level of concentration displayed on their faces. Whatever was inside the animal-skin-covered balls, he deduced, scared them. He had heard rumours that Tomos had been helping Master Engineer Gwen develop a range of deadly projectiles and a new catapult to hurl them. As a general rule, Luis preferred to use siege engines against a fortified position. He would have to see for himself if their inventions could change his mind.

"You know what the engineers call those balls?" asked Seren, shielding her eyes from the intense light of the Twins.

He flashed her a boyish grin. "Knowing engineers, something crude."

Seren groaned. "I'm serious. It's almost like they revere them. They call them godsbreath."

"Godsbreath? As in the tales of the battles between Enora and Velak?"

She nodded. "If Tomos were here, he'd smugly quote the whole passage." She stretched her arms out wide as if she were a bard in mid-flow. "Where Velak and the First unleash their streaks of fiery death upon the Hen Rai."

Luis cleared his throat. "And how, after giving himself to Enora, did Velak's Master of War and sword brother, turn against the dark one and sacrifice himself by setting fire to the sky to destroy the power of the First'."

Seren's jaw dropped. "And I thought Grimbard was the orator out of the three of you?"

"That's how Treharne's warden used to read passages from the Book of Enora. She might have been frail in body, but her voice was something to behold."

"Do you believe that it really happened? The Final Battle?"

Luis pulled his fingers through his moustache in thought. "Personally, I think it's all a metaphor for what was most likely years of bloody wars between the two religions. We create gods, goddesses, demons and sorcery to control the population and make sense of what we can't explain. That's between you and me. The Communion take a dim view of such theories."

"Your secret's safe with me, Master of War," said Seren, winking at him. "Actually, I agree with you. I don't have time for the notion of gods and goddesses, but I sometimes wonder if Enora, Gaius Galerius and Velak really existed."

"Perhaps they did," he said, taking one last look of the engineers loading the godsbreath balls. "Do you think Tomos' creations will keep the Mendari at bay?"

"From what he's told me about them, absolutely."

"Come on," said Luis, encouraging his horse forward. "I really need to see these in action."

42

A GIFT FROM A GOD

"Are you sure you're all right in there?"

"For the third time, yes."

"There's no need to get cross with me, Tomos. I'm only thinking about you."

"I know, but I'm feeling so much better since..."

"Since?"

"Oh, never mind." *Can't a man empty his bowels in peace?*

"I just wanted to let you know your aunt is on her way. If you need me, I'll be on the South Wall Battlements finding out how that fool, Ironfoot, managed to allow a full-scale riot in his jail."

"You really don't like him, do you, Uncle Kurzon?"

"No, I certainly do not—especially his unwavering compassion for the lower castes. It won't be the first time he's failed to take a hard stance on them to protect the kingdom."

Don't you mean the Communion and their antiquated caste system? "I'm sure you'll be able to find a solution that's agreeable to both of you."

"Humph. I doubt it."

Nothing good will come from that confrontation. Tomos listened to his uncle's footsteps trail off before hearing the bedchamber door slam shut. He eased off the wooden board and cleaned his rear with a handful of hay. "Ah! That's bloody sore." *Well, at least I'm not shitting in my own bed anymore.* Dropping the soiled hay into the circular hole cut out of the solid plank of wood, he shuffled to a basin of freshly poured water and stared at his reflection in the mirror on the wall. *That's odd.* He leaned in closer to get a better look and rubbed his jaw, twisting his head to view both sides. *Never seen that before.* He pulled back and squeezed his shoulders, noticing how firm they were. The door to the bedchamber opened and then closed. *Must be Aunt Yanna.* He washed his hands and reached for his robe. Tying it loosely around his body, he opened the door leading to his bedchamber. "Good afternoon, Aunt Ya—"

He froze to the spot, unable to speak, his mind whirling, his stomach churning, barely managing to look at her piercing blue eyes for more than the briefest of moments. "K-Kaitlyn?"

"Hello, Tomos." She stood in the middle of the room wearing a red woollen robe, embroidered with an endless looping pattern of gold thread that decorated the hem of the garment. Her long brunette locks trailed down her shoulders, stopping just short of her waist.

"Y-you can't be in here. They'll catch you."

"No, Tomos, they won't. I've got friends in high places now."

"Who?"

"It doesn't matter who they are, just that they made sure we won't be disturbed."

He stared, wide-eyed, as she bit her lip and edged closer to him— each mesmeric step stoking the embers of his desire for her, almost extinguished by his illness and his father's betrayal. "I-I don't understand."

"It's very simple, Tomos," she said, stopping a hair's breadth from his awakening body. "I have a message for you."

"What message?"

Her eyelashes fluttered and the corners of her mouth curled up into a sensuous smile. She leaned in close, allowing her breast to brush past his chest, and sent a shivering wave of pleasure across his skin.

"The message is in two parts," she said, caressing his earlobe with her lips, her breathing slow and steady, in total contrast to Tomos'.

He inhaled her luxurious scent, picturing the rose beds of the royal gardens in Caerniras on a warm summer's day.

Then, with the lightest of touches, she slipped a note into the pocket of his robe. "That's the first part. Read it once I've left."

"A-and the second?"

She drew back to face him. "He offers you a gift to prove to you he can grant you your deepest desires. I am that gift."

"He sent you?"

Keeping her eyes on him, she untied the bow that fastened her robe and allowed the garment to slip off her shoulders and fall to the floor.

"Oh, Kaitlyn," he said, casting his gaze to where her clothing had fallen.

"Don't be shy, my prince," she said softly, eyeing the bulge forming under his robe. She approached him, running her fingers across his brow and down his cheek. Stopping under his chin, she gently lifted his head to allow his eyes to feast on her nakedness. "I never realised you had such strong features."

"N-nor did I until today."

"I wonder what else has changed?" She slid her other hand between the folds of his robe and stroked the length of his erection. Her eyes widened. "Aren't you full of surprises?"

"W-what are you doing?"

"Why? Don't you like it, my prince?" she asked, raking her nails across his exposed flesh.

"Stop it," he rasped, pushing her away. "And stop calling me that. I don't care if you're his gift. You're not that kind of girl."

Kaitlyn's sultry expression melted away in an instant. She ripped her robe off the floor and ran into the privy, slamming the door behind her. From within, she sobbed.

Tomos pulled his robe tight around him, unsettled by the turmoil of desires affecting his body and mind. He sat on the bed, head in his hands, and groaned. "Velak's balls—and I hope you bloody well heard that."

After a few minutes, Kaitlyn emerged, fully clothed. Her icy-blue eyes, usually so vibrant, were now bloodshot and swollen. Silently, she walked to his bedchamber door and straightened her robe. She paused and looked at him, wringing her hands. "You'll probably never see me again, your highness."

"Why?"

"She'll punish me for this...or make me do something far worse."

"Who will?"

"If I gave away her identity, my family would be in great danger. Just make sure you read the note. At least I got that right."

"Wait. Just tell her you did everything you were supposed to do."

"She'll know I'm lying," she said, lowering her eyes. "Women know such things."

"Well, what else can you do?"

"Nothing—apart from actually going through with it."

"We could," he said, reddening. "I-if you wanted to?"

"I thought you didn't want me?"

"I've wanted you since the first day I laid eyes on you, but not as a gift from *him*. I hate the thought of you being made to do something like this—it makes my blood boil."

She smiled and sat beside him on the bed. "If you knew the truth, you'd call the guards and have me arrested."

"No, I wouldn't."

"Yes, you would, Tomos." She kissed him on the cheek, stood and walked to the door.

"Will I ever see you again?"

"I don't know. Just remember to read the note. And if you really feel the way you do about me, say nothing of this to anyone. Otherwise, she'll find out and bad things will happen."

"I won't tell a soul."

"Goodbye, Prince Tomos."

As the door closed behind her, Tomos rubbed his forehead, trying to work out what had just taken place. Everything about it was wrong. Who was the woman who had so much control over Kaitlyn? Was she really working for Velak? Common decency implored him to be wary of anyone who would use a young girl like that; but what if Velak could make him well? Was it worth the risk? *The note.* He rummaged through his pocket until he found it. Unfolding it, he read it aloud.

> "As the night watch begin their duty, the Pathfinder will be waiting for you at the inner gate of the North Tunnel. From there, make your way to the outer gatehouse where you'll be provided with your means of escape and the start of your new life."

Slipping the note back into his pocket, he shook his head and sighed. *I can't even take a shit without feeling faint. How in the goddess' name am I going to walk to the gatehouse, let alone embark on a journey to who-knows-where?* He checked the bamboo clock and knitted his brows. *That's strange—it's almost an hour since the last episode.*

The door creaking open broke his concentration.

Velak's balls—Aunt Yanna. He dived into bed, pulled the covers over himself and closed his eyes. He heard her light footsteps draw close to the bed.

"Get strong, my special nephew—I see great things ahead of you."

At least someone believes in me.

43

THE EYES OF THE TRAITOR

Seren lounged against a large mound of straw, allowing the warm springtime breeze to caress her bared skin. She broke off a stalk and idly chewed on it, waiting for her companion to join her. Eventually, Luis appeared from around the corner of the thatcher's workshop, red-faced and panting.

"Some guide you are."

"Well, you will insist on speaking to every person you meet."

He came up beside her, sagged into the flaxen stack and took a moment to recover. "I make it my primary task before a battle. I look each warrior in the eye and thank them for their service and offer them Enora's blessing."

"I thought you didn't believe?"

"No, I don't; but many of them do. They want to be sure that if they fall to a Mendari blade, they'll pass through the Veil and find themselves as a new light in the Void—a Child of Enora."

"If it's that important, why isn't the Communion here to do it?"

"Another thing you missed in your studies?" he asked, frowning at her. "Your father stopped the practice at the end of the Mendari War."

"Why?"

"When your father made the decision to accept the Mendari surrender, the Communion spoke out against it and turned many clansguard against the king. As you can imagine, Rodric came down hard on any form of dissent, expelling those unwilling to conform from the Clansguard Caste."

"Goddess. I didn't know that. What happened to them?"

"Some roamed the lands offering their swords for coin; others drank themselves into an early grave. Many, however, turned to the Communion and enlisted into the Grey Cloaks."

Seren spat on the ground. "When I'm queen, I'll disband every barrack of their fanatical order."

"No, you won't."

"Velak's balls, I won't!"

"You won't because if you do, you'll lose your uncle's support, and if that happens, you'll lose the other clans."

"They wouldn't dare."

He lifted his coat of mail and searched inside his gambeson pocket until he pulled out a sofran. Flipping it across to her, Seren plucked it out of the air.

"Very generous of you, but I get the feeling you're about to lecture me."

"Someone needs to," he said. "It's all about coin, Seren. Take Kurzon's fiercest opponent in the Council of Clans, Sorcha. The Galgari and Zirani were squabbling for years until your father united the clans. It doesn't take a discerning person to see the enmity between the chieftains. Yet if you try to move against the Grey Cloaks, Sorcha wouldn't think twice about siding with your uncle."

"Why would she do that if she dislikes him so much?"

"For two reasons. First, even though she respects your father more than she distrusts Kurzon, you have yet to earn her trust; and more importantly, Zirani coin keeps the Mines of Belith working. The Galgari rely on the mines as much as they do on the sea to prosper. She won't risk losing his money, or even worse, having to sell the mines to him."

Seren lashed out at a clod of earth with her foot, sending a powdery cloud up into the air. "What's the point of being queen if you have to bend to the wishes of your chieftains?"

Luis snorted. "Why do you think there's only been a handful of noteworthy monarchs throughout the history of Northern Tarania?"

She remained quiet for a moment, then shifted her position to face Luis. "It's clear to me I need people around me who'll give me sound, honest advice—people like you." She reached out and held his hand. "Thank you for everything you've done for me."

He reddened and looked away from her. "You don't need to thank me, your highness." He released her grip and reached down to rub his stump. "Come on, I'm seizing up, and I really want to see those siege engines." He stared up at the battlements. "I suppose there's no easy way to get up there?"

"We can either use the gatehouse stairs, or we can use the ramps."

"Which one's quicker?"

Seren pushed off the mound and turned towards the South Wall. Casually teasing the ends of a braid that had unravelled, she considered which route would be less arduous for Luis. She concluded that the steep steps of the gatehouse would likely be more of a hindrance to him—not that she dared say that to the fiercely independent veteran. "Probably the ramps."

"I knew you were going to say that."

Either side of the tunnel rose a broad slope that led up to the siege engine placements and battlements. On the one nearest to them, a team of horses laboured to haul one of Tomos' behemoth siege engines up onto the platforms.

Luis slowed his pace and tugged on his ear. "Perhaps we should use the other ramp? I don't fancy that thing rolling down on top of me."

"Well, at least one part of your body wouldn't get crushed."

"Ah, I wondered where Princess Piss Pot had gone."

She punched him half-heartedly in the arm. "Don't worry, she's still here, old man."

"If someone else says *old, bloody, man*," he scoffed, reaching the bottom of the slope. "I can still whip your skinny arse, my girl."

"Prove it," she said, sprinting past him, slapping his rear with the flat of her sword.

"You cheeky little—"

279

As Seren reached the top of the slope, she turned, hands on hips, and grinned from ear to ear. "Hurry up, oh great Master of War, or the battle will be over before you get to the top." Luis said nothing. She saw his laboured movements—more of an awkward skip than a run. Her grin faded, watching in awe, as Luis, with gritted teeth and tortured face, faltered towards her. *No wonder warriors follow you.*

As he arrived at the top, Luis collapsed onto the ground, wheezing. "That's going to hurt later on," he said, rubbing his stump.

"At least you've got one good leg."

He stopped what he was doing and peered up at her. "You know, I've heard that saying before."

"I'm sure you've heard all sorts of insults, Luis."

"Oh, yes. I could fill a book with them; but like you, she never meant it in a bad way."

"She?"

"Yes...your mother."

"Oh, I didn't know that," she said, holding her hand out to pull him off the floor. "It seems like you were close to her."

"Rodric never told you?"

She shrugged. "What do you think?"

"I loved your mother very much. She was a sister to me in every way but blood." Reaching into his pocket, he pulled out his pipe and favourite leaf. He struck his lighter a few times, but the wind up on the battlements quickly dispersed the sparks.

"Here, let me help." Seren cupped her hands around the flint block.

"Thanks," he said, finally lighting the contents of the bowl. He drew in some smoke, leaned on the battlement wall overlooking the interior of the fortress, and released the fumes into the air. "In those early days, the four of us were inseparable. Your father and mother, me, and...well, you know who else."

"Makes his betrayal all the more painful." Walking up beside him, knife in hand, she began to scratch a picture into a patch of yellow lichen growing on a large block of dressed stone. She smiled as she noticed Luis watching her out of the corner of his eye. Eventually, she blew on the stone, revealing a pair of oval eyes staring up at her. "What do you think?"

He stared straight ahead.

"Aren't you curious about what it is? Look."

He glanced at it. "Not really."

She frowned. "What's got into you?"

Luis shrugged.

"You're no fun at all," she said, scrunching her nose at him. "They're the eyes of your bard. Since that night in the jail, I haven't been able to stop thinking about them. I've never seen eyes that colour before."

"Oh, I don't know," said Luis, tapping his pipe upside down against the ledge of the wall. "Amber eyes are common outside of Northern Tarania."

"I didn't know that."

"Why would you? You've never been further south than Vedana."

"Princess Seren, War Master Ironfoot."

The pair turned to see Gwen, Rodric's Master Engineer, head across the battlements towards them.

"By the goddess, Gwen. How long has it been?" asked Luis, throwing his arms around her.

"Too long, my friend. I couldn't believe it when the young prince told me you'd become Belanore's sheriff. How did that happen?"

"It's a long story that I'll tell you one day over a pint of Red. How's Callum? I haven't seen him since...Belith."

"The incident at the mines changed him," she said, flicking her eyes towards the princess. "He's mostly working away these days. At least I've got my Kaitlyn."

"Oh, yes. How is she after that business at the tavern?"

"She doesn't tell me much. I assume she's feeling better as she left the house early this morning." Gwen sighed. "That girl. I try my best to bring her up right, but she's a free spirit." She faced Seren and swallowed. "Your highness, I can't believe that she lured your poor brother into that terrible place. Please pass on my sincere apologies to the prince and the king."

"I don't think my brother needed much persuading," said Seren, grinning. "Kaitlyn's a beautiful girl—the image of her mother."

"That may well be the case, your highness, but it doesn't excuse her behaviour." Seren turned to find Uncle Kurzon striding up the slope towards her. "The only thing the king or the prince requires of you, Gwen of the Skilled Caste, is to keep that girl in her place...or I'll get someone to do it for you."

"Velak's balls! You can't help yourself, can you?" said Luis, stepping towards Kurzon.

"No," said Seren, pulling him back by the arm. "Leave it."

"And how's the Archwarden? Are you still licking her arse?"

"Tread carefully, Ironfoot. The Communion is not as weak as you'd like to think." Kurzon paused, looking out in the direction of Belanore. "How you think you'll be able to cope with the Mendari when you can't even prevent a riot in your own jail is beyond me."

"I'm sure the riot's been dealt with by now."

"Really? That's not what I heard. I heard that the whole of Belanore is in an uproar and your clansguard are unable to contain it."

Luis' face flushed crimson. "Who told you that?"

"Someone who knows how to deal with the lower castes when they forget their place."

Luis edged closer to Kurzon. "Who?"

"Warden Elgar."

Luis clenched his fists and glared at him. "You have no authority to use the Grey Cloaks against the common people."

"I do when their actions directly threaten the Grove of the Goddess. I thought you'd be grateful—one less blunder to clear up."

"My clansguard are trained to use non-lethal methods to deal with the townspeople. If your Grey Cloaks march out fully armed, the town will resist. It'll be another Belith."

"Good. Then there'll be less treasonous scum to worry about."

"You bastard."

Ignoring Luis, Kurzon addressed Seren. "I tried my best to convince your father to allow me to choose someone else to command the fortress, but his ties with his sword brothers still run deep. How he could allow him to regain his position is beyond me; but then again, your father allowed that reptilian-eyed traitor to walk away free."

"Reptilian?"

"Yes. Grimbard's amber eyes. Extremely rare and never forgotten. Just like the cold-blooded eyes of a snake ready to strike."

Seren rounded on Luis. "You lying, conniving bastard! No wonder you reacted the way you did to the bard in the jail. It was him —Grimbard."

Luis blanched. "Please, Seren, I can explain." He reached out his hand to her.

"Don't touch me." She spun around and marched towards the slope. Halfway down, Luis' sweaty bald head appeared above her.

"Where're you going?"

"Where'd you think? Belanore."

"You can't go there. If you find him and provoke him, there's no telling what he'll do to you."

She paused and looked up at him, her face a mixture of betrayal and anger. "Stay away from me. I never want to see you again."

Luis stared at the last place Seren had been visible before he lost her in the hubbub of the central area of the fortress. *Oh, no—what've I done?*

"So let me get this right," said Kurzon, joining him beside the wall. "Not only did you allow a riot in your jail, but harboured your traitorous sword brother in the cell next to my niece? You've gone too far this time. The king will be furious."

"No, he won't. He already knows."

Kurzon snorted. "Why does that not surprise me?"

"What was I supposed to do?" said Luis. "He said he had vital information about the Mendari and would only speak to Rodric."

"What information?"

"A far-fetched story of unbeatable warriors and of an invisible creature that steals children. All lies."

"Do you think he's working for the Mendari or acting on his own?"

"I don't know; but he's lived a long time in the South, so anything's possible. She cannot be allowed to face him." Luis punched the palm of his hand and beckoned the nearest clansguard to him. "Instruct all clansguard that Princess Seren must not be allowed to leave the fortress. She's to be escorted back to the Great Hall and not allowed out for any reason. Let her sit with the prince."

"And tell Lady Yanna to speak to her," said Kurzon. "It seems my wife is the only one who can reason with her."

As the clansguard rushed off to carry out her orders, Luis pushed off the wall and turned to face a sheepish-faced Gwen. "Well, what are you waiting for? Show me your new weapons."

"Oh, of course, War Master. Please, follow me."

As Gwen scuttled off towards one of the new catapults, Kurzon grabbed hold of Luis' arm to hold him back. "Once the battle's over, I'll take this up with the Archwarden."

Luis wrenched his arm away from Kurzon's firm grip. "Do what you want, Zirani, but perhaps we should win the battle first?"

Without another word to each other, they neared the closest of the four siege engine platforms. "Well, apart from the obvious fact that they're much bigger than a standard catapult, what's so special about these?"

Gwen beamed. "It's a beauty, isn't it?"

"If you say so. So how does it work? And keep it simple—I know what you engineers are like."

"Of course, War Master. You see the treadwheels?"

Luis nodded.

"Well, a team of engineers run inside them to lift the counterweight," she said, pointing to a massive block attached to one end of a long beam suspended in the air.

"I see—and the other end of that beam has a sling on the end of it?"

"Yes, that's right. We attach a projectile to the sling and then release the brake, holding the counterweight in place. The beam is rotated by the force of the falling counterweight, whipping the sling and the projectile towards the target, doubling the distance of the older engines."

"Impressive. How long does it take to reload?"

"About ten minutes."

"That's too long—it needs to be faster. The Mendari aren't going to wait on the plain while you take your time to reload."

"I'll see what I can do, but some of the new projectiles that we've designed have to be handled with care."

"Yes, I saw some godsbreath being loaded onto a cart. I wouldn't want to be in those engineers' boots."

"It's not just the Warrior Caste that put their lives at risk during a battle," said Gwen, flicking her eyes towards Kurzon.

"Can I have a demonstration?"

"Of course, War Master. It would be my pleasure. The catapult's ready, we just need to load the projectile."

"I want to see what a godsbreath can do."

"But War Master, we have a limited supply. Perhaps a different kind?"

"No. I want to see godsbreath. Load it up."

"Yes, War Master," said Gwen, turning to the engine's team to give them their orders.

Kurzon sidled up to Luis. "You see what happens when they get too friendly? They question your orders. That's a slippery slope, Master of War."

Luis refused to take the bait and focused his attention on the siege engine. *If these beasts can keep the Mendari further away from the walls, perhaps I could form the main army on the other side of the Valtara? The remaining Woodland bows and higher-powered crossbows would still have the range to provide cover, even across the river. Hmm...I wonder?* "So do these things have a name?"

"Soulstealers," she said, keeping her attention on the massive machine. "They're called soulstealers."

"Who came up with that name?"

"Who do you think?"

"That boy and his books," said Luis, chuckling. "Are you ready?"

"Yes, War Master." She raised her arm into the air. "On my command."

Just as she was about to lower her arm, a guard in the outer gatehouse shouted, "Rider approaching!"

Curious, Luis made his way to the edge of the wall and scanned his eyes over the plain to locate the rider.

"Are they one of our warriors?" asked Kurzon, joining him.

"They're a warrior for sure, but not one I was expecting to see," said Ironfoot, discovering the colour of the rider's plaid. "He's Taleni. Someone made it out of Vedana alive."

44

ENEMY AT THE GATES

Cai's eyes darted across the South Wall Battlements, counting over a dozen crossbows trained on him. *This is a mistake. They'll fill me with bolts for sure.*

"Lower the drawbridge and open the gates. He's Taleni," boomed a commanding voice somewhere above him.

He let out a sigh of relief and pulled up on the reins, waiting for the drawbridge to lower.

Ever since leaving Vedana, Cai had been on edge, especially during his journey through the forest. He had barely ridden across Midway Bridge before the sounds of riders heading south had passed his hidden position within the mist. More than once, he could have sworn that he witnessed the faces of his dead comrades scowling at him within the swirling tendrils of dense cloud. If he could have galloped through the undergrowth, he would have, but the thought of riding into one of Derwedd's fathomless tar pools forced him to endure the scornful reproach of the dead. After all, it was what he deserved after the betrayal of his chieftain and his king.

He stirred out of his introspection as the hulking mass of the South Gate Drawbridge creaked and groaned, lowering itself across the final third section of the crossing, until the vast wooden deck came to a halt in its horizontal resting place.

Cai swallowed hard, still in two minds whether to spin his horse around and flee to some distant backwater village and see out the war in total anonymity; but Amira's face appeared within his mind, and he knew he had only one choice. He coaxed his mount onto the bridge and made his way over each section until he reached the raised portcullis gate and the oppressive South Tunnel. As he urged his horse into the gloom, the gatehouse chains took the strain of the massive weight of the drawbridge, heaving it back to its upright position. *There's no going back now.*

After a few minutes, he emerged into the open air and was immediately surrounded by a detachment of clansguard. Standing in the middle were two men. Cai recognised the taller and younger of the two from his gold-plated scale armour, emblazoned with a hawk and the four-colour plaid cloak that hung over his shoulders. *Lord Zirani.*

The other man appeared dull and tired, standing beside his dazzling companion, with his battered, patched-up mail shirt, plain cloak and braccae. The afternoon light of the Twins reflected off his bald head and, from his awkward stance, he likely carried an injury.

Both men appraised him with a look that reminded him of Lord Taleni. The kind of look that gave you the unpleasant feeling that all your secrets were known to them. He remembered his manners and dismounted, kneeling to the floor.

"No need for any formalities, clansguard," said Lord Zirani. "War Master Ironfoot and I are more interested in what news you bring of Lord Taleni and his younger daughter, Lady Amira."

"War Master Ironfoot," said Cai, standing to attention. "Swordstorm told me so much about you."

"Hmm," said Ironfoot, folding his arms. "How about you tell us your name and what happened to you?"

"Yes, sir. My name is Cai, adopted son of Alun Swordstorm...or at least I was."

"Swordstorm's dead?

"Yes, War Master," said Cai, fighting back the tears. "Kaine killed him."

"I'll make that bastard pay for everything he's done."

288

Not if I get to him first.

"Why don't you start at the beginning," said Lord Zirani. "And don't spare the details."

"Yes, lord." Cai gave his account of everything that took place since leaving Vedana with Lady Amira until he revealed what happened to Lord Taleni during the night. He left out the part where he slit his own lord's throat.

"So even Aedan 'the Defiant' couldn't hold back Kaine's horde," said Lord Zirani. "Which means we have to assume that the king and the Named will find the Mendari safe behind the walls of Vedana."

"Or that they're sweeping north and have already engaged our forces."

"By the goddess, I hope you're wrong."

"Which is why I want to mobilise the rearguard and form up on the south side of the Valtara. If the soulstealers have as much range as Gwen claims, then we can pulverise the Mendari before annihilating them with our superior infantry and cavalry, supported by our ranged units from the walls. It's our only way of ensuring a safe path back for the king and the Vanguard...if they survived."

"I don't know, Ironfoot. It's a considerable risk sending all of our warriors out onto the plain."

"If we can't stop them here, then we'll never stop them. We have to hit them with everything we've got."

"Well, if I was in command, I'd keep them back." Lord Zirani returned his attention to Cai. "And what of the Communion and the Sacred Grove?"

Cai lowered his eyes as the pungent smell of charred bodies resurfaced within his mind. "Kaine sacrificed the wardens and the Grey Cloaks in the Great Hall courtyard and destroyed the Sacred Grove."

The Zirani chieftain bowed his head, closed his eyes and mouthed a prayer to the goddess. He looked up and wiped a tear away. "I knew many of the faithful of Vedana."

"Are you surprised?" said Ironfoot. "That's why we need to stop him here before that scene repeats itself all across Northern Tarania."

Lord Zirani nodded, straightened his attire, and addressed Cai.

"What happened to Lady Amira? Did she share the same fate as her dear father?"

"No, lord—she's alive."

Ironfoot eyed Cai. "She's alive? So why didn't she escape with you?"

Cai's heart pounded; his life depended on the reaction he would get from what he would say next. "I-I didn't escape, War Master."

In one swift movement, Ironfoot levelled his sword at Cai's neck. "What?"

"P-please, I can explain," said Cai, faltering. "I was released by Kaine. He gave me a letter for Lady Yanna Zirani concerning her sister and was told to deliver it to her personally."

"Velak's balls, you will!"

"Calm down, Ironfoot. The lad's been through enough without you terrorising him."

"You've got a short memory," hissed Ironfoot. "You know the Mendari are known for their tactic of assassinating nobles. How do we know this boy isn't going to slit you or your wife's throat the minute he gets a chance?"

"Sir, I'd never—"

"Don't even breathe, son." He nodded to two of the detachment. "Search his horse, then search him."

"I suppose it's better to be cautious," said Lord Zirani. "It's a pity you weren't like this with Grimbard."

"Grimbard? My father's friend?"

"Never you mind," said Ironfoot, narrowing his eyes at Cai. "I don't know what it is, but something's not right about you."

"I-I've got nothing to hide, War Master."

"Well, even if you did, we'd find it, one way or another."

Cai paled at the thought of the 'other' way.

After a few minutes of searching, one of the clansguard handed Ironfoot a sealed letter. "This is it?"

Cai nodded.

"Sir, we also found this." The warrior held Boar's Rage out to him.

Ironfoot's face darkened as he sheathed his own sword and took hold of Swordstorm's blade, holding it aloft. "One of the greatest swords ever made; but you already knew that, didn't you? Such a treasure could make a man turn against his own."

"I-I already have a sword."

"Doesn't stop you from selling this one for a fortune."

Lord Zirani coughed. "The letter?"

"Perhaps you should read it first?" said Ironfoot, handing it to the chieftain.

"Goddess, no. Yanna would never forgive me if I did," he said, turning to make his way back to the Great Hall.

"What shall I do with the boy?"

"I thought you were a sheriff? Hold him and see what else you can find out."

Irritated, Ironfoot mouthed a curse towards the departing chieftain, then signalled to the most senior clansguard in attendance. "Take the boy to one of the storerooms and keep him under guard. No rough stuff...yet."

"You can't do this. I'm Taleni," said Cai, as two burly clansguard gripped him by his arms.

Ironfoot slapped Cai on the shoulder and looked him dead in the eye. "And that's about the only truth you've said since you've arrived. Take him away."

Cai sagged his shoulders in defeat. He was doomed if he told the truth and doomed if he lied. So, with nothing to lose, he did something he thought he'd never do—he prayed to Velak. He prayed that the god would deliver him out of this mess and allow him to complete his mission. The only thing that mattered to him in this horrid world was Amira.

45

A FAVOUR FOR A FRIEND

"Let me out, you bastards!" yelled Seren. She beat against Tomos' bedchamber door until her palms ached. "I'll have your heads for this." She slumped onto the solid wooden surface and wept. "Why won't they let me have my vengeance?" A delicate, reassuring hand rested on her back. If anyone else had touched her, they would have regretted it in an instant, but not her.

"The guards are only following orders," said Yanna. "Your uncle and Ironfoot are thinking of your well-being."

"If they were, then they'd let me go. They don't understand what it's like to constantly dream of taking your revenge on your enemy, just to wake up and realise that they're still out there, alive." She flicked her hair off her face in annoyance, only to curse when it fell back over her eyes.

"Let me help." Yanna untied the offending plait of flaxen hair that had unravelled from her fury. "I'll have this sorted in no time."

Seren remained silent, except for the occasional sob escaping. The repetitive weaving combined with Yanna's firm yet comforting grip allayed her rage, if not her profound sense of injustice. No-one, not even her personal servant, Carys, was permitted to touch her hair. She might not have remembered her mother plaiting her locks, but the instant anyone came close to her, an overwhelming surge of loss would engulf her. But this time it was different.

"There. All sorted," said Yanna, resting her hands on Seren's shoulders.

"Thank you." She reached back and squeezed her hand. "You're so kind to me."

Yanna kissed the back of her head. "You know, you're not the only one who misses your mother. Kurzon often cries out in his sleep for his sister."

"I-I didn't know that."

"It's true. Losing Isabelle haunts his sleep, even to this day."

"Well, if it does," she said, sniffling. "Why doesn't *he* go after him?"

"For the same reason he won't allow you to go: he fears him."

Weakly, Seren punched the door. "But I may never have a chance like this again."

"Please, Seren, don't go after Grimbard. Let the clansguard find him."

Twisting around to face her lover, she narrowed her focus on Yanna's pleading eyes. "But it should be me who stands against him."

"No. I don't want you to die." Yanna caught hold of Seren's face with her trembling hands, pressing her body in tight. "Don't you want to live now that we've found each other?"

Seren glanced across to Tomos lying in bed at the far side of the room.

"Don't worry about your brother. If he was going to wake, it would've been from your raging assault of the door," said Yanna, turning Seren's face back towards her. "Not even Velak could wake him."

"But what if he does? He'll see us like this."

"He won't." Yanna kissed her softly on the lips and eased her leg between her thighs.

Seren's lithe, powerful body quickened. "Stop it. I know what you're doing."

"And is it working?" mouthed Yanna, kissing her again, but with

293

greater ferocity. "I'd leave Kurzon and steal you away to some distant part of Tarania if it kept you from Grimbard."

"You'd do that for me?" gasped Seren, tilting her head back, allowing Yanna to run her moist, warm lips along her neck. She moaned, breathless from her love's lightest of touches.

"That," said Yanna, rubbing her thigh against Seren's aching mound. "And so, much, more."

The gates of Seren's heart flew wide open, unable to hold back the growing realisation of what was happening within. Her body trembled, sensing her braies cling to her inner thigh, saturated from her escalating excitement. The hatred for Grimbard, although ever present, gave way to other desires, other emotions, and her new obsession—Yanna. Once again, she fell under the spell of the woman before her. Running her fingers through Yanna's auburn locks, Seren uttered three words that welled up from within her soul. Three words she thought she would never say to another soul. "I love you."

"I love you, too," purred Yanna. She guided Seren's hands over her breasts and across her stomach, pushing them firmly between her thighs. "Touch me."

Frantically, Seren fumbled with the outer folds of Yanna's woollen dress until she found her chemise. She slipped her hands underneath and traced her fingers along her linen hose, up her calf, then over her knee until finally she whimpered with delight, reaching the warm nakedness of Yanna's soft inner thigh. Her pulse raced and her hand trembled, edging ever closer to Yanna's most intimate of places. She raked her nails across the last span of skin before pausing, biting her lip, her eyes widening.

"Stop teasing me," mouthed Yanna. She seized Seren's hand and thrust it tight between her legs.

"Yanna." Seren spun her around, rammed her hard into the door, pulled her dress off her shoulder and bit into her exposed, tender skin.

"Harder," Yanna hissed. "Don't hold back. Take your anger out on me."

Seren whimpered. Then, channelling all the years of pain and anger that had festered within the depths of her soul, she sank her teeth into Yanna's flesh.

Instead of reeling, or shoving her away, Yanna gripped Seren's head and held it firmly in place. Her body shuddered from the pain. "Harder."

"Open the door!"

Seren froze. "It's Kurzon."

As a guard turned the key, the pair scattered, urgently tidying their attire. The next moment, the door flew open and in stepped Kurzon, holding a sealed envelope in his hand.

"For the sake of the goddess, Kurzon," said Yanna, seething. "Show some compassion for your nephew."

"I'm sorry, but this is important. I've news for you." He looked at Yanna, then snapped his face towards Seren, snarling. "I swear, if you've laid one hand on Yanna because of your foul mood, I'll—"

"What in the goddess' name are you talking about, husband?"

"Look at yourselves. You've both got blood on you."

Seren wiped the blood from her mouth and watched in horror as Yanna placed her fingers against the crimson patch that had appeared against the pale blue woollen fabric of her dress.

"What have you done, Seren?"

Her expression darkened. She tensed her muscles, clenched her fists, and said, "None of your damn business."

"It *is* my business when it involves my wife," he said, squaring up to her.

"One of the guards accidentally elbowed her in the mouth when they brought her in."

Seren spun around to find Tomos sitting up in bed.

"Is that true, Seren?" asked Kurzon, flicking his eyes between her brother and her.

From behind Kurzon, Yanna widened her eyes at Seren.

"Y-yes."

Kurzon faced Yanna. "And what about the blood on your shoulder?"

"For the love of the goddess, husband. I comforted the poor girl.

She just found out she spent the night in jail with that traitor, Grimbard."

He turned to Tomos. "Is that right?"

Tomos nodded.

"If I—"

"Enough, Kurzon. Don't you think it's time you explained the reason for your rushed entrance?"

Kurzon sniffed, then nodded. "Yes, I suppose you're right. There's been a development."

"What do you mean, 'development'?" asked Yanna.

"I've news about Amira."

The colour drained from Yanna's face. "Have they found her? I-is she dead?"

"No. She's alive."

"Thank the goddess," said Yanna, sagging her shoulders in relief. But then she frowned, staring at the letter. "What's that in your hand?"

"A letter from Vedana, delivered by a young Taleni warrior."

"Someone survived?" asked Seren.

"In a manner of speaking," said Kurzon. He held the letter out towards Yanna. "It's addressed to you."

"For me? From whom?" she asked, taking the letter from her husband.

"Just open it."

"W-why won't you tell me who it's from?"

"It's from Kaine, isn't it?" said Tomos.

"Yes, it is."

Yanna's legs gave way. She crumpled to the floor, clutching the letter to her chest. Kurzon dashed to his wife's aid, kneeling beside her, and held out his hand. "I'll read it for you," he said, kissing her tenderly on the cheek.

Seren's eyes widened. She bit her lip and reached down to the hilt of her sword.

"Seren."

She ignored her brother, edging closer to Kurzon, the glint of steel appearing from out of the scabbard.

"Seren!"

She twisted towards Tomos, scowling. "What?"

"Come here...now."

With one last withering glare at Kurzon, she reluctantly walked across the room and stood beside Tomos' bed. "Well?"

"Come closer. I don't want to raise my voice."

She snorted, then knelt beside him and turned her ear towards his mouth.

"I just wanted you to know, your secret's safe with me."

She scrunched her face. "What secret?"

He nodded towards Yanna. "*That* secret."

"Velak's balls! How much did you see?"

"Let's just say I now know what lies under a lady's dress."

She cursed.

"And don't forget, I just lied for you."

She glanced over to the kneeling couple. "He doesn't deserve her."

"Maybe, but they're married, so there's nothing you can do about it."

"Well, when I'm queen—"

"When you're queen? You'd turn the Zirani and what's left of the Taleni against you, let alone endure the wrath of the Communion."

"I-I didn't think of that." For the second time that day, she grimaced at her naivety. She pulled back to look at him. "It's good to know you'll be there to do the thinking for me."

Tomos looked away.

"What's wrong?"

"I-I'm leaving."

"Leaving? What do you mean, you're leaving?"

"Shhhh," said Tomos, flicking his eyes towards Kurzon and Yanna. "Keep your voice down."

"You're only just recovering from a bout of fits that almost killed you." She prodded her finger against his head. "Did the illness damage your brain? Besides, you can't leave—you're a prince of Northern Tarania."

"Yes, I can," he said, slapping her hand away. "And you can't stop me."

"Velak's balls, I can't."

"You won't, or I'll reveal your little secret to Uncle Kurzon."

"You wouldn't dare," she said, through gritted teeth.

Tomos, with a glint in his eye, opened his mouth to speak. "Unc—"

She shoved her hand over his mouth. "Fine."

He flicked his brows. "I knew you'd see it my way."

Pulling her hand away, she asked, "Why, Tomos? Is it because of what Father did, or is it me?"

Tomos' expression darkened. "Father's abandonment certainly helped me see things clearly...but, in truth, you're also responsible for my decision."

His words cut deep. "Tomos, if—"

He reached out for Seren's hand and gripped it. "Listen to me. Goddess knows we argue a lot, but I want you to know, I'm proud of you, dear sister. A-and I envy you."

Seren shifted uneasily and played with the plait Yanna had repaired. "Why would you want to be like me? I'm a mess and a disgrace to Father. What's there to be proud of?"

"Isn't it obvious? You're a strong and fearless warrior. You live your life as you want to live it—not like some exotic pet that's cherished, but never allowed out of its cage."

"And look where it's got me?" she said, pulling her dagger out of her belt and peering into the reflection of her crooked, bruised nose. She noticed a remnant of Yanna's blood drying above her top lip. She flicked out her tongue and swallowed it. "If it weren't for her, I'd be just as caged up as you are."

Tomos shook his head and diverted his glazed eyes away from his sister.

"What have I said now?"

"Don't you understand? Ever since that night, I've been bound and fettered by the good intentions of those around me. Father obeys Madoc as if he was a god. He comes and goes as he pleases. Does anyone actually know where he goes when he travels for months on end? Well, I've had enough. I'm sixteen, not a child. It's time I started to make decisions for myself."

"I don't think I've ever heard you so forthright. I like it," she said, scruffing his hair. "And you're wrong about me—I understand. You weren't the only one enslaved that night. It's just that my prison's inside my mind."

Tomos tilted his head. "That's odd."

"What is?"

"That's the second time I've heard that expression today."

"When was the first?"

"Hmm. Let's just say it's someone who believes they have my best interests at heart."

"Sometimes, Tomos, you say the most peculiar things. That's why I love you," she said, punching him in the arm.

"And I—"

"You need to read this."

They looked up from their huddled conversation to find Kurzon standing at the foot of the bed. His expression chilled Seren to the bone. She took the letter out of her uncle's hand and read it.

"Lady Yanna Zirani

"Vedana is now in the hands of the Mendari, and your father is dead. If you want to avoid the same fate happening to your sister, then you must convince your husband to agree to the following demands:

"You and your husband must be present at the Stones of Valtara at the Great Conjoining. There you will both take the Mark of Velak and renounce the whore goddess. At that point, you will be reunited with your sister. On returning to Keld, you must order your warband to return to Zirani.

"If you agree to these terms, then the Zirani clan will be spared the cleansing of the Enorian blight that will follow our victory at Keld. And, as a further token of my good will, your father's body will be returned.

"However, failure to meet these demands will result in Lady Amira being sacrificed when the three gods combine. Both bodies will be hung above the gates of Vedana, where their rotting flesh will sustain the birds of the air until only their bare bones remain. Any attempt to rescue your sister will result in her suffering greatly before she is sacrificed.

"Finally, the young warrior who brought the letter must not be harmed, or there will be grave consequences for your sister. Remember, Lord Velak sees all minds, hearts and deeds.

Kaine."

"The Great Conjoining? That's tomorrow!" Seren glanced at Tomos, who had slunk lower into his bed the further she read through the letter. "Well, you're the clever one. What in the goddess' name are they to do?"

Tomos lowered his eyes and rolled away from her. "I-I don't feel so good."

"What?"

Tomos said nothing.

"You're unbelievable." Annoyed, she looked at Yanna and then at Kurzon. "You can't agree to his terms."

"Velak's balls, I will! I'd never renounce the goddess. Better to die fighting than bow the knee to Kaine and his dark god."

"But she'll die if we don't," said Yanna.

Kurzon shrugged. "We're damned if we do and damned if we don't."

The room fell silent, apart from the woeful sound of Yanna's intermittent sobs.

I can't just sit here and do nothing. Seren stood and walked to where Yanna was slumped on the floor of the bedchamber. She crouched in front of her and lifted Yanna's head to look at her. "I'll go. I'll rescue your sister and bring her back to you. If I die during the attempt, so be it—at least you'll be safe."

"You can't go," said Kurzon. "And knowing you, as soon as you're out of the gates, you'd double back and head to Belanore to find Grimbard. Besides, you're the heir to the throne."

"Grimbard can wait. Amira can't. I thought the prospect of me succeeding my father repulsed you?"

"Do you really believe I'd want you to die?"

"Maybe not you, but if it benefited the Communion—"

"Enough. I won't listen to another word of blasphemy spewing out of your mouth." He strode towards the door. "Yanna, we need to speak in private. And you," he said, spinning on his heels. "You'll stay here to look after your brother. Don't even think about leaving, or you'll have another elbow in your face." He opened the door and waited impatiently for his wife.

As Yanna got up, Seren gripped her arm and pulled her close. "Don't worry, I'll get her back to you—I promise."

"If you do, I'll leave him and will be yours forever."

Seren's eyes brightened. "It's as good as done."

"Hurry up, Yanna. We've little time to decide what course of action to take."

Yanna raised her eyes, then sighed. "Come back safe."

As the couple left the siblings to themselves, Seren rounded on Tomos. "What in the goddess' name were you playing at earlier?"

Tomos opened his tearful eyes and stared at her. "I-I can't say. But I've got a bad feeling about all of this."

"You don't say."

Wiping his eyes, he said, "One thing I know is that you need to get out of the fortress as much as I do."

"For once, little brother, I have to agree with you."

46

THE MARK OF VELAK

Adorned in a loose-fitting white robe, Amira, feet weighed down with a multitude of fears, stepped between the folds of heavy curtains and entered the Sanctum. Arranged around the circular room were a dozen wrought-iron floor sconces that sent a myriad of dancing shadows across the carpeted floor and encompassing fabric walls— floor to ceiling tapestries depicting scenes from the teachings of Velak, she assumed. At the heart of the Sanctum sat a smooth cylindrical stone altar. Resting on its deep brown surface was a large terracotta bowl, and carved deep into the stone was a glowing fire pit that spat tiny sparks into the incense-infused air. Behind, resting on a pedestal, was a speaking-glass. She shuddered, wondering if Lord Velak himself would witness the ceremony.

On detecting her presence, the Scions, standing in a semi-circle towards the altar, glanced at her impassively before returning their attention to the middle of the room.

Amira had met many formidable chieftains, warlords and warriors throughout her life. In all those years, not once had she felt overawed or threatened in their presence. Yet standing within the Sanctum in the presence of the five Scions of the First was entirely different. The grotesque image of them holding the severed heads of the men and women of the Taleni Elite Guard still haunted her thoughts.

She realised that one of the Scions was still looking at her. Juran smiled when she met his gaze and motioned for her to join him.

"When the ceremony begins, you need to stand between Rask and me," he said, pointing to a place between himself and a gaunt-faced warrior standing to the left of him.

Amira glanced at Rask out of the corner of her eye, recalling what Yanna had written about him. From the southern coastal settlement of Gol Stolrem, Rask had the most terrifying appearance of all the Scions. Yanna had tried to describe Rask's bald tattooed head covered in verses from the teachings of Velak, but seeing him in the flesh, with his full black beard, furrowed brow and deep-set, wolf-like eyes, Amira's skin crawled in disgust. Even worse was Yanna's recollection of how Rask would torture Enorian captives, carving the teachings of Velak into their heaving chests with his red-hot blade. And if any of those poor souls were inked, he would flay their tattoos away from their flesh to add to his infamous book of skins.

The warrior turned to face her, grunted, then returned to his silent vigil.

"I don't think Rask's as thrilled to see me as you are."

"Ignore him. He's just annoyed Kaine let the boy go without consulting the rest of us."

"Annoyed? I didn't think anyone would dare show any defiance to my father."

Juran chuckled. "Rask likes to test Kaine's patience, but I doubt he'd ever challenge him. Besides, he'd have to get through Aderyn first."

"Which one's Aderyn?"

Juran pointed her out. "She's Kaine's sister."

"I didn't know he had one."

"Adopted sister. Banan brought her back as a young child from a raid intending to keep her as a slave, but over time she became part of the family and eventually they adopted her."

"Auntie Aderyn," said Amira, smiling.

"I wouldn't call her that just yet. She hates Northerners even more than us Mendari."

"She's not from Mendaria?"

"No. She's from the North."

"Really? Which part?"

"Apart from her, only Kaine knows."

Amira frowned. "Why all the secrecy—"

Juran snapped to attention as her father appeared at the Sanctum's entrance. He flicked his eyes towards the place she was supposed to stand. She stepped in place. *Be brave, Amira. You can do this.*

Acknowledging no one in the room, Kaine approached the altar and blessed the bowl using the tongue of the First. Held in his hand was the most sacred of all artefacts of their faith: the Sword of Velak. It was a double-edged blade, long and slender, with the end tapering to a needle-thin point. The pommel of the sword plateaued at the top and had a pattern embossed into it. Amira strained to see it more clearly, but it was too dark in the room. Reverently, Kaine dipped the pommel into the bowl, then lifted it up, and slid the sword, hilt first, into the fire pit. Whatever was coated on the pommel sizzled in the heat. After a few moments, he picked up the bowl and turned to face the assembled group. He lifted the container high into the air, closed his eyes and prayed. "Oh, great and mighty lord. Hear the cries of your people whom you have chosen to carry out your will in this land. Accept this offering of the Taleni lord's blood as a token of our love and devotion to you." He opened his eyes. "Whom do you serve?"

"Velak. His body was slain but his spirit endures."

Kaine nodded, then walked over to Rask.

"State your name and your provenance?"

"I am Rask of Gol Stolrem, Scion of Praetorian Draganov."

"Declare your sacrifice, Rask of Gol Stolrem."

"I wear the Armour of the First."

"Show your obedience to him."

Rask pulled at a clasp at the front of the collar of his armour. The hiss of a snake escaped from within. Then he ripped open the black, skin-tight fabric, and pulled it down to his waist to expose his torso.

Amira gasped as Rask's legs buckled, his breathing shallowed, and his lungs rattled.

Teeth gritted, he said, "M-my pain...for him."

"Through sacrifice, obedience and pain you earn his mark." Kaine dipped his finger into the bowl and traced over the image of the Circle and the Cross scarred into Rask's flesh above his heart. "You have reaffirmed your devotion to him. Replace your armour, Scion of the First."

Amira paled as she stared at the Sword of Velak buried hilt-first in the fire pit. *Is he really going to use it on me?*

As her father moved on to the warrior to Rask's left, she forced herself to recall what Yanna had written about them.

Okita of Amaryth was the youngest member of the Scions of the First. Amira wasn't like her sister, who found both men and women attractive, but even she indulged in Okita's delicate hazel eyes and the rose undertone glow to her beige skin. Of Okita, Yanna had written:

'Do not underestimate her as a warrior or consider her youth to be a weakness. As in the ways of her ancestor, Praetorian Masuda, Okita was trained in the art of combat as soon as she could walk. She killed her first Taranian at ten and became her town's protector four years later. And, like all the Scions, she trained with the Sept of Shadows, in Gol Zaram.'

Flanking Okita was Alvar, who, if not in the same room as her father, would have been considered the greatest in physical stature of all the Scions. Like many of his kin, he wore a neatly plaited beard that was tied together under his chin. The sides of his golden blond hair were shaved, with only the top allowed to grow, flowing down his back. Yanna had noted that, just like his descendant, Praetorian Rasmusson, Alvar braided strands of hair from his defeated foes into his golden mane.

Next to Alvar was Aderyn. Apart from Yanna's brief physical

description of the middle-aged woman, Juran's information was as much as she knew about the tall, lithe warrior from the north.

Then there was Juran. From her grandfather's stronghold, Yanna claimed that the dark-skinned, curly-haired Kelarian had grown up as an orphan on the streets before being taken to The Sept of Shadows. The secretive guild was said to have been responsible for the assassination of Queen Isabelle Niras and many other Northern nobility. From the conversation she just had with the amiable warrior, Amira struggled to perceive Juran as a cold-hearted killer. She silently cursed her naivety, knowing that all the Scions were killers; even so, Juran seemed different, as if there was a part of him that didn't fit the life he now led.

Five unique but equally deadly individuals brought together by the expressionless man now standing directly in front of her. The moment she had been dreading ever since learning about the ceremony had arrived.

"Will you give yourself freely to Lord Velak?"

Her mouth dried. "Y-yes."

"Louder."

Be brave, Amira. "Yes."

"Then you must take his mark to be truly his." He turned to Aderyn. "Prepare her."

His two words sent a wave of panic through her mind. She dug her nails into her hand as a distraction, but as she watched her father return to the altar, replace the bowl and withdraw the Sword of Velak, her legs gave way—glowing white-hot at the end of the sword's pommel was the Mark of Velak.

"Get her up and keep her still."

"No, father!" she cried, as Alvar and Rask hefted her to her feet. Aderyn unlaced her robe and pulled it down to her waist. She struggled to hide her nakedness, but the warriors held her firmly in place.

"Calm yourself, child. To become Mendari, you must take the Mark of Velak."

"P-please, Father. Don't do this to me, I beg you!"

Kaine's mouth twitched. He drew in close to her. "I warned you not to make a scene. Take the mark willingly, or you'll leave me no choice."

"I can't do it," she said, blubbering—tears and mucus streaming from her eyes and nose.

Kaine stiffened. "Then you leave me no choice." He stepped away from her. "You disgrace our family with your snivelling desperation to shun such an honour. I was wrong to believe that you could turn to Velak—you have too much of the North still within you." He flipped the sword in the air, grabbing it by the sizzling hilt. "If you will not take his mark," he said, his voice trembling, "then you must be cleansed from our land. You must die."

Amira screamed, closing her eyes as a puddle of urine pooled around her feet.

"No, Kaine!"

She opened her eyes to the thinnest of slits. Juran stood in front of her with his hands raised, gripping the hilt of the Sword of Velak.

"Juran, I swear, I'll carve you up myself if you don't let go."

"She's your daughter, Kaine. You can't do this. She needs time to learn our ways."

"Get him off me."

Aderyn and Okita wrestled Juran to the floor, still yelling in protest.

"I'll deal with you later," said Kaine, scowling as he focused his fury onto Amira. "At least I'll still have one daughter who'll honour me."

"Stop!" boomed a voice that reverberated from behind the altar. The ethereal outline of a man, filled with thousands of luminescent colours, flickered above the altar. Immediately, Kaine and the Scions prostrated themselves towards the ghostly image.

"Lord Velak, you honour us with your presence. I-I will deal with my daughter's insolence and—"

"Silence, Kaine. Your devotion to me is admirable, but I reveal myself to you now to stop you making a grave mistake."

"I-I don't understand, lord. Have I not followed your teachings in this matter?"

"It is true that your daughter has spent too long with unbelievers to understand the gravity of refusing my gift and, as my word dictates, she should be cleansed. However, as your daughter is a direct descendant of Praetorian Lynch, she is of greater value to me alive than dead. And did she not complete her mission with the Pathfinder?"

"Yes, she did, lord."

"Then, on this occasion, I will show her mercy. Scion Juran sensed my concern and challenged you when no-one else would do so. He is correct in that the girl needs to be taught the ways of our people. So you will send her to the Sanctorum in Gol Zaram, and there she will learn what it is to be Mendari and to serve me. And you will not punish Juran, but thank him for his timely intervention."

"Yes, lord."

"Also, you will send a Scion to track the Pathfinder and the Vessel as they make their way towards my tomb. I have sensed the conflict in both. Should they stray from the path I have laid out for them, they will need to be shown the errors of their ways."

"I will send Rask, lord. He has a talent for such a task as this."

"Excellent." Velak turned to face Rask. "You will report directly to me."

"You honour me, lord."

"Now prepare yourselves for battle. The Enorians are waiting for you at the edge of Derwedd Forest. Make them suffer for their love of the whore goddess."

"We will, lord."

"Victory is within our grasp. Seize it with both hands and a joyful heart." The image of their god vibrated for a moment before vanishing into the wisps of incense trailing through the air.

Kaine sprung off the floor and squared up to Juran. "It seems Lord Velak favours you. If you're so concerned about my daughter, then you can escort her to Gol Zaram."

"And then what?"

"Then you'll oversee her teaching and training," he said, flicking his scathing eyes at Amira. "And if she fails, not even Lord Velak will stop me from ripping that suit off your back and watching you shrivel and crumble into dust."

Juran jutted his chin out, keeping his eyes fixed on Kaine. "Anything else?"

"Yes. You can take charge of the caravan transporting the Chosen. They leave within the hour. Now take her and get out of my sight before I change my mind."

"Father."

Kaine spun around and slammed the pommel of the Sword of Velak into the carpet beside Amira, burning the Circle and the Cross deep into its fibres. "You'd better have that burned into your chest by the next time I see you, child."

Juran barged past Kaine and held out his hand to Amira. "Let's get you out of here."

She left the Sanctum, whimpering. Taking one final look over her shoulder, her father had gathered the remaining Scions around him, not even giving her a second thought. *I hope I never see you again.*

Still seething, Kaine addressed the remaining four Scions assembled around him. "It's time. Rask will travel with the horde but will begin Lord Velak's task as soon as he's over the Valtara. Alvar will command in my absence, and Okita will be his second."

They nodded in understanding.

"By nightfall, their vanguard will be annihilated and our horde will be on its way to the gates of Keld. And remember, bring him to the Stones of Valtara by dawn. The Great Conjoining approaches, my friends. For the glory of Velak."

"For the glory of Velak."

He turned to Aderyn. "Come on, little bird. We have scores to settle."

47

LINGERING LIES

Kurzon's head swirled with the words contained within Kaine's letter. No matter how he broke the situation down, he could not see a way out other than to comply with the Mendari leader's demands or abandon Amira to a most horrible death. With no solutions in sight, he and Yanna headed for the only person who could shed further light on Amira's situation: Cai.

Accompanied by half a dozen of the Zirani Elite Guard, they approached the storeroom where the young Taleni warrior was held. Kurzon winced as a woeful groan spilt out from within. "What in the name of the goddess is going on in there?"

"War Master Ironfoot is preparing to interrogate the prisoner, lord," replied the clansguard, standing guard at the entrance.

Yanna, her complexion ashen, gripped her husband's hand. "The letter, Kurzon. Stop him before it's too late."

"Out of my way," said Kurzon, barging past the bewildered guard. He flung open the door, marching inside, with Yanna close behind. "Ironfoot!"

On entering the room, illuminated by a single, shuttered window set into the wattle and daubed lime-washed walls, the furnace-like heat and stench of sweat assaulted his senses. Sacks of grain had been cleared to make a space in the centre, which was where the young Taleni dangled, strung up by his arms.

Ironfoot, his back turned to the visitors, finished securing the rope holding Cai in place.

"For the love of the goddess, Ironfoot. I thought you were just going to hold him?"

"I changed my mind," said Ironfoot, turning to face them. "Lady Zirani. I'm surprised to see you here."

"What have you done to him?"

"Nothing, yet," he said, scratching his head. "Why the show of concern for him? The boy's certainly keeping secrets." He pulled Cai's head up by his hair. "You've already met Lord Zirani. Well, this is his wife, Lady Yanna, the sister of Lady Amira."

Cai squinted out of his bloodshot eyes. "Y-you look so alike."

Ironfoot caught him with the back of his hand.

"Ugh!"

"Didn't Swordstorm teach you how to speak to a lady?" He nodded to a clansguard standing to the side of Cai. "Remove his tunic."

"No," said Yanna. "You can't hurt him. He'll find out."

Ironfoot held up his hand to the clansguard. "Who will?"

"Here," said Kurzon, giving Ironfoot the letter. "You'd better read this."

The Master of War took the letter and perched on a nearby stool. He cursed, moving the parchment away from his face. "My eyes aren't as good as they used to be. Just wish I had one of those expensive reading stones."

"Use Kurzon's," said Yanna, impatiently.

"If you insist, my dear," said Kurzon, failing to hide his annoyance. He reached inside his tunic and handed Ironfoot a flat-bottomed, convex glass sphere. "Don't you dare drop it."

Ironfoot's mouth curled into a smile, nodded his thanks and began to read. His expression grew darker the further he read. As he finished, he looked up at Kurzon and shook his head. "Surely you're not going to agree to his demands?"

Kurzon raised his hands in exasperation. "Well, what other choice do we have?"

"We can start by getting this boy to spill his guts," said Ironfoot, pushing off the stool. He stood in front of Cai and pulled back his fist.

"No! I won't allow you to endanger her life," cried Yanna. "Kaine has spies everywhere. If he finds out that you've harmed the boy, he'll make Amira suffer for certain."

"Then what would you have me do, Lady Yanna?"

"A word in private?" She eyed towards the door and walked outside.

As Ironfoot followed Yanna, Kurzon nodded to the guard, then joined them out in the light of the Twins.

"I want you to let the boy go," said Yanna.

"Let him go? But he's lying through his teeth."

"I have to agree with Ironfoot. If we can squeeze something out of him, it may give us some advantage."

"You know I'm right about Kaine's spies. And you've said many times," she said, focusing on Kurzon, "that the People's Alliance are working with the Mendari."

"Pure speculation," said Ironfoot. "Why would they choose to strike a deal with Kaine?"

"See, that's your problem, Ironfoot. The lower castes can do no wrong in your eyes. Yanna's right—the People's Alliance are at least in contact with the Mendari, and there are rumours that one of the taverns in Belanore is a base of operation."

"So we just let him loose and follow his trail?" said Ironfoot. "See which tavern he enters and arrest everyone inside?"

"Why not? Kaine needs him alive. And don't forget that Grimbard is still at large and could very well be Kaine's main piece on the board in Belanore. I'll wager one hundred sofrans that he's the one Cai's come to see. We wait until the boy has made contact and then take them all—the wider the net, the bigger the fish." Kurzon paused, pulling on his plaited moustache. "And, if we capture Grimbard, then perhaps Kaine will consider a hostage trade?"

"He might consider it if the traitor has vital information that he wants," said Yanna.

"And what about the townsfolk?" asked Ironfoot. "Dealing with rioters is one thing, but arresting innocent people?"

"It doesn't matter what you think. This is now a matter of the security of the realm." Kurzon narrowed his eyes at the Master of War. "I warn you, Ironfoot: don't cross me on this."

"If I—"

"Stop it, both of you." Yanna turned to Ironfoot. "You have enough to worry about with the Mendari horde moving north, and you," she said, fixing Kurzon with a look that he knew only too well, "need to find a way to follow Cai without raising his suspicions."

"I'll put a clansguard on his tail."

"No. Too obvious." She tapped her finger on her lips in thought. "I think I have someone who'd be perfect."

"Who?"

"Someone who's just come into my employment." She returned her attention to Ironfoot. "So, Master of War, will you set him free?"

Cai rubbed his wrists, wincing at where the rope had chafed his skin. Just another bruise to add to the many he had received over the past few days. His possessions had been returned, and he had been given some privacy to dress. As he struggled to pull his chainmail over his head, he realised he was no longer alone.

Ironfoot sat on the stool, holding Boar's Rage in one hand and Cai's sword in the other. He held them up to the light shining through the window. "You know, when Rodric commissioned Boar's Rage and Red Mist, I never thought I'd see a sword to match them in my lifetime. I was wrong. Your sword's outstanding." He ran his eye down the edge of Cai's blade. "I'm no weaponsmith, of course, but I'm sure Bethan of Vedana would be impressed. It might bear none of the intricate decorations of Boar's Rage, but I doubt she could fashion such a blade."

He sheathed the sword and offered it to Cai. As Cai took hold of it, Ironfoot refused to let go, pulling him off balance. Boar's Rage sang as it moved to a hair's breadth of Cai's neck. "I can smell your deceit, Cai of the Taleni. Your secrets linger around you like a foul-smelling odour."

Terrified on the inside, Cai held his nerve, keeping his eyes fixed on Ironfoot's.

The Master of War snorted and released his grip, sheathing Boar's Rage. "But not everything about you is a lie, is it?" He stood and wandered to the window. Hands held behind his back, he peered up into the sky. "The last time I met Swordstorm, he told me about the boy he'd rescued from a shipwreck on the west coast of Taleni, whose only possession was a sword that was a match for his own." He pivoted on his good leg and studied Cai. "I do not doubt that you are that boy, but I know that Kaine's sent you here to be more than just a letter bearer. What's he got on you, son? Whatever it is, we can work it out, turn it against him."

"I told you before. He chose me because he knows that I'm honour-bound to protect Lady Amira and will do anything to keep her safe." That much was true.

"Anything, Cai? Does your devotion run deeper than duty? Is it love? You said it yourself; you'd do anything to keep her safe—even betray your own people?"

Cai turned away from Ironfoot's penetrating stare and walked to the storehouse door. He paused. "None of this matters. No matter what you do, Kaine will win."

As Cai stepped outside, into the mid-afternoon air, he shoved his hands into his pockets and frowned. *What's this?* He pulled out a small piece of parchment. Making sure no-one was looking, he opened it and read it.

'Go to the inner gate of the North Tunnel as the night watch begins their duty. He will meet you there.'

Cai closed the note, then whistled softly. He had prayed to Velak for help, and now he was free and about to make contact with Prince Tomos. Mere coincidence or divine intervention? He shrugged.

The guard at the entrance to the storehouse approached him. "War Master Ironfoot offers you the hospitality of Keld's clansguard refectory."

Cai nodded.

"Then he expects you to never set foot inside Keld again."

Cai snorted. "Don't worry—after tonight he'll never see me again." *They'll all be dead by morning.*

48

THE PEOPLE'S ALLIANCE

For over five hundred years, the hill fort of Hythe was the seat of power in Nirasia. The sprawling fortified settlement commanded views as far south as Keld, an intimidating reminder to would-be invaders that crossing the Valtara would exact a heavy price. Yet the only invader slipping into the abandoned fort that day was an elderly she-wolf long cast out of her pack.

She stood on her hind legs beside the dilapidated South Gate, barely hanging on its hinges, scanning for any movement within the walls. Her open display would have cost her dearly in other places inhabited by the creatures who walked on two legs, but not there—for none of their living would dare stray inside with the constant wailing and groaning rising from within the largest cave of wood and stone standing in the centre of the two-leg den.

Sensing no movement within the ruins, she padded her way towards the ramshackle building, welcome protection from the heavy spring downpours. She headed to a window where the shutters had rotted away from their fixtures and deftly vaulted inside. As her eyes quickly adapted to the reduction in light, she spied a plump rat scurrying into the shadows. She ignored it, knowing that tastier treats lay deeper within. The woeful sounds of the dead grew louder, vibrating through the flagstone floor; yet she showed no sign of concern, increasing her pace, nearing her prize.

In front of her, she came upon a spiral stone stairwell that descended into the depths of the Great Hall. The stench of death always greeted her at this point; she proceeded all the same. As she reached the bottom, she sensed the pain and torment inflicted in the many windowless rooms she now passed—lingering scents that only the creatures of land and air could detect. Scores of faceless two-legs, their lives snuffed out in the most horrendous of circumstances.

She broke into a run. Her drooling tongue flapped, cascading a trail of saliva behind her. The door loomed out of the darkness—the door that always promised delicious treats and a full belly. Just as it looked as though she would crash heedlessly into the ironclad barrier, she pulled up and pawed at the rusting surface in front of her, then backed away and sat to wait. She listened to the swirling hum she knew came from the other side of the door, as if a swarm of angry bees filled the cave within, ready to burst out of their captivity. Then, every so often, the low drone was accompanied by a serpent's hiss that she had fled from the first time she had heard it—but not anymore, for she knew what lay within. Cocking her head to the side, she discerned a sound that was familiar to her. It reminded her of the howls that the male wolves sang in the night when she was still with her pack—deep and even long notes that ended in slides that drifted off into the Void. She sprung up on all fours, wagging her tail, as the melodic song drew closer, whimpering as a clang of iron was followed by the grating groan of the door swinging open.

"Hello, old girl. I wondered when you'd turn up," said a welcoming voice, standing in the doorway. "You nearly missed your treat." The two-leg slid a large bowl of raw meat across to her and crouched to the ground. "Did you know that you're the only living thing to have seen this place? Obviously, my measures to ward away the living have little effect on you." He scruffed her fur. "Well, at least I know my secrets are safe with you." Muzzle soaked in blood, she tucked in her tail to show her submission to her two-legged benefactor.

Leaving her to enjoy her feast, the two-leg stood and walked back inside, continuing to howl his unusual song. For a while, she blissfully devoured the bloody banquet until only bare bones remained. Even then, she refused to leave anything for the vermin watching hungrily from the shadows, gnawing on the marrow until the unmistakable sound of the serpent's hiss snapped her attention back to the two-leg. He reached inside the object responsible for the frightening noise. He retrieved two identical fleshy objects and disappeared from view. Her curiosity aroused, she crept forward towards the door until she reached the threshold, the closest she had ever been to the two-leg's den.

"You're feeling brave today, old girl."

She looked in the direction of the voice, but could not see the two-leg. So, tentatively, she placed a paw over the threshold, and then another, until she stood in the middle of the cave.

"No need to be shy. Have a look around."

The room did not interest her—he did; but there was something different about his odour. He smelled different. Narrowing her eyes, she pulled back her ears and straightened her tail parallel to the stone floor.

"Right. I'm ready to leave."

As the two-leg reappeared, she pulled back her lips, revealing her incisors, and snarled at him.

"What's got into you?" He looked at his hands and then stroked the matted beard covering his face. "Oh, of course, you've never seen me like this," he said, crouching down. He avoided looking into her eyes and stretched out his hand to her. "No need to be frightened. It's still me."

She took a sniff of his hand, then licked it, retching immediately, desperate to get rid of the unpleasant taste. The two-leg chuckled. "Strange, isn't it? Imagine having to wear it for hours on end."

Feeling more confident, she moved closer and nuzzled the two-leg. "That's better," he said, scratching her under her muzzle. "I'd take you with me, but I don't think King Rodric would be happy with a fully grown she-wolf roaming around the place."

He stood and lifted the long sleeves of his tunic, revealing a slender black object strapped to his black-skinned arm. With the lightest of touches, the object flickered into life. Staring into the light, the two-leg groaned and rubbed his forehead. "How the hell did he manage to get to Belanore? Show me Tomos' movements since I left Keld." He flicked his finger over the light, then cursed. "Twice in three days...they must be making their move." He grabbed a leather bag and a staff from beside the door. "I'm bloody glad I packed the horses earlier." He clucked, then paced over to a table and picked up an object that the two-legs liked to tie around their bodies. She noticed something long hanging from it that looked like the thin branch of a tree; but this branch was perfectly straight. The two-leg gripped the top of it, which was wrapped in the skin of a dead animal, and slid out a thin, shiny stick that gleamed in the unusual light of the two-leg's cave. "Good as new...I can't wait to see his face."

She drew close to it and sniffed, noticing that the stick's surface contained swirls of cloud.

"Oh, no you don't." The two-leg slapped the stick back into the branch. "You'll slice your tongue off if you get any closer." He walked to the cave entrance, then turned back to the she-wolf. "Come on. You can't stay in here."

She obediently loped out through the entrance and waited patiently for the two-leg to lock the iron door. As he marched down the corridor, she followed him, only for the two-leg to spin around, his face stern. "Stay here. You can't come with me." Rummaging inside his bag, he found a few strips of dried meat and tossed them in front of the iron door. "That'll keep you busy for a while." She turned towards the door, but then paused and looked down the corridor. The two-leg had vanished, leaving the faintest of scents in his wake. She looked at the meat and then back to the last place the two-leg had stood. Then, wagging her tail, she lay in front of the door and rested her head on her front paws. Now, she would wait and guard her new den until her alpha male returned. She had found her new pack.

Branock crouched behind an outcrop of rock below the southern entrance to the abandoned hill fort. What was once the centre of power for the Nirasian Clan was now a haven for all manner of beasts, and, as many believed, the place where Govannon's spirit restlessly searched for its decapitated head.

Camping for two restless nights outside of the cursed earth mound did little to dissuade Branock otherwise. Hythe was not for the living, but it was the living for whom Branock and his followers lay in wait. He was sure of one thing: he would fight Govannon himself if it helped their cause.

While he waited, he considered why he risked his life. The People's Alliance began as a peaceful organisation, campaigning for the rights of the lower castes. For years, the Communion sought to destroy the Alliance, but when Queen Isabelle took up their cause, the lower castes believed things were about to change; that was before the Day of Sorrows. The assassination of the queen plummeted King Rodric into spiralling grief, losing his grip on reality and the needs of his people.

After eleven frustrating years of a cycle of demonstration, negotiation and reneged agreements, the Alliance had no other choice but to instruct its members to put down their tools and strike. Miners, ironworkers, builders, engineers and even the merchant guilds joined as one to send a clear message to the higher castes and the Communion: that enough was enough. For six long months, the Alliance held firm, knowing that the effects of the strike were causing severe problems for the clan chieftains and the Communion. Violent clashes between workers and warriors were frequent but non-fatal, thanks to the recovering king taking counsel from his Master of War, Luis Ironfoot. He convinced the king that bloodshed would be catastrophic for the kingdom and could lead to a revolution— something that the Mendari would take advantage of. That was before the capture, torture and execution of three clansguard at the Mines of Belith.

Enraged, King Rodric shunned Ironfoot's counsel and turned to his brother-in-law, Lord Kurzon Zirani, and his harsh solution to lower caste disobedience: deadly force. Two hundred miners died during the infamous massacre on that dark day. So as Branock and his small group of followers lay in wait, he expelled any superstitious fear from his mind. For the man they hunted was a prize worth enduring the spirits of the dead for—a man who had the power to bring King Rodric Shieldbane to his knees.

At last, their quarry emerged from the abandoned fortress and made his way on horseback, down the winding south-facing earthworks. The figure wore a hooded, full-length grey tunic that seemed a poor choice of clothing for travelling in the mid-afternoon heat. *Stupid old fool. We'll be on him before he knows it.* Branock signalled to the rest of the group to mount up. It was time.

After a short descent, the rider reached the bottom of the incline and headed towards the Great North Road. Branock dug his heels into his horse and hurtled towards the unsuspecting rider. The rest of his group followed, screaming and shouting at the tops of their voices. Strangely, their target never so much as looked behind or increased his pace. *Goddess. Is he deaf as well as stupid?*

Finally, as the eight riders encircled, the figure pulled up on the reins. "Good afternoon to you all. Out for a leisurely ride after the first spring rains?"

Branock trotted forward and levelled his spear. "You can drop the pretence, old man. We know who you are."

"And who exactly do you think I am?"

"You're Madoc the healer, personal physician to King Rodric's son, Prince Tomos. That's who you are."

"I am him," said the old man, sliding off his hood. "Is there someone ill among you who needs attention?"

Branock laughed. "I think you should be more worried about your own health, old man."

"That's an odd thing to say, son. Why should I be worried? Do you know something I don't know?"

"When she said you were strange, I didn't realise you were completely crazy."

"Who told you that? I'd like to have a stern word with them."

"Let's just say she told us that the prince's illness is far worse than anyone knows and that you're the only one able to keep him from the Veil. I'll wager the king would do anything to get you back."

321

Madoc scanned the group. "Hmm. You're not bandits or Mendari. I know who you are. You're from the People's Alliance."

Branock chuckled. "Maybe you're not as far gone as I thought. Patrick, take his reins. I need to get away from this accursed place."

"I'm not going anywhere with you."

"You don't have a choice, old man."

Patrick dismounted and made his way towards the old healer, but stopped as Madoc dismounted awkwardly and limped towards the stocky ironworker. He stared at Patrick from his doubled-up stance.

"I was hoping you'd see sense, but if you really want to do this, come and get me."

The group looked at each other in astonishment. "There're eight of us, old man," said Branock. "Make it easy on yourself. Come quietly, and no harm will come to you."

"Only eight? You should've brought more."

"Enough of this foolishness. Patrick, grab hold of that dithering old fool."

"I'm warning you, son, don't touch me."

"What are you gonna do about it?" said Patrick, bearing down on the old man.

As Branock watched impatiently, he could have sworn that Madoc's crooked back straightened. *What in the name of the goddess is happening?*

Just as Patrick grabbed hold of Madoc's arms within the oversized robe, he turned towards Branock, dumbfounded.

"What's wrong?"

"I told you—you should have brought more." With lightning speed, Madoc seized Patrick's arm and twisted it around, forcing him to bend over. Then, with one swift kick to the stomach, the man from the Alliance dropped to the floor, heavily winded. Madoc looked around the remaining group. "Who's next?"

"Get the bastard. Just don't kill him."

Dismounting, they armed themselves with clubs and spread out around Madoc. They edged towards him, aware that their comrade was still on the ground, curled up in agony. Two of the group launched themselves at the healer from opposite sides. Just as one of the pair slashed down with her club, Madoc slid to the side of her and drove his arm down onto her extended arm. She screamed as the bones in her lower arm shattered. Madoc pulled her around and rammed his knee into her chest. She groaned and fell to the floor. Just at that moment, the other attacker slammed his club into the back of Madoc. It should have put him down, but he didn't even flinch. Instead, without even turning to face his opponent, he drove his foot hard into the face of the Alliance man—the power of the kick so great that the man landed several feet from where he had been standing. Seconds later, another four of the Alliance lay wounded on the floor. Not even breaking a sweat, Madoc turned to face Branock and waved him on. He swallowed hard and charged.

In what seemed like a blurring nightmare, Branock found himself flat on the ground with Madoc's boot pushed hard into his chest. The healer had put down all eight of the group in less than a minute. He was no novice with a sword, staff or his hands, but how Madoc fought was like nothing he had ever seen before. "What are you waiting for? Kill me."

"I'm in no mood to have your blood on my hands; but if you don't answer the following question truthfully, I'll make you and your comrades suffer in ways you could never imagine. Do you understand?"

"Y-yes."

"Good. Who told you about the prince?"

Branock's eyes widened. "I don't know. I was never—Ahhh!"

"Don't lie to me. I'm in a hurry, but I'll take my time to get an answer from you. Who?"

"Goddess, forgive me. It was Master Engineer Gwen. She told us about the prince."

"Did she? I wondered why she was getting so friendly with him."

"Who are you?"

Madoc smiled. "If I told you, you'd never believe me. Now go to sleep." With one flick of Madoc's boot, the leader of the People's Alliance lost consciousness.

Madoc remounted his horse and prepared to resume his journey back south. He estimated he would reach his destination an hour or two after midnight. *Well, as long as I don't run into any more disruptions.*

Just as he was about to leave, he noticed a wide tear in his robe across his knee. Concerned, he glanced back to the eight injured men and women lying on the ground. He considered his options and shook his head. Even if they had seen the black material underneath his robe, they would not have understood what it was. He hated wearing it, but war was coming and whatever the outcome, the safety of Tomos was of paramount importance. Nothing else mattered to him.

So he's been enjoying the pleasures of Belanore? Sneaky little bugger. And I bet I know where. It's time I had my first taste of the finest ale in all Tarania—or so he keeps telling me. It's time to visit the Renegade Tavern.

49

THE BELANORE MASSACRE

Tarek slid his old sword out of its scabbard and took a few practice swings. It was heavier than Red Mist, but it was all he had. In truth, the blade was made with good steel and it had never failed him during the Mendari War. Knowing the uncertainty of his situation, he was pleased to have a weapon he could rely on. He sheathed the blade and glanced at the woman pacing the boards of the Renegade Tavern.

"How many are out there now?"

Mari edged open the shutter and looked towards the end of Main Street where the Grove of the Goddess stood. "Around fifty very pissed-off townsfolk. I can't see how many clansguard there are, but I'd wager not enough to handle our lot."

"Which is why I'm sure there'll be reinforcements sent from Keld."

"It's not the clansguard I'm worried about—it's the Grey Cloaks."

"Well, whichever it is, I'm their main target. So do us both a favour and sit your wrinkly old arse down over here so we can get on with business."

"Wrinkly old arse?" She looked over her shoulder at her rear, contained in the pair of old braccae she wore. "There's nothing wrong with my arse, love." She made her way to the booth that Tarek was using to change into his armour and waved her hand at his crotch. "Speaking of wrinkly old bits—does it still know how to work?"

Tarek tugged on his belt to take the weight of the chainmail. "It works just fine."

"That's good to know." She fluttered her lashes at him and leaned across the table. "My bed's just as warm as it was when we were young. We could always—"

"No, Mari, I can't."

She reddened and stared down at the table.

"It's not you—my heart belongs to another."

She slumped into the seat opposite him. "I never thought I'd see the day to hear those words coming out of your mouth."

"It's true, Mari. But now she's dead because of Kaine."

"I'm sorry for your loss, love." She lifted a jug off a serving tray and held it towards him. "A drink of Mendarian wine to remember her?"

"Goddess, no. I've had my fill of that stuff for a lifetime. Besides, I'll not mourn her loss until I avenge her."

Mari poured one for herself, leant back in her seat and raised her cup. "To the one who stole the heart of Tarania's greatest lover." She drained the cup, then nodded to the sword hanging from his hip. "So what happened to Red Mist? I thought it was indestructible?"

"That's what I thought," he said, thinking back to the moment Kaine cleaved his blade in two. "It's lying in pieces amidst the bones and ashes of Nabaya."

"You left it there? I thought it was priceless?"

"Swords can be replaced—people can't."

Mari smiled at him while refilling her cup. "You're right there, love."

He drummed his fingers on the surface of the table, then set his eyes on hers. "I've delivered his message, stirred up the lower castes and betrayed my sword brothers. Surely, I've held up my end of the bargain?"

She swirled the ruby-red contents of her cup and took a sip. "My contact says that he's pleased with the progress you've made, but he's got one final task for you to complete."

He slapped his hands down hard on the table. "I won't kill anyone for him. Not even if it means never—"

"That's not what he wants you to do."

"Then what?"

She dipped her hand into the pocket of her tunic and slid an object, wrapped in a plain piece of cloth, across the table to him. Tarek stared at it, then at Mari. "What is it?"

"Just bloody open it and see for yourself. And be careful—it's delicate."

Carefully, Tarek opened the cloth and gasped as he recognised the object. "No. I didn't bargain for this," he said, scraping his chair back and standing. "The boy'll die without it."

Mari shook her head. "The contact made it clear to me that the prince isn't the target. The loss of the amulet won't kill him."

"I'm sure Rodric would disagree." He leaned forward, looming over her. "So, who's the target? The king? The princess?"

"They didn't reveal that."

"Bastard." He slumped back into his seat. "So what does he want me to do with it?"

"He wants you to bring it to him at the Stones of Valtara before Ulena rises in the east."

Tarek's eyes grew wide.

"What?"

Ignoring Mari, he pulled out a knife from his belt and began to scratch into the surface of the table.

"Hey! You'll have to pay for that."

He flicked his eyes up at her. "I'm sure your Mendari contact will cover the cost."

She made a face, folded her arms and read what Tarek had carved into the wood. "Dawn at the Stones on the Day of the Conjoining."

"Who's that for?"

"Never you mind."

"I will bloody well mind if you mess this up for us."

Tarek slipped the amulet into his gambeson pocket, tucked the knife into his belt and leaned back in the chair. "Us?"

"You heard me."

"I'm just trying to work out why the People's Alliance would think siding with Kaine would be any better than how things are now?"

"It's simple, love. Kaine's promised to destroy the Communion and disband the caste system."

Tarek grimaced. "And what about those who refuse to renounce the goddess?"

"That's their choice; but at least everyone gets to choose."

Tarek squeezed the sides of the table, turning his knuckles white. "Ask me again when you've witnessed loved ones torn to pieces in front of your eyes."

"It's too late, now—the Mendari horde will soon be at the banks of the Valtara."

It's not the horde I'm worried about. Tarek frowned. "Speaking of the Valtara—how in the goddess' name can I cross without using the South Gate Drawbridge?"

"That's what I asked."

"And?"

"They said for you to wait at the willow copse just east of the fortress, and you'll be able to cross. Be there as Ulena descends into the Netherplain."

Tarek frowned. "Not even the Galgari could navigate the Valtara during these heavy rains."

"Just be there."

"But how—" Before he could continue, the noise from the crowds outside erupted into the shouts and screams of battle. Tarek gripped the hilt of his sword and spun around in his seat. "What in the goddess' name?" He rushed to the window and peered through the shutters. "Velak's balls, Mari, you were right: Grey Cloaks."

"I told you they'd get involved," she said, rushing over to join him.

"The tavern's not safe, Mari. You need to leave with me now."

"But they're my people, and I can fight."

"Then you'll die along with them. Look."

The townspeople were no match for the well-armed and disciplined Grey Cloaks. Cutting them down without exception, the Communion warriors chased after the survivors as they fled for their lives. A man and woman struggled towards The Renegade, supporting a badly wounded man between them. Close on their heels were four Grey Cloaks, one of whom slowed and loosed a crossbow bolt. The injured man groaned as the bolt sank deep between his shoulder blades. His head slumped and his legs gave way, slowing the others down.

"They won't make it," said Tarek, unsheathing his sword.

"You can't go out there."

"Just get ready to barricade the door as soon as I return."

Quickly, she unlocked the door and opened it. Gripping his arm as he slid past her, she said, "Not even you could take on that many."

Tarek grinned. "But I'm not on my own, am I?"

He launched into a sprint to shield the townsfolk from the advancing Grey Cloaks. As he passed the pair carrying their friend, he grimaced as he realised that the man had already crossed the Veil.

He slowed, assessing the four warriors now moving towards him. Three of them were armed with a spear, an axe and an oval shield bearing the triskelion with a circular iron boss riveted in the centre. The fourth carried only a crossbow and an axe. Under their grey cloaks, they wore well-made gambesons that covered the top half of their bodies.

Seeing his mail, they fanned out and held their ground. One of the Grey Cloaks spoke. "We've no quarrel with you, clansguard. Step aside, and no harm will come to you."

"And what about them?" asked Tarek, nodding behind him. "Will they have the same mercy extended to them?" Out of the corner of his eye, he noted the one armed with a crossbow was reloading it.

"Why should you care what happens to a bunch of lower-caste scum who threatened the Grove of the Goddess?"

"You could've arrested them, instead of slaughtering everyone. Aren't we all Northern Taranians?"

The Grey Cloak spat on the floor. "So you're one of them? A sympathiser, like that cripple, Ironfoot?"

"Careful, son. That's my friend you're talking about. He might only have one good leg, but he'd slice you all into pieces without breaking into a sweat."

The Grey Cloak sneered at him. "I'd love the chance to gut that blasphemous fool, but he's not here. So you'll have to do."

"One last chance to turn and leave with your lives."

"Kill him."

They never learn.

All but the warrior aiming the ranged weapon moved in as one, shields protecting their torsos and spears held ready to thrust. *Impressive. They've been well drilled.*

A crossbow bolt cracked loose and whistled through the air. From the short distance between them, the point would surely penetrate even the strongest riveted mail. Yet Tarek did not flinch. He closed his eyes and swept his sword in an upward arc, splitting the deadly projectile into two pieces. He leapt, plucking the arrowhead out of the air, and hurled it at the astonished bowman. A split second later, the lethal piece of iron pierced the warrior's thigh. He barely had time to cry out in pain before he realised Tarek was sprinting towards him. The other three, responding to their comrade's plight, launched their spears in panic. Tarek dropped to the ground as the three spears soared overhead. Two of them fell harmlessly into the caked surface of the street; the other thudded into flesh.

The bowman stared down at the spear, skewered deep into his chest, as blood seeped out of his mouth, but Tarek was not finished with him yet. He sprang off the floor and gripped hold of the dying Grey Cloak, twisting him around to face the three remaining warriors, now armed with their axes.

"How do you like my new shield, lads? Fancy taking a swing at it?"

They looked at each other, unsure of what to do next.

"I warned you to turn and run, but it's too late now. My old friend's awakened, and he's such a greedy fellow." He released a guttural roar that even the Communion warriors dispatching the remaining townsfolk could hear. Ramming the dying Grey Cloak into the middle warrior, Tarek swiped at the exposed shin of the warrior to his right, severing it from his leg, then combined it with a lightning-fast thrust into the middle warrior's neck. They crumpled to the floor in grim succession.

Ignoring their screams, Tarek flicked his sword towards the

remaining warrior, cascading the blood of his fallen friends onto his face. "Are you ready to die, Grey Cloak?"

The warrior stared at his fallen comrades and then at Tarek. "I-I'm ready to meet the goddess."

"Good. Send her my regards." Just as Tarek prepared to attack, a crossbow bolt whistled past his ear. He glanced up the street and cursed as scores of warriors hastened to join the fight. He snarled at the whimpering Grey Cloak. "Look at me, boy. The next time you see the face of Tarek Grimbard, it will be the last moment of your wretched life. We'll finish this dance—I promise." Then he turned and raced back to the tavern as a barrage of bolts were loosed towards him.

Behind, he heard the young Grey Cloak shouting, "It's Grimbard!"

"Mari, open the door."

She pulled it open, just as Tarek dived in, closely followed by several bolts that smacked into the tavern's doorframe. She bolted the door and pushed a table up against it.

Panting, Tarek turned to the couple holding the hands of their fallen friend, who was laid out on one of the tavern boards. "I'm sorry for your loss, but if you want to live, you need to leave now."

"We're not leaving," said the woman. "This is our home. We won't get bullied out of it by the Communion."

"Then you'll die."

"We know."

Shaking his head, he turned back to Mari. "Come on. We need to leave."

"I'm not going."

"Mari, so help me, I'll knock you out and carry you down that bloody tunnel myself if you don't shift your arse."

"I'm not going, love," she said, handing the couple a pair of blades.

"I can't protect you, Mari. I have to leave."

"I don't want your protection, Tarek. Before you go, I want to know one thing."

"What?"

"If Kaine killed your wife, why in the goddess' name are you helping him?"

Tarek closed his eyes and sighed. "Because he's got my son."

"Oh, love." She hugged him. "I knew it had to be something like that." Kissing him on the forehead, she straightened and fixed her tearful eyes on him. "Now piss off and save your son."

A moment later, the Grey Cloaks were at the door, hammering at it. Tarek hesitated.

"Go," said Mari, pushing him away from her. "That door won't hold them back for long."

"I'll never forget you...or your ale."

She forced out a smile. "Keld's finest."

"No, Tarania's finest." He spun around, strode to the booth, grabbed his pack and ran to the back of the bar. He shifted a large barrel to reveal a trap door that led to the tunnel that Mari used for smuggling contraband in and out of the tavern. With one last glance at his old friend, he pulled up the door and dropped into the darkness.

As he stumbled his way through, he stopped in his tracks, hearing the tavern door smash open above him. He scrunched his eyes tight as the fighting began, only to be cut short by the dying screams of two women and a man. "Go well into the Void, my dear friend."

After several minutes of wading thigh-deep through stagnant, putrid water, he emerged from the other end of the tunnel, just outside of Belanore's palisade. He looked back towards Main Street, now deathly silent after the horrors of the massacre. *Such a waste of life.* He spat on the ground in disgust. The man in black had told him that the only way he would ever see his son again was to stick to the plan, no matter what. So, with that in mind, he turned his back on Belanore, gritted his teeth and headed for the mighty Valtara.

50

THE LINES OF BATTLE

Manon shielded her eyes from the late afternoon glare of the Twins, scanning the low rise of the carpet of green stretching out in front of her, where the land met the sky. For a while, it seemed to Manon that her vigil would extend long into the evening. Then, through the stillness of the air, vibrated the faintest tremor. *They're here.*

As the first banners of the Circle and the Cross came into view, she forced a smile onto her face and walked her mount along the five rows of heavy infantry patiently waiting to meet the Mendari horde.

For Yanna's plan to work, the enemy needed to believe that the Northern Taranians were there to fight, which was why five hundred Named had formed a shield wall that covered the plateaued hillock that emerged out of Derwedd Forest's tree line.

Hidden within the trees, ready to protect each flank, was a unit of light Galgari-Zirani cavalry, supported by Belgar mounted archers. Sorcha commanded the right, Rory the left, leaving Manon in the centre to command the shield wall.

Within the lines, a few of the younger Named gasped as a vast forest of spears appeared as a bristling outline against the cloudless sky, finally revealing the sheer size of the Mendari horde. The veterans of the Mendari War, unfazed by such a sight, remained still and silent, their eyes set directly in front of them.

Her horse struggled to hold its footing on the edge of the hillock's steep slope, now a morass of half-baked mud, teeming with insects. Reaching halfway down the line, she pulled on the reins and wheeled her horse to face the Named. Within, her stomach knotted as the image of the mutilated Taleni Elite Guard consumed her mind. *I pray to the goddess that I'm wrong.*

"For those of you who've never seen one, that," she said, pointing towards the approaching army, "is a Mendari horde." She paused, examining their reaction to the increasing rumble of the oncoming enemy. "Does it frighten you, knowing that thousands of Mendari take the field against us?"

The Named, as a collective voice, responded, "No."

Her smile faded. "Well, it frightens me. Not because I'm a coward, but because I'm terrified of what will happen to the people of Northern Tarania if we fail. Your friends, families and neighbours, all at the mercy of Velak and his vengeful followers." She paused, allowing her words to take effect. "And we will fail if we underestimate Kaine. Just ask any Taleni, if you can find one that survived. So, my brothers and sisters, it falls to us to provoke the beast until it rears up onto its hind legs, bares its fangs and reveals its true nature to us. Stay true to our grim task and execute it as only you can —for you are the bravest and mightiest warriors in all Tarania. Who are you?"

"The Named."

"Who do you fight for?"

"Rodric."

"And what do you offer the Mendari?"

"Death! Death! Death!" yelled the Named, smacking their weapons against their shields, as the dremon horns of the Northern Taranian army bellowed their rasping monotone howl in response.

She unsheathed her sword and raised it high above her head. "For the goddess, Northern Tarania and the king."

The Vanguard roared their response. "For the glory of a warrior's death."

Dismounting her horse amid the rapturous cheering, she armed herself with an oval shield and a kladimos, and took her place in the centre of the front row. Beside her, a young Zirani warrior turned around in annoyance as a rough hand gripped him by the shoulder. When he realised who it was, he paled, nodded and quickly changed positions with the veteran who now stood beside Manon.

"Your words convey so much passion, spirit and strength, my love. One can only imagine what other pleasures your lips could bring."

Without looking at the speaker, she groaned. "Goddess, Fergus— I'll throw myself onto the first Mendari spear I see if you don't shut up."

"Deny it all you like, my Lady, but I know you want me as much as I want you."

"I always thought the wrong brother bit his tongue off."

"That cuts deep, my love."

She ran her fingers down her kladimos, stopping at the tapered end. "I think this will cut deeper."

Fergus roared with laughter. "I love our little games, but alas, I'm here at the command of my dear brother."

"Why?" she asked, allowing her eyes the briefest of glances at the Belgar champion.

"He's worried about you. And so am I."

"Worried? Why?"

"Because you sense the same oppressive state of the forest as we do. What happened to the Taleni Named was not from a sword, spear or bolt."

"So you don't think I'm losing my mind?"

"No, I don't. And neither does Kilien."

She bristled. "I thought he made his view clear to me at the Council of War."

"You know what he's like. For someone with no tongue, his words can still leave their mark—for good or bad."

"Or maybe he said what everyone else accepts as the truth?"

"I don't believe that and nor should you."

"But when the king himself believes my premonitions are sending me down the same path as her, it's—"

"Well, he's wrong. And he shouldn't have dismissed your counsel at the clearing. Is he that desperate to fight Kaine that he would ignore the concerns of his chieftain?"

She nodded. "He's so consumed with revenge that he can't see that something else is at work. Something dark and powerful, hidden from mortal eyes."

"Which is why I'm here, Manon. We'll face the darkness together."

Flustered, she scratched under her eye patch. "You're Kilien's champion. Protect him."

He shook his head and smiled, staring intensely into her eyes. "Not today. I'm your champion."

She blinked, unsure how to respond to him.

"I'll take your silence as permission," said Fergus, softly. He stared out towards the Mendari. "Looks like they're almost in position."

Without another word, Manon turned to face the oncoming enemy. She checked that her helmet was sitting firmly on her padded cap and that her chin strap was tight. *Any moment now, they'll charge.* She readied herself. *Why aren't they charging? They always charge.* She peered through a gap in the shield wall, watching in disbelief as the Mendari advanced in three orderly, distinguishable units, halting as one at the single blast of a Mendari horn. They stood in silence—uncharacteristic silence, bar the sound of a multitude of banners flapping in the grassland breeze and the occasional whinnying horse. Then, out of each cohort appeared a warrior dressed from head to toe in black armour, unlike anything that Manon had ever seen.

To the far left stood a figure whose frame suggested that of a woman. She held a curved longsword that kept its width throughout the length of the blade. In the centre, a huge warrior casually rested his immense body on a formidable double-handed axe. Finally, on the far right, completing the trio, was a lanky warrior who wielded a pair of identical blades similar in length to a kladimos. Manon's eyes narrowed as the Mendari levelled one blade directly at her and slid the other across his stomach.

"That bastard will pay for that," hissed Fergus, stepping out of the line.

She grabbed his cloak, pulling him back. "Don't be a fool! Get back in line."

"But he insulted your honour."

"How in the goddess' name have you survived so long with that kind of thinking?"

Fergus grinned. "I knew you really cared about me."

Before she could admonish him any further, the warrior in the centre raised his axe high above his head, then swung it down hard. With a roar that shattered the unnatural silence, the middle red and black cohort surged past their commander and charged towards the Named shield wall. Behind them, scores of crossbow bolts soared up, whistling through the air, arcing down towards the Named.

"Aerial attack!" bellowed Manon. Immediately, each of the Named hefted their shields above their heads just as the first of the deadly barrage descended onto their lines.

Misery from above, the bards called it—an apt name, Manon considered, as an iron-tipped bolt pierced her shield. Its objective was to make the Named cower, allowing the unchallenged advancement of the Mendari horde—a tactic that Manon had employed many times. For the inexperienced and undisciplined, sheltering from a ranged barrage was not only miserable but infuriating, as no warrior wanted to meet their end at the point of an unknown archer's bolt. Where was the glory in that? Watching their friends and kin die around them would allow the Red Mist to grip hold of many a warrior, causing them to break out of the shield wall, full of rage; but this was the Named. Even as the occasional bolt slammed into the flesh of a comrade, they bided their time, until the Mendari aerial assault ceased, for fear of hitting their own advancing warriors.

"Prepare spears!" she commanded, as the first of the Mendari reached the base of the hill. *Just a few seconds more...* "Fifth row, loose!" The volley of spears rushed over her head and plunged into the disorganised mass of Mendari bodies struggling to find their footing. As they found their mark, scores of warriors fell into the quagmire—those still alive, screaming, cursing and writhing in agony.

One such warrior held out her hand to her comrades, begging for them to come to her aid. Manon sneered in disgust as they not only ignored her but threw her body up the slope, stamping onto her back to support their footing. The macabre scene repeated itself across the Mendari line and, step by gruesome step, the enemy ascended the slope.

"Fourth row, loose!" Again, the spears carved into the Mendari, slowing their ascent, until the next wave of attackers took the place of the fallen. With only a couple of spear lengths between them, Manon yelled over the tempestuous din, "Extend!" As one, the front line of the Named planted their left feet just over the brow of the hillock, angling their shields down towards the first of the Mendari almost at the top.

"Brace for impact!"

Across the line, Mendari fury collided with Northern Taranian discipline, as shield clashed upon shield, iron struck against iron, and the deadly game of brute strength thundered into life.

Hemmed in on all sides, Manon dodged a speculative axe swing that found the slightest of gaps between her and Fergus' shields. She stabbed her pointed blade up into the armpit of the exposed arm, severing mail, skin, bone and muscle. Even before the warrior's weapon had slipped out of his incapacitated hand, she drove the kladimos deep into his neck. She watched the Mendari's life drain away, to become an upright corpse buffeted by the crushing swell of warriors surrounding it.

The line's holding, but their numbers are increasing. "On my command!" she shouted to her signaller standing directly behind her. The warrior sounded two short notes on the dremon horn. Immediately, the Named roared their understanding.

"Push!" As soon as the signaller relayed the command, the whole of the shield wall shunted forward, forcing the front line of the Mendari down the slope and into their comrades. With no solid ground to stand firm on, the shock wave ripped through the Mendari, sending them sprawling.

"Crouch!" The front line squatted behind their shields.

"Loose!" A final volley of spears from the second and third rows plunged into the mass of filthy bodies, desperately trying to gain their footing. The heavy losses that the Mendari middle cohort were suffering would have lured a less experienced commander to signal a counter-attack down the hill; but Manon stayed silent. *Is this all you've got, Kaine?* She spat on the floor and cursed.

"I thought you'd be relieved," said Fergus, wiping away the sweat from his eyes. "It's clear that apart from splitting into cohorts, nothing's changed from the way they fought in the war. It's all they know—use their greater numbers to smash into our centre and try to tire us out."

Before she could reply, Mendari horns blared the signal for the remaining two cohorts to advance. As if the Mendari commanders had heard Fergus' criticism, the cohorts fanned out, ready to attack the flanks.

"Oh, that's different."

Manon spun around to her signaller. "Send in the cavalry."

51

PROTECT THE FLANKS

As the dremon horn reverberated through the outskirts of the forest, Sorcha raised her war cry and dug her spurs into her horse's side. Leading the light cavalry at a controlled canter towards the right flank, the mounted Belgar archers peeled away from the main body to get further behind the Mendari. Realising the new threat, the warriors on the fringe of the Mendari lines quickly formed a shield wall against the oncoming cavalry, the front row planting their spears into the ground, holding them up at an angle.

Goddess, they've learned. She snapped out of her unexpected revelation as the Mendari launched a combination of crossbow bolts, spears and darts towards them. As one, the cavalry pulled their kite shields in front of their horses' heads and ducked under, just as the first projectiles thudded all around them. She cursed as she heard a rider and their horse collapsing into the grass to the left of her. The supply carts and healers shadowing the cavalry would have to tend to the fallen. Sorcha's mind focused on one crucial decision: whether to make a turn or pass behind the Mendari cohort. Such decisions came naturally to Sorcha, but the Mendari's newfound organisation worried her. If she executed a turn, they would be vulnerable to a ranged attack, but if she opted for the pass, they would take longer to replenish their spears from the supply cart and allow the cohort time to outflank the Named shield wall. Almost on them, she made her choice and prayed she was right. *We'll just have to take the chance on the turn.* She need not have worried, as scores of Belgaran arrows ripped into the fringes of the enemy lines, causing mayhem.

Thank the goddess they're on our side. "Loose and turn left!" she shouted to her signaller, Manus. As he relayed the command, Sorcha lowered her shield, picked out a Mendari warrior sheltering from the barrage of Belgaran arrows, and launched her spear. Then, without waiting to see if her aim was true, she deftly guided her mount at a right angle to the left, sweeping her shield over her exposed side, and held her breath. Behind her, the mounted Named followed her lead and headed for the nearest supply cart to rearm, while the Belgaran archers covered their retreat.

Grabbing a new spear from the cart, she called her warriors around her. "Let's keep them guessing. We'll execute a feint and see if we can draw them out after us. I can't wait to see their faces when they discover that the Belgarans can turn in the saddle and shoot back at them."

"Yes, Lady Galgari."

As she urged her horse towards the enemy, she called back, "And keep your bloody shields up."

Six sorties later, Sorcha waved away a healer as blood oozed from a nasty gash to her spear arm. Even though they had killed countless Mendari, the cavalry unit had paid the price: only two-thirds of their original number remained. Still, they had so far been successful in their primary objective—stopping the Mendari cohort from outflanking the Named shield wall. She just prayed that Swiftblade had enjoyed the same success on the left.

"Lady Galgari. Look."

She craned her neck to see where Manus was pointing towards in the distance. "Velak's balls. Cavalry."

"Since when did the Mendari fight on horseback?"

"Another one of Kaine's improvements. If they get past us, this will turn into a massacre." She turned to the most senior Belgaran warrior. "Leave me ten of your best archers and take the rest to keep the Mendari infantry from flanking our shield wall."

"Yes, Lady Galgari."

"My lady!" called a weaponsmith, sat on top of the cart. "Perhaps now is the time to try out Prince Tomos' compact crossbows?"

"Do they work?"

"Uh, there are a few teething issues, but—"

"That's good enough for me. Hand them out. We need to get back out there."

The Named cavalry fanned out into a single line with the ten Belgaran mounted archers positioned just behind them. By Sorcha's estimates, the Mendari cavalry outnumbered her mounted warriors by at least two to one, opting for a similar formation to the Named, but at least three rows deep. As she assessed the dire situation, her eyes lit up as she realised the Mendari's tactical error. *They're packed too tight and they're in full gallop.* She called back to the mounted archers. "Fan out and aim at the horses in the front line. But wait for my signal."

As the Belgar raced off, she spat into the wind. *Just because you can ride a horse, doesn't mean you can fight on one. Now you'll learn the hard way.*

The ground thundered as the Mendari hurtled towards the Named, roaring their god's name as they levelled their spears at their sworn enemy. The Named remained silent, keeping their line in check, holding their mounts to a controlled canter.

That's right: the faster, the better. Just a bit closer, you bastards. "Now!"

The command blared out, and the Belgar loosed their arrows, slamming deep into the sides of the Mendari horses. Sorcha smirked as the Mendari quickly learned why skilled riders never charge in such tightly packed lines. The result was instant. Wounded, the enemy horses collapsed, forming insurmountable obstacles for the riders following them. Those still standing veered hysterically into the surrounding riders.

It was then that the Named cavalry surged into the gaps that had formed, thrusting with their spears and smashing riders off their mounts with their shields.

The Mendari reeled in panicked confusion, made worse by the constant hail of arrows unleashed by the Belgar. The Southern cavalry commanders tried desperately to gain some order within their ranks, hurling threats and curses at those that seemed on the verge of fleeing.

"Crossbows! Aim for their commanders."

The Named rounded on the disarrayed Mendari and fired at close range at the warriors most likely to be the leaders of the cavalry unit. They didn't stand a chance. Even though they outnumbered the Named, the leaderless Mendari turned and fled the field of battle.

Without a moment to lose, Sorcha wheeled her mount around and surged towards the enemy infantry. The battle was far from over.

52

THE BEST-LAID PLANS

All along the line, the Named continued in their grisly task of dispatching the enemy. Manon struck out with her kladimos, burying it deep into the groin of a snarling Mendari warrior in front of her. She must have severed an artery, for as she withdrew her sword, the discharge of slick, crimson blood showered those around the dying Mendari. Out of the corner of her eye, she detected a swinging movement to her left. As she threw her shield in its direction, she howled in pain as the top of it shattered into pieces from the impact —the force so great, she lost her footing and fell into the soup of mud and bloody entrails. By instinct, she pulled what remained of her shield over her body, as the same war hammer smashed into the yellow and black paint of the wood. Her shield-arm dropped to the floor, lifeless. She reached out in panic, realising that her right hand no longer held the kladimos. Her fingers found the hilt, then she winced as a heavy boot kicked the blade away. Above her loomed a massive Mendari, hefting his fearsome war hammer over his head, ready to smash her brains to a pulp.

This is it. I'm going to die.

"No!" cried Fergus, diving at the Mendari. The pair tumbled over the brow of the hill and out of sight, down into the mass of the living and the dead.

"Fergus!" Manon dragged her battered body to the edge of the slope and stared down. The mud so thickly covered the writhing heap below, she had no way of identifying him. "Fergus. I-I'm sorry."

A moment later, Ovantae warriors surrounded her. "Get her out of here!" ordered her signaller.

"No. I can't leave him down there," she said, as a pair of warriors pulled her through the ranks of the Named towards the safety of the forest. "Let me go."

"You can't go after him, my lady. It's too late."

"Get your hands off me." She struggled to her feet, took two steps and collapsed.

"My lady, if we don't disengage as planned, we'll be overwhelmed."

She pounded her fist into the mud. "Very well. Sound the retreat."

Kilien rubbed his aching back against the crook of the mature cedar tree that had been his hiding place for the last few hours. Impatiently, he had observed the course of the battle from his high perch, fretting over any Mendari advance and cursing the poor decisions that his peers had made. When he witnessed Manon being dragged away from battle without any sign of his besotted little brother, he reluctantly prepared to climb down and take command of the centre. Then, as the Ovantae dremon horn droned its short repetitive pattern, he stood, bracing his feet between the branches, nocked an arrow and waited.

Below, the Named as one turned and disengaged the Mendari, scuttling towards the trees, covering under their shields for protection. He nodded to the Woodland Warrior closest to him, who whistled a signal to the other Belgarans hiding within the canopy. Silently, they drew their bows and waited for their lord's signal.

He smiled with satisfaction, as across the Mendari line, the enemy hesitated for the briefest of heartbeats to allow the slightest of gaps between them and the Named. Then, picking out one of the first Mendari to step onto the plateau, Kilien released the bowstring, sending the arrow straight and true, puncturing through the warrior's chainmail and through his breastbone. The dying warrior looked up into the trees. His eyes grew wide in terror as a storm of one hundred and fifty arrows tore over the heads of the Named and ripped into the advancing Mendari. Wave after relentless wave of the deadly projectiles inflicted carnage on the enemy that remained on the slope. In the space of a minute, almost one thousand arrows had been unleashed from the bows of the Woodland Warriors. As Kilien signalled the archers to cease, only the bodies of the wounded and the dead remained. Also, from his elevated position, it seemed as if Swiftblade and Bloodrage had succeeded in pushing the two other Mendari cohorts away from the Named flanks.

They've had enough. We could turn this into a victory. Yet even with that glimmer of hope in his mind, the three black-clad commanders reemerged from out of the horde and ascended the slope littered with the dead.

Cocky bastards. He drew his bow back as far as his restricted space allowed him and released an arrow towards the huge warrior with the axe. The arrow, capable of piercing the strongest of chainmail, bounced off the warrior's chest plate. *That's impossible.* Signalling the Belgar to resume their aerial barrage, he shook his head in disbelief as the three continued their climb, unfazed and unharmed from the hail of arrows assaulting them. As they stepped onto the plateau, they stood still, facing the onslaught, and raised their hands to the forest. Behind them, the entire Mendari horde clashed their weapons onto their shields and cried, "Reeeaperrrrr! Reeeaperrrrr! Reeeaperrrrr!"

What in the goddess' name are they doing? Behind, he heard the first of the Named set off on horseback, making their way towards the king at Midway Bridge. More darted through the trees underneath him. He turned back to the plateau, expecting the last of the Named to have made the tree line. *What?* The remaining Named halted their escape and craned their necks up above the canopy into the diminishing light. He cast his eyes above him just in time to witness the sky darken as hundreds of squawking birds burst out from within the forest and escaped across the plains. Below him, four-legged beasts of the forest hurtled past the bewildered Named: rabbit, boar and deer, beside fox, wolf and bear—predator and prey, unified in their terror of an unseen danger.

A shadow crept across Kilien's mind. The hairs on his neck prickled as if he stood directly under a thunderstorm. He apprehensively turned to face north. The great cedar, from its roots through to its evergreen leaves, trembled as a tumultuous roar ripped through the forest.

"Reeeaperrrrr!" the Mendari called in response.

Goddess. Is this what Manon sensed? Frantically, Kilien waved his arms to attract the surrounding warriors, but they too were struck with fear of the fearsome sound of whatever was approaching. Now more than ever, he wished he could speak, to yell to his comrades to run for their lives. Then, just to the north, as if the forest itself had suffered a mortal wound, the screams of the Named erupted from out of the trees. Their torturous cries increased in volume until, cascading all around the Woodland Warriors, descended a torrent of bloody gore—the remains of the Named.

Every second, the screaming drew closer to the edge of the forest. Even his Woodland Warriors, who were experts in the art of concealment, shrieked in abject agony as the mysterious, malevolent beast tore into them. Helpless, he stared in horror as one warrior's stomach exploded from within as an invisible force ripped her from her hiding place and drew her up through the canopy.

I'm next. Kilien dived off the crook of the cedar, just as the same hidden power drove into the bark of the branch where he had been standing. He caught hold of a branch a few feet below and swung with all his might, releasing just as the beast severed the branch in two. There was nothing to break his fall; he tumbled until he thudded to the forest floor.

Dazed, he scrambled onto his hands and knees. To his right, he spotted a rotten hollow in a toppled tree trunk about ten feet away from him. He sprung to his feet and sprinted in its direction, diving for its safety. Just as he caught hold of the outer edge of the hollow, he flinched as something hard coiled around his boot and yanked him back. He gritted his teeth, pulling with everything he had to shake off the hidden force. His muscles throughout his arm burned, but he refused to let go. The bark cracked. He needed to act. With his free arm, he pulled out his sword and reached behind him, stretching until he managed to push the tip of the blade under his boot fastenings. With one last desperate lunge, he severed enough of the strapping to loosen his boot. As it flew off his foot, he slid into the stinking recess, rolling through the decomposing mulch until he hit the back of the hollow. He spun onto his back, pushing his feet onto the roof, and heaved with all his might to rock the rotten trunk onto its side.

It was then that he finally saw what hunted him. Ripping his boot to shreds, a tendril of vibrating air raised itself up off the forest floor as if it were a serpent ready to strike.

Come on. Move.

It darted for Kilien, covering the short distance as fast as an arrow loosed from his forest bow.

With one last muscle-tearing effort, the trunk rolled just enough to close the opening. He held his breath, waiting for the beast to pulverise the rotten trunk and skewer him, just like it had done to the Named.

Why aren't you attacking? Although muffled, he could hear the metallic drone that the creature made, slithering across the trunk until it left in search of other victims. *It can't see me.*

53

FOR THE GLORY OF A WARRIOR'S DEATH

Sorcha reared up on her horse. She stared open-mouthed towards the forest, listening in disbelief at the harrowing screams spewing out from within.

Manus pulled up beside her. "Those bastards got around us."

"It can't be the Mendari. We had scouts right throughout the forest. We'd have known."

"Then what, my lady?"

She did not respond, for the answer to his question revealed itself to them in a way that defied belief.

As if from a ghost story told by a bard, a massive shimmering form appeared out of nowhere, hovering like a cloud above the forest canopy. From within the form, twelve rippling tendrils of air snaked into the forest, weaving its way through the trees.

"What in the goddess' name is that?"

"I don't know, Manus; but it's slaughtering the Named. We've got to help them."

A deafening roar erupted out of the apparition, and it raised its tendrils from within the treetops to reveal its grotesque quarry. Skewered on each tendril writhed a great number of the Vanguard, still alive, their pitiful wailing for such brave and noble warriors igniting a fury deep within Sorcha.

The Mendari horde fell to their knees and cried, "Reeeaperrrrr!"

So that's the name of your foul beast.

The Reaper bellowed, whipping its tendrils towards the plain, flinging the unfortunate Named through the air—their broken, mutilated bodies crashed mercilessly to the ground.

Sorcha's face flushed, her nostrils flared, and her eyes grew wide with outrage, as a cloudburst of blood fell upon the battlefield. The Mendari raised their faces into the deluge and bathed in the bloody remains of the Named. Then, as quickly as it appeared, the indistinct, shimmering form of Reaper faded from view.

Manon was right. She signalled to a pair of Ziranian warriors. "Ride as fast as you can to the king. Tell him everything you've witnessed here and implore him to retreat behind the walls of Keld."

"Yes, my lady."

As they set off, she turned to the remaining cavalry unit. "So, Kaine shows his hand at last. I do not know if the beast will return, but I will fight to save our brothers and sisters, nonetheless. Who's with me?"

The remaining riders looked anywhere apart from into her fierce eyes.

"Manus?"

The signaller pulled his attention away from the worshipping Mendari and met her unspoken plea for help. "If I'm to die today, let it be by sword, axe or spear, not by that accursed creature. I'll ride with you."

Then, one by one, the rest of the warriors nodded in response.

"I wouldn't have blamed you if you'd turned and fled this place. So know this: no bard will ever be able to express how proud I am to have fought with you this day." She removed her longsword from her scabbard and raised it above her head. "For the glory of a warrior's death."

"For the glory of a warrior's death."

With a final nod of gratitude to Manus, she spurred her horse away from the hill. Relying on the hope that the Mendari would believe that they were retreating from the field, she would cut through the forest fringes to avoid detection and reach the remaining

Vanguard before it was too late. To her far right, she caught sight of Rory's mounted unit also heading for the forest. *Let's hope you're less of a two-faced bastard than your lord.*

The Red Mist bubbled within her. No longer was she Sorcha of the Galgari. She was Bloodrage and woe unto the unfortunate souls that dared to stand against her.

Overwhelmed, Manon stumbled out of the forest, allowing her most trusted warriors to lead her away from the massacre that had just taken place within the trees. Never did she believe that her foreboding would come to pass in such a catastrophic moment of destruction. The blood of the Named spattered her from head to toe, and her right arm remained numb from the impact of the Mendari's war hammer. Out of the many Named that had entered the forest less than thirty now stood on the hillock. *No wonder the forest grieves. How can it be whole when its trees are ripped from their roots, its creatures are driven out from its borders, and it witnesses death on such a massive scale? What chance do we have against such power?* She craned her neck, peering up through the blood-drenched canopy. *Where have you gone?* That worried her more than anything else. With such a weapon, Kaine could strike out against the North with impunity.

"It looks like your cavalry has had enough. No matter. They'll be dead before the day is over."

You don't know Sorcha. She turned towards the owner of the unmistakable southern accent. Appraising each of the three black-clad commanders of the Mendari horde, she steadied her voice and spoke with as much confidence and authority as she could muster. "If you were a man of honour, you'd speak to me face to face, not behind a mask. Are you scared of an arrow piercing your eye?" she goaded, lifting her eye patch to reveal her hollowed-out socket. "Or are you so ugly that you dare not reveal your face, fearful of the derision you'll receive?"

The three warriors in black laughed.

As the warrior in the centre tapped his shoulder, the remaining

Named gasped, witnessing the helmet melt away to reveal the man's head. His appearance took Manon by surprise—his long blond hair and piercing blue eyes were in sharp contrast to the monster that she had imagined dwelled within.

"Lady Ovantae, I guarantee that apart from your small group, none of your warriors survived the Reaper's cleansing. It senses all things, just as we do."

"You have me at a disadvantage, Mendari. You know my name, but I don't know yours."

"I am Alvar of Gol Zaram, commander of Lord Kaine's host. This," he said, pointing to the shortest of the three, "is Okita of Amaryth, and to my left is Rask of Gol Stolrem. We are Scions of the First."

Manon shrugged. "Am I supposed to have heard of you?"

"No, my lady; but I've certainly heard of you. Your skills in combat and your exploits against my people are well known to all Mendari."

"And now you come to avenge a member of your kin that died by my blade?"

"On the contrary, I offer you a way to save you, your warriors and your clan."

Come on, Sorcha. Where are you? "What are your terms?"

"Lord Kaine offers you the same choice as he gave the Champion of Taleni: renounce the goddess and the king, and turn to Lord Velak."

"And what of the other clans?" she asked, stalling.

"If they turn to him, then they too will be spared."

The two other warriors in black snapped their moulded helmets away from the hillock and into the forest.

Alvar chuckled. "Well played, my lady; but as I told you already, we sense all things, including your approaching cavalry."

A moment later, Rory's riders burst out from the left of the plateau and bore down on the three Scions. Okita ran towards them, her sword sheathed at her side. The two foremost riders levelled their spears at her, intending to run her through. Just as they made their killing thrusts towards her chest, she sprang into the air, ripping the spears out of their hands, somersaulted over their heads, and drove the iron tips deep into their backs.

As the warriors fell to the floor behind her, she landed deftly onto the ground and reached behind her back with both hands. Then, with one fluid mirrored motion, she threw a pair of three-pointed projectiles towards the nearest riders; the razor-sharp, steel blades sliced deep into the necks of their horses. Their mounts reared up and unseated them, dumping them in a heap onto the ground. Okita ignored the fallen warriors, continuing to target the rest of the cavalry's horses with the vicious triangular weapons. When she had finished, not one rider remained in their saddle.

One warrior struggled to his feet, but flinched as a deep red cut spread across his throat. As blood pumped from out of the wound, Rask appeared out of nowhere behind the dying man. He snarled from within his helmet, then blinked out of view, only to reappear behind another of the Named.

"Behold the power of Lord Velak," said Alvar, stretching out his hand towards his black-clad comrades. "You should've accepted my offer, Lady Ovantae. As you're so keen to see my face, I'll make sure you get a good view of it when I take your head." He slid his axe off his shoulder and advanced on the thirty-strong shield wall.

"Stand your ground!" cried Manon.

Alvar roared, breaking into a run. He hurtled towards the shield wall with an unnatural acceleration, smashing into it with the force of a fully grown bear. As the battle-weary lines of the Named scattered from the impact, Alvar swung his axe, carving into the disorientated Northern Taranians. He twirled and swayed in a deadly rhythmic dance, majestic and invincible. Yet he failed to spot Sorcha hurtling towards him from out of the forest.

She thrust her spear into the middle of his back, sending the giant Mendari sprawling into the festering mud. She pulled up beside Manon, as the rest of her riders searched for any survivors.

"Get on," she said, reaching down to Manon. She wrenched her onto the back of her horse, steered it towards the forest and dug her spurs into its sides.

Glancing behind, Manon gripped Sorcha's shoulder. "That bastard's still alive."

Spear in hand, Alvar glared at them, very much alive and

353

unharmed. He roared, then launched the spear. It ripped through the air and punctured deep into their horse's rump. It collapsed, sending Manon and Sorcha hurtling onto the forest floor. Dazed, they scrambled to their knees, just as Alvar reached their position, towering above them. Sorcha lunged for her sword, but he kicked it away. She pulled out a dagger and stabbed it into his thigh. With a look of utter contempt, he swatted it away, then raised his axe over his head.

"Unlucky, Galgari."

Just as he drove his weapon down towards Sorcha's defiant face, a second black-clad warrior rippled into view in between Alvar and his intended victim.

"By the whore goddess, Rask. Get out of my way."

"No, brother. I want them alive."

Alvar's eyes bulged, his breathing shallow, every muscle in his face taut. "Not this time."

"Let him have his fun, Alvar." Okita walked up to them, dragging an unconscious Rory behind her. "I've even brought you a present, Rask."

Alvar relented. "As you wish." He jabbed Rask in the chest. "But make sure you're at Keld before the break of dawn."

"Don't worry, brother. I'll be there." He smirked at Manon and then at Sorcha. "Once I've had my fun."

54

CROSSING THE VALTARA

The last sliver of Ulena's bright golden disc slipped under the Southern Belith Range in the west. Kilena was not far behind his twin, choosing a more southerly exit into the Netherplain, below the distant tree line of Derwedd Forest. Perched in the boughs of the willow copse, thrushes, dunnocks and robins released their songs into the chill of the waning light, their melodies rising above the rumble of the surging waters of the Valtara.

Tarek slipped off the trunk where he had been resting and crouched at the edge of the raised bank. He picked up a pebble lying in the grass and tossed it out across the surface, its splash masked by the sounds of nature surrounding the copse. "Well, Ulena's gone to bed, and not a boat in sight." He snorted. "As if anyone would attempt to navigate a boat on the Valtara at this time of year." He knew it and so did the fortress, as not one patrol had headed his way since he had been there. "What're you up to, Kaine?"

Frustrated, he grabbed another pebble and tossed it as far as he could, but froze as it clanged against something metallic in the middle of the river's channel. *What in the goddess' name was that?* He sprung up and dashed down to the beach until he skidded to a stop at the water's edge. Warily, he gripped his sword's hilt and stared across the rolling current. He shrugged, seeing nothing unusual; but as he turned away from the river, an immense impact on the water's surface rose above the thundering torrent that made him stop and rip his sword out of its sheath. The hairs on his neck bristled. He was not alone. Another mighty splash—closer—the shock wave pulsing across the beach, transforming thousands of pebbles into a writhing carpet of stone cockroaches.

Tarek swallowed hard and turned, as every bone-jarring vibration brought the creature of his nightmares ever closer to him. He slid his sword back into its scabbard and outstretched his arms. "Come and get me, Bwgan."

The water's surface scythed in two, as the invisible force that had taken everything he loved slithered its way towards him. The shimmering limb slid around his boots, and coiled itself around his body until, cocooned, the Bwgan hoisted him into the air.

Tarek gripped onto the coil to steady himself but pulled away in disgust. He stared at his blood-smeared hands and shuddered. "You've been a busy little bastard, haven't you, Bwgan?"

A deep, resonant voice boomed with laughter from within the rippling air taking form above the Valtara. "Bwgan?" The coil lurched Tarek over the river and drew him towards the centre of the shimmering. "Now that's a name for the Reaper I haven't heard in a long time."

With all of his will, Tarek forced his fears deep within and allowed his dark companion to surface and give him strength. "Whatever your name is; you butchered my wife in front of my eyes." He spat into the shimmering. "And I *will* have my revenge."

"That's not fair, Grimbard. Do the families of your victims curse your sword's name or yours? The Reaper has no concept of right or wrong. It follows the will of its master—just like your sword."

"Then who are you, if not the Reaper?"

"You're in no position to make demands," said the voice. The coil jerked him in so close that Tarek's skin rippled from the oscillating air writhing in front of him. "Do you have the amulet?"

"Yes, I've got the damn amulet. If anything happens to Prince Tomos—"

"No harm will come to the prince; nor will anything happen to your son, as long as you hand over the amulet to Kaine by Ulena's awakening."

"But it's almost thirty miles to the Stones. It'll take me at least ten hours to get there walking through the night."

"Then you'd better steal a horse or sprout wings," said the voice, chuckling. "I'd get the Reaper to take you, but it has work to do."

Tarek's stomach knotted. "What kind of work?"

"You know the answer to that question, Grimbard."

"The children."

"Yes, the children."

"Why do you want them?"

"Because they have been chosen to bring life to that which was dead."

"And my son? Is he one of them?"

"Enough questions, Grimbard. Time to fly."

The coil pulled away from the shimmering mass and tossed him onto the southern side of the Valtara. As Tarek scrambled to his feet, a rush of wind surged above him and then only the sound of the river remained. His mind reeled from what had just taken place. He could just imagine the faces of his audience staring at him in disbelief at his story. Before that terrible night in Nabaya, he would have shared their scepticism. He considered the voice that had spoken to him. If it wasn't the Reaper's or Kaine's, whose was it? He flinched inside, then gulped as if the final piece of a puzzle slotted into place. "Velak's balls! He's real."

55

NOT THROUGH THE PRIVY

Tomos peeked out from behind the privy and glanced at the bedchamber door. He snapped his attention back to his sister kneeling beside the wooden bench with the circular hole, and slapped his hand against the doorframe. "If you don't hurry, we'll get caught."

"I'm working as fast as I can," she said, scrunching her nose as she lowered the makeshift rope of torn bedding and clothes into the privy. "Do it yourself if you think you can do better."

He ignored her and took another look outside. "I can't believe you talked me into this."

"*Into* being the perfect word for where we're going," said Seren. "Goddess, Tomos. Your shit stinks."

"Well, if I knew we'd be using it to escape, I'd have defecated lavender and rose petals just for you, dear sister."

"You're such an arsehole, Tomos."

"Another pun? You're on a roll."

"And you're full of—"

"Shit?"

She snorted. "Someone's back to their usual form."

"Surviving a near-death experience does that to you. Although, if Uncle Kurzon walks through that door, I'll be well and truly—"

358

"Stop worrying. He's too busy with Kaine's letter and that Taleni warrior." She looped the end of the rope around the heavy stone plinth supporting Tomos' wash basin and tugged at it. "That should hold our weight."

"*Should*? Like how the guards *should* stay away from this side of the Great Hall?"

She glowered at him. "I've told you already. The guards'll be watching all the doors and windows. There's nothing on this side, apart from the shit heaps—which is why they hate going past it on patrol."

"Lucky them."

She stood, hands on hips, and wrinkled her nose. "I preferred it when you were unconscious."

"That's low, even for you."

"You deserved it," she said, her stony-faced expression turning into a grin. She stared at him for a few seconds, then frowned. "Are you sure you don't have *any* of the symptoms you had in the night?"

He rolled his shoulders and stretched his back. "I sometimes get an unpleasant tingling sensation through my body, but it doesn't last for long." He rubbed the back of his neck. "And best of all, my skin's stopped itching."

"You certainly look better. In fact, I don't think I've ever seen you look so...healthy."

The unforgettable image of Kaitlyn standing naked inside his room burst into his mind. *You're not the only one to notice.* He played out the moment she slid her hand inside his robe and caressed him. *Why did I stop her?*

"Tomos."

"What?"

"Concentrate."

"Oh, sorry. I-I'm just wondering how I could feel so much better after being a hair's breadth from the Veil."

She shook her head, mumbling.

"What's the matter?"

"Are you sure you want to do this? You've never travelled on your own before, and the hinterland can be dangerous, even for someone like me."

"I know. But I've set my mind to go. I need to do this."

Seren nodded and patted him on the shoulder. "Well, if you're so keen to leave, you can go first," she said, eyeing the circular hole, just wide enough for them to pass through.

"Fair enough."

"Really? You're not going to argue?"

"No, Seren. I'm done with this life. The sooner I'm gone, the better."

He stepped over to the plinth, picked up the knotted rope and climbed onto the privy. "There's a phrase I remember reading in the books of the Hen Rai that seems rather appropriate for this moment."

Seren huffed. "You and your bloody books—what phrase?"

"Up to your neck in—"

"Shit?"

He stared into the hole and nodded. "Oh, yes," he said, trying not to gag. "And knowing what came out of my arse last night..."

"Lavender and rose petals, Tomos; lavender and rose petals."

A few minutes later, Tomos emerged out of the narrow shaft set inside the corbel jutting out from his side of the Great Hall. Although it was too dark to see, he knew that the rope dangled directly above a steaming heap of excrement and hay—the produce of the inhabitants living with him in that part of the building.

Holding his breath, he listened, making sure no-one was near. *Why did I agree to go first?* He closed his eyes and released his grip.

Gracelessly but silently he fell into the fetid pile below. *Urgh! And there was me fretting over the bar at The Renegade. I'll never get this stench out of my nose.*

"Hey!"

He glanced up at the outline of his sister swinging above him. "What?"

"Move your arse before I flatten you."

"Wait—"

Too late. She dropped through the air and landed on top of him, sinking him deeper into the stinking pile.

"You did that on purpose," said Tomos, pushing her off his chest. She wriggled around to face him. "Are you grinning? Why—"

With a clump of hay in her hands, she shoved it in Tomos' face and giggled. "I always said you spoke a pile of shit."

"Urgh." He lurched over, spitting chunks of excrement and straw from out of his mouth. "Hilarious. See how you like it." He slapped a heap into her hair and rubbed it in.

They glowered at each other in a silent stand-off, until unable to contain themselves, they burst out laughing.

"Did you hear something?"

The siblings snapped their eyes to the far corner of the building as two silhouetted guards stood looking in their direction.

"Came from that pile of noble shit."

"Noble or not, I'm not sticking my nose anywhere near it."

"Aye...probably a rat. Come on. Our duty's nearly over."

"That was too close," hissed Seren, watching the guards disappear from view.

Rattled, Tomos bit his nail, then screwed up his face in disgust. "Urgh. Let's get out of here."

They silently rolled off the dung heap and slipped into the shadows.

"How are we supposed to avoid detection smelling like my bloody privy?"

She smiled at him. "You'll think of something, my clever and extremely annoying little brother."

Tomos cocked his head to the side and grinned. "Isn't it ironic that now we're likely never to see each other again, we've finally found a way to get on?"

"Who said I got on with you?"

His grin faded. "Oh..."

"Come here." She wrapped her arms around him. "Oh, goddess. We really do stink."

"I'm going to miss you, Seren."

"I'll miss you too, Tomos," she said, pulling back from him, her eyes filling with tears. "I hope you find whatever you're searching for."

"And I hope you find a way to rescue Amira. And please, be careful. If you get caught, the Mendari will do terrible things to you."

"One impossible task at a time, little brother. First, I need to find a way to get out of the fortress."

"Same here."

"Take care, Tomos," said Seren, turning towards the South Wall. "Maybe one day we'll find each other again."

"Seren."

"What?"

"For the glory of a warrior's death."

She turned and faced him, her expression serious. "For the glory of a warrior's death."

As she faded into the darkness, Tomos' heart pounded with great excitement and pride. *She said it to me. Maybe there's a chance, even for someone like me.* He took a whiff of his clothes, almost gagging. *Well, as soon as I stop smelling like my own privy.*

56

THE COST OF FREEDOM

Cai sat on his own. He stared into his bowl of beef stew and stirred it with his spoon, making random swirls in the thick layer of fat lying on the surface. Apart from a few mouthfuls, he had hardly touched it. He took a sip of ale and looked across the long, narrow room where he sat.

The other clansguard within the refectory had kept well away from him, eyeing him with unveiled disdain. *It seems as though my reputation precedes me.*

He locked eyes with a surly veteran momentarily, before casting his eyes back to his lukewarm soup. He groaned as he heard a stool scrape back, followed by a set of heavy footsteps that increased in volume until a figure stood over him and darkened his view.

"I don't care what Ironfoot says, a filthy traitor like you doesn't belong in here."

Cai ignored the warrior, preferring to stir his soup.

"Don't you dare ignore me, boy." The clansguard slammed his hands so hard onto the table, the soup exploded all over Cai.

Cai took a deep breath, wiped the mess off his face and looked up. "I've got no quarrel with you."

"But I have with you...and so do they." At that, every warrior within the refectory stood and faced Cai. "You're not welcome here, traitor."

"Fine," said Cai, pushing his stool back. "I wasn't hungry, anyway." As he marched to the entrance and opened the door, he paused. "Enjoy your meal. It may well be your last." Slamming the door to a tirade of abuse, he wrapped his cloak tight around his body and headed for the North Gate Tunnel. *The sooner I'm out of this place, the better.*

Almost an hour later, Cai grew increasingly on edge as the night watch had already started their duty, and still there was no sign of Prince Tomos. He kicked a stone hard against the side of the tunnel. *If he's backed out.*

Then, from out of the darkness emerged a flaming torch that flickered in the draught flowing through the tunnel. As it neared, Cai realised that its owner wore a hooded cloak that hid their identity. Whoever it was, they were unarmed, but Cai was in no mood to take any chances.

Drawing his sword, he said, "If you value your life, you'll come no closer."

"Don't be alarmed. I'm a friend."

A girl? "A friend within these walls? I doubt it."

She laughed. "I know what you mean, but it's true. My mistress is Kaine's contact in Keld."

Cai cursed. "So Kaine sends young girls to do his bidding? How noble of him."

"I know what I'm doing. And I can look after myself."

"I'll take your word for it. So where's Prince Tomos? Has he lost his nerve?"

"I wouldn't worry; he's always late."

"Sounds like you know the prince well?"

"You could say that."

He strained to recognise any distinguishable features under the concealing hood. "So how did a young girl like you get mixed up in all of this?"

"It's a long story," she said, sliding her hand inside a fold in her cloak, but keeping her eyes fixed on Cai. "But I'm sure you already know it's impossible to say no to Kaine."

He stayed silent, more concerned with her actions. As she started to remove her hand from the pocket, Cai stepped towards her, his sword positioned defensively in front of him. "Whatever you have in your hand, take it out slowly and hold it out to me."

She chuckled. "No wonder Kaine chose you." Holding out a bag of coins and a folded parchment towards him, she said, "Give the money to the guard in the gatehouse and he'll open the outer gate for you."

Relieved, he took the items from her, then frowned. "What about the rest of the guards?"

"Don't worry about them; they've been dealt with."

"You killed them?"

"Goddess, no, nothing as drastic as that. I poured a sleeping draught into their stew. They'll be out for hours."

"How did you manage to walk into a gatehouse full of clansguard? Unless..."

She stayed silent.

"You bastard, Kaine."

"I do what I'm told, no matter what. Otherwise, they'll..."

"You don't have to say. I know what they're capable of." He slipped the money into his pocket, then unwrapped the parchment. "A map? I thought *I* was the map?"

"All I know is that you're to travel to the place marked on the map to meet with the People's Alliance."

Cai studied the map until he found a small cross marked twenty miles north of Keld at the foot of the Southern Belith Range. He looked up and frowned at her. "Why are the People's Alliance working with the Mendari?"

"I don't know; but Kaine's sending one of his best warriors to meet you there. They'll protect you on your journey."

"Protect?" Cai shuddered inside. "That's not the word I'd use. Did he say which one?"

Footsteps approached from behind. "

Hello. Is that you, Pathfinder?"

Cai spun towards the tunnel entrance. "Prince Tomos?"

"Yes. Are you the Pathfinder?"

"That's what Kaine told me—if I can believe anything that comes out of that lying, scheming mouth of his." Behind him, something thudded onto the ground. He whirled back to the girl, ready to strike at any unforeseen danger. "Hey! Where'd you go?" The girl had vanished, leaving only the sizzling torch resting on the ground in front of him.

The prince walked up beside him. "Was someone here?"

"Yes, a girl. Sent by one of Kaine's agents."

"Kaitlyn."

"She didn't give me her name, but she said you were acquainted."

"Yes, we are—I mean, were, friends."

"By the looks of it, she's in way over her head. I'm sure they've made her do some terrible things."

The prince looked away from him. "Yes."

"And knowing how ruthless they are, you willingly meet me here in the night, even though I could be an assassin?" He waved his sword towards the prince to add weight to his words.

The prince scoffed. "If Velak wanted me dead, he could've killed me earlier today."

"Why? What happened to you?"

"A story best kept for the comfort of a campfire. So, do you have a name, apart from the Pathfinder?"

"That's not important. How do you know about the Pathfinder?"

"It was in the message I received." He rummaged inside the pack slung across his shoulders and pulled out a small piece of parchment. "Can you read?"

Snatching it out of the prince's hand, Cai said, "Of course I can read." He picked up Kaitlyn's torch and held it close to the note.

"So, Pathfinder, do you know where we have to go?"

"Yes, to begin with; but after that I'm not sure.

Kaine said something about where Velak's spirit lies imprisoned and a slumbering creature...a leviathan."

"That's all you know?"

"Unfortunately,"

said Cai, grimacing. "He said Velak would reveal the answers to me as we travel."

The prince nodded. "I think I know what he means."

"Well, I'm glad you do. Otherwise, how in the goddess' name are we going to work out where to go?"

"Well, I'm leaving no matter what, but it's not too late to change your mind."

Cai sighed. "I've no choice." He sheathed his sword, picked up his pack and eyed the prince. "What puzzles me is why you would choose to leave your family and position behind. What have they offered you?

"Freedom."

"Freedom from what?"

"Everything."

Cai's eyebrows twitched in surprise. "It seems as if we have a common reason for taking this path." Torch in hand, he strode deeper into the tunnel.

"Wait a moment!" called the prince, chasing after him. "We can't just walk into the gatehouse and ask them politely to open the gates. We need a plan."

Pulling out the bag of coins, Cai turned and tossed it at the prince, who caught it cleanly in mid-air. "Good catch."

"It was, wasn't it? What's this for?"

"And I thought you were the cleverest person in the kingdom? Figure it out. By the way, my name's Cai."

A short while later, Prince Tomos handed over the bag of coins to the only guard left awake in the outer gatehouse. Just as Kaitlyn had promised, the rest of the guards snored, unaware of the pair of young men that had crept their way across the room seconds earlier. The three of them stood at the top of the stairs that led to the outer gate.

The grizzled clansguard licked his lips as he felt the weight of the bag. "I've raised the gate just enough for you to squeeze under. On the outside, you'll find two saddled horses and a week's supply of rations, as requested by your pretty young lady friend."

The lewd look in the clansguard's eyes confirmed Cai's suspicions. He wasn't the only one to have seen it.

"What did you do to her?"

"It's what she did to me I remember. Besides, your highness, why would you be so concerned about a little slut from the Skilled Caste?" Again, the clansguard licked his lips. "And let me tell you, she was very skilled indeed."

The prince snapped. "You bastard." He rammed the clansguard up against the wall. Cai raced behind Tomos, gripping his shoulder to prise him away, but reeled back winded as the prince elbowed him in the stomach with incredible strength.

The guard groaned as Tomos tightened his grip, but had enough presence of mind to reach for his dagger. "You'll pay for that, you snivelling little shit." He slashed the blade across the prince's face. Tomos flinched as the tip tore a nasty gash across his cheek. Hissing, he gripped the clansguard by his arms and threw him down the steep stairs beside them.

As the guard landed on his head, Cai grimaced, hearing the man's neck snap from the impact. "Velak's balls!" He grabbed Tomos' arm. "You've killed him."

The prince narrowed his eyes at Cai. "He deserved it." He ripped Cai's arm away with his free hand and squeezed it. "Don't you ever put your hands on me again." He spun away and descended the steps, kicking the contorted corpse of the clansguard as he passed.

Astounded, Cai pulled back his chainmail, gambeson and the inner layers of his sleeve, flinching from the hand-shaped bruise appearing on his skin. *Goddess! He's as strong as a Scion. Maybe stronger.*

57

DESPERATE DEEDS FOR DESPERATE TIMES

Luis leaned on the South Wall battlements and stared out into the distance. He drew in a deep draught of smoke through the lip of his pipe and exhaled a steady white plume out over the fortifications. As the wisps of smoke dispersed into the chill of the night, he craned his neck and marvelled at the thousands of tiny pinpricks of lights scattered throughout the Void. He wondered how many clansguard also looked up into the night offering a prayer to Enora, desperate to be found worthy and allowed to join their ancestors should they die in the battle to come. Luis had no interest in dwelling on such concerns—he had enough to worry about. Not one person had crossed the featureless plains since the young Taleni warrior had arrived earlier that day. *We should've received some news by now.* Not for the first time, the thought that Grimbard's story held a portion of truth gnawed at him. Had the undisciplined, headstrong Mendari of old evolved into something else? Something unstoppable?

He winced as cold steel slid against his throat. "Oh, bollocks. I always thought a Mendari blade would kill me. Good evening, your highness."

"The Three Orphans of Treharne. The king who deserted his family, the champion who betrayed his queen and the war master who lied to the girl who put her trust in him."

Luis closed his eyes and sighed. "I lied to you to stop you from doing something reckless, Seren." He snorted. "Well, that plan turned to shit."

"It wasn't your decision to make."

"So for that reason, I deserve to die? My throat slit and my body shoved over the wall to plunge into a watery grave in the Valtara?"

"No. I need you alive—at least for the moment." Seren pulled him away from the wall and shoved him towards the entrance to the outer gatehouse stairwell.

"Where are we going?"

"You'll find out soon enough." She forced him through the stairwell entrance and down the spiralling steps until he stood in front of the door leading to the outer gatehouse guardroom. "Open it. And don't try anything stupid. I *will* hurt you."

"I do not doubt that."

"Move!"

Luis opened the door. The guards within the room snapped to attention, then, one by one, they noticed the blade across his throat. They drew their weapons.

"Easy, clansguard. The princess and I had a slight misunderstanding that I'm sure we'll sort out. Isn't that right, princess?"

She ignored him. "You there," she said, pointing at a warrior nearest the exit to the tunnel. "It's Morag, right?"

"Y-yes, your highness."

"Go to the stable and fetch my horse, Gwyn. Bring him to the inner gate."

The warrior flicked her eyes towards Luis, looking for confirmation.

"Don't look at him. Do as I say, or the War Master dies. Go."

Morag opened the door and hurried down the walkway.

"The rest of you, throw your weapons in a pile on the floor and face the wall."

They looked at each other, hesitating.

Seren nicked Luis' skin with the blade.

"Ahh!" he hissed. "Do as she says."

Swords, axes and knives piled into the middle of the room. As they turned to walk to the wall, Seren pointed at two of them. "Not you two. Raise the outer portcullis, then lower the drawbridge."

"Goddess, Seren. You're not thinking of rescuing Lady Amira? You don't stand a chance."

"And she doesn't stand a chance if we just wait here and do nothing."

"We are doing something," he said, straining around to look her in the eye. "We have a plan that can save her."

"What plan?"

"We believe the Taleni warrior was sent by Kaine to make contact with Grimbard. If we catch them both, we can force Kaine to agree to a hostage swap—them for Lady Amira."

Above them, the guards cranked the pair of windlasses, heaving the immense outer gate aloft.

"No," said Seren. "It'll be too late by then." She shouldered him towards the tunnel exit. "Bar the door behind us. And I swear, if anyone tries to follow us, there'll be consequences."

Once outside on the walkway, the gatehouse door slammed shut, and the crossbeam snapped in place.

"Why are you so desperate to risk your life for Amira?"

She shoved him forward. "Move!"

They made their way along the torch-lit walkway, suspended across its length by hundreds of ropes fastened to the enormous crossbeams supporting the tunnel. It swayed after every awkward footstep Luis made. He cursed as his iron leg jammed between a gap in the wooden planks.

Seren jabbed him in the back. "Keep going."

He snorted. "You try walking across this with one bloody leg."

"You can walk faster than this—you're stalling."

"Stalling?" Luis wriggled his leg free, then peered over the edge, down into the tunnel. "Any faster and I'll decorate the tunnel floor with my guts."

"Velak's balls. I'll throw you over myself if you don't bloody move."

Luis spun around to face her. "It's not too late, Seren. We can work this out."

"In your own words, Ironfoot, bollocks to that."

They walked the rest of the way in silence until, after a couple of minutes, they came to a set of steps that led to the tunnel floor. After an awkward descent, Luis stepped under the suspended inner portcullis and emerged onto the southern tunnel courtyard. It was deserted.

"What now?"

"We wait for Morag."

"You know she's probably raised the alarm?"

"What if she has? No-one's going to attack me, the heir to the throne; especially when I've got a knife to your neck."

"Don't be so sure, especially when your uncle's involved."

"He wouldn't dare."

Luis laughed. "I doubt he'd hurt you, but I wouldn't put it past him to order a Zirani archer to shoot an arrow in me. Or maybe he'll call your bluff and see if you've got the stomach to do the deed yourself?"

She leaned in close to him and hissed, "I'll do whatever it takes."

They waited in silence until the clopping of hooves announced Morag's arrival. She appeared out of the darkness with Seren's horse, Gwyn, tethered behind her. Within a few feet of the pair, she released the reins and backed away from them. Gwyn, sensing his owner, trotted up to Seren and nuzzled her.

"Good boy." Just about to mount, Seren glanced up, noticing movement in the murder holes of the gatehouse above her.

"I told you so."

"Seren!"

She whirled around and grabbed Luis from behind.

Kurzon and Yanna hurried towards them, escorted by a dozen Elite Guard.

"What in the goddess' name are you doing, girl?"

"Don't come any closer. I swear I'll kill him if you do."

"I couldn't care less if you slit Ironfoot's throat, but your father would. So drop the knife and try for once to behave like a princess."

"Piss off, uncle. I've had enough of everyone telling me what to do: we both have."

Kurzon narrowed his eyes. "What do you mean, 'both'?"

"I mean Tomos. He's had enough of you all; he's leaving."

"Leaving? Seren, if you've talked your brother into doing something stupid, I'll—"

"I didn't do anything. My clever little brother did it all by himself."

"By the goddess, he's barely recovered from almost passing through the Veil." He called one of the Elite Guard over to him. "Find the prince, before he injures himself or worse."

"Yes, lord."

"I told you to look after him," said Kurzon, glaring at Seren. "I just hope for your sake they find him before the People's Alliance or a Mendari assassin get to him."

"At least he gets to choose his own destiny."

"Yet again, you dishonour your father and those who care deeply for you. If you weren't the princess and my niece, I'd order—"

"Kurzon, let me speak to her," said Yanna, taking hold of Kurzon's arm.

He shrugged. "As you wish, but if she lays a hand on you—"

"She won't," said Yanna, stepping forward. "Can I speak to you, your highness?"

"Yes; but only you."

She approached them, close enough so that they could speak quietly without being overheard.

"Forgive me, War Master, for I believe Princess Seren is acting on my behalf."

"What do you mean?"

"We've become close over the past few days, and I believe she feels compelled to act on my behalf."

"But you—"

Yanna flicked her eyes towards Seren. "Let me finish, your highness." She continued, "In truth, War Master, I think you and I know that apprehending Grimbard and arranging a meeting with Kaine is highly unlikely before the appointed time."

Luis narrowed his eyes at Yanna. "Where are you going with this?"

"To put it bluntly, my sister's only chance of survival is a rescue attempt, however low the odds of success. As Princess Seren has led many rescues of Taranians held by all manner of brigands, she is the person most qualified to make such an attempt."

"You ask too much of her, my lady. Yes, she's skilled in this area, but this is Kaine we're talking about—not a bunch of desperate thugs wielding axes and pitchforks. And on all those missions, she led the Elite Guard. If she goes on her own, they'll both end up dead."

"I'd rather die trying than cower behind these walls."

"Then you'd better slide your dagger in deep, princess, because I won't let you go while I'm still breathing, and neither will your uncle."

"But I need to go for *her* sake."

Luis stared into Yanna's eyes, and finally understood. *You're the one she's in love with. And now you take advantage of that love by sending her on a suicide mission to rescue your sister?* He glanced across to Kurzon, arms folded, staring at Seren with a thunderous face. *I wonder how much you know?*

Yanna reached across and gripped Luis' arm. "War Master, you're in command of the fortress. Order the clansguard to stand down and let Princess Seren do what she desperately wants to do. I'll deal with Kurzon. He'll listen to me."

"Oh, I'm sure he will, my lady," he said, easing his arm out of her grip.

She frowned. "What do you mean by that?"

Ignoring her question, he took a deep breath and sighed. "What if there was another high-value individual who could tempt Kaine into a hostage swap?"

"Who?"

"Me. Am I not celebrated as the mastermind behind the successful campaign in Mendaria? I'm sure Kaine would love nothing more than to get his hands on one of the Three Orphans of Treharne."

Seren spun him around, pushing the blade up against his chin. "Why would you sacrifice yourself like this?"

The sound of a dozen archers drawing their bows filled the small enclosure. "Lower your bows, you fools," cried Kurzon.

Ignoring the surrounding furore, Luis said, "It's like you said earlier. You put your trust in me, and I failed you. I won't disappoint you again, especially when there're those that desire to manipulate you for their own selfish gain." He wondered whether his pointed words found their mark in the mind of the woman standing behind him.

Seren's knife fell to the floor as her resolve melted away. She collapsed into his arms, sobbing. "I'm sorry. I didn't know what else to do." Staring up into his eyes, she said, "You know I didn't mean what I said."

"Well, you had me worried for a moment; but I told you, I'll probably end up dying from a Mendari blade." Speaking clearly to the assembled warriors, he ordered, "Stand down." Then, turning to Yanna, masking his newfound mistrust of her, he said, "Get your husband—we need to act fast."

58

THE CLEANSING

Every nerve and fibre in Manon's arms throbbed as she dangled from the coarse rope fixed around the branch high above her head. Her feet, bound at the ankles, brushed against the forest floor, almost close enough to bear her weight; but no matter how much she wriggled and stretched and swayed, her feet never came close to providing a second of relief from the agony pulsing through her body. Only after witnessing Rask's attention to detail in his art of torture did she realise that it was just another means for the warrior in black to ensure that his prisoners suffered throughout every moment that remained of their miserable lives.

She opened her eye, sensing him approach. For a tall man, he made little noise on the carpet of moss and twigs that covered the small forest clearing where he had set up his camp of terrors. If she had dared to hope, the lightness of his gait could have been that of a Woodland Warrior, of Kilien or even Fergus; but how could either of them have survived the events of the previous few hours?

As she peered up through her sweat-soaked hair, her heart sank. Rask's gaunt, unforgiving face scrutinised the remaining Named in the flickering light of the ring of flaming torches staked around the perimeter of the clearing. Of the nine that had been captured, only Manon, Sorcha and Rory were left. The other six poor wretches flayed by Rask's ceremonial blade lay as a mass of smouldering carcasses being greedily devoured by the Scion's pack of hunting dogs.

"Wake him up."

A warrior hurled a bucket of water into Rory's face. He lurched up straight and wide-eyed, coughing and spluttering. The Champion of Zirani stared at the remains of the Named, then set his eyes on Rask. "Call yourself a warrior? You're nothing more than a murdering, torturing bastard."

"Shut your snivelling mouth, Enorian," said the warrior holding the bucket. He swung it hard into Rory's face. "You address Rask, Scion of the First, and you will cower before him."

"Don't you dare, Swiftblade. Remember who you are," said Manon, through gritted teeth.

Rory faced her and opened his mouth into a bloody grin. "I'm a child of the goddess." He turned back to the sneering Mendari warrior and spat the bloody contents of his mouth towards him. "And I go gladly into her loving arms."

The Mendari drew back the bucket to strike him again, but stopped as Rask commanded, "That's enough. I want him fully conscious." He turned his attention to Sorcha dangling between Rory and Manon. "Wake her."

The warrior refilled the bucket and emptied it over Sorcha, but the chieftain remained unresponsive.

"Looks like Lady Galgari isn't as tough as the bards would have us believe. Give her a helping hand."

As the warrior drew close to Sorcha, Manon's lips curled into a sly smile. She watched as the Mendari gripped hold of Sorcha's short spiky hair and pulled her head back. She mumbled something under her breath.

"What did you say, bitch?"

Again, she mumbled.

He pushed his face into hers, "If you've got something to say, whore, say it to my face."

Sorcha's eyes snapped open. She lurched forward and clamped her mouth around the warrior's nose, biting deep into the cartilage.

He shrieked, digging his nails into the chieftain's cheeks to prise her away. Other Mendari rushed to their comrade's aid, delivering blow after blow to the chieftain's body; yet she ignored the pain, biting harder until, with one final wrench of her head, she tore the warrior's nose clean off his face. The Mendari, hands clasped around his oozing wound, staggered away from her, howling. Her face smeared in blood, she spat what was left of the warrior's nose onto the ground and smirked at him.

"I'm gonna kill you for that, bitch." The Mendari ripped his axe out of his belt and lunged towards Sorcha but flinched, staring down in shock as Rask's blade split through his chest.

"No, you won't."

The Mendari tried to mouth a response, but slumped to his knees, then keeled over—his final expression that of bewilderment.

The Scion stepped over the twitching corpse and retrieved his blade. He nodded towards Sorcha. "Well played, Lady Galgari. I'll enjoy testing your resolve later on."

"Why not now, Mendari?" she said, licking her lips. "Afraid I might enjoy it?"

"No; but I prefer to leave the best until last," he said, making his way towards Rory. "After all, Swiftblade's only a champion."

Rory's mouth twitched into a sneer. "Piss off, you southern piece of shit."

Ignoring him, Rask stepped behind the bound warrior, examining the many tattoos inked onto his body, raking his blade across his back until he stopped between the Ziranian's shoulder blades and tapped the knife twice on a tattoo obscured to Manon.

For the briefest of moments, she was sure she detected the Mendari's expressionless face crack. *What was that? Pain? Sadness?* Whatever it was, Rask hid it quickly.

"You've amassed an impressive number of faces, Swiftblade. Almost as many as Grimbard or Swordstorm. I wonder, do you remember this one?" Again, he tapped the flat of his blade in the same place on Rory's back.

Manon's stomach churned. Her uncanny intuition blared like a dremon horn within her mind. "He's playing games with you, Rory."

378

"She's right, Swiftblade. Don't give him the satisfaction."

Rory grinned at Sorcha. "What's this? Lady Galgari showing concern for Kurzon Zirani's champion?"

"Don't flatter yourself. If he kills you, then I'll never know if I was good enough to beat you."

Rory chuckled. "I almost forgot about that. What do you say, Scion? Surely you'd enjoy watching us fight to the death?"

"That's a tempting proposition, Swiftblade; but I asked you a question," said Rask, resting the tip of the dagger against Rory's skin. "Do you remember this tattoo?"

"I've taken so many of your miserable heads, how am I supposed to know which one you mean?"

Rask patted Rory's shoulder. "Then let me help you remember." The show of emotion that Manon had spied on the Scion's face reappeared. He smacked the butt of the knife with his palm, severing Rory's skin with the tip.

Rory hissed between clenched jaws. He arched his back and balled his fists, as the Mendari carved his way around the nameless face on his back.

His skinning complete, Rask stepped in front of Rory and thrust the tattooed face in front of the bulging eyes of the man from Zirani. "Do you remember him now, champion? Do you remember taking his head? How he begged you not to kill him in front of his son?"

Squinting, Rory licked his parched, cracked lips and croaked, "Oh yes, I remember." He looked at Rask, then back at the tattoo. "Come to think of it, he does look a lot like you."

Rask's face flushed and his lips drew back, revealing his snarling, yellowing teeth. He took half a dozen shallow breaths, then, with his eyes bright in the gleaming torchlight, he thrust his blade into Rory's stomach. "For my father."

Rory's body convulsed, and blood seeped out of his mouth, as Rask twisted his dagger deeper inside his abdomen.

"Feel." The Mendari ripped the blade hard across the champion's stomach. "My." He prised the wound wide open with his black-gloved hands. "Pain!" Rory's intestines slumped into a grotesque, steaming pile next to his feet.

379

Rory tensed every muscle in an effort to remain silent.

"You're right, Swiftblade. I *am* a monster. I became one the day you took my father's head."

Trembling, Rory glared at him. "It...was...war."

"Oh yes, the glory of war. What is it you Enorians say? 'For the glory of a warrior's death'?" He turned towards a campfire in the centre of the clearing where another five Mendari warriors huddled. His hounds sat attentively towards their master, tails wagging, tongues lolling out of their mouths. "There'll be no glory in your death." He whistled to his dogs. They bounded across the clearing in the forest towards the raw guts strewn across the ground. With spine-chilling growls, the pack descended upon Rory, ripping, gnashing and pulling his intestines in all directions. Rask slid his blade next to Rory's heart. "Plead for mercy, and I'll give you a swift death."

"No!" cried Manon. "Don't give him the satisfaction of hearing you beg."

Rory's body reeled in a bone-breaking fit, and his eyes rolled up into his head, as the hounds fought over every bit of offal; yet he still managed to wrench his head around to face Manon. "S-sing with me. 'Far in the past, when the world was young, the gods came down from the Void above.'"

Manon and Sorcha, fighting back their tears, joined him, refusing to be cowed by the threats of violence against them. "'They spun their lies, and they promised us hope, of a home in heaven, with lives full of love.'"

Just as they reached the second verse, the hounds yelped in distress, reeling from a volley of arrows thudding into their muscular, bloodied bodies.

"We're under attack," yelled Rask, running towards the mass of animals writhing within the guts and gore from Rory's insides. Then, all around him, the air whistled with a second volley of arrows, felling his warriors and their horses in a matter of seconds. He dived to the ground and slapped the collar of his armour as the hidden archers aimed for his head. The slides snapped into place just as an arrow slammed into the back of where his exposed head had been. Jumping to his feet, he spun in a circle amid the continuing barrage.

"Where are you?" He smacked the side of his helmet. "Whore of a goddess. What's the matter with this damn thing?"

Noticing his erratic behaviour, Manon stared at the Scion. He made to run to the left, but then stopped and swivelled to the right. Whacking his helmet even harder, he cursed, then in a blur he sped off into the forest, still hounded by a hail of arrows.

They were alone. A dog whimpered, struggling to stand within the slick, crimson morass strewn in front of Rory. The Champion of Zirani hung limp. Stringy strands of blood, saliva and mucus stretched from his chin, then broke loose, falling to the ground.

"By the goddess, Rory. Are you still with us?"

"Y-you can't get rid of me that easily," he croaked.

Sorcha shook her head in disbelief. "You're a tough bastard, Swiftblade. I know you're desperate not to fight me, but this is going too far."

He laughed, then broke into a coughing fit that Manon thought would finish him; but he turned to Sorcha and scrunched his face. "I-I suppose I should take that as a compliment?"

"You should." She faced Manon and closed her eyes.

"N-now if only I could die with a sword in my hand."

Manon's ears pricked up as the same soft padded footsteps from earlier drew close to their position. "By the goddess, he's back."

Then, silhouetted by the flames of the central fire, the well-built form of a man came into view. *That's not Rask.*

As his features became distinct, he appeared to be covered head to toe in a layer of caked mud. "Velak's balls—that bastard'll pay for this."

"F-Fergus? Is that you?"

"Indeed, it is, my love."

"But how? I saw you fall."

"That's a story that'll have to wait." He rushed to her side and cut through the ropes holding her in place. As he severed the last binding, she collapsed into his arms, holding him tight.

"I thought I'd lost you."

His eyes gleamed in the light of the torches, and he smiled. "I'm always going to be here for you, and more, if you'd let me." He lowered her gently to the ground, raced over to release Sorcha and turned to face Rory. "What're we going to do about him?"

"I'm dying, you idiot. Not deaf."

"Sorry, brother. Is there anything I can do for you?"

"The goddess calls to me, Finesmile. Find me a sword, so I can meet her with my honour intact."

"I'll do better than that," said Fergus, looking over to the campfire. "I'll get *your* sword."

"I'll help you," said Sorcha, limping after him.

While they were gone, Manon cut through Rory's bindings and lowered him to the ground.

He grabbed her arm as his body shook and he stared at her through glassy eyes. "Don't let him out of this forest alive."

"I won't. And if I survive, I'll make sure that every bard in Northern Tarania sings of your bravery and sacrifice."

His mouth broke into a smile. "I-I'd like that."

"You have my word."

"Here." Sorcha placed Rory's sword into his hand, squeezing it tight, and then stepped away."

"Not so fast, Bloodrage. We've got unfinished business." Hands shaking, he positioned the blade over his heart. "Will you help me?"

"It would be my honour," she said, her voice wavering.

Fergus drew beside the dying champion and placed his hand on his shoulder. "We're all here for you, Swiftblade."

He nodded to Fergus, then at Manon and then finally, he locked eyes with Sorcha. With a deep rattling breath, he said, "For the glory of a warrior's death."

"For the glory of a warrior's death." Then, as she eased his blade deep into his heart, Rory's head slumped forward and he breathed no more. "Go well through the Veil and up into the Void, Rory Swiftblade, Champion of the Zirani."

Silence fell. Manon imagined her fallen comrade striding through the Veil and taking his place of honour up in the Void, illuminating the darkness with his glorious light.

Behind her, someone clapped. "Very touching."

They all spun around to find Rask marching towards them with his two deadly blades outstretched either side of him.

"Get behind me," said Fergus, drawing his sword.

Rask cocked his head to the side. "You're a big bastard. Where've you been hiding all this time?"

Fergus ignored the Mendari. "Go. I'll hold him off as long as I can."

Rask laughed. "Haven't you realised? None of you are a match for the Scions of the First. The Armour of the First can see your moves before you know them yourselves."

"But it didn't see him," said Fergus, jutting his chin behind the Mendari.

Rask whirled around just in time to see a warrior wrapped in a mud-soaked cloak throw a clay container onto his breastplate. It smashed, cascading a thick, sticky liquid onto his armour.

A split second later, a burning arrow fizzed brightly through the darkness, hitting the Mendari warrior square in the chest.

"Get down!" cried Fergus.

Rask exploded into flames. He flayed his swords in dizzying arcs, stumbling blindly, until he tripped over and collapsed onto the ground.

"Who in the goddess' name is that?" said Manon, staring at their unknown rescuer.

Fergus grinned at her. "Who do you think?"

"Kilien?"

Kilien grinned.

Fergus embraced his brother and turned to the chieftains. "Come on—we need to go."

59

QUEEN BEE

Rodric ran his fingers through Cadarn's mane and scratched behind his ear. The stallion, corralled with the rest of the horses of the Named, nuzzled into his shoulder and swished its tail in response. "What happened to them, boy? And where are those bloody scouts? They should've reported back by now."

Many hours had passed since Manon had led the Vanguard down the Great North Road. Even with her recent erratic behaviour, Rodric never doubted that the chieftain would send word of any significant developments taking place at the edge of the forest. Yet no-one had entered the clearing; not even a riderless horse. In fact, no living creature had been seen for hours—something that the more superstitious warriors within the Named had declared to be a bad omen. Publicly, Rodric had played down their misgivings in a light-hearted, reassuring manner, yet within, Manon's warning rang in his ears. And it was not only the Named that had grown uneasy.

He scanned the lines of horses tethered in the centre of the northern side of the clearing. *You'd never think we almost lost them earlier.* He looked up into the treetops and listened. Apart from a light breeze rustling the new spring growth of leaves, there was no trace of the disturbing gust of wind from a few hours earlier that tore through the canopy, sending the horses into hysterics.

Leaning in close, he patted Cadarn's head and said, "I don't know what you think you heard, but it was just the wind blowing through the treetops." He took a final fleeting look into the forest and shivered. "Yes...just the wind."

"I've got to leave you now, boy, but I'll be back." He left the corral and headed towards the defensive line set out along the northern bank. As he neared his warriors, a clansguard approached him holding an object wrapped in a deer hide.

"Sire, here's the item you requested."

"Thank you." Rodric took hold of the heavy bundle and unwrapped it to reveal Shieldbane. "Hello, old friend."

"It's incredible, your Majesty."

Rodric smiled, remembering the first time he had laid eyes on the weapon, not much younger than the rosy-faced, fair-haired warrior standing before him. "What's your name, clansguard, as I can't remember naming you?"

"I-it's Gryff Pureheart, sire. Lord Zirani named me...umm...during your—"

Rodric held up his hand. "Please don't fret, Pureheart. It is I who should feel shame for my absence from my people, not you. Besides, Lord Zirani named you well."

Gryff reddened. "He said that it complimented the meaning of my birth name."

"Which is?"

"Fierce, sire. He told me that the Communion needed devout warriors like me to protect it from those that would harm it and offered me a commission with the Grey Cloaks."

Rodric's expression darkened.

The warrior blanched at Rodric's change of mood and quickly added, "B-but I refused, sire. I wanted to serve in the Named, just like my mother and father did. There is no greater honour."

For the warrior's sake, Rodric forced out a smile and observed the sigil woven into Gryff's gambeson. Emblazoned on his chest was the representation of a large cat, with golden fur and black spots all over its body. "Is that a lynx?"

Gryff nodded. "My family owns a farm close to the border with the Belgar. In the winter, when there are meagre pickings in the forest, many a lynx venture onto our farm and attack our livestock. Believe me when I say there's nothing more terrifying than cornering a starving, desperate lynx. They're—"

"Fierce?"

"Yes, exactly that," said Gryff, peering down at the sigil. "May I ask you a personal question, sire?"

"You may."

"Why did you choose the wren for your sigil and not Shieldbane?"

Rodric ran his finger around the elaborate circular design etched onto his scale armour. Encircling the triskelion were the six clans of Northern Tarania with the wren positioned at the top. "I chose the wren because every time I send a Mendari through the Veil, I want that tiny bird to be the last thing they ever see."

"Why, sire?"

"Because the Mendari were responsible for my dear sister's death, and I wear the wren in honour of her name." For a moment, Rodric stared off into the distance and wondered if he had spilled enough Mendari blood to atone for his sins. He sniffed and returned his attention to the weapon in his hands. "So, Gryff Pureheart, do you know what Bethan of Vedana said when she saw Shieldbane for the first time?"

"No, sire, I don't."

"She said, 'I've never seen any form of metal or alloy like this before. It shouldn't even exist'." He held out the weapon to the warrior. "See for yourself."

Gryff traced his fingers across the legendary silvery-grey weapon that had reputedly been handed down from Banan's earliest ancestor. "It's like the weaponsmith trapped swirls of smoke inside the metal... it's magical."

Rodric beamed. "Yes. That's exactly how I first described it to Bethan." He laughed. "I won't repeat her reply to that." Gripping Gryff by the shoulder, he said, "Fight well, Gryff Pureheart."

"For the glory of a warrior's death, sire."

"Yes. For the glory of a warrior's death."

Alone again, Rodric's smile faded, knowing only too well that Gryff's story was not unique. How many warriors had taken up Kurzon's offer to join the Grey Cloaks? Were the rumours true that their numbers now swelled to the thousands? A threat to his rule?

He studied the weapon that had been the catalyst for his unprecedented rise to power and a direct challenge to the Communion's influence. Standing at three-quarters the height of Rodric, it was a weapon that in the right hands could wreak carnage across the battlefield. On one side of the metal head was a hammer that was used as a blunt-force weapon, and on the other end was a long, vicious spike, designed to puncture plate and mail with ease. His thoughts carried him back to the ambush that took place twenty-eight years ago. A pang of guilt throbbed under his armour, exactly where Banan's face lay tattooed onto his skin. *He offered it to me freely. I could've refused, should've refused.* He spat onto the ground and shook off the remorse that weighed heavily on his shoulders whenever he dwelt on that life-changing event. *No...no matter how it came to me, it's mine.* He gripped hold of the weapon's smooth, untarnished handle. "And we will join with the Red Mist and weave a dance that not even that bastard Grimbard could ever match." Sliding a hand inside his layers of clothing, he retrieved Isabelle's ring. He kissed it. "I won't keep you waiting much longer, my love."

Slinging Shieldbane over his shoulders, he ambled his way towards the bridge, taking his time to spare a word of encouragement for the warriors who saluted him as he passed. He even took a bowl of beef stew from one of the cooking stations, soaking a large chunk of bread into the flavoursome juices. He swallowed it down whole in one greedy gulp. Then, as he wiped his moustache clean, he detected agitated voices arising from the front of the defensive line. Concerned, he tossed the bowl into the grass, signalled to his Elite Guard and hastened towards the commotion. They formed a protective cordon around him, shouting to the warriors in front to give way to him, until they emerged out of the ranks of clansguard and stood in front of the river.

Rodric called out to the sentry, scanning the southern tree line. "Report."

"Rider approaching from the south, sire."

"Just one?"

"Yes, sire."

Illuminated by the flames of the torches placed around their defensive position, the rider, flopped forward in the saddle, allowed their horse to navigate the vicious caltrops and stakes littering the southern side of the clearing.

"Sire, it's one of the scouts."

As the horse trotted across the bridge, Rodric caught hold of the reins. Two of the Elite Guard eased the injured scout out of her saddle. She winced as they laid her on her side.

"She's taken a black-feathered bolt through her shoulder blade," said one of the warriors.

Rodric knelt beside the failing warrior and held her hand. "What's your name, clansguard?"

"B-Beca, sire." Her body tremored from every word she uttered.

"Shhh, Beca. Save your strength. Just nod or shake your head to answer. Do you understand?"

She nodded.

"Do you know what happened to the Vanguard?"

Again, she nodded.

Rodric bit the corner of his lip, then asked, "Are they still alive?"

A tear rolled down her cheek, then she shook her head.

He closed his eyes and considered the catastrophic consequences of losing so many of the elite of Northern Tarania. He lamented their loss —not just for the spilling of their blood, but because he could no longer challenge Kaine on the battlefield. There was a choice to make: either retreat to Keld or do the unthinkable and agree to Kaine's proposal and give himself over to his enemy. He wiped his face with the back of his hand. "One more question, I promise. Where are the Mendari now?"

Widening her eyes, Beca raised her head and said, "They're everywhere." Her head flopped back into the grass, and the final spark of life within her eyes faded out of existence.

"Go well into the Void, Beca of the Named, and take your place of honour with the Children of Enora," he said, closing her eyelids.

"Sire!"

Rodric snapped towards the voice of the sentry. "What now?"

"Lights appearing to the south."

Rodric sprang off the ground and stared in the direction of where the sentry was pointing. "Where? I can't see—" His words trailed off into the distance, as a tiny pinprick of light appeared out of the darkness. Another joined it, then another, and another, until, in a matter of seconds, like a swarm of synchronous fireflies hatching from their pupae, a thousand flickering flames soared brightly into the blackness of the night.

"By the goddess. Aerial attack!" he bellowed, tracking the Mendari bolts arcing against the backdrop of the Void, hissing and sizzling, plumes of smoke trailing behind each of them as they hurtled towards the Named. He gripped Isabelle's ring. "It seems I'll be joining you sooner than I thought, my love."

———

"Sire, you must take shelter," begged an Elite Guard, tugging at him from behind.

Rodric kissed Isabelle's ring, stuffed it under his armour and backed away from the oncoming threat, unwilling to give the Mendari the satisfaction of seeing him turn and run. Finally, clear of the bridge, his Elite Guard swarmed around him and hefted their shields into a protective shell, just as the first of the fiery bolts slammed into the planks of the crossing.

Bolt upon flaming bolt rained upon the two hundred men and women of Niras, thudding into the caked earth, thumping into shields, and as their cries betrayed their misfortune, striking into the flesh of the Named.

Rodric gnashed his teeth, as every cry of agony drove a spear of anguish deeper into his soul. The Elite Guard hissed curse after curse as the hairs on their skin shrivelled from the heat of the fires burning through the wood of their shields. They would soon be defenceless against the incessant barrage of fiery bolts, but within the span of a couple of minutes, the attack ceased, with the last of the bolts fizzing harmlessly into the river.

It was at that moment, when the surviving Named threw down their smouldering shields and peered through the clouds of smoke, billowing all around them, that they discovered a new threat—a threat they had not expected—a threat that came from the north.

Rodric pushed his way to the rear of the beleaguered Northern Taranian line and stepped out into the open. Barely fifty feet away from him stood a wall of Mendari infantry, stretching from one side of the clearing to the other. From a concealed position within the enemy ranks, a man's deep voice barked a command. The Mendari, as one, shifted their circular shields into an interlocking pattern that sent a deafening crack into the night air. Then, with a great roar, they took a step forward and levelled their spears at the Named.

With most of the shields destroyed by fire and the Mendari blocking the way to their horses, Rodric could neither form a shield wall nor launch a mounted counter-attack. He spun around and scanned across the river. If he acted now, the Named could escape across the bridge before the Mendari closing in from the south could cut them off completely. At least they could escape into the trees and make a stand in there. It was better than a dishonourable death by drowning or being cut down by a black-feathered bolt. Yet nothing could have prepared him or the Named for what happened next.

From over the ranks of the Mendari flew a great number of clay jars that smashed all around the Named, their liquid contents igniting into great fireballs on contact with the burning bolts and shields littering the ground. Rodric covered his eyes with his forearm as a blast of fire engulfed the warriors in the lines behind him. He dived away from the flames, rolled to a stop and stared back in revulsion—his brave, unflinching warriors screamed in terror, thrashing and rolling their burning bodies across the earth. Some poor souls, in desperation, hurled themselves headlong into the tributary, only to sink into the depths, weighed down by their heavy armour.

From out of the inferno, a figure staggered towards Rodric—their flesh and skin bubbling and melting away from their bones like fat in a red-hot pan. Collapsing to their knees, the figure raised their smouldering head to Rodric and reached out their grotesque hand towards him. "Kill me!"

Horrified, Rodric gawped at the grim aberration, then gulped, recognising the blackened image of a lynx, barely visible on the warrior's armour. "Gryff."

"Kill me!"

Rodric withdrew his dagger. He leapt towards Gryff, ready to put the tortured warrior out of his misery. Almost beside him, he glanced up, detecting the sound that had ripped through the trees hours earlier. It thrummed high above his head. *It's getting closer.* Something metallic slid past his ear. He skidded to a stop, tensing every muscle. It trailed down his neck and coiled itself around his torso.

As one, the Mendari cried, "Reeeaperrrrr!" Then they smacked their shields in a riotous frenzy.

A new level of dread flooded through Rodric. He flung his head back and gaped into the Void, but saw nothing through the suffocating plumes of smoke swirling above him. *What manner of evil is this?* He pulled with all his strength to release his trapped hand that held his knife, but his efforts were in vain. The coil tightened its grip around his body. He looked into the tortured, ghoulish remains of what was Gryff's face and mouthed, "I'm sorry."

Then, with an acceleration that felt as though his skin and bones were ripped away from his guts, Rodric ascended, away from the wailing, writhing bodies of the Named, until the only scream he could hear was his own; then even that faded. The ice-cold air burned the back of his throat, and his heart raced as it fought against the incredible ascent, pushing his blood down towards his legs. Sensing that his pumping muscle was losing the fight, his body did the only thing it could do to preserve his life. His muscles relaxed, his head drooped, and he passed into a semi-conscious state.

Events from his life flashed into his subconscious. He cowered within his mind as he relived the shame of failing his mother and his sister, the guilt of secrets that he had kept, and the moment his wife took her last breath. He cursed his life, berating himself for the mistakes he had made, and then he wept: wept for his mother, wept for his sister and wept for his beloved Isabelle. It was strange that even after so many tears, he knew that within the fog of his recent memories, a new traumatic event demanded his grief. *Why can't I remember?*

Then within the twilight of his mind, someone spoke to him—a woman—her voice soft and delicate yet rich in tone. A vaguely familiar voice that he had not heard for many years. Each syllable drifted through the darkness, rekindling a hope that had almost perished.

"Rodric."

"Isabelle?"

"Yes, Rodric. It's me. Open your eyes."

Rodric's mind spiralled into a dizzying blur. The voice of his late wife called out to him again. "Don't be afraid, my love."

"I-I always hoped your spirit lived on in some way, but I never believed in my most lucid of dreams—"

"Just open your eyes and you'll see."

He opened his eyelids into the smallest of slits and gasped. "T-the Void."

Like a ship drifting across the calmest of seas, Rodric also floated; but his sea was the blackness of the Void, and all around him shone the twinkling lights of the Children of Enora. One yellowy orange light, directly in front of him, glowed brighter than any other. It was so close that if he stretched out his hand, he was sure he could touch it. "Isabelle. Is it really you?"

The light pulsed. "Yes, Rodric. You passed through the Veil, and now you stand at the crossroads between the Void and the Netherplain."

"So this is what it feels like to cross over." He willed himself to move towards her welcoming light, but he remained fixed to the spot. "Why can't I cross? Is the goddess angry because of my lack of faith?"

"Your lack of faith is the least of your sins, my love." She giggled. "You abandoned your sister to die in the flames of Treharne, lied about your past and made a pact with the man in black. How can such a man expect to ascend into the Void?"

Rodric stared dumbfounded into the light. "I never told you about those things."

"No, you didn't." There was a change in Isabelle's voice. It was subtle at first, but then, as she burst into laughter, her voice, so melodic, yet uncharacteristically bitter, deepened into a stern, masculine tone. The light grew in size, and changed from yellowy orange to red. "I know your deepest, darkest secrets, King Rodric Shieldbane. Secrets that not even your precious sword brothers know the full truth of."

"What's happening? Where's Isabelle?"

"Haven't you worked it out yet? She's not here."

"No. I heard her voice. What've you done to her?"

The force holding Rodric jerked him towards the light, making Rodric shield his eyes from its throbbing glare. "She's where you left her, fifteen years ago—crumbling to dust in her tomb, outside the walls of Caerniras."

"No," said Rodric, his bottom lip quivering. "She lives among the Children of Enora."

"No!" boomed the voice. The light swept forward, pulsing into Rodric's eyes at a blistering rate. "I know it's hard for your primitive mind to comprehend even the most basic scientific concept, but I'll try to explain it to you. Those bright lights are not the spirits of your ancestors. They're massive balls of gas that have been burning for millions upon millions of years—just like Ulena and Kilena, except very far away."

Rodric gawped at the light. "By the goddess." *Tomos was right.*

"Hmm. It seems to me you've heard that before."

"Who are you?"

The voice chuckled. "Be careful what you ask for, King Rodric. You might not like the answer."

"Enough of these games. You dare torment me about my wife and my beliefs, but hide your face from me like a coward. I demand that you show yourself to me."

"Very well. If you insist; but don't say I didn't warn you."

All around Rodric, the air vibrated. The pulse swept over him and through him, shaking every bone in his body. Then, as if the Twins burned their rays directly into his eyes, seven circular lights encircled the one that had hovered in front of him. "What are you? The Bwgan?"

"All legends contain an element of truth, but the reality is far worse than any creature a bard could conjure up in their tales of horror. Tell me, King Rodric, do you know what it feels like to see something so terrifying that you loosen your bowels?"

Rodric swallowed hard and flared his nostrils. "Just show yourself."

"Behold the Reaper—the real Bwgan."

The coil lurched Rodric away from the blinding lights, until, as if from out of a child's worst nightmare, the hideous form of the Reaper appeared before him.

The Reaper's bulbous, metallic-grey head scrutinised Rodric with its multitude of brightly coloured red eyes. Eight heavily armoured legs curled inward below its main body, and positioned all around its elevated abdomen sat a dozen perfectly shaped semi-spheres that glowed in the darkness. From out of the domes, eleven metallic limbs stretched out into the Void, coiling around each other in a slithering, mesmerising dance. *Where's the twelfth?* He lowered his gaze, then trembled, finally discovering what held him tight—the twelfth limb coiled around his body. It was as wide as a fist, and possessed the same smoky surface of Shieldbane. *It's hideous.* The voice was right. Ever since that dark day of the raid on Treharne, Rodric had vowed to face every adversity thrown at him head on, but nothing could prepare him for what he now saw. Never had he known such impotence as in that chilling moment of paralysis.

The voice boomed with laughter. "Lost for words, oh great king?"

Rodric steadied his breathing, then asked, "W-what are you?"

"In simplistic terms, the Reaper is like a worker bee, responding to the wishes of the queen of the colony."

"I-I don't understand. If you're not the Reaper, then who are you?"

"Come on, King Rodric. Who else would know the secrets of your past and be powerful enough to command a creation like the Reaper?"

"Kaine?"

"Kaine! You dare compare me to a mere mortal?"

"Mortal?" Rodric gulped a surge of vomit back down his throat. "Then you're a god?"

"Yes, King Rodric. To you, I am a god."

"No! The gods don't exist."

"I'm surprised you'd say that."

"Why?"

"Because you made a pact with one...the one who betrayed me so many years ago."

"Who?"

"Gaius Galerius."

"Galerius...but that means you're—"

"Yes, King Rodric. I am Velak. Now fall."

The Reaper's lights blinked out of view, and the coil suspending Rodric high above the land released its grip. He fell, plummeting towards the ground. He bit into his tongue, willing himself to wake from his lucid nightmare; but still, he fell. As his stomach pressed up against his chest, he battled to keep his eyes open, unwilling to lose consciousness, knowing that he had only seconds left before discovering if Velak's revelation about the Void was true. For one brief moment, his vision sharpened, and he perceived details that clawed at the layer of an occluded memory—something important—something that needed to be remembered. As the wall of amnesia collapsed inside his mind, two words hit him like a bolt through the heart: burned alive. Then he gasped. His recent memories surged up from the depths of his subconscious, and the full extent of the loss of his beloved Named screamed inside his head. Grief-stricken, he snapped his eyes shut, and amidst the sound of the whistling air, cried, "Whatever's next, I'm ready to join my brothers and sisters."

But Velak had other ideas. From out of nowhere, the Reaper's coil lashed itself tight around Rodric's groin and lurched him away from imminent death, suspending him barely a few feet above the clearing. He stared in horror at the scene below him. The carcasses of the Nirasian Named had been piled into a smouldering heap, and circling the macabre mound were the Mendari—so many that their numbers stretched deep within the forest. They cried, "Reeeaperrrrr! Reeeaperrrrr! Reeeaperrrrr!"

The Reaper bellowed in response. Then, releasing its hold on Rodric, it dropped him onto the mountain of the dead and soared up into the air, disappearing from view.

Rodric sprawled among his comrades and friends, entangled in their charred remains. He spewed his guts until nothing was left in his stomach.

The Mendari howled with laughter. They hurled abuse at him, mimicking the horrific sounds that the Named had made as they perished.

Rodric sensed the change building up within him. Not even the Reaper, with its dreadful appearance, could have subdued the Red Mist rising from deep within his soul, famished and ready to feast. His eyes widened, his pupils dilated, and his heart raced, coursing red-hot blood throughout his body. He rolled off the mound, pulled Shieldbane from off his back and held it out towards the thousands of Mendari facing him. "I am King Rodric Shieldbane. Are there none among you who will offer me the honour of a warrior's death?" He waited, prowling across the line of shields.

"I will fight you."

Rodric snapped his eyes in the direction of the deep, southern voice hidden within the ranks of Mendari. "Show yourself, so that I can see the only Mendari with honour among your pitiful ranks."

In front of him, the Mendari parted to allow a black-clad warrior to enter the ring of shields. On sight of him, Rodric froze to the spot. His legs weighed like lead and his hands grew clammy. Within him, a shocking revelation wrestled with the Red Mist. "You?"

The warrior planted a double-handed axe into the ground and leaned on it. "Whoever you think I am, King Rodric, you're mistaken, for we've never met."

But that would mean Grimbard's telling the truth. There's more than one Wraith Warrior. "Then, who are you?"

"I am Alvar of Gol Zaram, Scion of the First. And I would be honoured to take up your challenge, oh great king."

"I've seen your kind fight before. Not even Grimbard could match you for power, speed and skill." He paused, and pointed to the remains of the Named. "But I'd rather die by your axe than the way those brave men and women did. Where was your precious honour when you watched them burn alive?"

Alvar shrugged. "At least they died in battle, which is something I cannot say for your chieftains."

Rodric's nostrils flared. "What do you mean?"

"Defeat me, oh great king, and with my dying breath, I'll tell you every last detail of how Sorcha of the Galgari and Manon of the Ovantae begged for their lives as my brother, Rask, flayed the skin from their backs."

Rodric, lost to the Red Mist, roared in fury, then hurtled headlong towards the warrior in black. Alvar remained still, watching the king's raging charge, as if he merely stood in a street watching people pass him by. Just as Rodric launched into the air, hefting Shieldbane over his head, ready to smash it down onto the Mendari, a flash of black rammed into his side, sending him hurtling into a patch of churned-up mud. Before he could find his feet, a second, shorter, black-armoured warrior stamped onto his chest, sinking him into the quagmire, then stabbed him in the neck with a needle-thin blade. He tried to resist, to stand; but the warrior was strong. His body numbed, his head swirled and his eyelids drooped. "P-poisoned...I don't want to die like this."

"Don't worry, King Rodric. I'm not going to kill you. That's an honour reserved for someone else."

"Wh—" His voice left him and into the spiralling darkness he descended.

Alvar smacked the side of his collar to lower his helmet and stormed over to Okita, still pressing King Rodric into the ground with her boot. "What in the whore goddess' name are you doing?"

"You know our orders. You could've killed him."

He slammed his axe into the mud. "You know I'm perfectly capable of beating him without killing him. He sent out the challenge, and I answered. It was the honourable thing to do."

She rounded on him. "You and your haughty sense of honour." She grabbed hold of Shieldbane and thrust it towards him. "Just because you wear that armour doesn't make you invincible. You accepted the challenge of one of the most formidable warriors of the North, knowing full well that he held a weapon capable of smashing your stupid head into a pulp."

Alvar went to reply, but thought better of it, catching sight of the fear in Okita's eyes. Scowling, he barked at a pair of warriors waiting to the side with two horses that they had commandeered from the Named. Nearing them, one of the horses tugged hard against its reins and trotted towards the prostrate king, dragging a warrior unceremoniously behind it. As the Mendari clapped and hooted at the warrior's expense, the chestnut stallion prodded and nuzzled King Rodric in an attempt to gain his attention.

Alvar raised his voice to address the Mendari. "Behold. The tyrant king's horse will carry him to his doom." His mood brightening, he tilted his head towards Okita. "When was the last time you rode a horse?"

"I think you know the answer to that," she said, smiling.

"You'd better get started if you want to get there before daybreak. It's at least thirty miles to the Stones, and you know what he's like if he's kept waiting."

"Never mind that, where's Rask? He should be here by now."

Alvar looked to the southern tree line. "Yes. He's having far too much fun. If he's not with me by the time I reach Keld, I'll call it in and send the Reaper to find him." Then, as King Rodric was bound and secured onto the back of his mount, Alvar helped Okita onto her horse. He looked up at the raven-haired warrior, and caressed her gloved hand.

Okita reddened. "Stop it. They'll see." She pulled her hand away from his. "If Kaine were to find out—"

"He won't."

"Don't be so sure."

"What if he did? I'd protect you."

"I don't need your protection," she said, punching him in his breastplate. "Try not to get yourself killed while I'm not around to save your skinny arse."

Alvar grinned, then nodded. "For the glory of Velak."

"For the glory of Velak." Okita dug her spurs into the horse's flank and headed off to the east. *Some things are worth dying for.*

60

MATTERS OF THE HEART

Kilien knelt in front of his brother, close to where a handful of Woodland Warriors raked over a dark trench circling the perimeter of the secluded dell where they hid. In the centre, Sorcha and Manon sat silently, hugging their knees, frozen to the bone, each one lost in their own misery from the catastrophic events of the day.

"Goddess, man. How much longer?"

Kilien pressed his fingers to his lips and narrowed his eyes, noticing a clean patch of cloth on his brother's cloak that he had missed. Spitting onto a handful of forest mulch, he mixed it into a cold, sticky paste and applied it to the spot. Nodding in satisfaction, he signed, "Done."

"Well, as plans go, this one, dear brother, is utter shite," said Fergus, trying to stop his teeth from chattering. "I mean, if it wasn't enough for you to smother us in this stinking filth, you then expect us to offer ourselves as bait? I reckon that fall from the tree's messed with your head."

"So, we just let him get away with it? Is that what you want, little brother?"

"No." Fergus' eyes darted to the pair of chieftains, before returning to match his brother's knowing stare. "What?"

"She's a warrior and a chieftain. She knows the risks."

"But her arm's not fully recovered."

"Even so, she's still the fastest runner out of all of us."

"This is insane." Fergus pushed up onto his feet and trudged deeper into the dell.

Watch where you're going, you fool. Kilien sprung to his feet and rushed after him. He lunged at Fergus and grabbed him by his cloak, wrenching him backwards.

"What in the godd—" Fergus stared down and swallowed hard. "Shite. That was close."

Flaring his nostrils, Kilien gripped his brother by the shoulders and spun him around to face him. "Idiot. You know we'd never get you out if you fell in there."

Concealed by a thin layer of forest dirt and rotting leaves resting on a row of branches lay a deep, oozing tar pit. An eye-watering belch of sulphurous air wafted up from its depths, violating Kilien's nostrils.

Fergus scrunched his nose and snorted the mucus out from each nostril. Avoiding his brother's gaze, he reached inside his hood and scratched his neck. "I suppose I should say thank you. I-I'm just not thinking straight after everything that's gone on."

"I know your head's not in the right place, little brother. It's over there," he signed, pointing to Manon.

"I-I can't help it," said Fergus. "I sense her warming to me. If I could persuade her to leave now, with me, then maybe—"

"If she knew you'd put her life before ending that Mendari monster, she'd never speak to you again. And what about me? What about Sorcha and the rest? Would you abandon us in our time of greatest need?"

Fergus dropped his gaze. "No, I would not.... But how can we possibly win against a god?"

"He's not a god, he's a man—and that means we can kill him."

"You really think this will do it?" asked Fergus, staring down into the trap.

Kilien nodded. "Not even a fully grown bear could get out of this. The more it struggles, the more it gets trapped, until it dies of thirst, hunger, or gets eaten alive."

Fergus spat onto the flimsy facade. "That bastard deserves all three after what he did to Rory and the others."

Kilien clasped his brother's arm and looked him straight in the eyes. "He dies tonight. I'll stake my life on it." Then, leaning in close, he kissed Fergus on the forehead.

"Yes, I love you too, you bastard," said Fergus, returning the gesture. "And don't worry, I'm not going anywhere. Besides," he said, flicking his eyes towards the pit, "I owe you one."

"Only one?" Grinning, Kilien glanced over to the centre of the dell, noticing that the Woodland Warriors had completed their task. "Come on—they're ready."

Returning to the rest of the group, Kilien's heart sank as he thought of all those who had lost their lives during the battle. He scanned across the forlorn remnants of the eight hundred strong Vanguard. *Fergus is right—I must be insane to think we can kill him.* Yet after twice evading Kaine's new weapons of warfare, he was sure that the disgusting mantles of filth hanging around each of their shoulders might be the only thing separating them from a grisly death at the hands of Rask. Even so, he apprehensively peered through the canopy of ancient crowns obscuring the Void, and offered a brief prayer to Enora, begging her to hold back the rain that was so frequent at that time of year.

"I'm still not happy about running without my armour," said Sorcha, inspecting the riveted rings of her chainmail folded across her lap.

Kilien smiled sympathetically and signed, "Your armour will only slow you down, and anyway, it's useless against his blades."

She threw her hands into the air. "Then maybe I should just strip off and run naked through the forest."

"Velak's balls, Sorcha," said Fergus, inspecting a vine lasso that one of the Woodland Warriors had given him. "Not even Rask would attack you with your skinny white arse on show."

Laughing with everyone, she stood, cricked her neck, and stepped beside the Champion of the Belgar. She slapped him hard on the shoulder and whispered something into his ear.

Fergus darted his gaze towards Manon before glaring back at the Galgari chieftain. "That's not fair, Sorcha."

She shrugged and said, "It's the truth." Then, pivoting on her heels, she returned to her seat beside a bewildered Manon.

Unimpressed by the spectacle, Kilien wagged his finger at the smug-faced chieftain. *As if Fergus isn't already preoccupied.* He puffed out his cheeks. *I've prolonged this long enough. It's time.* He beckoned his surly brother to stand beside him, to interpret his words.

"Brothers and sisters, it is plain to see the sorrow and loss scarred across your faces. But do not take out your frustrations on each other; take them out on that black-clad brute that lurks in the forest, lying in wait for us." He paused and peered up into the night. "I swear by the precious name of Enora that I'll not allow this day to end in regret— the regret of knowing I let that barbaric, torturing fiend leave this forest alive. Rory Swiftblade and the others who died at his hands must be avenged. Who's with me?"

Without the slightest murmur, the group rose to join the brothers on their feet. In the hush of the dell, they placed their hands on their hearts and said, "For the glory of a warrior's death."

"I expected nothing less," he said, smiling at each of them. "Then there's only one thing to say: good hunting."

As the group hugged each other farewell, Kilien nodded to the woman approaching his brother from behind, and with a final grip of Fergus' arm, he left them alone, melting into the gloom of the night.

———

Manon sidled beside Fergus and peered up into his hood, where she could just make out the whites of his eyes. Before, she had been able to dismiss his overt affection and lurid suggestions of bedtime activities, but since the battle she felt a tangle of feelings towards him. She tried to convince herself that it was from the trauma she had suffered, but deep down, she knew, whether she liked it or not, that a new emotion bubbled inside—an emotion that grew every time she thought of him. "What did she say to you?"

"Who?"

"You know who," she said, prodding him.

"Oh...um...n-nothing that you need to concern yourself with, my love."

"Fergus Finesmile. I saw you look straight at me right after she spoke to you."

He shivered, dramatically. "I love it when you say my name like that. Do it again."

"I know what you're doing, Belgaran." She gripped hold of the lasso and pulled him in close. "What did Sorcha say?"

He lowered his eyes, and after several awkward seconds, said, "S-she said, I should use the lasso on you, as everything else I've tried has failed to capture your heart."

Loosening her grip, she fell silent, as her mother's disapproving face flashed into her mind.

"What? Tell me? We could be dead before the morning. I need to know."

"Is that what you think I am? A quarry you can catch?"

"No. Of course not. I'd never think of you like that."

Manon snorted. "She was right. You're all the same." Striding off towards the trees, she cursed, berating herself for allowing Fergus to get past her defences. Her mother's words rang loud and clear inside her mind: *'Men are fickle creatures, weak-minded and rotten to the core— even the good ones. Heed my advice. Never let one steal your heart.'*

Above the dell, hidden in a tree, Kilien looked on as Manon fled his brother's gaze. Fergus stamped his foot into the forest floor and cursed, following the outline of the woman he had loved ever since he first laid eyes on her. As he stomped up the slope towards the valley entrance, passing below Kilien's position, he said, "I hope you enjoyed the performance?"

Velak's balls, Fergus. I've got enough to do without keeping my eyes on you. The Belgar chieftain scratched his nose in thought and considered Manon's difficult childhood. Everyone knew of Stefan Ovantae's brutality to Manon and her mother, and how Branwen rose up against him in a bloody civil war. Goddess only knew what effect watching her mother bury a sword deep into her father's heart would have had on her. And then, with her mother's unbridled animosity towards the advances of suitors, no wonder she held Fergus' affection at arm's length. But his brother wasn't Stefan. Yes, he had the swagger of a champion, and a smile to lure any woman to his bed; but he knew, without any hint of doubt, that Fergus loved Manon with every fibre of his being. So, concluding that nothing would bring his brother out of his unrelenting, lovelorn state of mind, he did two things. First, he prayed.

Blessed Enora, I ask that you protect all of us this night; but I pray especially for my brother and Manon. You know my brother's heart is honourable and true. I ask that you will help Manon see what I see. And should their lives be threatened this night, I willingly pledge my own in exchange for theirs. I pray this in your glorious name.

For his second action, he slipped out of the tree and walked through the dell, only stopping when he found a patch of ground that sprung beneath his feet. Withdrawing his knife, he knelt and dug into the earth, until the coal-black, seeping tar that he sought bubbled up through the hole. Then, finally, he unclasped his cloak and coated it in the sticky, molten pitch. *Tonight, the hunter becomes the hunted.*

61

THE HUNT

Rask searched across the vertical shades of dark blue illuminating the tree trunks of the forest. In the background, lighter shades of blue showed gaps in the trees while, scattered in the foreground, similar tones displayed the new spring growth of leaves and vegetation close to his position.

It was a strange sensation, hunting in a forest so bereft of life; but within his helmet, he smirked, knowing that his prey would light up like a bonfire within the canvas of blue surrounding them. So even with the knowledge that the intense heat from the sticky tar had damaged his suit's ability to cloak, Rask set to his task confident about the eventual outcome.

The thin black glass attached to his arm vibrated as yet another message from Alvar appeared on the screen. He imagined the look on his comrade's face as, once again, he failed to respond. *He'll just have to wait. I won't leave this place until I hunt every last Enorian down.*

He paused in his introspection as a red light flashed across his visor, warning him of movement to his left. Spinning towards the direction of the threat, he sliced his blade in an arc, splitting the incoming Belgar arrow in two. "Nice try," he said, locking on to the bright red form of an Enorian barely one hundred feet away from him. The figure darted off to the left. Rask's body tingled with excitement. *Now it's my turn.*

He crouched low to the ground and crept towards them, taking his time, acutely aware that every brush of a branch or snap of a twig thundered in the hush of the forest. The Enorian, now knelt beside a large tree looming up into the night, nocked another arrow. *You need to find me first, Enorian.*

As he took another step, a shrill whistle pierced the silence of the forest. He spun, plucking a knife from his belt, making ready to throw. *That's strange.* Nothing but blue stretched out in front of him. He turned back to the archer. Again, only blue met his gaze. Frustrated, he smacked his helmet. *Wait.* He tracked to the right until, as he had thought, a faint glow of red spilt out from behind the giant tree trunk. He bared his teeth. *Now I have you.*

Picking up his pace, he pushed through the undergrowth, keeping the wide girth of the trunk between him and his prey. Then, mere feet away, he pounced, soaring past the tree. He twisted his body in mid-air and launched his knife. It thudded into the dark blue of the tree, the hint of glowing red nowhere to be seen.

"Impossible." He head-butted the side of the tree, strewing shards of bark in all directions. *First, the cloak, now the sight?* Wrenching the knife out of the bark, he crouched to his knees and inspected the ground. *That's strange. Someone was definitely here. So how could they...no. They'd never work it out; they're too stupid to understand.* He heard a second whistle, coming from deep within the forest. A moment later, a second bright red form sparked into view. "So, you want to play games?" he bellowed. "Very well. All the more pleasure for me." *No more stealth. Time for the chase.*

The forest blurred into streaks of cobalt blue as he expertly navigated the tangled, uneven terrain of the forest, bearing rapidly onto his quarry. Almost there, he dropped into a brook thick with cattails and rushes, blocking his view. He plunged into the water, sprung onto the bank and vaulted through the thin, blue stalks, skidding to a stop within a small clearing. *Not again.* He flew into a rage, punching the side of his helmet repeatedly. "*Work, damn you.*" He whirled around, ready to strike, as the faintest of sounds registered inside his helmet. Marching into a dip where a large tree had fallen on its side, he stamped on a thick, dead branch, not caring if the Enorians heard him. "You can't run forever! You're only postponing the inevitable." Inside his visor, yet another glowing red image of a warrior flickered into view, about three hundred feet to the north.

A woman's muffled voice called out in the dark. "What's the matter, Rask? Need a minute to catch your breath?"

"Well, if it isn't Lady Ovantae. You owe me a tattoo."

"If you want it, come and get it."

As she sped off to the north, Rask whistled inside his helmet. *She's fast. I'm going to enjoy this.* Then, howling like a wolf, he raked his feet across the dry earth and tore out of the clearing, shouting, "I'm coming for you, Manon of the Ovantae! I'm coming!"

Heart racing, Sorcha allowed herself to finally breathe, as the warrior in black raced out of sight, disappearing into the darkness. She silently emerged from behind the fallen tree, tightly wrapped in her cloak, and looked in the direction of the hidden dell. *We've almost got him. It's all down to you now, Manon.*

Unburdened by her armour, Manon hurtled out of the thick forest undergrowth and onto the winding track leading to the entrance to the dell. She took a corner at full stride and counted to ten in her head. *Now!* She sprung into the air, clearing the fallen birch that lay across her path, and accelerated down a straight section that she knew was clear of obstacles. Then, from behind her to her left, a baleful howl wailed from within the trees. Startled, she pushed harder and faster than ever before, burning her lungs, punishing her bones and stretching every muscle inside her body to the point of snapping. For the briefest of moments, she thought she had lost him. Then, almost at the final bend, she glimpsed a dark shadow speeding through the trees to her right. *He runs like the wind.* She took a longer look but saw nothing. *Where—*

"Run, Manon, run!"

Goddess! He's right behind me. She panicked, looking over her shoulder. *Nothing. Where is he?* She turned back just in time to check her speed as she hit the curve, but yelped as her ankle twisted. *Not now. Not when I'm so close.* Wincing with every painful stride she took, she willed herself forward, ever closer, nearing her goal. Then, with one final chest-pounding effort, clasping her injured arm tight to her body, she hobbled towards the entrance. Cresting the slope, she mistimed her stride and lost her footing, tumbling down into the hidden depths. Her vision spinning, she struggled to her feet, staggering and swaying towards the concealed tar pit, her only thought succeeding in her task. She would go no further. Taking one final laboured step, her ankle buckled, sending her sprawling back onto the floor. Wheezing for every breath, she clawed on her belly towards the back of the dell, but froze, and shuddered, for she knew she was no longer alone.

Launching off the top of the slope, Rask soared like a hawk, with his blades outstretched as if they were talons, and descended onto his prey, stamping hard on her injured arm. The chieftain grunted through gritted teeth but did not scream.

"Brave to the end, eh? I'm intrigued, Lady Ovantae. Why would you run down here, straight into a dead end?" Sheathing one of his swords, he moved the other in an arc around the dell until he stopped, levelling it on a large patch of darker blue further inside the valley. He eyed the indentations of multiple footprints surrounding the patch and chuckled. Confident that they were not alone in the dell, he raised his voice. "You bunch of devious bastards. You dare lay a trap for me?" Grabbing hold of Manon by her injured arm, he yanked her towards the trap. He sneered over his shoulder, hearing a joint pop out of its socket, and growled, "Let's have some fun."

Reaching the dark patch of ground, Rask swept his blade across the covering, hacking branches, leaves and mud into the deep hole meant for him. Then, with the greatest of ease, he hefted Manon over the precipice, dropping her for the briefest of moments before jerking her back up. Again, she grunted. Again she did not cry. Instead, she spat on his visor and sniggered.

Wiping away her spit with his sword arm, he said, "If it weren't for the fact that I want your tattoos, I'd gleefully drop you to your oblivion."

"Do what you want, Mendari. But know this: you're not getting out of here alive."

Rask laughed, detecting the red glow of a figure approaching from behind. "You think that big, mouthy bastard can take me?"

"Put her down, you spineless prick."

Without turning around, Rask chuckled. "Seems like you've got an admirer. What'd you think, Manon? Shall we find out how much he really loves you?" He tossed her away from the pit. "I'd tell you not to move a muscle, but I think we both know you're not going anywhere."

Unsheathing his other sword, he twirled his blades through the air with electrifying speed and sauntered towards the yellowy-red figure standing before him. "I've been looking forward to spilling your guts all night."

Idiot! I knew he'd do something stupid. Kilien paced across the tree line, hidden from view. *There must be another way? Think, Kilien, think.* He closed his eyes, then sighed. *No. There's only one way left. I knew it would come to this.*

Stepping out into the open, he crossed the hidden trench that circled the dell and signalled to the three Woodland Warriors hidden at key positions around the perimeter. They emerged out of the darkness, covered in their cloaks, whipping their lassos around their heads, aiming for the warrior in black, but Kilien shook his head and waved his hands, frantically. The warriors, so used to hunting in the night, had no problem seeing him, but they hesitated, unsure of his command.

Frustrated, knowing every second mattered, he mimicked using a lasso and pointed to Fergus. Their uncertainty allayed, they nodded obediently, changing target, and unleashed their lassos.

"What the—" growled Fergus, spinning around, as each loop slipped expertly over his head.

Taking the strain of each vine, the warriors heaved the incensed champion away from the Mendari, now standing still, shaking his head.

"Get these off me, you bastards, or I'll gut you myself."

"No, you won't, little brother," said Kilien, dashing across the clearing. He placed his hand on his brother's shoulder. "They're acting on my orders."

"B-but why, Kilien? You know she's in trouble. She needs me."

With a nod of his head, Kilien signed, "Yes, she needs you...alive."

Turning to look across to Manon, he placed his hand on his heart and pointed to his brother.

Whether it was physical pain or an emotional response, she grimaced, then gulped, "I-I want to...it's just—"

Kilien smiled softly and mouthed, "Just try."

"By the whore goddess, it doesn't matter who faces me—you'll die all the same."

Kilien eyed the Scion. *Not this time.* Then, his eyes glistening inside his hood, he signed, "Goodbye, little brother." He turned to face Rask.

"No!" yelled Fergus, pulling with all his might against his bindings. "I won't let you do it." But no matter how hard he laboured, the warriors held him firm. He sank to his knees, sobbing.

Rask raised his swords towards Kilien. "So you're Kilien Severedtongue? This day just gets better." He tilted his head. "Where's your sword, Chieftain of the Belgar?"

Kilien, with the gut-wrenching cries of his brother in his ears, stepped forward and raised his hand. *I don't need a sword when I have fire.* Whipping his hand down, several bright yellow lights appeared out of nowhere, like tongues of fire dancing in mid-air. He sneered, watching Rask spin left and right, finally detecting the dark curved line surrounding his position.

"Whore of a goddess!" Rask dived towards the line, but the fiery arrows descending from their elevated positions were faster, thudding into the dark markings, instantly exploding into a screen of searing flames.

Rask reeled away from the flames, edging closer to the tar pit. He smacked the side of his neck in an attempt to retract his helmet. "Open, you useless piece of shit."

Kilien sneered. *For the Named!* He flared his nostrils, gritted his teeth and then, pulling his cloak out wide, like the wings of a bird, he broke into a run. Almost upon the Mendari, he launched into the air. A pair of flaming arrows hissed from the trees, smacking into his heavy cloak of thick, flammable tar. Like the wings of the fabled phoenix, his cloak burst into flames.

Then, just as Rask's helmet finally lowered, he cursed, seeing Kilien descend on him at the very last moment. He twisted towards him and lunged both blades deep into Kilien's chest.

But the Red Mist had already ascended, and the feast that was promised would not be denied. Kilien's life drained from him. He smiled with satisfaction, sensing the collision. With his last breath, he wrapped the flaming cloak tight around the Mendari, and let his body's inertia take its course. Over the precipice they plunged, and into the fathomless pit they descended.

The explosion that followed shook the ground where the remaining Named stood. All around them, pockets of flames erupted as the fire spread throughout the tar field that lay beneath the ground. Sorcha hurtled through a section of the fiery curtain and sprinted over to Manon, hauling her onto her feet. "We can't stay here. We'll be burned to death."

Manon nodded, weakly. "Where's the rest of them?"

Out of the fire and sulphurous smoke emerged Fergus,

surrounded by the remaining Woodland Warriors. "Get off me! I want to see for myself."

Manon limped up to the champion and raised her hand to his tear-drenched face. "No, Fergus. He's gone."

"We need to go, now," said Sorcha. "Cover yourselves with your cloaks."

As the others leapt through the flames, Sorcha turned back to the inferno of the pit and thumped her chest in one final salute to the bravest man she knew. "Farewell, you fearless, insufferable gobshite. Take your place of honour in the Void. You deserve it. For the glory of a warrior's death."

Then, with one long leap, she flew through the curtain of flames and rolled to a stop. She patted herself down, and straightened, meeting the eyes of each Woodland Warrior still restraining the distraught Champion of the Belgar. "Warriors, is it customary to treat your chieftain in such a way?"

First, they frowned, and then, as the reality dawned on them, they released their hold on Fergus and knelt before him.

"All hail, Fergus Finesmile, Chieftain of the Belgar," declared the warriors.

Fergus closed his eyes and shook his head. "No...not like this. It should've been me."

62

LIKE FATHER, LIKE SON

Wrapped in a blanket, Amira hunkered in front of one of the many fires littered across the encampment, irritable and bleary-eyed. Beside her, a warrior snorted, mumbled an obscenity, then rolled over, pulling his blanket over his head. She stared at him, envious of his ability to sleep. Why, after the horrendous events of the day, was she denied the chance to forget it all, just for a few hours?

What happened after leaving the Sanctum remained a blur to her. She vaguely recalled riding through Vedana's south gatehouse, along with an armed escort and six wagons containing what she now knew to be the Taleni children harvested by the Reaper. Then, as twilight heralded the invasion of a storm of midges onto the southern trade route, the caravan left the road to make camp on an exposed beach on the south shore of Lake Grimlin.

Between the bitter northerly wind sweeping across the lake and the sprigs of bog myrtle that a kind caravan driver had given her, the tiny, vicious insects no longer plagued her. Yet they had left their mark. She dug her nails into her arm and scratched at the small red lumps littered across her exposed skin. *Urgh! Will they never stop itching?* She pulled off a leaf from a sprig wrapped around her wrist and crushed it between her fingers. *What did she say? 'If the bites get sore, rub the resin over your skin, and you'll feel much better in no time at all.'* She sniffed it. The sweet fragrance was potent, yet pleasant. *I suppose it's worth a try.* She picked some more leaves and made a salve, applying it to her inflamed skin. As the soothing properties of the plant took effect, she drowsily stared into the firelight, and gradually, her eyelids drooped, and her muscles relaxed.

"At last," she said to herself, her body accepting the tender caress of sleep. Her mind was not so readily allayed. Events from the past few days flooded her lingering consciousness, as her inner voice judged her actions and found her guilty. *But I did what he told me to do.*

Her conscience replied, *'You mean this man?'* The image of her scowling father burst into her mind. He towered over her, the Sword of Velak poised for the killing thrust. *'This is the man you put your trust in?'*

But he was so loving, so tender...Before—

'Yes, before—before you made Cai fall in love with you, before he slid a knife across Aedan Taleni's throat for you, before he betrayed his king for you. And now he'll die for you. Foolish little girl. Corrupted by the man you call Father.'

She shuddered, bolting upright, sensing a dark figure step from out of the gloom and into the light of the fire. "Father?" She rubbed her eyes, then sighed with relief, realising it was Juran.

"Can't sleep?"

She shrugged. "How can I sleep after all that's happened?"

"Be thankful to Velak that he spared your life."

"But it wasn't just him, was it?" She hesitated, trying to find the right words. "I never got a chance to thank you."

"You don't have to thank me."

"He could've killed you."

"Well, what else would you expect me to do?"

"I don't know what you mean."

Juran frowned, then asked, "He didn't tell you?"

"Tell me what?" Before Juran could reply, a child's cry broke through the crackling of the fire and the resonating snores of the nearby warriors. "Juran, what didn't he tell me?"

The warrior pushed his finger to his lips and tilted his head to listen. The child cried out again—their voice more like a wild animal than that of a person. Juran's expression darkened.

"What's the matter?"

"I'm not sure," he said. "I'd better take a look."

"Can I come?" she asked, holding out her hand to him.

"No. This doesn't concern you."

"Oh, come on, Juran. I doubt there's anything that'll shock me after—"

He shot her a look that silenced her. "Stay here." He turned from her disappointed gaze and slipped into the darkness.

Frustrated, she tossed the crushed leaves into the fire and watched them boil, blacken and shrivel to nothingness. Although she did not want to cross the only person in the world who she could trust, her inner voice whispered, *'Time to make your own decisions.'* She wavered for a second, but her guilt overcame her reluctance, as she thought back to when Keila had given her the doll. Decision made, she heaved her tired frame off the pebbles, tightened her cloak around her body and headed in the same direction as Juran. She slipped her hand under the blanket and into her robe pocket, just to make sure the dolls she had recovered from Keila's home in Vedana were safe. *If there's even the slightest chance you're alive, I'll make things right. I promise.*

As she picked her way through the mass of dozing travellers littering the pebble beach, she flinched. A whiplash cracked from the direction of the children's tent, followed by a child's pitiful wail. *What're they doing to them?* She broke into a run, stumbling over the uneven surface of the pebbles, until the large, circular tent came into view. The whip cracked once more and across the remaining distance, deeper voices growled, taunted and laughed. *This is barbaric. I have to stop this.*

Juran, already at the tent, spoke to a pair of warriors guarding the entrance. He glanced back the way he came, nodded, then slipped inside.

Incensed, she hurtled towards the entrance. Seeing her, the guards crossed their spears, blocking her way. One of them called out to her. "You can't go in, my lady. Scion Juran's orders."

Skidding to a halt, she caught her breath and glared at them. "Don't you know who I—" She stopped speaking as the lashing and the taunting ceased.

"But the boy was out of control, lord. If I hadn't put the whip—" A sickening crack broke out from within the tent. The guards outside craned through the gap in the folds of the entrance, keen to know who had incurred the wrath of Juran.

Now's my chance. Amira ducked under the crossed spears and dived inside the dimly lit room. She stopped in her tracks, gaping at the scene before her. Juran stood in the centre of the room, surrounded by the terrified children, trembling under their blankets. At his feet lay a lifeless guard, his neck snapped, while two other warriors prostrated themselves in front of him.

Crouched behind Juran was a boy of eleven or twelve. His tunic was torn to shreds and rivulets of blood trailed off his back from being whipped. Shielded underneath him was another boy—a thick-set lad who looked as though he had received a severe beating.

The pair of guards burst through the folds of the entrance and gripped Amira's arms. Juran's disapproving gaze bore into her. "I knew you couldn't help yourself. Let her go, and take him to the healer." A guard staggered towards the entrance, clutching his hand to his chest, as blood pumped from a stump where his thumb had once been.

Tugging away from the pair of rough hands, Amira glowered at the guards. "You should all be ashamed of yourselves. They're only children. Taleni children. And they're my responsibility, especially after—"

Juran cocked his head, then scratched his beard. "Yes, you're right. They're only children. So what shall I do with these?" he asked, nodding in the direction of the pair of warriors face down to the ground. "They held the boy down, while this one," he said, kicking the corpse on the floor, "lashed into him. For it is written,

'Those who raise a hand against The Chosen will suffer greatly for their wickedness'."

"I don't care what you do with them, as long as you do it away from here and there's no more killing. These children have been traumatised enough."

Juran nodded, then addressed the remaining warriors within the tent. "Know this. If I hear of any of you mistreating The Chosen of Velak again, you will answer to me." He summoned one of the other warriors over to him. "Get the body out of here and clean this place up." He pointed to the warriors lying on the floor. "And take them out and give them forty lashes—a mercy they do not deserve."

As the warrior barked orders to the other guards, Amira walked towards the boy.

"Be careful," warned Juran, catching her arm. "The boy's blood still boils with the Red Mist."

"But how can one so young possess such rage?"

"This one can. So be careful."

She knelt in front of the boy at a respectful distance. "I won't hurt you. I just want to help you." The boy turned to face her. She pulled all the leaves off her sprigs of bog myrtle and mashed them into the soothing paste. Rubbing some on her arm, she smiled and said, "It stings a bit, but it'll take away the pain." She moved her hand towards him, but he flinched and hissed at her. "Please, I want to help you."

"He won't answer you," said a young girl emerging out of the shadows. "He only speaks to me and the boy lying on the floor."

Amira blinked. "K-Keila?"

Keila curtsied. "Hello, Lady Amira."

"When I saw the cart hurtling through the forest, I thought the worst had happened."

Keila lowered her eyes. "The worst did happen, my lady."

"Your mother and father?"

"Yes."

"What happened to them?"

"A demon came onto the plain and ripped them to shreds before it took me. And the next thing I remember is finding myself a prisoner with these."

"The Reaper. I'm so sorry, Keila." She dipped her hand into her pocket and pulled out the pair of dolls. "Here. I found these in your room in Vedana. I thought you'd like to have them."

Keila's eyes grew moist. She took hold of the dolls and cradled them to her chest. "Thank you."

"It's the least I could do for you."

"But, I don't understand, my lady," said Keila, frowning. "How are you here? Have they taken you hostage?"

Amira looked away from the girl's questioning eyes. "Something like that." She sniffed, then turned back to her, smiling. "What's important is that I've found you...all of you," she said, looking at the boys. "So, Keila, will you help me dress your friends' wounds?"

Keila nodded.

"And do your friends have names?"

"The boy on the floor is Lars, and this one," she said, scruffing the crouching lad's corded locks, "is Dagan."

63

A DANGEROUS GAME TO PLAY

Seren glanced across at her companion. He stared out into the distance, puffing plumes of smoke into the northerly wind spilling down the slopes of the North Keld Range, across the Valtara Estuary and up onto the narrow pass they waited on. "It's not too late to change your mind."

"If there were any other way, I'd grasp at it," said Luis, the glow in the bowl of his pipe illuminating his face. "But like I've told you every mile since we left Keld, this is the only way I get to see you walk away."

"But he'll kill you."

"Probably."

"Probably? Why are you so indifferent about this? Do you want to die?"

"We all die one day, Seren. And if it's my time to go, there's nothing I can do to stop it."

"At least let me go with you? I can watch from below the ridge and—"

Locking eyes with her, he leant across the saddle, his lips pursed and his brows furrowed. "No means no, Seren."

"You're insufferable." She stroked Gwyn behind his ears and stared glassy-eyed out into the night. The Valtara Estuary roared in the darkness, hundreds of feet below the narrow pass hugging the side of the East Keld Range. The lower slopes of the vast chain of mountains rose gently to the south, thick with fir, larch and pine, silent spectators bearing witness to Luis' journey of self-sacrifice.

To the east, Golanos bathed the Endless Sea with her yellowy radiance as she traced a high arc across the Void, descending towards the horizon. Soon, Ulena would rise out of the waters, and for the briefest of moments, she would embrace her daughter and withdraw her light and warmth from the world below. But tomorrow's reunion would be different—for Kilena would seize his chance and catch his sister unawares. Taranians called it the Great Conjoining. Whether Enorian, Mendari or Wildlander, such an event where the gods displayed their awe-inspiring power could not be ignored. Many prayers, curses, offerings and sacrifices would be made as Tarania fell into the shade. An icy chill shot down Seren's back. If she could not stop Kaine, then Amira's blood sacrifice at the Stones would send a tremor of panic throughout the goddess-fearing North, and make the Mendari leader's plan of conquering Northern Tarania a far simpler quest.

The Stones of Valtara lay on a plateau that jutted out into the estuary, half an hour's ride from where they waited. *If we don't leave soon, we won't get there in time.* "Where's that damn rider?"

"She'll be here, Seren. I just hope that my name's enough to bargain with."

"I suspect that depends on whether he despises you more than forming an alliance with the Zirani clan."

"Oh, he hates me. That I know for sure." Luis took a deep drag of his pipe and exhaled. "And as I'm about to save your reckless arse from certain death, I want you to listen to what I've got to say, whether you like it or not."

Seren groaned. "If it's about Grimbard—"

"No, it's not; it's about Lady Zirani."

"Yanna. What about her?"

He jabbed his pipe towards her. "I know something's going on between the two of you."

"I-I don't know what you mean."

"Seren, if there's one thing I've learned during my time as Master of War and as the Sheriff of Belanore, is that I can read people very well. You're lovers."

Seren blinked, gawping at him.

"I thought as much." He tapped the ash from his pipe against his iron leg, then locked his stern gaze onto her. "That's a dangerous game to play, Seren. After everything I've told you about your uncle—"

"He doesn't deserve her."

"That's beside the point. He barely tolerates you now. How do you think he'll react when he finds out about your affair with his wife?"

"I don't care what he thinks, and neither does she."

"Really? Even if it puts your legitimacy to rule in further doubt? And don't get me started on what the Communion will think of your frolicking."

"But my life makes more sense when I'm around her," she said, pushing her hand against her chest. "Am I not allowed a sliver of happiness after everything I've been through?"

"Of course; but you must understand that there'll be grave consequences if you're discovered."

"It'll be worth the cost."

Luis' nose twitched. "Whose cost? Hers? I don't see her risking her life for her sister, but she's happy to send you, the woman she loves." Under his breath, he mumbled, "I guess it's right when they say, 'Love is blind'."

"I heard that. Is that what you think? That she's using me?"

"I don't think, Seren—I know she is."

"You're wrong, Luis. She'd never do that to me. She loves me."

"I hope you're right, Seren, because I doubt your father or I will be around to protect you from Kurzon's wrath."

An awkward silence descended between the pair. She would not disrespect Luis by telling him he had no clue about matters of the heart—especially with the sacrifice he was about to make. How many more of those that she cared for would fail to see another day? A pang of guilt pulsed through her, knowing that her father's chances of surviving the trap that Kaine and his spies had set for him were slim at best. *At least Tomos is safe. Which is less than I can say for Amira.*

Time dragged its heels for Seren. She picked at the ends of her braids and gnawed her nails down to the quicks. There was nothing worse for her than having to stay still. She hated it. It gave her time to dwell on the past. If only she had some memories of her mother before that terrible day, then she would not need to numb her senses with drink, or any other vice she could indulge in. But now she had Yanna, and she would do anything to spend the rest of her life with her and make new memories. All she had to do was free Amira.

"Someone's coming," said Luis. A set of hooves pounded around the curve on the pass and headed towards them. The rider pulled up on the reins, swung off her saddle and marched in front of the Master of War.

"Good to see you back safe, clansguard. Report."

"Thank you, sir. Kaine will accept the exchange at the appointed time on one condition."

"What condition?"

"Princess Seren must accompany you."

"What? How does he know the princess is here?"

"I don't know, sir, but those are his terms."

"Well, he can shove his terms up his arse."

Seren reached across and gripped his arm. "Please, Luis. Amira's only nineteen. We can't leave her to the cruelty of the Mendari."

"What's stopping him from taking you as well?"

"I'd like to see him try. And we've brought more than enough clansguard to cover us from the ridge."

"No, Seren. I'm doing this for you, not Amira. Either you agree to stay away from the Stones or we turn back this instant."

She glowered at him. "But he'll kill you both."

"Seren?"

"You're a stubborn bastard. Very well, Luis. I give you my word."

"Come on," he said, spurring his horse forward. "Dawn isn't for a few hours. Let's make camp below the plateau and see what we're up against. Besides, if I'm going to die, it might as well be on a full stomach."

As Seren watched him ride into the distance, she slipped her hand into her pocket and pulled out the small bottle of sleeping draught that Yanna had given her. "You're not dying today, Luis Ironfoot."

64

THE SIEGE OF KELD

Surrounded by his Elite Guard, Kurzon scowled at the throng of warriors blocking his way up the rampart to Keld's southern battlements. He flared his nostrils and smacked his fist into his palm. "Don't tell me it's another fight?"

"I believe so, lord," said one of his guards. She stood on tip-toes and looked into the throng of warriors in front of her. "Belgar and Ovantae this time."

"Idiots! Don't they know we're under siege? Break it up, then find me the most senior Named from each clan and tell them to meet me up there," he ordered, pointing to the nearest siege platform.

"Yes, lord."

A host of Mendari horns blared to the south. *By the goddess. They're close.*

The Elite Guard took little time to deal with the squabble, ramming their shields in between each of the culprits. With the way cleared, Kurzon bounded onto the battlements and weaved his way towards the platform where one of the soulstealers sat. He passed a group of clansguard novices swarmed around a supply cart piled with baskets of arrows and bolts. Taking them off the fletchers, they ran off to drop them beside the warriors taking their place across the wall. Further along, he skirted around a cauldron of steaming water sat over a fire pit, its underside glowing bright orange from the heat of the flames. Many more stretched out across the battlements, ready for pouring on any attackers who successfully crossed the Valtara.

Then, striding onto the platform, he took a breath, faced south and stared into the night. He pulled his long blond hair away from his eyes, buffeted by the unrelenting north wind, and mouthed a prayer to the goddess. A sea of flames stretched out before him, so vast that Kurzon saw no end to the east or to the west. *I warned you not to go, but you had to listen to Yanna. Your stubbornness has cost you your family, your throne, and the lives of your people. Goddess help us all.*

"Slow down," warned a woman behind him. "You drop that and you'll engulf everyone within a hundred feet in flames."

He glanced over his shoulder to find Gwen of the Skilled caste glaring at a pair of engineers struggling with a large, round projectile. "Should I be concerned, Master Engineer?"

She scoffed, eyeing the Mendari horde. "I think you've got enough to be concerned about...Lord."

"Careful, Master Engineer. You may have found favour with the king and Prince Tomos, but not even they'll be able to protect you from your open insolence against a member of the nobility...that is, if the king survived the battle."

"Then perhaps you should pray to *your* goddess for his safe return?"

Kurzon frowned. "*Your goddess*? That sounds like blasphemy, Master Engineer."

She shrugged and returned her attention to her engineers.

"Don't you dare turn your back on me," he said, gripping the pommel of his sword.

"Lord, you called for us?"

"Yes, I did," he said, still glaring at Gwen. *I'll deal with you later.*

"Do you have news of the Vanguard?"

He turned to them, his face ashen-white. "We must assume that we're all that remains of the Named, and that..." He lowered his eyes. "The king and the other chieftains are most likely dead."

"But surely, lord, there may still be a chance, however slim?"

"Only the goddess knows the answer to that; but what I know is that tensions are running high between the clans, my brothers and sisters. I want you to speak to your warriors and remind them we cannot defeat the enemy if we're divided."

"Can you blame them, lord?" asked one veteran, clothed in the green and brown of the Belgar. "Not even during the Mendari War did we see such numbers against us. We're in the twilight of our warrior years, and many of the others are untested in battle."

"What's your name, clansguard?"

"Ffion, lord."

"Did you take part in a siege during the war?"

"Yes, lord. I fought at Amaryth."

"Amaryth...a brutal affair. Tell me, Ffion of the Belgar, how did Lord Kilien force the Mendari to surrender?"

"He starved them out. Took two months, but they eventually surrendered."

"And how did he feed his army?"

"He sent foraging parties out into the surrounding area to gather food."

"Precisely. So, clansguard," he said, pointing to the advancing enemy. "How many Mendari stand against us this night?"

The warrior stared out across the plain. "I-I'm not sure...ten thousand?"

"At least that. And even if they stripped the land from here to Vedana, do you think they would have enough food, this early in the year, to feed all those hungry mouths for a few days, let alone weeks or months?"

"No, lord."

He paced across the line of warriors and clasped his hands behind his back. "We have all the resources of Northern Tarania behind us and the swollen banks of the Valtara in front to keep them at bay. So believe me when I say that the Mendari will come at us with great haste. They will surge across the bridge, carrying ladders long enough to cross the final third of the Valtara and attempt to reach the walls. No easy task when our archers rain down death from above. And even if they succeed in their endeavour, they'll meet our iron and steel on these battlements," he declared, drawing his sword.

427

"Veterans and novices, standing side by side, driving the followers of Velak from our walls, casting them into the surging torrents of the Valtara. And so shall it be, if we turn once more to the teaching of the Communion and the loving embrace of the goddess." He fell to his knees. "Join me, my brothers and sisters, and pray to the goddess to deliver us from our enemies."

The warriors followed his example. Then, like an expanding ripple on the calm surface of a lake, nobility, warriors and skilled also bent the knee in submission to the goddess. *Hear our prayers, blessed Enora. Reveal to them your glory in their greatest moment of need.*

He rose to his feet, raised his hands above his head and bellowed, "This is a holy war. A war against a false god, and..." He paused as he caught sight of Gwen glowering at him. "And a war against those who would undermine the pillars of our faith. Now prepare for battle, and may the goddess grant you a warrior's death."

As the defenders roared their response, the Named saluted him and left to join their clans. Kurzon called over to Gwen. "How far can your engine hurl one of those things?"

"Around six hundred feet. Maybe more with the north wind behind us."

"Good. Begin your bombardment on my command."

She nodded.

"And Master Engineer."

"What?"

"I want your engines firing every five minutes."

"But that's impossible. I told War Master Ironfoot—"

"Ironfoot's not here—I am. Anything more than a five-minute reload and I'll start launching your engineers over the wall."

"You—"

"Wouldn't dare? Ask the miners of Belith that question. The ones that survived the massacre. Five minutes, Master Engineer, and not a second longer." With a final withering glare at the Master Engineer, he moved to the edge of the platform and scanned the battlements. A thousand archers stretched either side of the outer southern gatehouse, supported by just as many heavy infantry. A further two thousand clansguard waited at the inner gate, ready to repel an assault through the South Tunnel. He would not send them onto the plain as Ironfoot had advised unless the Mendari fell into disarray.

As the horde drew to a halt on the plain below, well out of reach of the soulstealers, the defenders waited, speaking to their comrades in hushed tones. Braziers crackled and spat in the quiet, sending wafts of fragrant smoke across the battlements. Kurzon drew the sweet incense of burning grey birch into his lungs and closed his eyes. For a moment, he stood looking up at the face of the goddess within the Sacred Grove of Belanore. He shivered in awe, sensing her presence. *Truly, you are with us this night.*

"It's not like them to hold back," said one of his Elite Guard.

Kurzon cast his eyes across the horde and searched for signs of activity. *Nothing. Come to think of it, I can't see any siege engines or even ladders. How can they possibly—*

"Reeeaperrrrr!" cried the Mendari, smashing their weapons against their shields, like a sudden clap of thunder.

What are they saying?

"Reeeaperrrrr!" Again, they hit their shields.

Reaper? What in the goddess' name is a reaper?

Out of the darkness, shattering the silence, arose a roar so terrible that Kurzon took a step back. The Mendari exclaimed the name one last time, then surged forward, shouting their fearsome cries of war.

He spun around to Gwen. "Now!"

The Master Engineer waved a torch in the air to signal the start of the bombardment, then stepped away from the soulstealer as a member of her crew ignited the godsbreath. She took the trigger off an engineer and, with one sharp tug of the rope, the switch snapped loose. No longer held in place, the counterweight plummeted to the floor, whirling the arm in a forward arc, hurling the flaming projectile over the cowering heads of Kurzon and his Elite Guard. The godsbreath roared in flaming fury. Three more projectiles arced towards the Mendari, leaving pluming trails of smoke in their wake. Then, as the godsbreath smashed into the advancing lines of warriors, four flashes of bright yellow light erupted across the plain. A fraction of a second later, Kurzon flinched as the thundering booms of the explosions vibrated throughout his body. Domes of flames spread out across the ground, igniting all that stood in their way. He stared in disbelief at the destructive power of the godsbreath, the screams of the Mendari reaching even the heights of his lofty position. Turning to Gwen, he said, "Again."

He watched as engineers ducked into the treadwheels, facing away from the plain. On Gwen's command, they walked, concentrating on keeping their footing and rhythm. The arm, made of the trunks of two large ash trees, creaked as it lowered towards the back of the machine where two other engineers cranked on a pair of winches.

"Hurry!"

"We're working as fast as we can."

"Work faster," he said, returning to face the oncoming Mendari. The first rows of the horde were almost at the Valtara. *What're they going to do—swim across?* "Signal the archers to begin." His signaller blared out the command.

As the first volley thrummed from a thousand bows and crossbows, two of the soulstealers loosed their flaming projectiles towards the oncoming horde. They soared through the air, ready to send countless more Mendari to their horrifying deaths. Yet as they descended towards their targets, the missiles slowed to a halt in mid-air, then lurched back towards the fortress.

"Goddess...take cover!"

The first slammed into the earthworks below the South Wall, the impact shaking the battlements as if an earthquake had struck. The second projectile roared over the battlements, struck a soulstealer, and engulfed the entire platform in a raging fire that singed the hairs on Kurzon's moustache.

"Get down!" yelled Gwen. "The cache's going to—"

A second explosion, dwarfing the first, blasted off the cart of godsbreath stored at the back of the platform, spewing timber, stone and flaming projectiles everywhere.

Kurzon dived to the floor just as a blazing godsbreath decapitated a guard barely a few feet away from him. Sprawling to his feet, he watched in horror as the projectile exploded into the packed eastern battlements, killing anyone within its deadly radius. Two more blasts boomed from within the fortress. He staggered to the back of the platform just in time to witness a firestorm consume the two thousand clansguard waiting below. "By the goddess. Get those fires out!"

"I'm not sending my engineers into that inferno. Not until the fires die down."

Kurzon charged towards Gwen. "Are you disobeying a direct order?"

"You'll kill even more people if you send them into those flames."

Kurzon's eyes bulged, and he gnashed his teeth. He gripped the hilt of his sword. "I've had enough of your—" He stopped. The terrifying roar rumbled once more on the plain. He whirled to the south. The soulstealer on the far western platform unleashed another godsbreath. It, too, hung in the air, but as it hurtled back, it detonated. As the fireball expanded, a bizarre shape flickered into view, then disappeared.

"What in the goddess' name was that?"

"Nothing good," said Gwen. "Light the godsbreath." She waited, the trigger held taut in her hands.

"What are you waiting for? Loose."

She ignored him.

"I swear I'll cut you down if you disobey me one more time."

"I know what I'm doing."

"You'll kill us all!"

She matched his glare, then pulled hard on the rope, sending the godsbreath fizzing through the air. "Come on, you bastard. Catch the damn thing." Once again, the missile froze in mid-air, but this time it detonated on contact. "Yes!"

A second thunderous explosion boomed, extinguishing the fireball engulfing the hidden terror hovering in the air. Then, as the shock wave spread across the plain, it snuffed out the torches of the Mendari and the fires of the godsbreath, until only darkness remained.

The torturous wail that followed pierced the night air, as if a whirlwind carved its way across the plain. Kurzon clasped his hands over his ears and crouched to the floor, praying that the ear-splitting noise would end before it drove him mad. His prayer was answered—the high-pitched whine stuttered to a stop. A moment later, a tremendous crash thudded onto the plain.

Kurzon stood and looked out into the darkness, but detected no signs of movement on the plain. On the battlements, the damage caused by the godsbreath was horrifying to behold. Even the constant ringing in his ears could not drown out the moans and screams of the injured and the dying. He cast a look of unbridled malice towards Gwen. "You may have scored a small victory, but wars are won by soldiers following the chain of command. Observe." He turned to an Elite Guard. "Get the injured off the battlements and down to the healers. And organise teams to get those fires out, no matter the cost."

"Yes, lord."

"Then you've sentenced your clansguard to death," said Gwen, watching the warrior disappear into the chaos of the eastern battlements.

"That is the nature of war, Master Engineer."

Gwen did not respond. She stared out onto the plain.

"Even now, you choose to disrespect me?"

"But something's happening down there," she said, pointing into the darkness. "Look."

Kurzon scanned the plain until his eyes fell on what Gwen had seen—a pulsing red light that pierced the black of the night. He strode off the siege engine platform and pushed his way through the lines of warriors until he stood at the outer wall of the battlements. He studied the light. It moved. It was difficult to say for sure, but it seemed to Kurzon that the light rose up for a few seconds before falling back down. This pattern repeated itself for a few minutes until the light stayed up.

The Mendari, who had been silent since the explosion, cried, "Reeeaperrrrr!"

"By the goddess."

A rhythmic clanging cut through the clamour of the enemy, similar to the sounds the portcullis gears made in the winding room. What Kurzon knew for sure was that the sound was getting closer and the rhythm matched the erratic movement of the light. The glow grew in size and intensity. Kurzon's throat dried and his legs weakened as the shape of what approached finally appeared out of the darkness. He gripped the edge of the wall to steady himself. "Goddess, save us. What kind of creature is that?"

Cries of disbelief and terror echoed across the battlements. "It's the Bwgan!"

The creature, almost as tall as the South Gate Drawbridge, crawled on seven legs and dragged a mangled eighth behind it. Four plumes of smoke billowed from under its belly, leaving a dissipating trail in its wake. As it neared the Valtara, a dozen limb-like objects streamed out of a patch of glowing domes fixed to its back. It leaped into the air and landed in the middle of the river's channel, straddling the bridge.

Kurzon leaned out as far as he could, just in time to watch the limbs wrap themselves around the drawbridge. The creature lurched back and the whole of the South Wall shuddered.

No...it couldn't...not even with a thousand warriors could you bring that down.

Yet as the creature heaved a second time, the oak and iron of the drawbridge groaned against the strain. "How can—"

A woman screamed behind him. He spun around as the engineers surrounding the soulstealer looked at each other in shock.

"Where's the Master Engineer?"

"S-she was just standing right beside me, and then she..."

"She what?"

"Vanished."

"People don't just—" A shimmering form flashed in front of Kurzon and grabbed him by the arms. Then, in a blur of blistering speed, the form ripped him across the western battlements, through the outer gatehouse entrance and down the stairwell, until he was thrown onto the floor of the guardhouse next to Gwen.

"Don't move a muscle," said a strange-sounding male voice from within the rippling air. The shimmering form shot back up the stairs, barred the battlements door and returned.

Kurzon scrambled onto his feet, drew his sword and swung it into the apparition. "Get away from me, foul creature." The air writhed and his blade flew out of his hand, clattering against the wall on the far side of the room.

"Don't press my patience, Lord Zirani."

"How do you know my name?"

"That's not important." The shimmering diminished, revealing a tall, well-built figure dressed in unusual black armour with their head hidden by a smooth spherical helmet. "You need to listen to me —you have little time."

"B-but you shimmer like you're a spirit from the Netherplain, and you're as strong as ten clansguard," said Kurzon, looking the man up and down. "You're not of this world. Why should we trust you?"

"Because if the Reaper breaks into Keld, it'll slaughter you all and there'll be no-one to stop Velak from taking Northern Tarania. I want to help you stop that from happening."

"What *is* that thing you call the Reaper?" asked Gwen.

"A deadly weapon you must stop at all costs from entering Keld."

"But what can we do against such incredible power?"

"Look at what one projectile did to it, Master Engineer. Imagine what you could do with many."

"Well, we've got at least ten left. But if we detonate them so close to the tunnel, it could bring the whole of the South Wall down."

The man in black nodded. "Yes, it would."

Gwen gasped. "I see. We trap it inside, then detonate the remaining godsbreath to collapse the tunnel on top of it."

"Well done, Master Engineer."

"This is madness," said Kurzon, staring in disbelief at Gwen. "If we do that, we cut off any way for the survivors of the Vanguard to cross the Valtara."

Above them, a battering ram thudded against the upper gatehouse door. "Your warriors will be here soon, so listen." The man in black gripped Kurzon by the shoulders. "Do you honestly believe any of the Vanguard could survive such overwhelming odds?"

"W-we must hold fast and pray to the goddess that she'll deliver them safely through the darkness and evade capture."

"If you really knew Enora, then you'd know she wouldn't hesitate to blow the Reaper into oblivion no matter the consequences. If you truly want to protect your beloved Communion, follow Gwen—she has the same spirit as Enora." He turned to her. "Even if that passion is sometimes misguided."

She frowned. "I-I don't understand."

The man said no more. He vanished, leaving only a cloud of dust in his wake.

Kurzon wiped the sweat from his forehead, then rounded on Gwen. "If he really knew the goddess, then he'd know she'd never put the fate of her people in the hands of...someone like you.

Gwen met his glare.

"But it seems I have no choice in the matter."

A loud crack descended from above. Seconds later, a group of clansguard burst through the door. "Lord, we thought—"

Kurzon held his up hand, still staring at Gwen. "Never mind that. Give the Master Engineer anything she asks for. We've got work to do."

In the space of ten minutes, Gwen had organised a line of over fifty clansguard and engineers tasked with transporting the remaining godsbreath into the tunnel. The chain stretched from the remaining siege platforms, through the outer gatehouse and down to the tunnel floor.

Gwen stood in the centre of the tunnel, thirty feet away from the inner portcullis. From the other end, the drawbridge groaned as the Reaper heaved it inch by inch towards the Valtara. Above her, the battle raged. As a pair of warriors secured the twelfth and final godsbreath, she inspected the four clusters of projectiles positioned close to the inner entrance. In the little time that she had, Gwen had chosen to lay the godsbreath in clusters of three. The projectiles were stacked on top of each other and then tethered to two pairs of upright timber beams supporting the weight of the earth above.

If the initial explosion didn't destroy the Reaper, then Gwen hoped the blast would demolish the strong yet flexible yew timber caps and posts, collapsing thousands of tons of earth onto the monster. She patted the bowed timber upright. *You designed these well, Prince Tomos. I just hope three godsbreath are enough to destroy them.*

She dismissed her team and paced towards the inner portcullis that had been raised just enough for her to squeeze under to make her escape. Beyond lay the mass of smouldering bodies that were once two thousand clansguard. The cloth wrapped around her face did little to stop the stench of burned, acrid flesh stinging her eyes, carried into the tunnel by the freezing northerly wind. Between the dead and the portcullis stood Lord Zirani, with his Elite Guard arranged behind him. A group of hand-picked archers fanned out on either side of him, some armed with arrows wrapped in kindling, just in case the godsbreath failed to light in the unrelenting wind.

She reached the portcullis and peered through one of the holes in the latticed timber-work. Zirani stared back at her, stony-faced. "We're ready."

The chieftain nodded to his signaller, who blew a series of droning notes on the dremon horn. A clang echoed down the tunnel, signalling that the windlasses had started to lower the drawbridge.

In the distance, the Reaper roared in triumph.

Gwen swallowed hard. She strode over to the tunnel wall, removed a spluttering torch from its sconce and made her way to the furthest set of godsbreath. She held it to the underside of the lowest ball until flames licked around the tar-soaked covering.

A boom pulsated down the tunnel. *The bridge is down.* Then, from within the depths, the Reaper roared, its thundering charge nearing at an alarming rate. She hurried across to the adjacent set of godsbreath and with a trembling hand, she ignited them.

Glancing over her shoulder at the previous set of balls, she grimaced. *Shit!—they're out.* She hesitated, in two minds whether to move on to the next cluster or go back. She cursed, knowing that the archers would have great difficulty hitting the ones further inside from the portcullis. *It won't work unless they're all lit.* She ran back across the tunnel, skidded to a stop and wedged the torch under the ball. The ground beneath her feet rumbled. Dust and soil fell from the roof. She crouched to shield the struggling flame from the wind. It worked. The lower godsbreath burst into flames. *Two down, two to go.* She pulled out the torch, sprung off her feet and headed for the next set.

A heavy thud from behind shook her to her core. She stumbled, stretching her arms out towards the soft, sludgy floor. *Shit!* The torch spun out of her hand, sinking deep into the mud—the flame snuffed out with a hiss. As she scrambled onto her feet, she dared the briefest of glances behind her. She froze. A ring of red eyes appeared out of the darkness. Every second, the glow brightened.

She reeled away from the Reaper and sprinted for the portcullis. "Light them now!"

The archers rushed to the gate, aiming their flaming arrows through the gaps in the latticework. Bowstrings thrummed. Arrows hissed either side of her, slamming into the unlit godsbreath. Then, as she prepared to slide under the gate, a dremon horn bellowed and the gate plummeted to the ground. With the crash of ten tons of oak and iron resounding in her ears, Gwen slid into the portcullis and smashed her hands against the wood. "Raise the gate!"

The archers, their job done, rushed away from the nearing terror, leaving one man standing on the opposite side of the gate to Gwen.

With tears streaming from her eyes, she matched the man's contemptuous stare. "You bastard, Zirani. W-why?"

"Because you're everything I despise about the rot spreading through the castes."

"You'd murder me for that? For having a voice? Are we not all Northern Taranians?"

"I'd do anything to preserve the glory of the Communion." He flinched as the Reaper's roar echoed through the tunnel. "The Reaper nears. Renounce the People's Alliance and renew your faith in the goddess, and I will raise the gate."

"Never."

Zirani snorted. "Belligerent to the bitter end."

The ground beneath her feet trembled and the heat from the flaming godsbreath singed her skin. "You may silence me, but there're hundreds of my people who'll gladly take my place."

"Then I'll hunt down every last one of them." Zirani backed away, jabbing his finger towards her. "If you won't give the goddess your obedience, then you'll damn well give her your sacrifice." He looked beyond her, his eyes filled with sudden terror. "Time to die, Gwen of the Skilled Caste."

She spat at Zirani, then turned to face the bringer of her death. The Reaper's hulking, spider-like body emerged out of the darkness, filling the tunnel with its terrifying mass. Its eyes darted between the front two clusters of burning godsbreath. As if it sensed the danger, it backed away.

With death a certainty, a tremendous sense of calm flowed through Gwen. The man in black's words echoed in her mind. '*She has the same spirit as Enora*'.

She wiped her eyes, slid her knife out of her belt and struck the iron latticework. "Come on, you bastard! Come and get me." Again and again she struck it until the Reaper stopped. The lights of its eyes intensified and locked on her.

"Yes, that's right. Here I am."

The Reaper growled, then roared, launching itself at her.

She gripped the sides of the latticework, and as a burst of blinding yellow light flashed across her eyes, she bellowed, "For the Alliance!"

Brighter than a flash of sheet lightning, the godsbreaths' detonation expelled the darkness of the night. The explosion that followed unleashed a wall of inescapable power that hurled Kurzon backwards, throwing him reeling into the blackened corpses of the clansguard. Fragments of wood and iron shot through the air, slamming into the living and the dead.

Within the swirling clouds, Kurzon's hairs shrivelled from the searing heat radiating from the blast and he retched on the suspended debris filling his lungs. He rolled onto his back, pulled the knife out of his belt and hacked off a strip of his multicoloured cloak. He wrapped it around his face and coughed until he dispelled the irritating fragments from his lungs. Barely recovered, he winced, sensing a stabbing pain pulsing from his leg. He grimaced, staring at a shard of wood buried deep into his thigh. He knew enough about impalement injuries to know that removing the shard would only make things worse. So, cutting off a second strip of his cloak, he bit down and wrapped the fabric tight around his thigh, two inches above the wound. The tourniquet would limit further blood loss until the wound could be cauterised by a healer.

Goddess! The Reaper!

He clambered over the scorched mounds of his fallen comrades and stared into the smoke billowing out of the tunnel. As a gap in the ashen clouds widened, his stomach knotted, discovering that although a mass of rubble littered the entrance, the tunnel roof remained intact. He scanned for the Reaper through the smouldering rocks, timber and iron. *Did it work? Is it dead?* A boulder toppled from off a pile. Kurzon paled. He forced himself to stand, his thigh throbbing, his heart racing. *No.*

A pair of mangled metal tendrils emerged from out of the debris and stretched up to the remains of the upper section of the portcullis, coiling around the glowing latticework. The gate groaned as the Reaper heaved itself up onto what was left of its legs. The circle of lights flickered into life, and with a low-pitched growl, the Reaper staggered into the open.

Kurzon fell to his knees among the stench of death. "Goddess, save us."

A deep rumble emanating from within the tunnel made him look up. Earth, stone, and timber plummeted to the tunnel floor. *It's working.* The Reaper, sensing danger, limped further outside, whipping its tendrils towards those still alive.

"I beg you, goddess, hear the cries of your people. Deliver us from this evil."

High above the tunnel, the inner gatehouse swayed as if it were a ship buffeted by the sea, its foundations dislodged by the void left by the tons of earthworks now filling the tunnel below. A piercing crack filled the air, and the gatehouse toppled forward. The Reaper's eyes snapped up, intensifying into a single disc of light. It lurched forward, hauling itself away from the descending threat.

With his hands raised in worship, Kurzon cried, "Behold. The goddess sends her deliverance." Then, with tears flowing down his cheeks, he watched the gatehouse plunge into the Reaper, crushing it under tons of stonework and timber. "Got you!" A radial line of rubble tumbled out from its epicentre. "Goddess." He scrambled under the mound of the smouldering dead for protection. He ignored the stench of death and the thunderous wall of debris sweeping over him. The goddess was with him. Euphoric righteousness coursed through Kurzon. *You were testing me. Seeing if I still had the will to do what others balk at.*

After a few minutes, the perilous clouds dissipated. He emerged from within the dead and picked his way through the carnage between him and his destination. He stopped and turned to face those that still lived. "Do not be afraid, my brothers and sisters. We punished the blasphemer, and the goddess delivered us for our obedience." The survivors hugged each other, and offered prayers of thanks to the goddess. Then they followed Kurzon into the wreckage of the gatehouse, no longer fearful of the creature sent by Kaine to destroy them.

Kurzon climbed over a large section of masonry and halted. There in the rubble was the twisted remains of the head of the Reaper. An eye flickered into life. It creaked and hissed, setting its baleful gaze onto Kurzon. He crouched beside it and spat into the waning light. Then, finding the largest rock he could carry, he stood and heaved it over his head. "Let this be a warning to those who would stand against the goddess." He hurled the rock into the light. As he crushed it, a tendril rose up into the air. It quivered, swaying in the northerly wind. With a final, half-hearted lunge towards Kurzon, it dropped to the ground, lifeless.

The Reaper was dead.

65

THE STONES OF VALTARA

No fire would chase the chill of the night from Seren's bones high above the Valtara Estuary—not when they were so close to the Mendari. The twenty-strong party had turned north, leaving the dense slopes of evergreens behind them, and had made camp less than half a mile away from the silhouette of the plateau that led to the Stones of Valtara. The terrain between Seren and her destination stretched out as a swathe of coastal grassland, decorated by a vivid canvas of spring squill and thrift, their violet-pink patchwork tinted by the bluish light of Golanos in her full, majestic glory.

Seren sat on the bed of grass, hugging her knees, and stared up at the plateau looming up into the Void. *I'm sure I've been here before.* A lull in the northerly wind wafted the honeyed scent of thrift across her face. The familiar fragrance triggered a memory buried deep inside her subconscious, waiting to be remembered. She closed her eyes and allowed the memory to play out.

She rode on a horse between two long lines of slender stone monoliths. Ulena peeked over the horizon from behind, casting Seren's shadow through the middle of the stone avenue. She held her breath as a pair of arms grew out of the silhouette, yet her arms held the reins. Then she felt them wrapping tight around her waist— strong and protective, yet feminine. Her body trembled as she recognised the same ring that her father wore around his neck. "Mother?"

"Your highness?"

Seren flinched. She opened her eyes and snapped her gaze onto the warrior standing above her. It was Ellis—the lad who had shot a bolt at Luis from the gatehouse. Luis had insisted that he and his mouthy friend, Finn, be part of their escort. "We don't stand on ceremony here, clansguard. When we're on a mission, it's just Seren."

Ellis looked over his shoulder at Luis, making his way towards them. "I-I don't think War Master Ironfoot would agree."

"I wouldn't worry about Ironfoot," she said, retrieving the bottle of sleeping draught from her pocket.

"I-I don't understand, Your...I-I mean, Seren."

"You'll find out soon enough." She eyed the flask he was holding. "Did you have something for me?"

"Oh, of course." He gave it to her and hurried away.

Quickly, before Luis could see her, Seren opened the flask and tipped the sleeping draught into the wine. She shoved the bottle back into her pocket, just as Luis arrived, staring disapprovingly at Ellis.

"What's that trigger-happy dimwit up to?"

"Leave him alone. Besides, you wanted him here."

Luis rubbed his iron leg. "He's almost as good as a Woodland Warrior. If everything turns to shit, we'll need his skills for sure." He struggled to the floor and eyed the flask. "I thought you were trying to stop?"

"I am, but I thought, as it's likely to be the last time I'll see your ugly face, we could share some Mendari wine together."

"Mendari?" He grinned and accepted the flask off Seren. "Can't pass up an offer like that." He took a deep gulp of wine and offered it back to her.

She ignored him, looking towards the plateau.

"Having second thoughts?"

"No, it's not that. I'm sure I've been here before—with my mother."

It was Luis' turn to stay silent.

"You know something, don't you?"

He nodded. "A few days before she died, Isabelle brought you here to watch Ulena rise over the Sleeping Stone."

"I knew it." She turned to him, cocking her head to the side. "What's the Sleeping Stone?"

"It's the only stone in the shrine that lies on its side. The Hen Rai considered the times of the year when any of the gods touched the stone to be sacred; but once the Communion made Enora the principal god of Northern Tarania, the Stones lost their significance." He took another swig of wine, then yawned and rubbed his eyes.

"What else do you know about our visit?"

"I know your mother was excited for you to see the Stones," he said, smiling. "She knew so much about the old world. You'd be forgiven in thinking she was brought up as an Ovantae, not Zirani." He yawned again. "She raced up through the tiers, with you in front of her, galloping along the same winding path that the Hen Rai had taken a thousand years before. You both laughed and hooted, with the wind in your hair and not a care in the world. Then, just as you climbed the final ramp to the upper tier, Ulena rose from behind the Sleeping Stone, illuminating the ring of weathered stone giants that had stood guard for time immemorial. She said you cried with delight." He drank again from the flask. "By the goddess, this wine's strong."

Seren gnawed at a nail, watching Luis squint at her. "How do you know all of this? I thought you were in Vedana on the Day of Sorrows?"

"I was, but I hadn't left for Vedana when you were here. I was meeting with your father about something or other."

"So my mother told you?"

"Um..." He scratched his head, frowning. "No, she didn't tell me... I only just found out myself."

"Then who did, Luis?"

"S-someone else—someone who accompanied you to the Stones. They warned her. Yes, that's right—a warning about a plot to assassinate her at the Council of Clans.... But she wouldn't listen and begged them not to tell me or your father."

"Who, Luis? Who warned her about the threat?"

Luis rubbed his forehead and swayed. "Grimbard." He slumped prostrate into the dew-covered grass, staring up at her. "What have you done, Seren?"

She leaned down and kissed him on the cheek. "I almost killed you earlier—the one person who truly cares for me. A man who'd gladly sacrifice himself to save me? A wretched failure like *me*? No, Luis. You're not dying today—Northern Tarania needs you more than it needs me."

"Please...don't..."

"Sleep well, old man."

She patted him on the shoulder and turned back to stare at the plateau. *Grimbard warned her? Why would he do that if he was in on the plot? It doesn't make sense.* She would have to mull over Luis' revelations later—dawn was close, and it was time to act.

She stood and beckoned the warriors to gather around her. "Prepare yourselves, my brothers and sisters. Before Ulena breaks the surface of the Endless Sea, we free Lady Amira." She called Ellis and Finn over to her and nodded towards Luis. "I'm sorry for the deception, but I don't know you like I know the others. Prove yourself to me, and I'll speak to my father about awarding you your warrior names."

The pair's eyes widened. "Thank you."

"I want you to stay here with the Master of War. Bind him, but make sure he's comfortable. And no matter how much he threatens you, don't set him free."

"Yes, Seren."

"If things don't go our way, get him back to Keld."

As they hurried off to ready their horses, Seren clicked her knuckles and spat on the ground. *I'm coming for you, Amira. And should I get the chance, I'll kill Kaine, return to Keld and present Yanna with his head on a spear.*

The orangey glow bleeding into the Void on the eastern horizon heralded Ulena's arrival into the land of the living. High above the

Endless Sea, Golanos descended from her place of honour between the Children of Enora, gleaming in expectation of the reunion with her mother. Little did she know that her uncle lay hidden in the Netherplain, biding his time until he would catch them both unawares in their loving embrace.

Just like Kilena, Seren waited. She lay just below the ridge of the plateau surrounded by a tapestry of sea squill and thrift, and stared up at the tiered earthworks that rose up into the Void. She had no clue how many Mendari stood between her and Amira, but she would wager a sofran that Kaine held her on the highest of the two tiers, where the Sleeping Stone lay.

Apart from Ellis and Finn protecting Luis, the remaining warriors surrounded the Stones, positioned under the ridge, armed with heavy crossbows. Once Seren gave the signal, they would take out the sentries patrolling the base of the earthworks, then move up each tier covering her attempt to rescue Amira.

A glint of iron on her wrist caught her eye. She clucked. One flash of metal from Golanos' light and the rescue would turn into a disaster. She tugged at the sleeve of her gambeson to conceal her mail. All of her warriors had adopted the same strategy. They wore no helmets and carried no shields. Their exposed skin was covered in mud and their weapons coated with a mixture of grease, ash and the poisonous sap extracted from the flat, dark green leaves of the yew.

Yet even knowing that every preparation had been meticulously observed, Seren hesitated. Her failure would result in the death of a young woman, but it was the thought of Yanna's disappointment in her that terrified her the most—even more than her own death. She flared her nostrils and cricked her neck. *I promise you, my love, I'll return with Amira or die trying. It's time.*

She hooted an owl call, then dropped over the ridge and sprinted towards the earthwork that encircled the base of the Stones. The call rippled through her warriors, and the shadowy forms of those nearest to her bounded inward. When she got to the outer mound, she dived over its brow and slid into the ditch, splashing into an unseen puddle. She cursed at her clumsiness and scrambled up the inner mound. She held her breath and waited for any sound of alarm from the pair of sentries patrolling the western point of the lowest rings of monolithic stones. She heard nothing and released her breath in relief. The guards chatted for a moment, then walked off in opposite directions. Satisfied that they were far enough away from each other, she hooted once more. A pair of bolts whistled either side of her and thumped into the sentries, dropping them to the ground without the faintest of cries. The threat removed, she slid down the mound, sped across the open ground and slipped between the ring of stones.

Beyond the lower circle arose the sheer slope of the first tier—impossible to climb without the right equipment. There was only one way to get up—the way she had ascended the day her mother brought her to the Stones—the earthwork ramps. Two ramps led to the lower tier: one at the northern end, overlooking the Valtara Estuary and the other at the southernmost point. Hoping that the sound of the Valtara would help mask her movements, she turned left and hugged the slope northwards.

Her warriors had been deadly efficient. Every so often, she would come across a dead Mendari, their bodies pierced with multiple bolts, so it did not take her long to reach the gap in the stones that gave way to the earthwork ramp. It was deserted. Assuming that her warriors had hidden the bodies, she took a step out into the open, then froze: the glow of a pipe revealed the presence of a sentry heading down the ramp. She dropped to the ground, scrambled back between the stones and slowed her breathing, waiting for the sentry to fall—yet not one bolt whipped through the air. *Where are they?*

"Marta? Sander?" called the Mendari. "Stop fooling around." Receiving no reply, the sentry emptied his pipe, slipped it into a pouch and pulled an axe out of his belt. He edged down the slope until he reached the bottom and turned in Seren's direction.

Shit! She reached for her knife, but after a few seconds, the sentry turned and headed over to the other side of the ramp.

Now's my chance. Seren whipped the knife from her belt and vaulted out into the open, covering the ground swiftly and silently. Almost on to the warrior, a twig snapped under her boot. The Mendari spun in an instant and swung his axe in a sideways arc. Just as the blade severed her golden braids trailing behind her, Seren ducked, then tumbled to the ground, smashing into the warrior's legs. He reeled back, clattering into the standing stone at the edge of the ramp. He groaned from the impact but managed to thrust his axe out to block Seren's lunge with her blade aimed at his heart.

They leered at each other; only the rumbling Valtara and their laboured breaths bore witness to their deadly struggle. The knife point edged closer, and the Mendari knew it. He lurched his head at her, just enough for Seren to falter for the briefest of moments. The butt of the axe swung up and cracked into her temple. She stumbled back, dazed. A flash of iron from Golanos' light streaked across her face. She howled in pain, slumped to her knees, then rolled onto her side, clutching a hand against the gash oozing blood from her cheek.

The Mendari stood over her, then spat at her head.

She still held her knife, coated with the concentrated sap of the yew. One nick of the blade into his flesh would be enough. Yet as she waited for the Mendari to heft his axe for the final blow, he left—the jingle of his mail decreasing amongst the sounds of the Valtara. Seren struggled up into a sitting position and squinted in his direction. *Why did he spare me? And why is he leaving the Stones?*

A wave of dizziness washed over her. *I'm losing too much blood.* She opened a small pouch sewn into the side of her gambeson containing her field triage kit and emptied the contents onto the grass. First, she stuffed some yarrow leaves into her mouth and chewed it into a pulp. Then, opening a flask of alcohol, she tipped some into the palm of her hand and applied it to the wound. She hissed through gritted teeth, then spat out the yarrow and pushed it deep into the wound. Clamping the wound, she gripped one end of a strip of linen cloth between her teeth and bandaged her head as tight as she could manage. Finally, after securing the strip, she uncorked a small glass bottle of vinegar, honey and willow bark extract, and swallowed it down in one gulp.

She knew she should wait for the medicine to take effect, but the odds were already in favour of the Mendari. And now, in her condition and with no sign of her warriors, those odds were almost insurmountable. She cast her mind back to the times she had held her lover close after their moments of intimacy. It strengthened her. She unsheathed her sword, drove it into the grass and pushed with all her might to stand. *No matter what. I will find her, Yanna. I promise.* She turned to face the ramp and, step by grimacing step, she ascended.

Seren stumbled her way through the circle of stones that encompassed the lower-tier earthwork. The ramp leading to the highest level lay a quarter way around from her position, at the westernmost point.

Her face throbbed, but the yarrow had stemmed the bleeding, and soon the willow bark would ease her pain. The sooner the better, as she was sure the Mendari lay in wait behind the faceless leviathans she now passed. Yet she found no-one; and as she neared the ramp, she realised that apart from the wind whistling through the stones, her breathing and her muffled footsteps were the only evidence of any living thing being present. A gnawing sensation in the pit of her stomach warned her to flee while she still could; but how could she? Yanna would never forgive her. With that in mind, she willed herself onto the ramp and climbed up to the second tier.

The area between the highest circle of stone was similar in size to the Great Hall in Caerniras. It was perfectly flat and bereft of any vegetation, as if not even nature itself was permitted within the stones. At the eastern end, set between a gap in the circle, rested the Sleeping Stone. Either side of it stood a tall sliver of rock; but it was what hung between them that dried Seren's mouth and tensed every muscle in her body. Silhouetted in front of the brightening horizon slumped a hooded figure. Their arms hung taut from bindings tethered to the thin pillars and their feet brushed the surface of the Sleeping Stone, buffeted by the relentless north wind.

Rubbing her cheek, she looked from left to right. She was alone. The gnawing sensation intensified. She knew it was a trap, but who else could the forlorn figure be but Amira? Tantalisingly close to her goal, she stepped into the circle and crossed.

Reaching the Sleeping Stone, Seren slumped against the weathered rock to catch her breath and took a cautious look over her shoulder. Still, they were alone.

The figure within the cowl moaned. "Thank the goddess. Please, help me. They're going to kill me."

The accent, although mixed with the harsher vowels of the south, was that of a Northern Taranian woman. *It must be Amira. Her mother was from Kelaris.* "Is that you, Amira?"

"Yes. Who are you?"

"Princess Seren. I'm here to rescue you."

Amira chuckled. "Of course you are…. But who's going to rescue *you*?"

Seren frowned. "What?"

Amira bolted upright, flinging the cowl behind her with a backward flick of her head.

Seren staggered away from the stone, as the face revealed from under the hood was that of a middle-aged woman, her features partially hidden by her long, sweeping fringe. She levelled her sword up at the imposter. "Who are you? And where's Amira?"

The woman cocked her head to the side. "By the whore goddess, you look just like him. Makes me want to smash my fist into your pretty young face." She grinned, staring at the bandage wrapped around Seren's head. "Looks like someone's beaten me to it."

Seren snarled. "At least tell me who you are before I take your head."

The woman sniggered. "You even act like him."

"Who're you talking about?"

"Why, I'm talking about the only other surviving member of our little family, my dear."

"Our family?" Seren edged back.

"Oh yes, my dear. I'm surprised you can't see the family likeness."

"No. It's not possible. She died in a fire when the Mendari raided Treharne."

The woman grinned again, snapped her tethers as if they were made of straw, and vaulted off the Sleeping Stone.

Seren crouched into a defensive stance. "Stay back."

449

"But then you won't be able to see this," said the woman, sweeping her hair away from her face.

Seren gawped. Across the woman's face ran a diagonal scar from the bridge of her nose and down to her cheek. The skin around her ear was shrivelled and blotchy—clearly the effects of severe burns. "Eleri?"

"That's Auntie Eleri to you, my dear, but I haven't gone by that name in years."

"I don't understand. Why didn't you come home? And why're you here?"

Eleri unclasped her cloak, let it fall to the ground, and pointed to the Circle and the Cross painted onto her black breastplate. "I am Aderyn, Scion of the First, adopted sister of Kaine, and I will have my vengeance."

The Red Mist boiled within Seren. Not only had Aderyn betrayed her family and people, but had used Amira as a way of setting a trap for Yanna and Uncle Kurzon. *So be it. At least I've saved one of Aedan Taleni's daughters.* She screamed her battle cry and sprung at her aunt; but just as she scythed her blade towards the warrior in black's neck, Aderyn darted past her in a blur of incredible speed. She pivoted, stretching her sword out in front of her. Aderyn had vanished. "What in the god—" A powerful kick from behind sent Seren sprawling into the barren dust of the enclosure. She yelped as her cheek and broken nose scraped across the ground, but had enough presence of mind to scramble into a crouch.

"What's the matter, Seren? Too slow to catch your dear old auntie?"

Seren spun towards Aderyn's voice, staying silent. The throbbing of her wounds and the Red Mist coursing through her veins pounded in her ears. Being deaf and blind to her aunt's sorcery, she closed her eyes, slowed her breathing, slid the poisoned dagger out of her belt and pressed it into the ground. Then she felt it—the slightest vibration travelling through the compact earth, increasing in tempo behind her. She waited for a moment longer, then swivelled, swinging her sword into the rippling air that loomed above her. Her sword stopped dead, trapped in a vice-like force.

Now's my chance. She rammed her dagger into the shimmering where she hoped Aderyn's head was positioned, but the blade did not strike skin, flesh or bone—it struck something hard. The tip of the blade snapped.

Aderyn laughed. "Well played, dear niece. You'd make a fine assassin in the Sept of Shadows." The shimmering diminished, revealing the warrior, her head now enclosed in a smooth, black helmet. "I had a feeling you'd try something like that." She snatched the dagger out of Seren's shaking hand. "Oh, you're full of surprises. I'll save this for later." She slid the dagger into her belt, then knelt beside Seren. "I'll let you into a little secret—even if you'd drawn blood, the Armour of the First would've protected me from your primitive poison. Nothing that you possess can kill me." She looked up, and forced Seren's head around to face the western entrance. "Oh, look. We have visitors."

A figure wearing the same black armour as Aderyn entered the circle. He was an imposing giant of a man with cropped blond hair, who could only have been Kaine. His thunderous expression left Seren in no doubt that he was furious. He dragged a prisoner behind him. She cried in anguish, recognising the man from his unusual gait even before seeing his face.

"No, Luis. You were supposed to live."

Aderyn squeezed Seren's shoulder hard. "Oh, no, my dear niece. No-one's getting out of here alive—not even you."

As Kaine neared them, he snarled. "Whore of a goddess."

"What's wrong?" asked Aderyn.

The Mendari leader yanked on the rope tethered to Luis, flinging him across the enclosure until he slid into the Sleeping Stone with a crack—his iron leg lay on the ground less than a few feet away from Seren. She darted toward it, but Aderyn grabbed her hair and slammed her against the earth.

"Stay down, dear niece. He's beyond your help now." She pushed her boot into Seren's chest and folded her arms. "Well, Kaine?"

Kaine's face twitched. "They destroyed the Reaper." He growled the last two words.

"But how could they destroy it?"

"I don't know, but he'll be furious when he finds out." He strode over to the Sleeping Stone and loomed over Luis. "But at least I have the unexpected pleasure of your company."

Luis pushed up against the stone, flicked his eyes towards Seren, then looked up at the Mendari leader. "Let her go, Kaine. You want revenge for Banan and for the war, then take it out on me. She's suffered enough."

Kaine laughed. "You will indeed answer for your crimes against the Mendari; but how could you possibly believe that the Three Orphans of Treharne were a match for my father?" He crouched down, almost face to face with Luis, and bore his finger into the reddened skin of the Master of War's stump.

Luis grimaced, but did not cry out.

"My father's game with you was interrupted by the Thief who stole the Vessel. *He* defeated my father, took his head and weapon, and created the lie that is King Rodric Shieldbane."

Luis grew pale.

"Ah, so your precious sword brother never told you the truth? As for the princess, she will die today, along with her father and brother, at the hands of Aderyn."

Seren's eyes widened. "You've got Tomos...and my father?"

Kaine smirked at her, then bellowed, "Bring out the others!"

From all around the circle of stones emerged a warband of Mendari warriors. They were led by a woman with hair as dark as the night, who also wore the black of the Scions. She held three leashes in her hand—three leashes for three hooded prisoners.

Seren gasped for breath as Ulena broke the surface of the Endless Sea and cast her presence into the circle of stones. Her light revealed the identity of two of the prisoners in an instant: one bore the sigil of the triskelion encircled by the six clans of Northern Tarania, and the other wore a silver amulet around their neck. The third prisoner could only be that of a young boy or girl. She went to call out to them, but a shout to her left drew her attention.

"Dagan!"

Seren snapped her gaze to the man being forced to the ground by a pair of Mendari warriors. As he struggled to reach the prisoners, Seren shook to her core, recognising the colour of his eyes. *They're amber.*

"Let me go—I want to see my son."

"Don't press my patience, Grimbard," said Kaine.

"But you said I could see him once I did what you asked."

"Yes, I did. And now you've seen him, be a good dog and do as you're told, or you'll never see him again."

Grimbard glowered at Kaine, but nodded his compliance.

"You traitorous piece of shit!" screamed Seren. "I'll kill you and your son for what you've done to us."

Grimbard flicked his brows at her and said, "Remember your last visit to these stones, Seren. Then you'll know the truth."

She gaped at his words—a contradiction to what she had known all of her life and what she saw playing out before her. Something in Grimbard's eyes made her wonder if there were more layers of facts surrounding her mother's death than she had always believed.

Her father uttered something inaudible from under his hood.

"By the whore goddess, Okita," said Kaine, walking towards the Scion. "You must've stuck him with enough sedative to drug a horse."

"I had to give him more." Okita slipped Shieldbane off her shoulder and handed it to Kaine with a bow. "I would've got here earlier, but I was ambushed a few miles outside of Derwedd Forest. They maimed the horses, so I had to carry him the rest of the way."

"How in the whore goddess' name did anyone survive the forest?"

"I'm not sure; but by the accuracy of their arrows, they were probably Woodland Warriors. Which means they either escaped Rask or—"

Kaine seethed. He tapped his fingers rapidly on a thin rectangular object that from Seren's position looked like a small writing slate. It glowed white. "Rask, you idiot. Respond, damn you, or I'll send Aderyn to rip your armour from off your skin and carve your cock off as you shrivel into dust."

Luis laughed. "So you're not invincible."

Slowly, Kaine turned back to Luis. He lifted Shieldbane's hammer to his lips, closed his eyes and whispered something that Seren could not hear. Then, reopening his eyes, he kissed the smoky metal and looked upon Luis.

Seren trembled, fearing what would follow.

"It is both fitting and poetic that the same weapon that shattered your left leg be the one that shatters the right."

Luis snarled up at Kaine. "Then do it—and kill me while you're at it so that I never have to hear your snivelling voice again."

"But you can't die yet—there's so much more for you to witness." Baring his teeth, Kaine hefted Shieldbane above his head and swung it down hard onto Luis' right knee.

The sickening crack of bone pierced a shard of terror into Seren's heart. Inside her mind, she screamed, but not even a whimper escaped from her mouth. She would not disrespect the Master of War, who uttered nothing as bones splintered, muscles ripped and the egg-white-like fluid from the cartilage surrounding his knee exploded in front of him.

Kaine roared, "Scream, damn you!" He swung again, and again, until all that was left of Luis' lower leg was a pool of bloody pulp within the crater hammered into the powdery soil by Shieldbane.

How Luis stopped himself from howling in pain, she did not know, but by the end of the ordeal, the Master of War was slumped unconscious against the Sleeping Stone, deathly pale. *If you really exist, goddess, take him through the Veil while he cannot feel.*

Kaine spun around to face the scions. "Prepare them for the Great Conjoining."

"What about the Thief?" asked Aderyn, dragging Seren towards a standing stone.

"He knows he can't take all three of us. He'll wait until the darkness descends and will make his move for the boy then." Kaine looked over at the figure wearing the amulet. "I want at least one of you watching him at all times." As Aderyn and Okita headed over to the hooded prisoners, Kaine looked over to Grimbard. "He's your sword brother—you can clean him up. And if you have any thoughts of putting him out of his misery, I'll gut Dagan right in front of your eyes."

Seren watched as Grimbard gently lifted Luis onto his shoulders and carried him over to the stone next to her. He eased him down and kissed his forehead.

A warrior hurled Luis' iron leg over the edge of the tier. "He won't be needing that anymore." The surrounding warriors laughed.

Bastards. She turned towards Grimbard. Every fibre in her body wanted to hate him, but his eyes were as bloodshot as hers, and his gentle manner with Luis was not that of a man who hated everything but himself. Again, he was a contradiction.

He wiped the few strands of hair remaining on Luis' head away from his face, and quietly asked, "He told you about what happened at the Stones?"

"Yes—being here has helped me remember. You warned her about the assassination."

He nodded.

"Then it's all true? The mysterious woman in the tavern and being drugged?"

Again, he nodded.

"Do you know who she is?"

"No—it was dark in the tavern and I can't remember much about her."

"So if it wasn't you who betrayed my father, who in Northern Tarania was working with her?"

"Someone who had a lot to gain from all the deaths in the nobility."

"Maybe; but I wonder if my mother's drive for caste reform made her a target?"

"The Communion?"

"Why not?"

"Well, we'll never know unless we get out of this alive."

"Do you have a plan?"

He smiled. "I do—and I've got someone who's willing to help us."

66

REVELATIONS

Kurzon stumbled through his apartment door, staggered across the living room, and collapsed into the seat next to the window. He flinched from the movement. He had spent the last hour before dawn in the infirmary. Now, with his thigh cleaned and dressed, and dosed on vinegar, honey and willow bark extract, he considered their situation. *I need a drink.* "Wine."

His servant hurried over to a small table where he had readied a breakfast for him. Filling a cup, he asked, "Do you want me to prepare a plate for you, lord?"

"No. Just the wine, and fill it up."

The servant did as he was told, hurried over to Kurzon and handed it to him. "Do you want me to draw you a bath?"

"No. Just open the shutters and make yourself useful to the healers. Goddess knows they need help."

"Yes, lord."

As the servant opened the shutters, he coughed from a waft of soot and ash carried up from the carnage blanketing the southern side of the fortress. "By the goddess, lord. What happened down there?"

"We turned to the goddess, and she saved us from annihilation.

Give thanks to her and offer a prayer to all those brave men and women who lost their lives during the night."

"I will, lord."

Just as the servant opened the door to leave, Kurzon asked, "Where's Lady Zirani?"

"I-I think she's still sleeping. Do you want me to wake her?"

"No, let her sleep."

Alone, Kurzon gulped the warmed wine down in one go, then numbly stared out from his south-facing window. Victory over the Reaper would mean nothing if the thousands now encamped on the plains found a way to cross the Valtara and scale the walls. He thought of the Vanguard and Seren's rescue party. Even if they could lower the drawbridge, how would any survivors be able to pass the enemy without detection? He cursed, knowing that even then the thousands of tons of rubble that had collapsed into the South Tunnel had to be removed. For a moment he rued his decision to kill the Master Engineer—her expertise would have made reconstructing the inner stretch of the South Tunnel far easier. He threw his cup against the wall. *No. She was an affront to the goddess. Enora will provide a way for us. I'm sure of it.*

The door to the bed chamber squeaked open.

He sighed, knowing that his assessment of Seren's pitiful chances of rescuing Amira and returning to Keld would tear Yanna apart. "I'm sorry, my dear, but I—"

A sleeve of green cotton streaked before his eyes and wrapped tight around his neck. He gasped for breath, tugging at the arm to release the pressure to his windpipe, but no amount of gripping, punching or scratching made a difference. Lacking oxygen, his arms flopped into his lap and a veil of blackness enfolded him.

———

Kurzon's eyes snapped open as a sharp slap struck his face. He shook his head, then blinked at the blurred figure in green standing in front of him. Leaning forward, he squinted until the green blur sharpened into that of an elegant emerald dress that he knew well. He gasped. "Yanna?"

Stern-faced, she retrieved a small, rectangular object from a wooden box set on a table beside her and tapped a finger against its surface until a curious glow illuminated her face.

"What in the goddess' name are you up to?" He tried to stand, but his wrists and ankles were bound to the chair. "Damn you, woman. What treachery is this? Have you lost your mind? Guards!"

"They can't hear you, dear husband. They're being *entertained* by my servant. Now, be silent. He wants to speak to you."

"Who does?"

Kurzon's eyes widened as Yanna stepped to the side, revealing the spectral form of a man standing in the room. Vibrant colours flowed and shimmered within his translucent body, but there was just enough definition to make out the entity's eyes, nose and mouth. "Who are you?"

The entity smiled. "Come on, Kurzon, can't you work that out for yourself?"

Each resonating syllable of the entity's voice sent a wave of despair through him. One name burned itself into his reeling mind— a name that pushed vomit up into his bruised throat. "V-Velak?"

"Yes, I am him."

"Goddess, protect me from this evil."

Velak laughed. "She's not going to help you, Kurzon. All those years of praying to her, and she never heard one word you uttered."

"Why should I believe you, the god of lies and deceit?"

Velak snorted. "Believe what you want, Chieftain of the Zirani; but perhaps you'll think twice about disrespecting me once you've heard what I have to say."

Kurzon flared his nostrils and gripped the arms of the chair. "What do you want?"

"First of all, I want to commend you."

"Why?"

"You defeated the Reaper, of course. That I did not foresee."

"It was Enora who delivered us from your evil creature."

"Unbelievable—your primitive mind's so entrenched in dogma

458

that it cannot see beyond the teachings of her blasted book." He turned to Yanna. "We had a deal, child. I did as you asked and instructed Juran to protect Amira from your father. You promised me your husband's compliance in return."

"Just tell him the truth, lord. I promise you, he'll see it our way."

"For your sake, I hope so." He returned his attention to Kurzon. "Would you believe me if I told you I'm prepared to end this war?"

Kurzon creased his brows. "Why stop now when your horde is so close to overwhelming us? It makes no strategic sense."

"That's because you do not know what I know. It was my intention to defeat you in battle, not wipe every Northern Taranian off the face of the land."

"If that's true, then why did you allow Kaine to run amok through the Wildlands and Southern Taleni?"

"Yes, that was regrettable. I made Kaine believe that this was what I wanted, and equipped him with my power so that he could unite the tribes. But it also fuelled his lust for vengeance against the Three Orphans of Treharne and the one they call the Thief. His fanaticism is becoming a liability. If you agree to what I propose, then I'll deal with Kaine and ensure the horde return to Mendaria."

"Why do you care about saving Northern Taranian lives?"

"Because all life is sacred, Kurzon—especially that of the young."

"You'll forgive me if I find that hard to believe, coming from your lips."

"I will not lie to you—the blood of the innocent is stained deep into my hands, but never the blood of children, and always for the greater good."

"Whose greater good?"

"That is not your concern. What is, is saving the lives of all Northern Taranians—or should I say, the ones you *want* to save?"

"And how do I do that?"

"Let us make a truce."

The word floored Kurzon. "What kind of truce?"

"The kind that's beneficial to us both."

"To me?"

Yanna knelt beside him and drew her lips close to his ear. "You talk in your sleep, dear husband. I know how deep your hatred runs for those who defy the precepts of your precious Communion."

Velak stepped closer. "What if there was a way to remove the problem of the lower castes once and for all?"

"Go on," said Kurzon, leaning forward.

"I already told you: children are precious. Without them, those undesirable castes that you so detest will become extinct in a generation."

"I-I don't understand."

"It's quite simple. Agree to deliver one hundred children up to the age of sixteen to Vedana at the beginning of every cycle of Golanos, and I'll command the horde to return to Mendaria, leaving only a small garrison in Vedana commanded by one of my Scions. They'll stay to ensure that you fulfil your side of the bargain. Yanna will stay here as your wife, and act as my voice in the North."

"What do you want the children for?"

"I told you—for the greater good. They're very much part of my great plan."

"Which is?"

"Some truths are beyond comprehension, and better left hidden in the dark."

"Even if I agreed, I cannot simply round up children and transport them south. The king and the clan chieftains would turn against me...that's if they survived."

"I wouldn't worry about the king, Kurzon."

"Why? Is he dead?"

"Soon enough."

"And Seren?"

Velak nodded. "And so are the chieftains of the Galgari, the Ovantae, the Taleni and the Belgar. Northern Tarania needs a leader, Kurzon. As the sole surviving chieftain, it is your throne by right."

"No, there's Prince Tomos. I know he's missing, but I have clansguards scouring the land for him. I'm sure he'll be—"

Velak leered into his face. "No! You must call off your search. Tomos is not your concern."

"But he's my nephew—the only legitimate heir to the throne."

Velak's mouth curled into a smirk. "But is he?"

"What do you mean?"

"Correct me if I'm wrong, Kurzon, but only those who are of the Clansguard caste can ascend above their station to *legitimately* claim the throne?"

"Yes—as it has always been. Why do you ask?"

Yanna spoke again. "I know you lament the loss of your sister, and struggle to understand how a daughter of the Zirani could turn her back on the teachings of Enora. Your cries of regret wake me every night—cries of guilt for what you did to preserve the caste system."

Kurzon's face drained of colour. "She was poisoning Rodric's mind and that of the other chieftains. She had to be stopped."

Yanna held his hand tight. "It's time you knew the truth, my husband."

"What truth?"

Velak knelt in front of him. "Did you ever wonder why Rodric's only burns from that fire in Treharne were on the palms of his hand?"

Kurzon looked at Yanna and then at Velak. "He got them when he tried to fight his way to Eleri."

"No, Kurzon, he didn't. As Eleri screamed for her life, Rodric panicked and fled; but before he escaped, he opened his palms and pushed them into a red-hot timber beam until his flesh sizzled. And do you know why he did that?"

Kurzon's mouth dried and his body trembled. "N-no...tell me it's not true?"

"He did it to hide the brand he bore on his right palm—the brand of the casteless."

Tears streamed down Kurzon's face.

"If it weren't for Rodric, your sister would never have turned her back on the goddess."

Kurzon clenched his eyes tight, then, between sobs, he opened them and said, "I agree to your terms. Just promise me one thing."

"What?"

"Make him suffer."

67

THE GREAT CONJOINING

The Great Conjoining was almost upon the land of Tarania. Like three overlapping discs of scale armour, the gods of the Void merged. Golanos' silhouette descended across her mother's path, covering all but a thin crescent of her bright golden disc, while Kilena edged behind his twin from below. As the light diminished, the world held its breath. Even the bitter north wind lulled to the faintest of breezes, adding to the mystery of the once in a millennium meeting of the gods.

Seren gnawed at a fingernail, and stared helplessly at her father. He was bound to the stone to her right, slumped awkwardly against it. "Father? Can you hear me?"

At the sound of his name, Rodric listlessly turned in Seren's direction, mumbled something under his breath, then dropped his head to the side. A stringy tendril of saliva escaped from his open mouth and dropped into the dust. Whatever drug the Scion had given her father, it still held its grip on him.

A hiss from her left snapped Seren's attention onto the prisoner flanking her. Luis scrunched his eyes and bared his teeth, yet stayed silent. Since Kaine's brutal assault, the only time the Master of War had spoken was when he discovered Grimbard's presence, hurling every curse and profanity he knew at the traitor. She knew he deserved it after what he had done to Luis in Belanore Jail, but as she looked over at Grimbard's hooded son, bound against a standing stone on the opposite side of the circle, she was sure his actions were not driven by hatred for his sword brothers or by greed but by love. She lowered her eyes, thinking of Yanna, knowing exactly what a person could do in the name of love. She scanned the circle of stones, in the vain hope of discovering a young woman with flaming hair and bi-coloured eyes. *Of course she's not here.* Amira was either locked away in Vedana or dead—a fate they would all share with her unless Grimbard really did have a plan to save them.

Kaine climbed onto the Sleeping Stone, now illuminated by four braziers positioned at each corner of the massive rock. He raised his arms up to the Void. "Oh, great and mighty Velak," cried Kaine. "As we draw near to this moment when your godly kin gather together to form the Great Conjoining, we remember that you also journeyed through the Void to bring us your message of hope. Yet instead of accepting this great gift, the Hen Rai rose up against you, and through the betrayal of one of your own, robbed you of your body, and bound your spirit to a restless eternity. On this most sacred of days, we offer you the flesh and bone of your enemies as a sacrifice to honour the loss of your own." He lowered his hands and turned to where Aderyn and Okita held Tomos. "Prepare him."

Seren, along with every Northern Taranian, cried in horror as the Scions hauled Tomos onto the rock. They spun him around, then pulled his arms back against the two slivers of stones standing either side of the sleeping giant. Within the hood, Tomos moaned, but did not struggle. After fastening each wrist with thick cords of rope, the Scions removed Tomos' hood. His head flopped forward—his long, dark wavy hair rippled in the breeze like a veil of silk.

Gasps of wonder echoed through the ranks of Mendari. Seren glanced up, just as Ulena's sliver of a crescent disappeared under Golanos' loving embrace. Kilena was mere minutes away from slipping behind his sister, and then the world would plunge into the eerie darkness of the Great Conjoining.

The Mendari fell to their knees in a rocking trance, uttering the name of their god in a frenzied incantation. Yet the Scions stayed alert. They drew their weapons and scanned the circle.

Kaine stepped behind Tomos and held the Sword of Velak across the boy's neck. "We know you're here, Thief. Show yourself, or the boy dies."

Who in the goddess' name is he talking to?

The answer to Seren's question revealed itself as a shimmering form in the centre of the circle of stones. The agitated air turned black, then solidified into a figure standing head to toe in the same black armour that the Scions wore.

Kaine thrust his sword out towards the figure in black. "Did you think you could just slip past us and rescue the boy?"

"I could have; but instead I come to you with an offer," said the figure within the suit—their voice that of a man who sounded as old as the stones encircling him.

Seren clasped her bound hands around her mouth, hardly able to breathe. *I know that voice. But how in the goddess' name could it be him?*

"An offer," said Kaine, stepping in front of Tomos. "Are you out of your mind? What could you possibly offer me?"

"I offer you a chance to know the truth before it's too late."

"Truth about what, Thief?"

"That your god doesn't care about your petty vendettas, Kaine, or your holy war. They're a means to an end—to finish what he started a thousand years ago."

Kaine thrust out the Sword of Velak and pointed it at the man. "How would a despicable creature like you know the mind of a god?"

"Call off the sacrifice and I'll gladly share with you the dark truth that your *god* hides from you."

The assembled Mendari jeered and hurled curses at the man in black.

Kaine raised his hand for silence. "I'll give you some truths. It was *you* who stole the Armour of the First and the Vessel that was promised; and it was *you* who raised that coward and liar to be king, after *you* took the head of my father and made it look like Rodric's triumph." Kaine swung his sword around to Seren's father. "A man

464

who left his sister to burn, and hid his casteless identity to all but his precious sword brothers."

A collective cry of shock echoed from the lips of the Northern Taranians.

"Do you deny these things, Thief?"

"No, I do not."

The Mendari roared with rage.

Seren's stomach knotted. She turned to her father, seeing the same drugged figure as before. Yet as she faced Luis and then Grimbard, they both lowered their eyes from her questioning gaze. *Goddess, is it really true?*

"Scions." Behind Kaine, Okita and Aderyn slid their blades against Tomos' neck.

The man in black held his hand out to Kaine. "This is your last chance. Stop this madness or you'll leave me no choice."

"That's the first truth you've uttered, Thief. You have *no* choice." Kaine looked over his shoulder at Tomos. "We know how much he means to you. Remove your weapons and helmet, or they'll carve the boy right before your lying, thieving eyes."

"Please, listen to me. I can—"

Kaine raised his hand. "I don't give second chances, Thief."

"Very well, Kaine. You've sealed your fate." The man unfastened his belt, allowing it to drop to his feet. Then, tapping his shoulder, the helmet melted into the suit. A gasp of astonishment escaped from the mouths of the Northern Taranians. For even in the waning light, it was obvious to all who had met him that the man standing in the middle of the circle of stone was Tomos' healer, Madoc.

I knew it was his voice.

"Velak's balls."

Seren glanced across at Luis. "You knew?"

"No; but I bet my bastard of a sword brother did," he said, jutting his head up to Grimbard. "He didn't even blink when Madoc took that *thing* off his head."

She looked up at Grimbard. He leaned against a standing stone, his eyes fixed on Madoc. "I think they're working together, Luis."

"Oh, he's working with someone," said Luis, staring across at Kaine.

"You'd do the same if he had someone you loved."

He frowned at her. "I thought you hated him?"

"I should; but after what you told me and what I see in his eyes, I know there's more to my mother's death."

Grimbard glared at them and put his fingers to his lips.

Luis spat on the ground. "Maybe you're right, Seren, but until we all get out of here alive, he's still a treacherous, lying bastard."

Grimbard raised his eyes, then returned his attention to the healer, standing on his own in the centre.

Seren tucked her knees in tight to her chest as the wind picked up. A plume of ice-cold breath escaped from her nose. The Great Conjoining was almost upon them.

On the Sleeping Stone, Kaine signalled for silence, then said, "Take off the armour."

Madoc removed the unusual plate armour from his torso, then unfastened each section wrapped around his arms and legs, dropping them to the ground.

Kaine glanced up into the Void. Kilena finally slipped behind his sister. As the world descended into darkness, faint waves of light and dark washed along the barren, dust-covered ground and over the monoliths of stone. "Take off your suit."

Seren leaned forward and strained to see anything more than the faint silhouette of Madoc's suit within the darkness. She heard a sound like a piece of linen being torn into strips, and then something soft fell to the ground, piling around Madoc's feet.

"Throw it away," said Kaine.

The old healer did as he was told. Seren flinched as Madoc's armour and equipment thudded to the ground mere feet away from her.

Kaine raised the Sword of Velak towards the single, black disc outlined by a ring of light high above him. "And now, at the Great Conjoining, you will die."

The Mendari roared.

Kaine signalled once more for silence. "Now, my brothers and sisters, see for yourself what happens to one who removes the Armour of the First. Watch as our enemy's body turns to dust, and the wind scatters it to the four corners of Tarania."

The circle fell silent, with all eyes on the silhouetted shape of the old healer. His long, scraggy hair danced in the wind and the ethereal waves of light and shadow oscillated across his semi-naked body. Hidden in the unnatural darkness, corncrakes, nightingales and sedge warblers sang their songs of the night, making ready for their nocturnal activities.

Seconds turn to minutes; yet Madoc's dark shape stayed as still as a statue, and no cry of agony escaped from his mouth.

The Mendari grew restless, murmuring to each other.

"Silence!" bellowed Kaine. "It will happen...he promised me it would happen."

A flash of light from above signalled to the land below that Golanos was leaving the embrace with her mother. The darkness fled the light, and Mendari and Northern Taranians alike gasped at what they saw in the centre of the circle. Not only was Madoc alive, but his appearance defied belief: his body was in complete contrast to his face. Instead of aged, mottled skin, the healer's body was that of a man in his prime—powerful and toned.

Kaine vaulted off the Sleeping Stone, sped across to the circle's centre and pointed the tip of his sword at the old healer's throat. Madoc did not flinch.

From where Seren sat, Madoc almost matched the Mendari leader in both size and stature. Her heart rate increased, sensing a glimmer of hope.

Kaine traced the Sword of Velak along Madoc's peculiar features. "I don't know what aberration of a man you are, but no-one that is bound to the suit can survive without it."

Madoc shook his head. "You're wrong, Kaine. The suit was designed for a group of elite warriors, who tarnished this land over a thousand years ago."

"No. You can't be one of them. Only the spirit of Lord Velak endures. H-he would've told me—he knows and sees all things."

"Well, he didn't find me." Madoc gripped the back of his head and pulled off his face and hair as if he were a snake shedding its skin. The circle gasped as a dark-haired, olive-skinned man, with strong, chiselled features replaced the ancient healer that Seren had grown up with.

Kaine staggered back as if he had been punched in the stomach. "If it's true, then there's only one of the First who would dare stand against him; the one who betrayed him for her; the one who set fire to the sky; the one they called Gaius Galerius."

"I told you to take my offer." Madoc flew at Kaine, hitting him with a force that hurled him hard against the Sleeping Stone. The Mendari leader stood up, dazed, and reeled around to Okita and Aderyn. "Surround him."

They jumped into the dust, circling Madoc, ready to pounce.

"Lord Velak will honour us when he learns that we took the head of his greatest foe."

Madoc laughed. "Wrong again, Kaine. Enora was his greatest foe. And her ancestors are just as mighty. Now!"

Seren crouched into a ball as, all around her, warriors covered head to toe in black camouflage slipped from behind the stones and set on the unsuspecting Mendari. Arrows whistled through the air, thumping into flesh with the kind of accuracy that could only be that of the Belgar.

Grimbard bolted into the circle, and dived into the dust, skidding to a stop beside Madoc's armour. He scooped it up into his arms, ran back towards the edge of the circle and crouched in front of Seren. Slipping a knife from out of Madoc's belt, he cut her bindings. He cocked his head to the side. "Promise not to kill me?"

She snatched the knife out of his hand. "If you'd asked me that a day ago, you'd be lying in a pool of blood. Duck!"

He dipped his shoulder, just as Seren threw the blade deep in the eye of a Mendari poised to take Grimbard's head off with an axe. The warrior screamed, collapsing to the ground beside them.

Grimbard grinned. "I'll take that as *yes*."

Another massive figure loomed above them. She threw up her hands to protect her face, but no iron or steel struck her down. She peered between her hands and sighed with relief. Clansguard sped past the figure and formed a shield wall around the group, with a squad of Woodland Warriors providing cover.

"Shite, Madoc wasn't kidding when he said you were back, Grimbard. He told us everything...and I'm glad you're here, brother."

"Bloody hell, if it isn't Fergus Finesmile."

Fergus grinned at them, but paled as he discovered Luis' horrific injury and Seren's listless father. "We need to get you and the king out of here, Master of War."

"Never mind that, Fergus. How many clansguard are left?" asked Luis, straining to lift his body into a sitting position.

"We left Derwedd with twenty, but liberated ten of your rescue party being held in a camp a mile back inland."

"Let's hope that's enough to defeat Kaine and his Scions."

"Leave them," said Grimbard. "Just get out of here with your lives."

"Aren't you coming with us, Grimbard?" asked Fergus.

Grimbard shook his head. "Go on without me—I need to help Madoc free the boys."

Seren gripped his arm. "I'll get Dagan. Just bring my brother back to me safe."

He nodded. "I hope, when all this is over, we can talk."

She smiled. "I'd like that."

Grimbard unwrapped a binding of leather covering the sword attached to Madoc's belt, then slid the blade out of its scabbard.

Seren stared in awe at the blade. It barely reflected the light, and it contained the same swirling pattern that Shieldbane possessed. "Goddess. Madoc's blade is incredible."

Grimbard shook his head. "It's not Madoc's blade." He held it up to the waxing light of the Twins to reveal the shape of a wren formed into the hilt. "It's mine—reborn out of the ashes of Nabaya. It's Red Mist."

Tarek pressed his back against a standing stone, hoping that the enemy were too busy focusing on the clansguard to see him hiding stark naked outside of the circle. He hopped on one leg, edging precariously close to the sheer drop of the earthwork, slipped his foot inside Madoc's suit and pulled it over his shoulders. The thin, stretchy fabric was like nothing he had ever felt before. He gripped the strip of cloth next to his crotch and pulled it up to his neck, then frowned, stretching the saggy suit away from his body. *I can't wear this to fight. It's too—* He took a sharp intake of breath, as the fabric contracted and moulded itself to every contour of his body. It grew around his fingers, stretched over his toes, and just like Madoc had promised, it became a second skin.

Quickly, he strapped up his boots, then leaned past the edge of the monolith to peek inside the circle. The ground was littered with the dead and the dying, but to Tarek's relief, the fighting had drifted towards the western ramp, which meant that the Northern Taranians were making an orderly retreat. *Dagan.* He snapped his eyes to the empty standing stone, and frantically scanned the bodies to find one wrapped in the same ceremonial robe that he had seen on the children the night Nabaya burned. Finding nothing, he sighed with relief, knowing Seren had been true to her word.

In front of the Sleeping Stone, Madoc engaged the three Scions in a dizzying duel, which was remarkable as he fought them weaponless.

Just as Tarek prepared to enter the fray, a man roared behind him. Tarek whirled to face his assailant, but winced as a flash of iron streaked in front of him and smashed into his chest. He looked down, expecting to find his chest carved open from the cut, yet the fabric showed not even the slightest tear from the attack. The Mendari stood open-mouthed. Tarek smirked, then lashed out with a left jab towards the warrior's chin. The Mendari's head snapped back, then fell to the ground limp. Tarek stared in awe at his fist encased in the stretchy black fabric. Then, taking hold of Red Mist, he stepped into the circle. As he walked, he remembered Madoc's words the night he came to him after the attack on Nabaya: *'If Kaine delivers Prince Tomos to his god, then the fate of Dagan, the children and that of all Tarania will be in the hands of Velak'.* Tarek did not know if he could stop Velak, but he knew he could never rest until Kaine paid for what he did to Runa.

And even though everything he had done since returning to Northern Tarania had come at a painful cost, the opportunity to face Kaine once more was worth it. He snapped his eyes towards the man who had ruined his world. *I'm coming for you.*

"It's about bloody time!" cried Madoc, dodging a cut from Okita's blade. "Ready?"

"Never more so," said Tarek, edging closer to Kaine.

"Good—I was getting bored playing this game." He stopped moving, lowered his hands to his side and grinned. "Come and get me, girls."

Aderyn and Okita howled their cries of battle and surged towards Madoc, levelling their deadly weapons at the man of the First. With a hair's breadth between the tips of their blades and his unprotected body, Madoc darted out of the way and grabbed each weapon in his hands, thrusting them into each of the Scions' thighs. They screamed, then fell to the ground, staring in disbelief at their wounds. Madoc stood over them. "I've no desire to kill you; but if you try anything stupid, you'll regret it." He looked at Kaine's stunned face, and then at Tarek. "He's all yours, my friend."

Kaine snarled at Tarek. "Come on, Grimbard. Let's do this."

They ran at each other, launching off the ground. Their blades rang out from the shuddering collision, sliding into a deadly embrace at their hilts.

Kaine stared wide-eyed at the hilt of Red Mist. "That's impossible. I severed it in two."

"Madoc forged a new blade for it—one that matches your precious Sword of Velak."

"Ahhh!" cried Kaine, launching into a powerful combination of blisteringly quick thrusts and swings. Tarek matched each one, grinning from the effortless freedom he felt from wearing the suit.

Kaine disengaged and sneered at him. "You think you can master the suit merely by wearing it?" He slapped the side of the collar to summon the suit's helmet. "It's time for you to learn from a true master." His form dissolved into shimmering air.

Tarek lunged forward with Red Mist, but met only the dust swirling in front of him. He groaned as a sharp stab of pain lashed across his back. He spun around, slashing with his blade; but again, all he found was air.

"It takes months of training to master the power of the Armour of the First," said Kaine from somewhere in front of him. "And you don't have weeks, Tarek. Your death is moments away." A gust of wind flew past his left flank. "Ahhh!" Another cut—this time the black fabric of Tarek's thigh tore open, and blood gushed from the excruciating wound.

Tarek spun to Madoc. "Are you going to just stand there and watch him carve me up?"

"Listen to me, Tarek. The Red Mist within you is the same that flows in me, and my comrades of the First. It's a weapon, Tarek. For once, set it free—the suit will do the rest."

"It's too late, Tarek. Nothing can save you now. And then, once I've killed Madoc, I'll hunt your son down and rip his heart out of his chest."

Tarek's old friend rose up from within the depths; but this time, instead of controlling it, he let go. The suit responded. It thrummed with power, amplifying his untethered anger into a level of perception that he had never before experienced on the field of battle. The world around him slowed. The swirling dust of the circle hovered in hushed suspension all around him, and the beating wings of the birds of the air slowed to that of a funeral march. A cloud of dust a few feet in front of him parted. He dodged left, swept Red Mist to the side, and felt the blade connect with flesh. Kaine cried out. The Sword of Velak clattered to the ground, and his rippling form fell into the dust.

Tarek limped to the blood-soaked, shimmering figure fighting for every breath and knelt down.

Kaine growled through gritted teeth. "Let me hold his sword as I die."

Tarek said nothing. He slid Red Mist into the wound and thrust it up, severing the suit in two. The shimmering faded to reveal Kaine lying on his back, clutching his guts in a vain attempt to stop them spilling out. Tarek stamped onto Kaine's shoulder, and the helmet slid away.

"Let me get this right. If I remove the Armour of the First, your body will turn to dust, and the wind will scatter it to the four corners of Tarania?"

The Mendari leader stared up at him. For the first time since Tarek had laid eyes on him, the Scion showed fear.

"Not like this. I want to die as a warrior."

"A warrior's death is too good for you." Tarek ripped the suit away from the Scion's body. "For Runa."

As soon as the suit left Kaine's flesh, thick black lines appeared, criss-crossing his skin. Then he screamed as his body snapped into a spine-breaking convulsion. From within, bones creaked and cracked, and then his skin broke into flakes, carried off by the wind, disintegrating into dust.

With his final breath, Kaine snarled up at Tarek. "You'll never see your son again."

Tarek spat into Kaine's face. "Time to meet your father in the Netherplain." He stamped his foot onto Kaine's body. It burst into a powdery cloud. Then, as Tarek fell onto his back, exhausted, he stared up at the swirling canopy that was Kaine, Son of Banan and Scion of the First, and said, "To the four corners of Tarania you now go."

Madoc shielded his eyes and stared up into the Void, watching the final remains of Kaine disperse into a myriad of tiny particles. Death, even that of an enemy, saddened his heart. Like him and the rest of the First, Kaine was just another indoctrinated foot soldier, enlisted into Velak's relentless pursuit of an end that only he knew. If it were not for Enora, Madoc's eyes would still be blind to the injustices of the First—every enemy slain, every child taken, a step closer to the resurrection of the nameless ones who communed with Velak alone.

The sounds of battle had drifted further down the earthworks; from the ferocity he had witnessed from the likes of Fergus, Manon and Sorcha, he knew which side would take the day.

The hooded figure that had been tethered above the Sleeping

473

Stone now lay on the rock. Madoc sagged onto its edge and patted the boy under the ceremonial robe he wore. "You've been through a lot, son. Get some rest, before we get you home." He picked up the silver chain lying beside the boy, and prised open the amulet. A faint flicker of green light blinked up at him. *Damn you, Lucian. I should've known you'd figure it out.* He snapped it shut and slipped the chain over his neck.

A gust of wind sped across the circle. The boy squirmed under his robe, pulling it tight around his battered body. Madoc would have given anything to feel the cold against his flesh, but all he felt was the lightest of tickles trail across his skin. He closed his eyes, nonetheless, and enjoyed the moment of freedom, unburdened by the sweaty mask and heavy robe that was part of his persona as Madoc the Healer.

Beside him, Banan's weapon leaned against the stone, coated in what he suspected to be the crusted blood of Luis. He remembered vividly the moment he prised Shieldbane out of the dead giant's fingers, and thrust its cold, metal shaft into Rodric's hand. Since then, half a lifetime had passed for the king, but to Madoc it seemed as though the ambush in the glade between the Dunree Marshes and Borgen Forest took place barely a few weeks ago.

He glanced over at Tarek stretched out on his back, still wearing the Armour of the First. As he had suspected, the high levels of what the Northern Taranians called 'the Red Mist' coursing through Tarek's body were more than enough to allow him to tether with the suit. It still puzzled him how someone so far removed from the First could contain such a potent strain of the weapon, even surpassing the levels that Kaine and the other Scions possessed. Perhaps the Hen Rai were not as untainted as he had once believed? He considered what Tarek had told him about the night Dagan was taken. If Tarek could defeat Kaine only minutes after wearing the suit, then it stood to reason that Dagan, if trained properly, could become a warrior that even the First would consider a worthy opponent. He was sure that Velak had come to the same conclusion.

Silent and calm, Okita sat in the dust with her injured leg stretched out. Madoc had made sure his thrust incapacitated each of the Scion's movements; but as with all but the most critical of injuries, the suit had already started to repair the damage. He estimated he had mere minutes before both warriors were combat-ready again. If he was not going to kill them, he would need to find an alternative way to deal with them.

Aderyn wailed for her adopted brother. She lay prostrate on the ground and butted her helmet into the dust. She called his name repeatedly until, with her voice hoarse, she craned up at Madoc, and said, "I swear by almighty Velak, I'll make you suffer for this."

Madoc pushed off the Sleeping Stone, took hold of Shieldbane, and walked over to the Scion. "The owner of this monstrosity also enjoyed making people suffer," he said, swinging the war hammer through the air. "No wonder Banan and Kaine had no capacity for mercy—Lynch didn't." He spat the name out in disgust.

"That's not true. Banan showed me mercy and gave me a home."

"Is that what you call slavery? I wonder, Aderyn? Did Banan free you from being a slave and adopt you at the same time he started to recruit other Northern Taranians? When he discovered that your brother was gaining fame and standing as a warrior in Govannon's warband?"

"It doesn't matter what his motives were—I needed no persuasion to turn against Northern Tarania, or my brother. Did you know, Galerius, that the Wardens and the Grey Cloaks who ran the casteless camp I grew up within also showed no mercy? We were worth less than the beasts of the field to them." She pulled at a fold in the black fabric below her right wrist and held up her palm to reveal a pair of crossed lines scarred into her skin. "I was only eight when they tore me from my mother's arms and did this to me." She hid her hand. "And then, one year later, after my mother bribed a guard with the only thing she had left to barter with, we ran away and headed south. My mother believed that life would be better if we got over the border into the Wildlands." Aderyn staggered to her feet and rubbed her thigh. "We didn't even get out of Nirasia. The village watch from Treharne caught us and locked us in a hut, hoping to claim a reward from the Communion for our capture."

Madoc glanced right as Tarek came to stand beside him.

"Velak's balls. No wonder Kaine knew so much about that day."

"But there's so much more to tell, Grimbard," said Aderyn, stepping closer to the pair. "While you were outside playing warriors with Luis, some men of the village thought it would be fun to share my mother. They held her down and raped her right in front of us."

Tarek stayed silent and looked away from the Scion.

She snorted. "Oh, yes—a very different story to one you and your sword brothers tell."

"We believed what Rodric told us."

"I'm sure you did," she said. "I remember one man in particular. He lost control and beat my mother so badly that it took three men to pull him off her dying body. At least that part of Rodric's version is true."

"I'm sorry, Aderyn," said Madoc. "No child should witness such horrors that scar them for the rest of their lives."

"But I'm glad I can remember, Galerius." She slipped her hand across her collar bone. "Because when I sat in that tavern fifteen years ago and slipped the drug into *his* cup," she said, pointing at Tarek, "I saw in his eyes the unforgettable colour of amber that he shared with his father—the man who killed my mother." She slapped her hand against the suit and her helmet vanished. "Remember me, Grimbard?"

His breathing shallow, Tarek staggered forward. In his trembling hand, he thrust Red Mist towards the Scion. "It was you. You set me up."

"And you weren't even the main target—just a means to an end, and my chance to make you suffer for your father's deeds." Aderyn sneered. "It's time to finish what I started."

They both braced for Aderyn to attack, but she spun around, ran through the stones and launched off the earthwork. Madoc sprinted to the edge and looked over the tier. Aderyn was nowhere to be seen. "Shit."

"Go on. Do it. Cut me down."

Madoc whirled around and cursed. An enraged Tarek stood over Okita, about to plunge Red Mist into her chest. "No!" He sprinted into the circle and tackled Tarek to the ground. They wrestled, tumbling in the swirling dust, until Madoc found the fastener and ripped it down to Tarek's crotch. The suit sagged.

Tarek panted through gritted teeth. "None of them deserve to live."

"No more killing, Tarek. And never wear the suit again. It will eventually bond with your flesh, and you'll never be able to take it off." He stared over to the black strips of cloth and plate armour that were once Kaine's suit. "Or you'll end up like him." He got up off the ground and held out his hand to Tarek. As he lifted him up, he stared at the figure lying on the Sleeping Stone. "Get that poor bastard down to the others. You're too volatile to be around Okita. I'll catch up with you once I've dealt with her."

Tarek's eyes widened. "Goddess! Poor Tomos. I promised Seren I'd take him to her. I forgot all about him." He rushed towards the hooded figure.

Madoc called after him. "Bloody hell, Tarek, put some clothes on or you'll scare whoever that boy is half to death!"

Tarek skidded to a stop in a swirl of dust, turned and gawped at Madoc. "What do you mean, 'whoever he is'?"

"He's not Tomos."

"By the goddess. But that could mean that Dagan—"

Madoc nodded. "I'm sorry, Tarek. They fooled both of us."

"Then it was all for nothing?"

"No—I'm sure your boy's alive and well. He's probably with Lars and the other children on their way to Mendaria."

"Why Mendaria?"

"I don't know, Tarek. I think it's time I had a chat with an old friend."

As Tarek rushed behind the stones to find his clothes, Madoc collected his armour from around the circle and dressed. Then he picked up Kaine's armour and Lynch's chain and walked over to Okita. "For his funeral pyre."

"You're letting me go?" she asked, cautiously taking hold of the bundle.

"Yes," he said, crouching beside her. "If you share even the slightest amount of intelligence your ancestor did, then listen to me.

Masuda was my friend." He eyed the pair of discs hanging from the chain. "He wasn't like Lynch, who killed for pleasure. He did what he did out of honour and duty—which was why he could never bring himself to oppose Velak, even though he hated him with a passion."

"That's a lie. He was devoted to him."

"If you won't believe me, then dig deeper into his past. Find his old journals and read the truth from Masuda's own words."

"I've never seen any journals at our family home."

Madoc shook his head. "He would've kept them a secret—to protect his family from people like Lynch, and the First who survived the final battle, who stayed loyal to Velak."

"What would they look like?"

"All I can remember is that he loved to write with ink and parchment, just like you Taranians do now. Promise me you'll try to find them?"

Okita nodded.

"Good. Now go. And make sure you cloak, or you'll have to fight your way through a warband of very pissed-off Northern Taranians. Not even a Scion could match their fury."

She eased to her feet, nodded, and disappeared into the rippling air.

Alone, Madoc sat on the edge of the Sleeping Stone. He blew through his lips and stared down at Kaine's speaking-glass. "I've put this off for too long." He tapped onto the glowing glass. Within a few seconds, a form of iridescent, multi-coloured light appeared a few feet away, hovering above the dust-covered ground.

"Gaius Galerius—my tribune, my brother-in-arms, and my betrayer. I wondered when you'd call."

"Where is he, Lucian?"

"Far away from you, my friend. And now that he's separated from the amulet, you'll never find him."

Madoc sprung towards Velak and snarled into his face. "I know what you're planning, but his mind's strong and he'll fight you."

"Is that so?"

"Yes."

"Then tell me: why did he willingly walk out of Keld to go in search of me?"

Madoc seethed. "Because you seduced him. Like you do to everyone."

Velak laughed. "Not this time, Gaius. Before my link severed with him, I found him standing on a window ledge ready to throw himself out of the Great Hall and to his death in the filthy street below."

"You lie."

"No, I do not. The question you must ask yourself is why? Was it from the excruciating agony he suffered from the quickening, after your amulet suppressed it for so long? Maybe so; but I believe it more likely to be from the suffocating dungeon you built for him—sixteen years of being held captive, physically, emotionally and mentally. That could make anyone desperate to find a way out of their miserable existence."

"I had no choice—you would've found him otherwise."

"Well, you failed, and in the process made him hate you, and turn to me."

"If you hurt one hair on his head, I'll—"

"You'll what?" Velak's luminescent mouth curled into a smile. "Don't worry, Gaius, I'll take good care of him; and then when the time's right, I may even introduce him to *her*."

Madoc's legs buckled and his eyes widened. *She's alive.*

"Yes. It hurts, doesn't it? Knowing she's been alive all this time, so near but yet so far from her loving embrace?"

"You bastard."

As Velak's form began to fade, he laughed. "I'll give her your love. See you soon, Galerius."

68

BARING OF SOULS

A deathly hush had descended over the surviving Northern Taranian clansguard camped halfway between the Stones of Valtara and Keld.

Rodric hunkered beside the fire. He spun Isabelle's ring around his little finger, and stared into the dancing flames. It was hard to believe that only three days had passed since he sat with the clan chieftains discussing strategy at the Council of War. *If only I could go back—things would be so different.* It was clear to him that Kaine had known every detail of the agreed plan, which meant that someone in that meeting was a traitor and spied for the Mendari. Was it one of the Elite Guard, or a champion? Surely not a chieftain—they had all suffered loss at the hands of the Mendari. If not those, then who? Then he remembered what Luis had told him earlier about Seren's desperation to free Amira, sending her into the trap that Kaine had set for his family—all for the love of Yanna. The affair with Kurzon's wife was troubling in itself, but what if there was more to Yanna's interest in Seren? He knew she was a frequent visitor to Kelaris, visiting her grandfather. Could she have been compromised? Kurzon would be furious if he knew his thoughts. Rodric's stomach tightened as the image of the bodies of the smouldering Nirasian Named heaped into a fetid pile on the northern side of Midway Bridge seared into his mind. *I don't care who I offend—I will find the perpetrator and punish them, no matter what caste they are.*

Rodric's recollection of what happened after the events of Midway Bridge hid in a thick haze within his mind—the effects of the drug the Scion had stabbed him with. He remembered leaving the Stones, and how his warriors fought with such a rage that the Mendari stood no chance without their black-clad commanders leading them. But knowing that other Mendari could still be near, the chieftains pushed the beleaguered group further west, away from the barren coastal landscape and towards the lower slopes of the South Keld Range and the cover of the trees blanketing it. Then, after walking for an hour, they left the pass and ascended the slope, until they found a secluded clearing where they could recover their strength.

Despite the protests of his chieftains, Rodric refused to rest. He had walked through the camp speaking to every clansguard, thanking them for their strength, courage and loyalty through the darkest days to have befallen the kingdom. He promised them they would all receive their warrior names as soon as the ceremony could be arranged. Then, he sat beside dying comrades, singing the songs of Northern Tarania and whispering words of comfort as they slipped through the Veil and up into the Void.

Sharing some food with Sorcha, he listened to her account of the battle at the edge of Derwedd Forest, the bravery of Rory and Kilien's sacrifice that had sent him and Rask into the flames of a tar pit. Then he spoke with Manon in private, and apologised to her for dismissing her concerns and for not believing in her sixth sense. When he met Fergus, he consoled him and shared some memories of Kilien. By the end, only laughter escaped from their mouths, remembering the antics of one of the most charismatic and outspoken people they knew.

Not once in all the conversations did anyone question him about his past. It humbled him that these brave souls saw him for what he was: their king. Whether they could keep Kaine's accusatory words a secret from those who would dig deeper into his past was another thing entirely.

After leaving the chieftains, he put aside his duty as king and sought Seren. He wrapped his arms around her, told her he loved her, and said he knew that Isabelle was just as proud as he was for the way she had acted. Seren had paled, admitting that she believed she had failed Kurzon and Yanna for not rescuing Amira. In his heart, Rodric thought it highly unlikely that Aedan's daughter would have survived the massacre at Midway Bridge—which further strengthened his suspicions that Yanna was involved somehow. However, for the sake of his daughter, he suggested that Kaine had kept her within the walls of Vedana as a hostage. Seren had brightened at his words.

When Madoc and Tarek had arrived with the boy he believed was Tomos, he and Seren had wept when they discovered the truth. And then, as they sat together with poor Luis, whose leg had just been amputated, Rodric learned the staggering truth about Eleri. He sat dumbstruck hearing how she had survived the fire in Treharne, and that she blamed him for leaving her, and Tarek for what his father had done to their mother.

It was at that moment, sat with Seren and his sword brothers, that he swallowed his pride, and admitted that Eleri's story was true. He revealed to them that Tarek's Wraith Warrior had indeed intervened during Banan's ambush. In fact, Madoc, from his place of hiding, had watched all three of the boys while they were in Govannon's warband. That was how he discovered the chieftain's plan to kill them. He believed that each of them was destined for great things, but warned Rodric never to tell his brothers about him, and to never reveal the secrets of his past.

After giving them all a moment to digest his revelation, Madoc had turned to Tarek and invited him to share his story of what happened on the Day of Sorrows; and for the first time, Rodric knew it was the truth. He recognised the same pain in Tarek's eyes that he had in his—the kind that only those who have suffered great personal loss can discern.

And so, after restoring his bond with Tarek, and unburdening himself of the secrets of his past, he sat beside his sword brothers and chatted to them as if the last fifteen years had never happened.

"It makes no sense," said Luis. He puffed on his pipe, and blew out a sweet-smelling cloud of smoke from the pain-relieving concoction that Madoc had made for him. "Why allow them to live?"

"He has his reasons, my friend." Rodric glanced over at Madoc, clothed head to toe in the Armour of the First. Since completing his rounds of the injured, he had stood guard, scanning the surrounding area in case Aderyn returned. "Which is why he chooses now to heal, not kill."

"You should've seen him put down Aderyn and Okita," said Tarek. "By the goddess he was fast; and that's without the suit."

Luis jabbed his pipe at Tarek. "From what he told me, you showed some unbelievable skills. What was it like, wearing the suit?"

"It was like a heavy burden was lifted from my shoulders, and everything around me slowed. Then, when the Red Mist arose, I no longer felt the fabric of the suit against my skin—it *was* my skin."

Rodric glanced over at Tarek. "What will you do now?"

"Madoc told me the Mendari have been sending caravans of children back to Gol Zaram. I'll pick up their trail and see what I can find." He shook his head and cursed. "He warned me that Kaine would never let me see Dagan, but like a fool, I believed that lying bastard."

"You were desperate—of course you believed him."

"I know I can never understand what it's like to be a father," said Luis, staring at his pair of stumps. "But I would've gone willingly to Kaine if it meant protecting Seren."

Rodric gripped Luis' arm. "What you did, brother, will never be forgotten by me."

"Nor I," said Tarek. "In fact, I've already started to write a ballad about your exploits, my friend. There'll not be a dry eye in a tavern from Penglas to Glanmorden."

"I know what you can call it," said Luis.

"What?"

"*The Tales of Luis the Legless*," he said, stony-faced.

Flustered, Tarek looked at Rodric, then back at Luis. "I-I didn't mean to offend you, Luis. I-I—"

Luis started to shake, then the sides of his mouth curled up into a grin, and then blurted, "You should see your face."

"You bastard," said Tarek, wiping the sweat away from his forehead. "Just for that, I *will* use it as the bloody title."

"Yes! I can just imagine Kurzon's face when he hears it." Luis pressed his hands against his stomach. "Velak's balls, I've missed this."

"Yes, I feel the same way," said Rodric. He eyed a large flask resting against Luis' leg. "Brother, I hope you intend to share your Mendarian wine?"

"Bollocks. How'd you know about that?"

"I've always known." He gripped both of his sword brothers' shoulders and smiled. "Let's get pissed."

Happy and drunk, Rodric left his dozing sword brothers and picked his way through the clearing until he reached the sentry standing guard at the edge of the camp.

The young lad stood to attention.

"At ease, clansguard."

"Thank you, sire."

Rodric leaned over and frowned, then wagged a finger at the boy. "I know who you are. You're Ellis—the one who shot a bolt at War Master Ironfoot."

The lad paled. "P-please don't punish me, sire. It was a terrible mistake. I'll do anything to make things right with the Master of War."

Rodric slapped him on the shoulder. "I'm not going to punish you, son. I just wish I could've seen the bastard's face when you shot him."

Ellis smiled nervously. "It wasn't a pleasant sight, sire."

Rodric roared with laughter. "I have no doubt.... But since you're keen to make amends, you can escort the Master of War on his journey to Hythe."

Ellis' eyes grew wide. "H-Hythe, sire?"

"Yes, clansguard. Madoc believes he can help Ironfoot walk again; but to do so he must return to his home and treat the Master of War there."

"After what I saw at the Great Conjoining, sire, I have no doubt Madoc has the power to save him."

"Nor I, son, Nor I..." He glanced at a bandage wrapped around Ellis' arm. "Has he checked on your dressing yet?"

"Yes, sire. He just left before heading into the camp to tend to my friend, Finn. He took a Mendari bolt in the thigh."

"Well, I hope he makes a swift recovery. Now if you'll excuse me, I'd like to take a piss in private."

"O-oh, of course, sire."

Still chuckling, Rodric stumbled through the tree line, and walked into the forest, until he found a tree he liked. He relieved himself, then turned back towards the camp. The whistle of a bird warbled in the darkness of the forest. The song lasted for five seconds and ended in a trill. At first he ignored it, thinking it was a dunnock; but he heard it again, this time closer. He frowned. *What could make a wren venture out of the nest so late at night?* Then he froze, sensing he was not alone. He sighed, then turned around. "I wondered when you'd come."

The figure, all dressed in black, moved closer. The black helmet covering their face hissed, then melted away. Trembling, his sister stared at him.

"It took me ages to learn that blasted whistle, and you did it almost immediately."

"Such trivialities were below you, dear brother. Your head was full of joining a warband and earning fame and fortune. You obsessed over it—which is why, given half the chance, you burned your shame from off your right palm and left me to die in the flames of Treharne."

"That's not true, Eleri. I'd just seen our mother brutalised and murdered—I was terrified. And then when the Mendari attacked, I panicked; but I never meant to leave you there."

"And still the lies drip like poison from your mouth." From out of

485

her belt, she slid out a knife that had lost its tip. The blade was covered in a sticky, resinous liquid.

With tears streaming from his eyes, Rodric withdrew his sword. "Don't talk to me about lies. You lured Tarek away from my family with lies. Isabelle died because of you." He sneered at her. "Who helped you plan the attacks on the nobility?"

She smirked, then giggled. "Haven't you worked it out, dear brother? It was someone who was prepared to do whatever it took to preserve the Communion and the caste system...even if it meant killing his own sister."

Rodric's sword dropped to his side. He sank to his knees, trembling. "Kurzon."

"Yes—he arranged it all. Targeting all those who planned on voting to reform the caste system. Isabelle was supposed to be the only target of your family, but as you know, Tomos got hurt during the attack." She stroked his tear-stained cheek with her black-clad hand. "The thing is, dear brother..."

Rodric hissed through gritted teeth as Eleri plunged the blade into his thigh.

"The blade that was used by the assassin was laced with the same sap of the yew that now flows through you. Not even Galerius would've been able to save him. Your son died that night."

Rodric fought the poison as it spread through his body, pushing back the tremors building up from within. His mouth tightened, and his stomach muscles tensed. Foam bubbled from out of his mouth. "B-but—"

"But who's the boy you've raised as your own son for sixteen years?"

Rodric's eyes grew wide.

"You should ask Galerius." She leaned forward and kissed his forehead, then yanked down on the hilt of the knife and snapped it from the blade.

"Ahhh!" moaned Rodric, flinching in pain. "My sword!" He flung his hand into the forest undergrowth through blurry, bloodshot vision. "I need my sword!" He felt cold steel across his finger tips, but just as he tightened his grip, Eleri wrenched the blade away from him and threw it into the trees.

"There'll be no gathering of friends and family as you die, dear brother. No songs of valour or memories shared. No glory of a warrior's death for you." She pushed him onto his back, then cocked her head as she spotted something. "Awww...is that hers?" She ripped the chain holding Isabelle's ring away from his neck.

"No."

Eleri stood and slipped the chain over her neck. "A memento of our lovely reunion. Oh, and one more thing—Kurzon knows everything. He can't wait to welcome his niece with open arms. Goodbye, dear brother. Time to die."

Shade descended across Rodric's eyes. His heart pounded within his chest. His muscles convulsed, and he shook his head violently, until after spewing his guts, he drew his final breath.

Thank you for reading The Stones of Valtara.

Feedback

If you have a spare moment, it would be great if you could add a review on Amazon or on my Goodreads page.

Don't forget to visit my website

Head over to christopherclargo.com and join my mailing list to receive my newsletters and find out about opportunities to take part in beta reading and Advance Reader Copy promotions on future books.

There's also plenty more to discover on the website, including interactive maps and timelines about the land of Tarania and the people who live there.

Get in touch on Facebook

https://www.facebook.com/christopher.clargo.author

Printed in Great Britain
by Amazon

75948438R00296